RIVER RUN

RIVER RUN
A DELIA CHAVEZ MYSTERY

J. S. James

CROOKED
LANE

NEW YORK

Copyright © 2019 by Joseph J. Stowitschek

Published in the United States by Crooked Lane Books, an imprint of The Quick Brown Fox & Company LLC.

Crooked Lane Books and its logo are trademarks of The Quick Brown Fox & Company LLC.

Library of Congress Catalog-in-Publication data available upon request.

ISBN (hardcover): 978-1-64385-231-7
ISBN (ebook): 978-1-64385-232-4

Cover design by Lori Palmer and Andy Ruggirello

Printed in the United States.

www.crookedlanebooks.com

Crooked Lane Books
34 West 27th St., 10th Floor
New York, NY 10001

First Edition: November 2019

10 9 8 7 6 5 4 3 2 1

For Carole and Julie, always

1

The stench of decay wafted into the patrol car like an insult. Sheriff's deputy Delia Chavez fought an urge to roll up the window and hit reverse. The bodies on the porch didn't factor into the foulness. They were fairly fresh. The odor seeped in off the river, like it always did.

Too late to back out anyway. Deputy Craig Castner was already poking his boxy jaw into the opening, his forearm planted on her driver's side windowsill. "Wasted trip, Chavez. Suicide pact kinda deal."

She nodded, knowing Cast Iron Castner figured his tough-as-nails act had earned him his nickname, not the super-hard lump between his ears.

"Evening, Craig. Mind if I stretch my legs?" With a shove that forced Castner to take a step back, she got out and shut the cruiser's door.

With his feet set wide in the space between their cars, his thumbs hooked into his utility belt, Castner postured like an oversize turnstile against a background of red, blue and white flashes.

He'd gotten there first and she was deputy-come-lately, trying to horn in.

"It's Friday night, Chavez. Don't you have a truckload of *borracho* berry pickers to cuff and stuff?"

Delia bit her tongue and took in the river-bottom scene. *Take his shit. This could be the ticket.*

1

Both pairs of headlights shone on a rock foundation as high again as the first floor of the two-story wood frame it supported. Three of the four walls were overgrown with blackberry vines. The dilapidated house sat fifty yards from the Little Luckiamute River—not so little at sixty feet, bank to bank. A quarter mile below, it dumped into the much larger Willamette. Somewhere on the opposite shore, the Santiam River did the same. To Delia, this lowland junction of three rivers dredged up the rot of nightmares.

"Got things sorted out, Chavez." Every second or two, the strobing lights recast Castner's glower as either comical or garish. "Waitin' for Harvey and the ME to show up and confirm." Harvey Schenkel was senior detective in the Sheriff's Department.

Delia nodded, scanning a weed-infested yard full of woodpiles and clutter so rusted it would shame a junk dealer. "We have a bit of a wait, Craig. Charlie's out of state, and that leaves just Harvey."

Charlie Lukovsky was Investigations' other detective. Running short had become chronic, given a morale-busting, penny-pinching sheriff, a half-staffed patrol unit, and a two-person investigations division saddled with a six-person caseload.

"I heard." Castner's face was stone. "Some old coffin-filler at that Bethel nursing home kicked it from smoke inhalation. So?"

"So, Harv's there with FD, ruling out arson and—"

"And he sends Señorita Bachelor's of Law Enforcement to make sure I snap on my surgicals and preserve the crime scene."

Too late for either, she figured, but said nothing. With six years in grade, she was still Castner's junior deputy. He often accused her of using her education to jump seniority. In truth, she did lean on her degree. Otherwise, why had she sweated blood to earn the damned thing?

Detective next, sheriff not far down the road.

Castner backswept his arm toward the dark forms at the middle of a sloped porch. "Look, it's open-and-shut. Way those two oldies are slumped in their lawn chairs? Way the guns dropped? The woman looks like death warmed over. Her man prob'ly couldn't stand to outlive her." He flattened his hands across his heart. "'Life's over for us, sweetie. How's about we go out with a bang? Ready? On three,' ka-pow, ka-pow." He rehooked his thumbs on his belt.

"Maybe so, Craig. How about we go over what else you've found?"

Except for a grunt, Delia got no response. She reached in through her open window, pulled out a flashlight, rubber gloves, and shoe covers, and toggled the cruiser's high beams. With part of her protective wear snapped on, she brushed past Castner's elbow gates and made it to the front bumper before he tugged at her arm.

"Hey now, woman. You hold up. This is a goddamned waste of time."

Delia turned and burned a stare into Castner's hand, then his face. "I guess you haven't heard. Harvey specifically requested that I do a preliminary. Either we walk through the scene together or you wait here. Your choice."

Castner backed off, his eyes drops of lead. "Yeah? We'll see about that."

She stepped toward the wreck that the pair on the porch had called home. Behind her, the door to Castner's patrol unit opened and slammed shut. He was sure to be on the horn to Sheriff Gus Grice.

After all, Castner was Grice's nephew.

Confident Harvey had already run interference, Delia slipped on the shoe covers and eased her way up a dozen sagging porch steps. Too high for headlight beams to do any good.

The bodies were slouched in opposing lawn chairs as Castner had described, the male in bib overalls, undershirt, and a weathered fedora, the female in a faded housedress, one slipper halfway off her left foot. Had there been loving gazes, any sign of them was long gone. The pair had been dead for a day or more, judging by the sallow, waxen skin.

A deer rifle lay at the man's feet and a large-bore pump shotgun beside the woman's chair. Delia's Maglite lit up a puddle of sticky-dry blood beneath the dead man's torso. Gun-cleaning materials and loose .30-06 cartridges lay on a bench next to his chair. Beneath the ever-present river stink, the warm night held a lingering odor of butchery.

The man appeared near seventy, had a face like cracked leather and a tennis ball–size hole in his chest. A cascade of blood, now dry, saturated the lower portion of his bib. A dark-ocher pool had hardened on the porch floor, more than she'd have expected from a gunshot wound. Delia put her light on his face, and her body tensed. His corpse wore a look she'd seen too often. Run-ins with hard men were common in Delia's line of work, but even in death, this guy pushed a primal button. Like she'd seen him. Someone like him.

The quiver of familiarity passed. She shifted her light to the woman and sucked in air—not at the dark flower around the heart-level hole, but at the impact of long-standing damage. Careful not to touch the body, she teased back tendrils of gray and exposed a recently bruised forehead. The woman's face spoke less of old age than ongoing abuse—the sunken, beseeching eyes, the discolored skin, the buildup of calcium deposits on both cheekbones. The scarring from repeated damage and healing. And the silent scream that echoed within the cavity of her dead mouth.

Delia flicked the beam back on the man, down to his gnarled hands. Clublike. Each knuckle aping the rounded end of a ball peen hammer.

Her free hand found the butt of her holstered weapon. Her left shoulder twitched as if a demon had dug in, whispered in her ear. *Pull it. Shoot the bastard again.* Years of practice breaking up domestic squabbles hadn't dulled her loathing of abuse as blood sport. She fingered the Smith & Wesson's release strap—officially her backup weapon, in practice her sidearm of choice—and flicked a glance toward the idling patrol cars. Castner glared back from behind his dash lights. She let out held breath and forced her hand down to her side.

Castner's premise—two old, fast-failing fogies deciding they couldn't live without each other—had dissolved faster than a sand castle in a tidal wave.

She edged deeper onto the porch, spraying light over layered seediness. What was that word movie critics liked to toss around when they'd seen it all before? Cliché? The ambience here even beat out that *Tobacco Road* flick she'd wasted an evening on. Now there was a deputy Castner could relate to.

4

A screen door hung from a single hinge, the sill worn to a deep groove. Her light traveled over a clapboard outer wall gone without paint so long its weathered wood reflected an eerie, silver gray.

About to step in, she backed up and re-aimed her flashlight along the front wall, down into a narrow space between encroaching brambles and stone foundation. Something bladelike glinted back. She crouched at the side of the porch for a closer look.

Blade was right. It was the longest piece of cutlery she'd seen outside a meat market. A home-fashioned boning knife, slightly curved and slender. Below the handle, the first three inches gleamed. The remaining nine were coated in dark maroon.

Delia returned to the body of the old man. Using a pen point, she unhooked one side of his overall bib and folded it back. Next, she pried up the blood-starched hem of his shirt and exposed a horizontal gash—the main source of the blood puddle. She saw the guy yanking out the blade, flinging it off behind him, then staring in shock at the gusher he'd unplugged.

Good for her.

Method evident and motive congealed, Delia pressed on.

She played the beam down the front hallway and stepped past an open gun cabinet ringed with spilled shotgun shells, then through a doorway to her right. No blood spatters, no telltale drops suggesting the stabbing or shooting had happened anywhere but the porch. The inner walls were steeped in outside dankness. She flicked the kitchen's light switch and got nothing. She flash-lit a wooden table, scarred and burnt under hard use. Beside a lantern, a lined tablet and Bic pen rested at one end. The closest chair lay upended.

Delia swept the room, over cupboards painted institution green, across Formica countertops, gouged and ripped, yet neat and unknown-cluttered. Her beam traced along a row of drawers, all closed except one. That drawer stuck out at an awkward jaunt, its collection of knives awry. Castner must not have even glanced in there.

She scanned the linoleum floor, worn thin by foot traffic. Spilled kitchen matches littered a pathway ending at a potbelly woodstove with a nickel-plated base, its door ajar. She stepped closer and bent low over one clawed foot where the circle of light haloed a dried stain smaller than the tip of her pinkie. The spot was dark maroon, like the puddle under the old man.

She wedged the Maglite into the stove. The door swung open with a rusty screech that jangled her nerves.

Delia bent forward. A crumpled page, the same yellow as the tablet, lay atop the stove's dead ashes. She withdrew the paper by a corner, teased it open with her pen, and read by flashlight. The message appeared hurried, but written by a delicate hand.

Robbie,

Stay away. Willard made me write the postcard he sent you. That devil means to get even for what happened to Je—

Graceful loops flattened into a scrawled line as if the page had been yanked from beneath the pen point. Delia swallowed on a dry throat and straightened up.

Backtracking toward the front of the house, she mentally assembled the events of a last-straw scenario: *Devil Man catches Battered Woman writing covertly to someone she knows. Battered Woman's warning attempt is thwarted. She blows her cork, latches onto the first handle available in the drawer, and skewers Devil Man in the gut. Devil Man makes it to a lawn chair, tosses the knife, and loads the rifle he's been cleaning. Committed to finishing what she started, Battered Woman grabs up a new weapon from the hall gun cabinet, loads, and pursues.*

Back on the porch, Delia aligned herself directly behind the dead woman, her light trained on the body she assumed was Willard's. Facial crags remained deeply shadowed as if carved into granite.

Maybe they touch off at the same time, maybe not, but Devil Man's heart-shot drops Battered Woman into her chair.

At any rate, years of suffering were over. End of story.

Then why did it feel like chapter one?

"Told you it was a damned waste of time." Silhouetted in headlight glare, Castner stood below the porch, his arms locked across a data-entry keypad.

Delia came down the steps. Halting on the last, she faced him at eye level. "You sure did, Craig." She nodded back over her shoulder, toward the porch. "Got IDs on the victims?"

"Now, what d'you think?"

The grip-strengthening ball, always in her coat pocket, got a hefty squeeze. She cocked her head and waited.

Castner's eyes wavered. He tilted the keypad forward. Lips moving, he read silently off the display, then hugged the cranky device to his chest, like a pat hand. "Postman called it in. One Willard Lester Gatlin. The other's Rose Gatlin. Lived like hillbillies in this river-bottom skunk hole. Annie's trace pulled up a string of poaching convictions on the old man."

Annie Cox's official title was communications and dispatch officer. Unofficially, she covered the sheriff's butt and kept the place afloat. Polk County Sheriff's was not the tightest ship in Oregon's law enforcement armada.

Delia acknowledged his cooperation with a nod. "How about a Robbie? Maybe Robert?"

Castner's eyes narrowed. Chin jutting, he sighted down his nose. "You find somethin'?"

Delia said nothing. Let him wait.

The muscles in Castner's jaw bunched as he checked his precious database. "Missing-person report filed twelve years back. A son named Jesse Gatlin drowned in the Willamette. Nothing on anybody named Robert." The keypad disappeared behind Castner's back. "Your turn. What've you got?"

A fresh set of headlights approached the house. A mud-caked Ford F-350 four-by-four rolled to a stop and a lanky frame unfolded from it. Harvey. Allowing detectives to use personal vehicles was one of the Sheriff's budget slashing notions. So far, the specialized insurance offset any savings.

"Craig, you got here ahead of me. You go first."

Delia prowled the property and waited Castner out. If he hadn't been such a stink-flinger, she might've stopped him from making an ass of himself in front of Harvey.

The yard between the back of the house and the river was littered with everything from discarded animal bones to a single-wheeled deer-toting cart and overturned boats, all choked by weeds. Her light picked out an old outboard motor the color of sea kelp with cursive lettering in faded gold that spelled out *Elgin*. Her upper arms goosebumped. She blinked at the déjà vu sensation, there and gone in a flash. Unsettled, she faced away from the mess.

Lowland woods defined three sides of the open ground that sloped toward the river. An ancient weeping willow dominated the fourth, dangling its umbrella far out over the slow-moving current. Her light kicked back diamondlike sparkles between the tree roots. With each step toward the river, the disquiet crept higher, almost to her throat.

It's only water.

Thirty feet back was plenty. From behind, sounds of a radio dispatch drifted on the night air. Thankful for the Maglite, she narrowed the beam to its farthest reach.

The glitter at the base of the tree turned out to be broken bottle glass, the bark above so chipped and pitted with bullet holes she was amazed the willow had survived.

Farther up, her light picked out a band of discoloration where the trunk went from mud gray to nut brown. Its significance hit with a coldness that traced its finger along her spine. The last flood had climbed several feet above her head. No wonder the house sat on a built-up foundation. Images of angry currents surrounding her on that porch, swirling over its top step to rise above her ankles, drove that chill deep inside. Down to the ends of her toes.

Whoo-whoop.

Castner, signaling his exit.

Harvey called to her from the porch. She was up. This was her ticket.

Delia made to move but felt glued in place, slow to tear her eyes from that telling watermark or tamp down the feeling that her fate was at the whim of a river.

2

The boy's alive. It was a good shoot. The boy's alive. It was a good shoot.

Sheriff's deputy Delia Chavez typically put no stock in chants or mantras, but this one calmed her as she waited to find out how badly she'd screwed up. It kept her pacing the bus-size RV's aisle instead of kicking the shit out of every miserable piece of furniture in the place. Instead of kicking herself for letting her temper off its leash.

More than two hours had passed since the shooting. The medical examiner was gone and Camacho's body had been removed from this moss-covered wreck marooned out behind the oldest watering hole in Independence, Oregon. The other deps were gone, too—one returning the abducted boy to his mother.

Mostly unmolested. Mostly uninjured. After Delia had hugged his shakes away, told him he was okay. Hoped she wasn't blowing smoke.

Even the hard-core Sunday morning drinkers and card players had faded back inside the tavern's rear door. Only she and Detective Harvey Schenkel, who doubled as IA officer for the Polk County Sheriff's Department, were left inside the pigsty on cinder blocks, her in the living area, him working his way forward from the bedroom.

She paused near the bump-out in the RV's living space, eyed its recessed couch for cootie squatters, and opted to keep moving. She'd

9

take whatever Harvey dished out on her feet. Better coming from him than her Mexi-phobic boss, Sheriff Gus Grice.

Seven steps to the dashboard, turn, seven steps back to midbus. *The boy's alive. It was a good shoot.*

"Harv," Delia called. "We about done here?"

From him, silence.

Harvey had liked her investigative work on the Gatlin dual homicides back in June. She could tell he didn't like what he was seeing now, running his flashlight over the spray pattern again, slow-walking the entire gore-spattered hallway that bordered the galley. She'd had to coax the guy out of the bedroom somehow. To be sure of a clean kill. And not hit the boy.

Afraid of giving in to her demolition urges, Delia eased a hip down onto the arm of the fake-cowhide travel sofa. She propped her patrol hat on one knee and searched for distraction.

"How 'bout it, Harv?"

More silence.

The morning was bright, but with the lights out and newspapers plastered over every window, the RV's interior stayed murky. Unopened utility bills on the cedar chest–turned–coffee table explained the power outage but not those window coverings.

Delia's hand found a lock that had slipped free of her French braid duty-do. She wondered how messed up the boy really was while her gaze settled on a picture frame hung near the exit. She wound and unwound the strand of hair, sneering back at the canted rendering of the blue-eyed King of Rock and Roll. Messed up in a different way. Still got him dead.

Harvey's flashlight switched off, and the narrow hallway returned to the semi-murkiness she had fired her weapon into. She stopped fiddling.

Shambling forward, Harvey snatched two clear plastic bags off the only surface of the L-shaped kitchen counter that wasn't stacked with food-lacquered dishes. The labeled baggie held a metal object. The other, larger bag was empty. Three more paces and the big man halted his high-top Red Wings opposite the cigarette-marred coffee table.

The newspaper-filtered light cast a pall over Harvey's Afro-Dutch skin tones. He frowned in obvious deliberation, his shoulders rising and falling under a black sweat shirt grayed from too many wash cycles. Springy hair the color of a rusted scouring pad poked out from his Ducks Unlimited ball cap.

Delia started to get up, but he motioned her back down. She'd like nothing better than to blow this skank hole. She darted a glance at the crooked picture frame, then back to Harvey. "Pretty sure the boy's gonna be okay, Harv. Wolfed a couple of my granola bars once I got him settled down." She got back a nod acknowledging the morning's upside. But looking past his grim smile, the disappointment in his eyes made it clear she'd lost ground. Maybe his support.

"Did you find a weapon?" She had to know where he'd come down on the shoot, her second in less than two years. "I mean, besides what the guy had in his hand?" She folded her arms across her lap, swinging the hat in front of her shins, wishing that metal chunk into a snub-nose or even a buck knife.

Harvey lifted the labeled bag and squinted at its contents. "Only the metal comb." His forehead bunched into furrows. "Hardly lethal, huh, Dee Dee?"

She pulled her hat up over the flat of her lap. Good. Using the family nickname she'd told him about meant he wasn't going all official. "That steel comb flashed like a blade, sighting down the hallway." She supposed she could have put a kitchen knife in the guy's hand afterward, but she'd had to get the kid out of that nightmare. And she wasn't that kind of cop.

Harvey wanted more.

She raised her chin, brought the hat brim up, and made a slicing motion. "Asshole held it like a knife across the little boy's throat. You didn't hear that chicken hawk's words, his taunts."

He gently took the hat from her hand and set it on the cedar chest.

She braced her hands on her hips, ready to push off. "I need coffee. Need to get out of here. What say we do the Q and As back at the shop?"

His sight line dipped to her jackhammering leg. "You need caffeine like a hound needs fleas."

Harvey ripped the sports section off the closest window and settled himself into an easy chair. She guessed RV cooties didn't bother him much.

Bathed in sunlight, his dark complexion was back to the freckled warmth she was used to. His hands flipped outward in explanation. "It's likely the sheriff will be gunning for you, so I need to be ready when I walk into his office."

Delia breathed easier, nodding that she understood. Every department had a hard-ass or two.

Reaching into his windbreaker, Harvey pulled out writing materials, a stubby pencil, and a notebook that got swallowed in his bear-size paw. "Okay, run it past again, this time in low gear. Around eight thirty this morning, you responded to a 911 from this woman . . ."

Hands clasped, Delia leaned toward him. "Hernandez, Lupe."

"About her missing son . . ."

She nodded. "Carlito. Little Carlos. I've been to the mom's apartment three times this month. Lupe had a court order against her ex-boyfriend, because of his violent episodes, weird sex stuff." She cleared her throat. "Lotta good that did her." She poked a thumb down the hallway toward the kill spot, the bedroom beyond. "Nasty piece of work, Zedo Camacho. Came and took the boy from the day-sitter's yard after Lupe left for work." She nodded at the exit. "The guy was known to hang out at the tavern. I drove here and found out he'd rented the owner's motor home out behind the place."

Harvey flipped a hand, signaling for her to slow down. He'd written nothing. "Okay, Dee-Dee. Facts are important, but I need to know exactly what ran through your head. Accounting for your mental state will be crucial with the officer-involved-shooting review."

Delia stiffened. "Uh-huh. Well, I stepped out behind the tavern, headed for the Winnebago, and peeked in around the newspapers covering the window. I heard a high-pitched yelp from inside."

Harvey made his first note. From upside down, it looked like he added "probable cause" at the end. Then he waited, his patience helping to calm her a little.

"I tried the door latch, the boy screamed, and I drew my weapon."

"You didn't knock?"

Knock, hell. About ripped the damn door off its hinges.

"Sure. But then I stepped in and stopped there." She pointed to a throw rug at the center of the RV's cramped living area. "I heard crying from inside the bedroom. The hall was dim, but I could see okay down there." Delia motioned toward the narrow passage. "Camacho heard my shout and came out of the bedroom. He was this large shape with a head, holding a smaller one by the back of the neck. Harv, the kid was shaking like a leaf."

"You identified yourself."

She tensed. "Asshole identified me. '*Oye, mamacita,*' he said. '*Policía.*' Cupped his crotch and growled out, 'Bet I got a bigger gun.'"

"He could tell it was you?"

She shook her head. "Picked up on my uniform, mostly."

Harvey tapped his temple. "What went on up there when he said that?"

Delia glanced at the floor. *I wanted to storm down that hallway and boot that chicken hawk in his big gun.*

"I ignored it. Instructed him to let the boy come forward."

"You tried a talk-down first?"

"Of course I did." Had she? Her memory flashed on a little boy's face contorted in terror, Camacho shuffling him sideways.

"All right," Harvey prompted. "Camacho's in the passageway with the boy . . ."

"By the kitchen opening, now."

". . . beside the kitchen, still holding the boy at the neck?"

"Squeezing, Harv, making him squeal."

Harvey frowned. "Jesus. Then?"

"Camacho said, 'Back off, *chiquita*. Or the floor turns red with blood.' That's when he yanked a drawer open, whipped out something shiny, and held it close to the boy's throat. Honest to God, Harv, I thought it was a knife." Delia clasped her hands together, studying her chewed thumbnail.

Could have been a spatula, anything from that galley. But her trigger finger had turned it into a knife.

Harvey would talk to the boy. She hoped he'd back her up.

He patted her wrist, a brief touch. "That's what made you take the shot?"

She blinked at the whiteness in her knuckles. That, and blind fury.

"I was sure the boy was toast."

He sat up and capped his knees with his hands, the notebook disappearing under one of them. "The sheriff will point out you've collared this Camacho before."

"Right. Several priors. Three for domestic violence, one a possible snatch attempt on the boy. Camacho skated when Lupe refused to bring charges. She was scared spitless of him."

Delia Chavez hadn't been, not by a long shot.

Harvey wrote something, then double-traced a question mark after it. "The last mentioned being the most recent?"

"Harv, my run-ins were three of at least a half dozen 911s on this guy. Ask Castner. Ask the responding deps. We all had our eye on him."

"But you more than others. He knew you."

Delia maintained steady eye contact and kept her first thought to herself. *If he didn't, he was blind, deaf, and stoned.*

"Knew I was Latina and a cop. He was usually so wasted he couldn't have cared less whether it was me or anybody else pouring him into the back of a patrol car."

Harvey's eyes narrowed. "Well, he wasn't falling-down drunk this morning."

She said nothing.

The big man lifted the curved bill of his cap off his forehead, scratched at a woolly outcropping, and reset his cap. "That brings up the last shooting review. You'd had several run-ins with the shootee back then."

Delia bristled but held silent.

"As I recollect, it also ended with him taking a little boy—"

"Now that was ruled a clean shoot. I—"

He raised his hands in a *whoa-up* gesture. "Except this time, you shot the guy dead."

She glared down at him, only then realizing she had jumped to her feet.

"Dee-Dee, I gotta play devil's advocate. Remember? I was the deputy's rep on that board. Now I'm on both sides of it, and I'm expected to present the full picture. You know I'll back you, so long as I'm convinced you didn't target Camacho and the shoot was justified. So park your skinny ass and get on with the convincing."

Skinny ass. Delia clamped her mouth shut and tried to wrap her head around the notion. Harvey had a knack for deflating her with an off-the-wall remark. She let out a breathy laugh and eased her so-called skinny ass back down onto the arm of the couch. "Sorry, Harv."

"I've said this before, Dee-Dee, you've got potential. Way beyond some of the numbnuts in our department. You've got this drive, this fearless compulsion to . . . well, do what's right, corny as it sounds. Just don't go overboard with it." She almost blurted out that he hadn't stood helpless, watching *his* baby brother get stolen away. "And you've got to spritz whatever's burning inside. Above all, an officer of the law is required to keep his or her temper in check."

She smiled at the spritzing part but recognized the last as a direct quote out of the law enforcement practices manual.

Harvey opened the larger bag and held it out. "I need your piece."

She felt the burn steal back into her face. Like a good investigator, she squelched it with a curt nod and handed over her weapon.

The interview lasted another thirty minutes, him probing with needle-sharp questions, her answering, eyes fixed on the opposite wall, where that velvet Elvis sneered back.

Finally, Harvey yawned. "What say we blow this dump?"

On the way out, Delia straightened the picture.

3

A chill evening breeze sent dry leaves rustling through the backyard fence slats of Delia Chavez's leased farmhouse. Fifty feet beyond the place, she stepped out of a sauna hut, her bared skin teeming with goose bumps. The only sweat she'd worked up was mental, over the shooting inquiry board. Four damn days and no damn call, *si o no*.

Wrapped in a beach towel, she dashed up the flagstone walkway to the rear deck, where a bottle of Spanish red and a cedar hot tub promised better therapy.

Her white two-story rental sat near road's end just a mile west of Monmouth and at the edge of the Coast Range foothills. Delia savored the privacy of the house, if not the drabness. She was grateful to its Swedish owners, the Johanssons, who knew how to soak the stress out of their days. Grown too old to run the farm, they'd given her a bargain rate.

And there was Clawed, who'd come with the rental. The single-fanged Maine Coon was the scourge of the rodent-choked pastures that ringed the place. Who knew what he'd sunk that lost fang into?

She took the six steps three at a time and let the towel drop beside the landline she'd placed within reach of the tub—just in case. The ugly plastic cockroach phone was a gift from Uncle Tino. No way would she stuff it in a closet and hurt his feelings.

Hey, it had given her good news about Carlito. The boy's mom said he'd smiled a little and was sleeping better. Best of all, no nightmares. No more Zedo Camacho.

Turning down the heat, she eased over the rim and into the bur-
bling warmth. The hot tub was her nightly refuge. Not a half-bad spot
to sit out a paid administrative leave.

She reached over and poured a glass of Diablo Rojo, then took in
the sleepy towns dotting the valley below, their streets and buildings
hazy blurs in the dusk. A mile away, sprinklings of street and dorm
lights flicked on around the campus of Western Oregon University.
She absently traced a worry line across her forehead, peering down
at her alma mater, half wishing she'd picked a different major than
criminal justice. Darker thoughts pushed forward. Delia splashed
water over her face to sidetrack the image of a hole in Camacho's left
eye.

How long before she flipped the safety off the trigger again, the
one inside, coaxing her to squeeze off a round, send another kid-
molesting asshole to hell? *Two's your limit, right, Chavez?*

She felt a grazing bump against the back of her head, followed by
a rattling purr.

"Hola, Clawed. What headless present have you left at my patio
door tonight?"

Yeolph.

Smug-faced and self-absorbed, the motley-colored cat flopped
onto her towel, his inside motor as soothing as anything she had tried
that evening.

She tossed off the last of the red, slouched low in the water, and
let the warmth envelop her shoulders. Flattening her soles against
the tub, she felt heavy-lidded. After two sleep-deprived nights, she
wouldn't mind a catnap. So long as she didn't dream.

Collected light flickered inside her closed eyes. Soon, she drifted
off, and upward. Dream drifting. Over Wheatland Ferry and the
Willamette River. Toward the hop fields of Old Mission Bottom.

*Light swallows the dark. The sun sends yellow ribbons down to
where Mama and Papa are training hop bines. Big brother Enrique is
there, too, helping. I wave, but they don't see me. They smile at each
other. The sun warms them.*

Oh. The light flashes. The hop field slides away. I see a little girl by the big river, playing in mud. I float down to her, closer and closer. I swim inside her.

I look out from little Dee-Dee's eyes. My eyes. I feel warm, too.

Sun on my face. I lick up sun with my tongue.

"L-l-l-r-r-b." Sun and water. Drink the sparkles. No clouds in the sky. I can play awhile.

No mud on my Sunday dress or Mama gets mad. Keep little brother, Bebé Tío, close by, Mama say.

Oh, Tío must be hungry. I make mud tortillas for him. "Ta-ta, la-la." Add some water. Fingers squishy. Gooshy-gooshy.

Papa calls my little brother Bebé Tío, "Baby Uncle," because he is so smart. But I have English now. Tomorrow I go in the big school. Head Start is for little niños *like Tío. Mama is so proud. Mama say,* Bravo, Dee-Dee.

"La-la, ta-ta." Ooo . . . that rock is hot. I bake the mud tortillas.

"Tío, come and get your breakfast. Where are you, little brother? Are you in the willows? Come out now."

I don't see Tío. The sky goes dark. A cloud comes down. Cold and gray all around me. I don't hear him. I feel afraid. Mama say, Watch him close, Dee-Dee.

My heart feels big inside me. I run to look behind a log. Bebé Tío no está aquí. My cheeks feel hot.

"Tío, no peek-a-boo . . . Come here right now, or I spank . . ." Tiny needles stick the back of my neck. Don't take Bebé Tío by the fast water, Mama say.

"Tío, are you by the water? Ow!" The rocks make me fall down. The fog is thick.

Bump-de-bump inside. Is something breaking?

Better yell loud.

"Tí-í-í-o. Be-e-bé-é Tí-í-í-o." Go away, gray. My eyes make wet.

I hear Tío. I can hear him.

"I'm coming, Bebé Tío." I run fast. Tío screams. He is scared, too. I push at the willows. Wet stings my cheeks. My heart is tight.

Fast water pulls at my legs. I see my face on the water. I feel cold inside. Drops from my chin make circles on the river. I look up. A boat with a green motor makes waves. A man with a brown hat smokes a pipe. Bebé Tío is in the man's lap. Tío's legs kick the air. Kick at everything. Duck things fall out of a bag into the bottom of the boat. A gun with two barrels slides down inside the boat. The motor spits blue smoke on the water. The boat melts into the gray.

Bebé Tío is crying. He is going away on the river. I try to say my little brother's name, but it hurts in my throat. The gray fog eats Tío's cries.

I sit down in the water. I hug my knees. Oh-h, Mama will be mad. She will ask why Dee-Dee let Tío go to the river. She will not be proud anymore. My heart wants to come out of my mouth and fall in the river.

La cucaracha, la cucaracha. *I float outside me, up into the gray.*

La cucaracha, la cucaracha. *Dark swallows the light.*

* * *

La cucaracha, la cucaracha.

"¡Ay, Dios!" Eyes blinking in relief, Delia lunged for the phone.

La cucara—

She picked up and held the buglike receiver over the churning water, pushing back the dream-fear. For a moment she thought about hanging up, putting off possible bad news. Instead she pressed its yellow cockroach belly against her ear. "Yeah."

"Chavez, are you drowning or something?" It was Annie, the sheriff's right-hand man—who was all woman.

Delia sat up. "Nah, I'm in my hot tub. So, what's the word?" Tight friends now, she and Annie Cox were social opposites who hadn't gotten along at first. Delia had been raised in Aunt Matilda and Uncle Tino Flores's strict—Tino not so much—churchgoing household. Annie had been a military brat. She'd gotten around, and still did. Funny how that could fascinate even an Easter Catholic.

"You've got one of those? Have to come out and try it. Clothing optional? Mind if I bring a friend or two?" Annie's stalling wasn't a good sign. But then, her calls always started off with a heavy dose of light banter.

"Not if it's the Friday-night kind you pick up at MaGoo's."

"Party pooper."

Enough chitchat. "So what's the verdict?"

Quiet from the other end. Clawed yawned, the hooks on his paws kneading her towel into a rumpled wad. Forget she was neck deep in soothing heat, Delia's body felt drum tight. Her free hand had gravitated up near her throat.

"Big shouting match in the sheriff's office, but I read Grice's expression on his way to a potty break."

"And?" Delia owned one piece of jewelry, a silver crucifix on a chain. At the bottom of that chain, her twirling fingers gave the family keepsake a workout.

"Not happy. Schenkel followed Grice out, smiling. Signaled three-to-one and flipped me a thumbs-up—shooting justified."

She gave her family memento a hard squeeze before letting go. She was the only female officer on the force, the first Latino, and now the only deputy to weather two shooting inquests. Much as it cut across her vegetarian grain, she owed Harvey a prime rib dinner.

But the vote wasn't unanimous. Resentment crowded out her sense of relief. "Do I need to guess who the holdout was?"

"Grice was the dissenter, according to the note he dropped on my desk. Harvey is still negotiating."

"Negotiating?" Delia's yell startled Clawed. Recalling Harvey's warnings about threads connecting the two shootings—her "temper" for one—she lowered her voice. "What's to negotiate? Hell, I've already seen a psych."

"Penance. Sorry, but the sheriff has conditions. Insists you stay in grade and under his thumb for another six months. Says you need more seasoning."

Delia huffed. "I get any more seasoned and you can pop me in the oven for Thanksgiving."

Annie just sighed. No sense rehashing.

Delia pulled her French braid around and chewed at the dark tip.

"I heard Marion County's hiring. Maybe I'll jump ship."

She felt the sting of Annie's silence. It was no secret Grice was slow-walking through another election cycle and into retirement— a buck-passer who'd blame the department's lack of direction and a shrinking deputy roster on anything and anyone except himself. But Annie didn't need to point out how Delia's two shooting inquests inside two years, plus a lame recommendation from her superior, would stymie any serious job interview. Especially if he ran an update on her background check.

Her last had been six years ago. Before the Albuquerque police raided her older brother's custom car palace–turned–chop shop and shot a hole in Enrique's hip for resisting. His partner, Big Juan Diego, skipped out and made his way to Oregon. Ran a speed shop and tow service just down the street from the county courthouse. It would be no mental leap for Grice to find out she had an incarcerated brother. Or to figure out that Enrique's ill-gained money had put her through school. After beating herself up over the discovery, Delia had gotten to where she was okay with crime gains launching a law enforcement career. But would Grice make a big deal out of it? Hell yes, he would.

"Quitting is not like you, Chavez. Stick in there. Change is in the air."

Delia leaned forward, cocking her head. "Why, what have you heard?"

"Can't say yet, but something's bound to happen."

Delia waited for a second, but when Annie buttoned up, she stayed buttoned. "You said 'several conditions.' What else?"

"Night shifts, special patrol assignments. Part of keeping you under his thumb, I guess. Grice plans to throw scut work your way. Expect some crowd control assignments for a while."

Delia sat up, sloshing water over the tub's rim. "What crowds? We live in a backwater rural county, for godsakes."

"PETA protesters. Harvey thinks they're building steam to disrupt this year's hunting openers."

"That's the Staties. Fish and Wildlife. How do we figure in?" Delia knew from her trooper contacts that People for the Ethical Treatment of Animals' feeble attempt to break up last year's game hunting had been all bluster and noise, done mostly for TV exposure.

"County facilities are likely targets for this year's waterfowl season. Droves of duck hunters use our boating access ramps and— Uh, the sheriff's coming back. If he signs your reinstatement tonight, I should see you tomorrow evening."

Delia dropped the phone onto its cradle and slumped back into the tub. Her hoped-for jump to Investigations had just gotten sidetracked. She poured another Diablo Rojo and sucked it down, watching Clawed's tail switch.

"Whaddaya think, old boy, should I hang tough or job hunt?"

Meolph.

"I hear ya. Quit whining and take my lumps."

The big Maine Coon rose up and stretched. Then he showed her his fluffy backside and sauntered off into the night.

4

Polk County sheriff Augustus L. B. "Gus" Grice picked at the irksome growth alongside his left nostril and eyed the documents on his desk. He'd wasted half the morning combing through Delia Chavez's service jacket knowing he was going through the motions. It galled him to pull her off administrative leave when he really wanted to knock the pegs out from under that smartass. Her and her uppity criminal justice degree.

He had to admit, her incident report logs were extensive for six years in grade. His first six as a county-mounty had earned him a look and a disappointing send-back for another three in uniform. Nine goddamn years, just to make detective. Then Harvey Schenkel had shown up, recruited right in over Gus's head.

He smiled to himself. Well, his election upset had sure put the kibosh on that seniority-jumper.

He puffed up his cheeks and blew out. Pen in hand, he paged through Chavez's portfolio, hoping something he'd missed would pop up on its own. Zip from her shooting write-ups. *Background check's old but clean. No juvie record.* The lean family section was no surprise: wetback amnesia, with parents almost sure to be illegals.

His yellow pad stayed blank. Chavez and Schenkel had pulled off another ass-covering. Cursing under his breath, Gus signed off on the order to reinstate and slapped her portfolio shut. Next time. And there would be one.

At least Schenkel wouldn't dare put her up for detective anytime soon, not with her reassigned to back-county night patrol. For once, running short on deputies was a good thing.

His in-box load was light, a couple of callbacks and a stack of circulars. Gus picked up the first message slip and tensed. The words *U.S. Navy* flared like a beacon. His scalp prickled, struggling to kill the flashback. Once he'd gotten through the whole message, Gus relaxed. Somewhat. The note was from the president of the Oregon County Sheriffs' Association. A heads-up that a Commander John Bannock, U.S. Navy, might contact Gus and other sheriffs whose counties bordered the Willamette River.

Other sheriffs, not just Gus. Nothing about his time in Colombia.

A second message was from Perry Barsch, a county politico. No urgency there. He set both notes aside and moved on to the latest crop of wants and warrants.

The first handful dished up the usual: A pair of pharmacy B&E specialists working their way up the Valley. A scam artist running an investment scheme on the elderly. A ganja transporter who evaded State Police but left a rental truck with bales of Mexican merriment idling on an I-5 exit ramp. Gus shook his head at that one. No doubt the Staties'd crow to the media over their major drug haul.

Gus came to a federal bulletin and groaned. It was an FBI circlejerk, cautioning that ALFies—shorthand for Animal Liberation Front extremists—had infiltrated several PETA chapters. He skimmed the notice and found nothing pertinent to his jurisdiction. Local colleges had no primate labs to raid, no monkeys that needed liberating.

After PETA's fizzled attempt to ruffle hunters during last fall's opener, the group had gone low profile. Maybe the Feds were afraid ALFies would talk PETA into blowing up a processed chicken truck. Inject packaged fryers with vomit-green dye. So what was he supposed to do, talk the county's grocers into restocking meat counters with Tofurky? Patrolling the opening-day crowds alone at county marine parks was ass-pain aplenty. He pitched the notice into the circular file cabinet beside his desk.

The warm, scaly growth by his nose was a finger magnet.

The next item was an alert on a military fugitive thought likely to turn up in his jurisdiction. Perplexed, he skimmed the description beneath the smudged photo. AWOLs didn't normally make the U.S. marshal's most-wanted list. When he got to the bottom, Gus let out a low whistle. Before skipping out somewhere on the upper Amazon River, this Robert Bastida character had wrecked a U.S.-Colombian counterdrug-training operation. Gus knew from experience to insert air quotes before and after training with any Colombian riverine unit.

Time to fortify. Standing, he picked up his cup. The phone buzzed, causing Gus to take a longing glance toward his coffee alcove as he tapped the communications bay light.

"Hey, Annie."

"Aloha, Sheriff."

Gus chuckled to himself. Annie Cox had just gotten back from Oahu. He pictured her in a room at the Waikiki Pearl, her teased-out shock of high sorrel gushing across a good-size pillow. His mind's eye traveled lower, conjuring lighter wisps of red, curling over hip-hugging Victoria's Secret underwear.

"Change your mind, darlin'?"

"Sheriff, you know you're way too much man for me."

He chuckled. Earlier, Gus had sauntered past her com bay, floated his usual offer, and gotten back a wink.

The afterthought of that mock tease made Gus warm inside. Annie was old school. None of that "Help me, I'm being sexually harassed" garbage. The love exploits of his saucy-mouthed dispatcher were legend, and legend held she wasn't all that choosy.

Not that she'd yet chosen him.

"Well, Annie, you just let ole Gus know when you get tired 'a chasin' those young hotshots."

"Until I do, Sheriff, promise you'll keep breathing in and out?"

Gus gave out a lost-cause sigh. "You rang me, darlin'?"

"Right. The naval officer Tomlin referred to is on line one."

"Jeezum, but that was quick."

Settling back into his chair, Gus picked up the receiver and punched the flashing button. "Sheriff Grice here."

"Former petty officer third class, Augustus L. B. Grice?"

Gus felt that tingle along his hairline again. This officer had done some homework. Question was, how much? "Ye-es. A long time ago. What can I do for you, Commander Bannock, is it?"

"Have you received a U.S. Marshals warrant on a military fugitive?"

Gus's momma would've declared the man so whiskey-voiced you could wring out "hunnert proof." An offbeat cadence in his speech, too. Something not quite right.

"I have."

"Bastida, R., gunner's mate second class. The Bastard, for short. We suspect he used an alias."

"Who's this *we*?"

From the other end, Gus heard what he took for a stifled groan. The drawer of a metal desk opened, then slammed shut. Then repeated.

"My special operations detachment and the Colombian riverine unit we were assigned to. Our training and support mission was to deny the Caquetá and its tributaries to drug traffickers sending product downriver. The *cartelitos* protect smugglers for a cut. In our last operation, we inserted two squads that destroyed their key river island base. The Bastard went rogue, rammed and overturned one of our support boats, then boogied with the other. Fucking stranded us on that snake-infested island."

A thumping sound came from the other end, like a fist pounding dead meat. Back in his Navy days in South America, Gus had run across DEA-sponsored tactical units whose job was to inject fire into Colombian counterdrug units. Clearly, this officer's burner was still set on high.

"We extracted the hard way, but the damage was done. It goes unsaid, my operators would sooner bite the biscuit in a firefight than lose face."

"Commander, I understand your predicament, but this is clearly U.S. Marshals turf. Or NCIS. You should be talking with them."

"It has been three goddamn months." More meaty thuds.

"How's that?"

"Apparently, you have to kill somebody to earn the attention of NCIS or the Marshals Service. The Bastard's been low priority with both. Now it's on me and my detachment to get this bastard—and I'm convinced you're the one to help."

"Me?" The inflammation beside Gus's nose started to itch like chigger bites. "Hold on there. I surely am sympathetic, but—"

"Exactly what I thought once I looked into your service tours. Your picket ship practically straddled that cocaine sluice box at Barranquilla. In fact, I'm betting you're more than sympathetic."

Gus sat back in his chair, giving up, picking at the itch. *Think, Gus.* Everything Bannock had said so far could be pulled from military separation papers. Likely, that was all he knew. It was time to exit this conversation.

"Look, I don't know what you're getting at, but you're barking up the wrong tree. Now—oh geez." Gus made his chair squeak as he stood. "Here I am, late for a deputy debriefing. How about you leave your information with my dispatch center, Commander? And if my crew runs across anything pertinent to your fugitive, we'll be sure to include you in the loop. Best of luck on—"

"According to the Sheriffs' Association, you're up for reelection."

Bannock's sudden topic switch left Gus short for words, his ear tight against the receiver.

"Being a fellow Navy man and a former noncommissioned officer, I'm sending something you'll find interesting. Nostalgic, even. Look for a packet labeled *Amigos de Colombia.*"

The connection went dead.

* * *

Delia lingered near the com desk, tingling with visceral curiosity. Impatient for the string of dispatch calls to end. Grice still had to make her reinstatement official, so she'd shown up in street clothes—just in time to hear Annie relay something about a naval officer and a fugitive over her intercom link with Grice. Words rarely heard in a rural county sheriff's office were bound to set Delia's detecting antennae humming.

Annie lowered the headset mic and swung her way. "You know you're jumping the gun."

"Yeah," Delia said, rubbing at her arms. "Couldn't bang around the walls at home any longer. Hey, what was that I heard about the Navy and an AWOL?"

"Way more than a military skip-out. U. S. Marshals got a federal warrant on him."

"What about the officer?"

"From some base on the East Coast. Little Creek, Virginia, I think. Why?"

"I don't know. A feeling. Mostly curious." Delia sauntered off toward her locker room. "Let me know if you hear more, 'kay?"

"Remember what killed the cat."

"Yeah, and what brought her back."

5

Delia had one foot on a locker bench in the women's restroom, tying up her Danner high-tops, when the door swung open behind her and a fruity juniper fragrance announced Annie's presence.

"Got a minute?"

"A minute." Delia yanked the second bow tight and straightened up. "Still have to check out my gear for the shift. What d'you need?"

"Grice got a package labeled *Amigos de Colombia*. Just means 'Friends of Colombia,' right?"

"Yeah, or 'from Colombia,'" Delia said, reaching for her tactical windbreaker. "A tourist packet, maybe?"

Annie moved to the wash counter and started primping. "That's what I'd thought when he said as much. Grabbed it out of my hands and scooted into his office." She patted a loose coil into place. "Stormed back out ten minutes later, asking whether I had that naval officer's number. Cussed when I said I didn't. It took me a minute to remember that packet had a Little Creek, Virginia, postal stamp." She faced Delia with a coy smile. "Spooky, huh?"

"What?"

"How you and your little hunches get me so fired up."

Delia held her hands out with her palms up, the coat hanging off three fingers. "Hey, what can I say?"

29

She'd gotten an arm inside a sleeve and then paused, giving Annie the eye. "Don't get ideas, Cox. Could be a reason why Grice hasn't brought up this military contact or the fugitive during our briefings."

"Yeah, but what's to stop us from staying curious? Hunting up a little satisfaction on the DL?"

Delia shrugged, slipping the coat on. "Oh . . . loyalty? He is the sheriff of this county. The office commands respect."

Annie rolled her eyes. "Puh-lease. The guy's lost half his staff and is close to running the place into the ground. He pipedreams of getting reelected. You know, I could easily—"

"Just keep your eyes and ears open for now, okay?"

* * *

A week later, and for the umptieth time that day, Gus glanced at his desk clock. Five forty-five and no call from Bannock. He tapped the point of his pen on the notepad where he'd scratched in two words: *stick* in small letters, *carrot* in caps. The wait was exasperating. The com phone buzzed, making him jump, then pick up.

"Yeah, Annie."

"Sheriff, you have a call."

"That naval commander?"

"No, Perry Barsch."

"Oh, for cripesake. Bet he wants me to make another jail remodel pitch at the Dallas Rotary."

"Mr. Barsch didn't say."

"Put him through." Gus leaned back in his chair, clicking the pen. "Perry, how the hell are you? Keepin' happy?"

"Uh, no, quite frankly." Perry's ragged exhale rattled in the phone's earpiece. "Gus, I'm letting you know up front. Regardless of my objections, Republican leadership wants to back another horse in next year's election."

Gus clenched his jaw, heard a crack, and glanced down. Shards of black plastic littered his lap. The pen's filler tube was bent double between his thumb and his closed fist. In this county, the sheriff was

30

nonpartisan in name only. What's more, the county GOPs had a history of using the office as a pipeline into the state legislature. No reelection, no senate seat later on.

"Oh? And why in hell would they do that, Barsch? Somebody gunning for me from my own staff? Schenkel, maybe? He been lobbying you?"

Perry's answer came back evenly spaced. "No, Gus, it's all on you. The mess you've made of the department's budget won't stand public scrutiny, not to mention the staff you've driven off."

Gus sat up, feeling the festering sore at the base of his nose. How'd a county DA political hack get access to internal financial documents? How far back had he looked? His mind spun. Perry must have gotten word of another possible defection. Charlie Lukovsky, Gus's number two in Investigations. Charlie had seemed disconnected at the last situation debriefing. Right after he'd taken a three-day leave. And he'd done none of his usual clowning around. Not one lame joke.

Besides a limping investigative section, Gus was down to a skeleton crew of deputies. Rumors flew in the law enforcement community. Word got around. Even the reserve officer pool was drying up.

"Barsch, you wanted a small government advocate and you're getting it. Crime numbers are up, but I've kept a tight lid on staffing. For that, I expect a certain amount of budgetary leeway. You're not reneging on our agreement, are you? Because—"

"Don't force my hand, Grice. You and I both know you've taken way too many liberties on that agreement."

Silence followed, long enough to send needles of fear into Gus's scalp. So he'd padded travel expenses a little, dipped into the snitch fund now and then. Granted, quite a few more nows than thens.

"Where are you taking this, Barsch?"

Another pregnant pause. "Let's say, sometimes a person just finds he does his best work in the field. How about we meet at the Blue Garden for a drink and talk futures? If we don't see a way out of this, I can pull some strings over toward the coast, maybe Tillamook or Clatsop County—"

"Back to wranglin' cases? Bustin' backwoods tweakers? Like hell. Yours isn't the last word." He slammed the phone onto the cradle and hurled what was left of the pen at a wall.

Dirty son of a turd-floater.

Gus stomped over to the nook, yanked out the Bacardi, and stared at it. Nothing would be better than to lace his coffee with a hefty slug.

He'd borrowed from his pension fund a few times too many and needed to ride out another four-year term. A step backward was out of the question.

He stowed the unopened bottle in its hidey spot.

Back at his desk, Gus worried the scab off the sore and flicked it onto the carpet. Gradually, he worked his way around to truth time.

Perry was the last word.

Taking a long count to calm down, he lifted the phone and hit the speed dial.

"Barsch here."

"Perry. God, man, sorry I torqued on you. Real sorry."

Again a long pause. "Okay, but the message stays the same. Gus, you need an attention diverter. Otherwise, your prospects are grim."

"But not impossible." Gus could almost hear Perry shrug.

"What do I need to do?"

"Pull a big hairy rabbit out of a hat."

* * *

On her way out to the assigned patrol car and her last night shift for the week, Delia stopped by Harvey's desk, woke his Dell, and entered his password. The head of Investigations let her use it when the antiquated deputy-access system was cranky or slow, which was often. The screen had just brought up the shift schedule when a cardboard box plopped onto the desktop beside her. It overflowed with a compacted mixture of trash, including shredded, sliced, diced, and crumpled paper.

Annie stood close by. She had her arms folded, a big grin on her face. "Bet Colombia's in there somewhere."

Incredulous, Delia pushed the paper overflow back into the box. "Girl, what'd you do, toss Grice's office?"

"Nah. Theo, the custodian, has a stiffy on for me. Asked him real nice to set aside Tuesday night's paper discards. So how about we kill a cat and bring it back to life?"

"You do know I have a cat at home, right?" Delia pushed the lid-less box to the corner of the desk. "Take it away, back to . . . wherever."

"The dumpster? Don't you want to know what we've got here?"

"Not this way. Not without a solid reason—"

As if on cue, Grice tooled around a corner thirty feet down the aisle from them.

"*Mierda*. Distract him."

Annie complied, snatching up a folder and scurrying toward the sheriff. Meanwhile, Delia yanked open the desk's empty file drawer and crammed the box inside. Seeing that he was focused on the folder's contents, she eased the drawer shut, fumbled up a desk key, and locked the entire desk. Harvey wasn't coming back soon, so she pocketed the key as a reminder to herself to remove the box after her shift was over.

She didn't know why. She hadn't done anything, really. But a knot the size of a grapefruit had taken up residence in her gut as she stood and straightened her uniform, set her duty hat, and hustled out toward the waiting cruiser.

6

That same night, sheriff's deputy Delia Chavez was well into the doghouse shift when her radio squawked.

"Six-two. What's your loc?" It was the sheriff's trusty dispatcher.

Delia pressed her radio's send key. "South of the Independence–Coast Highway Y. Headed for the Octane Stop and a coffee break. What's up, Annie? Did the sheriff say anything about that box of paper?"

"We're good. But war's broken out again on the lower Luckiamute. Farmer alongside the Willamette greenbelt north of there is complaining about gunfire somewhere below his pastures. Afraid his Jerseys will stop giving milk with all that racket."

"Gee, I wonder who the racket-makers are?"

"Give you four guesses."

Twenty minutes and a long dirt-road drive later, the old Gatlin place once again appeared in her headlights. Dull glimmers showed from the windows as she cut a sharp right into the front yard, diagonally blocking a pair of vehicles. Both faced toward the Luckiamute. She knew the cars and their drivers, ran the plate numbers anyway.

Leaving the engine running, she flipped on the cruiser's halogen spotlight. By chance, it pointed at the big willow that bordered the river. She could just make out an empty longneck perched in its crotch. The mounds of broken glass at the base had grown considerably over the fifteen weeks since the Gatlin homicides.

She redirected the beam toward the front porch. A familiar foursome burst out of the abandoned house. Bryce Adkins, his twin brother Lonnie, and their two amigos. The guys approached, hands shielding their eyes. They stopped between her cruiser and the back of the ringleader's tricked-out Prelude.

She switched off the spot so they'd notice her slow headshake. She sighed for effect.

"Bryce, Bryce, Bryce," she said, scanning their faces. "The rest of you, too. What do I have to do to get through to you guys?"

Central High School's onetime quarterback was the first to lip off, spewing foul language and throwing in the tired complaint about having no fucking place to blow off steam.

Thirty seconds into his rant, Delia hand-signaled time-out for a call-in. She confirmed her location, making sure they heard there was another unit close by. Delia wasn't worried about these guys—she'd tutored two of them in grade school as a junior at Central High— being extra-cautious was part of the job.

When she dropped her hand, Bryce started in again. "This is all bogus, Chavez. You cops don't cut us no slack. Can't even night camp up at Helmick." He jabbed a thumb in the general direction of the state park a few miles up the Luckiamute. "Highway patrol ran us out, so we came down here."

"Camping, huh?" Leaving the headlights on, she cut the ignition and stepped out.

The pride of Central's former Panther offense shouldered up to their spokesman, each in an arms-folded, defensive posture. "Lotsa guys hang in this old house, Chavez." Brice was heating up, his block- ers crowding forward. "It's already a mess. So give us a break."

Delia unsnapped the tactical flashlight from her utility belt and swept their faces with a blinding glare. "I'll say it once. *Back. Off.*"

Bryce and his compadres shuffled backward until they were against the Prelude's trunk.

She lowered the light. "Everybody cool your jets. Doesn't matter if this place is abandoned and falling apart. You guys are trespassing."

Bryce shrugged in conciliation. "Sorry, Deputy. We're cool, but . . . well, this sucks."

"So does getting pried out of a sound sleep by gunfire."

They traded looks.

She aimed the light past the front of the Prelude and picked up brassy glints among the clumps of yard weeds. Lots of them. The groupings of expended casings were consistent with rapid fire. Very rapid fire.

"Somebody have a birthday? Get a new toy?"

No one moved. Nobody spoke.

"Let's have a look." She nodded toward the rear of the Honda.

"Uh, don't you hafta have a warrant or somethin'?"

She swept her light over the casings. "Not when I've got piles of probable cause." Then back on Bryce. "So open up."

Bryce fished keys from his pocket, inserted one in the lock, and paused. "Just doin' a little plinking. You know, gettin' ready for deer season 'n' stuff. Nothin' wrong with that." He popped the lid.

The trunk light came on, and Delia felt her eyes go wide. "Not unless you plan on decimating a herd." She'd expected maybe a hunting weapon equipped with a bump fire stock to simulate rapid fire, not AR-15s and 60-round magazines lying around. Both were older-model Colts, capable of accepting M16 fire control parts.

"Stand over there." She pointed toward the second vehicle, a Nissan pickup hiked up on tractor tires. The four complied, even though the highboy sat square in a giant rain puddle.

Making sure one of the ARs was unloaded, Delia retracted its bolt and dry-fired. Pulled the bolt again with the trigger depressed. The bolt closed, no click. They'd probably been modified for full automatic fire.

She turned toward the four. "Do you have any more weapons?"

Four heads shook. She had them show their waistbands, turn full around, and hike their pant cuffs. Next, she carefully scanned the insides of both vehicles, including the truck bed. Bryce used the time explaining, as much with his hands as his mouth. "Really, Deputy. Those are my dad's. Me and Lonnie kinda reworked them at his store. Y'know, Nimrods-R-Us? Got the paperwork there."

It figured that Bryce and his brother still lived with their parents. "I'll do more than that." Delia gathered up clips and rifles and stowed them in her brown-and-white. Then she squared off in front of them.

"Okay. Assume against odds the firearms check out as legal. I want to get something through those thick heads. The four of you are experienced hunters. Right? You all know how far a slug can carry from a long gun." They studied the puddle, as if polliwogs were about to wiggle out. "So then, what the hell were you thinking, shooting out across an open waterway?" The two who weren't brothers glanced at the twins, but that was all she got.

"I'm not saying some boater's crazy enough to chug around out there in the middle of the—"

"Ha." Lonnie's head snapped up. "Took off like a bat anyway, so we didn't—*umpf.*" Bryce had stifled his brother with a sharp nudge to the ribs.

"You have something to tell me, Lonnie?" Delia got back a tight-lipped mouth shrug.

She stared off toward the river a few beats, then back at their faces. "You guys are too young to mess up your lives getting hauled in for manslaughter or negligent homicide. Let alone possessing illegal guns."

She ran her light across the back of the deserted two-story. The house must've decayed five years in the months since she first climbed those porch steps. Chunks of roofing hung off the eaves. Blackberry vines probed through window frames bristling with glass shards. The bloodstained lawn chairs were gone, likely tossed somewhere into the yard. Delia pursed her lips, trying not to let grisly images trip through her head. Like a forlorn country song stuck in replay, she couldn't leave off speculating on the misery Rose Gatlin had endured inside those rotting walls.

"Look, guys, there's been too much tragedy here without somebody getting shot. Or knocking over a lantern and burning up in that tinderbox." Blank stares.

"What's up at the house?" She aimed her question at Bryce, who unfolded his arms and cleared his throat.

"Uh, nothin' much. Camp lanterns and a pony cooler. Snacks 'n' stuff."

Stuff. Delia canted her head. "Well, tell you what. Before we pay a visit to your dad and have a look at those papers, you need to hike back in there, dowse the Colemans, and collect your gear."

Bryce opened his mouth again, and Delia poured words into it.

"Because if I enter the premises and discover the presence of illegal substances, I guarantee you won't be happy campers."

* * *

A few minutes past three AM, Delia wheeled off Highway 20 into the lane between Rickreall Winery's floodlit parking lot and an unlit mom-and-pop store. She rolled to a stop beside what had to be one of the last pay phones anywhere, got out, and set her lunch on the hood. Besides gym workouts, her hip-slimming regimen consisted of a Vegan Delight pita, followed by dessert a la Annie. Maybe a blow-by-blow of her latest bar cruise. To avoid flapping ears, their chick chats took place via landline.

An hour and a half had passed since she'd followed Bryce and crew to his parents' house and awakened them. Mom was fairly passive, but Dad owned a gun shop and thus valued his relationship with local law enforcement. On his promise to reconvert the firearms for legitimate resale, she'd let Bryce's dad deal with the gang of four.

Leaning against the fender, she tilted her head up and inhaled a grapey essence she could almost taste. Trucked in from vineyards flanking the Coast Range, the crushings of first frost spiked the air. She tied into her sandwich, the pungent spiciness helping to chase off the memory-stink of river bottom and mildew that had hung over the Gatlin house, and a closed case. Except for the missing relative, whoever Robbie was.

Okay, so air-wine and vicarious sex made poor substitutes for the real thing. Both kinds were safe. And Annie could be . . . deliciously graphic. Too bad the men Delia's relatives tried hooking her up with were all big little boys.

She tossed the pita wrapper in a receptacle, picked up the phone receiver, and punched in the numbers.

"Polk County Sheriff's Office."

"Hey Annie, how 'bout capping your nail polish and helping me get through the last half of a super-dull night shift?"

"Give me a sec."

On hold, Delia removed her hat, let her French braid fall free, and reset the holding band. Grice insisted on a trooper's hat and hair tucked underneath. At shoulder-blade length, her choice of hairstyle honored a mother's wish and a memory. She'd kept it long since she was nine, since the day her parents were buried.

"Dried and buffed, Chavez. Done chasing young men around in the woods, are we?"

"*We?*" Delia chuffed.

"Uh. Gimme a sec." A bit of radio chatter followed, then Annie was back. "Have you talked with Charlie?"

"About what killed the cat and brought him back?" Charlie Lukovsky had ridden the sidekick detective desk since before Delia joined the department; knew Grice like the back of his hand. "Been meaning to, but he's been on leave. Now I hear he's going off duck hunting with his brother." She bit of the end of one of the carrot sticks that came with the sandwich.

"Not about that, but you'd better catch up with him soon," Annie said. "Remember the other night I let slip things were about to happen? Word has it Charlie's ready to jump ship."

Delia straightened up. "Charlie? Leaving?"

"Offered chief of police. Some small town in Minnesota, Montevideo, I think he said. Sure gonna miss the guy. Him and his left-field sense of humor."

The chewed bite Delia swallowed went down hard. "Me too, Annie." She'd interned with him during her law enforcement training. Now she regretted thinking the guy was too jolly. Too . . . comedic to make a first-rate detective.

A whiff of freshness wafted past. She inhaled deeply and flushed away the guilt for picturing herself a stepping-stone away from Charlie's desk. Leastwise, not before he was gone.

"That isn't the half of it. Harvey hit up the sheriff to shift you into Investigations on interim assignment."

Delia pressed the phone into her ear, as if she hadn't heard right. "Yeah? For real?" The boost from Annie's words lasted about two seconds before she slumped back against the cruiser. "Don't need to guess how Grice reacted to that proposal."

"Have to admit, a lot of yelling and desk-pounding went on behind the sheriff's door, clear up to the point Harvey walked out and slammed it. But he flicked me a wink as he passed by."

"Meaning?" Delia held her breath for a long second.

"Meaning either the sheriff's over a staffing barrel, or Harvey's caving to my charms. I'd pick the second if I didn't know the county board approved a freeze order on outside hires."

A coast breeze blew across Delia's face, cool and sweet.

"Not even one little woo-hoo, Chavez?"

Delia laughed. "Okay, here goes. *Woo-hoo!*"

"Ouch. I said little. Now, it's a done deal only if Charlie takes the offer, the sheriff stays desperate, and Harvey keeps winking."

Small thrills hat-danced a circle inside Delia's chest. "Think he will?"

"Keep on winking? Well, if I show Harvey a little more cleavage—"

"No, you randy wench. Will Grice wear down?"

"Don't see he has an option, what with the freeze on. Your time's coming, Chavez. Just hang in a little longer on doghouse shift, and make some collars."

As if on cue, Delia's spoiler alert kicked in along with a sudden urge to pace. Could her brother Enrique still gum up the works from his cell at Los Lunas? The short receiver cord kept her to a single step and turn. Annie's switch to a new subject had barely registered, but it was perfect for staving off a case of disaster diarrhea.

"Hey girl, been dying to fill you in on the latest. Met this ca-yute frat guy, last night at the Hind Quarter? Well, we—"

"The Hind Quarter? That steak-on-the-hoof sit-down in Salem? Annie, we know you're a manivore, but a carnivore, too?"

"Funny. Get off your veggie high horse or I'm not giving up one juicy tidbit."

"Fat chance you won't."

7

ONE WEEK BEFORE WATERFOWL SEASON

Dawn hadn't broken over the far tree line when Delia parked and switched off her county SUV at the crest of a floodlit boat ramp. Independence, Oregon, slept behind her. Down below and never asleep, the river glided past in black silence.

Two aged and starkly contrasting vehicles were backed to the water's edge. The rust-paneled Jeep Cherokee had a small flatbed trailer attached behind. The second was the pickup she'd been told to look for—a glimmering-red, fully restored Chevy Apache, pulling a small boat piled with brush.

Charlie and Zack Lukovsky sat in the Apache and seemed enthralled with the spectacle to their right. Shirttails flapping, the guy from the Jeep manhandled his drift boat onto the flatbed and clapped on the winch hook, shouting curses that reverberated through her closed windows. She had known both of the Lukovskys for years, but needed to question Charlie about Grice. Say a proper good-bye, too.

Delia was content to wait and watch until they were done at the water and away from the river.

She couldn't be sure, but when the guy with the Jeep ran around and jumped into the driver's side, the crotch area of his cargos looked soaked through.

The Jeep lurched up the lane, slowed when the driver saw her SUV, then rolled on by and out of the marine park. The driver's face was white as a sheet.

Back down the ramp, Charlie got out the driver's side and mouthed something to Zack, then plodded uphill.

Delia unlocked, swung her mobile data terminal to the center of the SUV's dash, and made room as Charlie slumped into the passenger seat.

"Hey, Detective Charles Lukovsky."

"Hey back, Deputy Delia Chavez. Long shift?" Though full-on coworkers, they'd stuck with that minor formality clear back from Delia's interning with him. She liked Charlie for that.

"Getting longer by the minute. Any idea why that Jeep bombed out of here?"

"The pants-pisser? Either he took sick or something out on that river scared the bejesus out of him."

"And not a full moon in sight." She shook her head. "Hey, is what I hear for real? Your gone in a couple weeks?"

His shoulders moved. "Couldn't pass it up. You know Grice. His ship taking on water and all."

"Yeah, besides wanting you to know how much I'll miss you, that's why I swung by. What's with him, letting the department slide downhill?"

"Beats me. It's beyond incompetence."

They watched Zack in silence for a while, unhooking boat tie-downs, unplugging lights, backing down until the trailer hubs sloshed.

"Has Zack done any writing since high school?" She hadn't seen him since after-school tutoring. She'd coached him through his senior paper while she finished college. Back then, it had been a toss-up between her first and second passions: teach English language arts at thirty-six a year or catch bad guys for sixty. Sixty won.

"Not a lick. Stickum notes on the fridge. Filling out salmon tags. He still talks about how you kept him from bagging high school, settling for a GED." Charlie shifted toward her. "He's pretty bent out of shape about his hunting and fishing partner and all-around sage leaving for Minnesota." He seemed to hesitate. "Mind checking in on him now and then?"

She gave Charlie a noncommittal shrug. "Yeah, maybe. If I run into him. We haven't even seen each—"

"Don't worry about it. Just if you happen to cross paths."

Zack's empty boat hauler made water trails up the ramp on its way to parking. The sun cleared the far bank, cutting a golden trail across the river.

Delia filled in their pause with the question that had hung around for days. "Speaking of Grice and 'beyond competence,' have you noticed anything unusual?"

"Like?"

The radio croaked. She squelched it. "Like, has he passed a U.S. marshal's warrant on to Investigations?" Harvey was at a law enforcement conference in Seattle, or they would've had a sit-down.

"Nope. Why?" By the halfhearted note in Charlie's voice, she could tell his head was already in Minnesota.

"He ever mention a naval officer who keeps calling?"

"Look, soon as I let Grice know I was moving on, he lame-ducked me." Charlie nodded toward Zack, then motioned downhill at the boat full of cut brush. "So, I figured I might as well be out with the ducks and my kid brother."

Charlie's *kid brother*, who had to be twenty-four or -five, strolled up to the SUV. Delia let him into the back seat and scrunched around so she could see both.

"Hi, Zack. Long time."

He slumped against the seat back. "'Lo, Deputy. Charlie try out his fake Norwegian accent on you? Tell you he's takin' a job in Minnesota? That I'm losin' halfsies on a bigger boat?"

The cage blocked Charlie's hand—from patting his brother's knee, maybe? "She knows, Zack."

"She know why we're building a duck blind just to hunt for nine or ten days?"

Delia said nothing. Watched Charlie inspect the back of his hands in the tense silence between them.

"Hey Zack," he said. "Remember a while ago you talked about applying for deputy sheriff?"

She glanced up. Charlie's idea of *checking on* expanded like a helium balloon.

His attention was directed at her. His coy smile, too. "You know, Deputy-soon-to-be-Acting-Detective Chavez here went through the Deputy Sheriff's Academy." She narrowed her eyes. *Thanks a bunch, Charlie.* His former intern owed him, and he wasn't shy about collecting on her debt.

Zack lurched forward, his fingers curling through cage openings. "How'd you do? Was it tough?"

"Pretty tough. Especially written requirements." She had to be careful not to pop that balloon. Float it off in another direction. "Done much writing since high school?"

"Some." To her surprise, Zack didn't sit back. "Funny duck-hunting stories, mostly. Like that Gordon MacQuarrie in Dad's old *Outdoor Life* mags." Charlie's eyes had gone wide, staring back at his kid brother.

"Nothing I didn't trash, so far." Zack opened his door and paused. "But hey, you might get a kick out of running upriver with us, seeing the drive-in duck blind we're building. You could fill me in on the academy."

Delia's hand flew to the ignition like a startled bird. "Sorry Zack, not my idea of fun. I gotta get a move on. We'll talk sometime." Her ears burned with the white lie.

Charlie levered the door handle, ready to make his escape. "Vell, Zachary, vee got to be goin' so vee can get after those mollards, you bet you."

"Don't start in with that Scandahoovian crap," Zack said, getting out. "just cause you're goin' back there. See you around, Deputy."

"Sure thing, Zack." She started the SUV.

Charlie got out and tipped his head back in. "Take care of yourself, A. D. Chavez. And thanks."

"You, too, Detective Lukovsky. And thanks a lot."

He eased the passenger door shut, a big grin across his face.

* * *

Gus Grice collapsed into his desk chair with a heavy thump. Head bowed and hunched forward, he stared at the age spots blooming on the backs of his hands. He was getting too old for this garbage.

Suspecting Charlie Lukovsky—his number-two investigator—had taken leave to hunt for greener pastures, Gus had run a what-if flag up the new-hire pole. Not one of the county commishes had saluted. Just the opposite. They'd directed him to fill all future openings from within. Then the SOBs informed him they'd ordered a line-item audit of the departmental budget, including asset forfeitures and slush pots. Pots he'd tapped far more than once.

Damn that Charlie Lukovsky. And damn that Perry Barsch for being right about those bastards coming after him.

Now Gus needed to cover his skim trail. He sat up, yanked out desk drawers, slammed them shut, opened more, and found the old refills. Twenty-sixteen on up to twenty-twenty. They had Day-Timer apps, but Gus preferred paper planners he could pencil in and back-date. Most important, erase as necessary. Pure gold when bean counters came looking for documentation. Load in snitch payoffs here, miles traveled there, and nobody would know the difference.

He hoped.

Gus was partway through his backfilling when the intercom buzzed. He mashed down the lighted button. "Not now, Annie." He'd instructed her to head off his calls and take numbers.

"Okay, Sheriff. But that naval officer you were asking about the other day is on hold."

"Kee-rist," Gus shouted, winging his 2018 filler across the room, where it hit the wall with a thwack.

When it rains, it shits daggers.

"Sheriff?"

He smoothed back wisps of hair, surprised at how clammy his scalp felt. "Put him through."

Familiar sounds issued from Gus's receiver—the bustle and chatter of people grouped into small quarters, the repetitious paper sounds coming from banks of copiers. Office noise, not training or operations.

"Commander Bannock? Okay if I call you John?"

No answer. Gus filled the void. "Say, uh, John. We kinda got off on the wrong foot the other day and . . . well, the past is long past, and—"

"Then you received my packet." The off-sounding voice again. The boozy slur.

"Well, yeah, John. Speaking of that, what do you plan to do with those old Navy files? You're not sending them anywhere else, are you?"

A throaty chuckle rattled back over the line. "Relax, Grice. Those were attention-getters. Mainly."

"Then how about the other two, uh, items?"

"All yours, and more. If we reach an understanding."

"About?"

"Bastida. The Bastard. About finding him and laying down some military justice. Call it a special operation."

"Special? How?"

"Taken care of by my unit. Except for people under your command, no other cops involved. That's where you come in."

"Me? And what army? John, I lead a small county law enforcement org. Hell, we're running so shorthanded, I've had to promote from within. No way are we equipped to go after some badass superwarrior who—"

"Shut. The. Fuck. Up. Listen to my offer."

Gus winced, holding the receiver out from his head. The wattage of Bannock's hissed earful was so powerful, he might as well have shouted. Blood heat rushed up the back of Gus's neck, sending prickles into his scalp. Nobody had talked to him like that since the goddamn Navy. If it hadn't been for those files and the two items, and that word *offer*, he'd have told Bannock to eat a big grubby one and slammed the phone into its cradle.

Gus listened.

"You find the Bastard. We do the going-after. My operators slip in, execute a snatch-and-grab, and slip out. Ghosts in the night."

Gus rubbed the itchy spot next to his nose. "My people just do the locating?"

Nothing from the other end. Not a man to repeat himself.

"Okay then, John. What makes you think this fugitive is here? Or would stick around, for that matter?"

"First, we learned that he's originally from Oregon. Second, we've traced him into Portland International by way of the Bahamas. And third, my guys tell me the Bastard had a permanent hard-on over some screwed-up family thing that happened way back when. Got so his nonstop muttering about some backwoods poacher drove them nuts."

A distant shout carried over the line, then scraping sounds, as if Bannock had pulled himself to his feet. Gus knew a barked order when he heard one.

The last of Bannock's words tumbled out in a low-pitched voice. "Gotta snap to. I'll leave you this bone to chew on . . ."

Again Gus listened, thinking it was a fine bone for sure. With extra marrow.

The line went dead.

Gus finished doctoring his old appointment calendars. To the dollar signs, he added flourishes.

8

No damn peace. Delia cursed her luck on the morning before she was slated to become acting detective. Lights and siren running, she floored her cruiser toward Buena Vista Marine Park while Castner screamed at her over the radio.

"Shots fired. Chavez, where the diddly-fuck are you?" Loud booms, followed by the background racket of revving car and boat motors, garbled his next words. "Holy . . . spent bird shot . . . comin' down like fucking hailstones. Get here, quick."

An ancient van of many colors coughed and sputtered past her, belching blue-black smoke. Moments later, cars stampeded from the fog-bound park as she entered and screeched to a halt near the bottom of the boat ramp—so close to the river of her nightmares that she froze in her seat. Castner's blue streak faded into ear mush.

There he stood, ankle deep in water and the aftermath of chaos. The stink of bird poop—chicken, maybe—tainted the air that wafted through her open windows. Yellow plastic buckets rolled in the backwash of camouflage-painted hunting boats hightailing downriver. Discarded antihunting signs littered the ramp and emptied parking lot. And the strangest of all: behind those hunters, a large watercraft slinked after them.

Rounded hulls with sides painted in a serpentine pattern, it reminded her of the tropics, its driver of something . . . fleeting, then gone. The boat seemed to gather mist, a cloaking veil that made Delia doubt what she was seeing.

The dark-toned man standing behind the steering console cut a Captain Ahab–like figure—overused but accurate, she thought—in his long black coat. The resemblance to that fictional character in the bow of a whaleboat was striking: the forward lean, the jutting chin. His fixation on the fog ahead. She half expected a white whale to breach the surface.

"Chavez, you hearing me?" Castner splashed toward her, his voice veering upward, close to soprano.

She shook off the image and got out. Jungle greens and river grayness came together as the boat disappeared into the water-hugging vapor.

"Can't miss hearing or smelling you," she answered. "Anyone hit? Injured?"

"Don't know. Don't think so. Both groups split so fast I . . . I—"

"Secure your weapon and calm yourself." Opening her cruiser's rear door, she patted the seat and backed off from his barnyard odor, thinking she might as well get into AD mode.

"Take a minute, then give me a full rundown."

9

DAY TWO OF WATERFOWL SEASON

Zack Lukovsky stood knee deep at the lower end of Needle Island, listening to the hornet's drone of his outboard motor fade into the o'dark-thirty gloom. His ants-in-the-pants brother, Charlie, just had to make the mile-long run to the island's upstream point, sure he'd find better shooting.

Zack knew different. He yanked off a glove with his teeth and untangled the anchor cords from a drake decoy that had drifted against a hen. Unless they were scared, real ducks didn't clump together. Fakes shouldn't either. He left the hen in place, unwound more anchor line, and gave the drake a heave into deeper water. The decoy held in the current.

Fringe ice crackled as he waded onto the gravel bar. His pick to hunt, not Charlie's. Forget they'd set out a humongous decoy spread. Never mind they still needed to throw together some kind of make-shift cover to hunt behind. No, his older brother had to wander, even after Zack told him Needle's upper end was a jumble of snags and shifting currents.

Charlie'd see it was unhuntable and motor back.

Zack snatched up a machete and bent low beside a willow thicket, hacking at young shoots, making them take the blame for the ruined duck blind he and his brother had spent damn near two weeks building.

51

Whack. Whack.

Best damned floating blind on the river. Pontoons shaped in a drive-in U. Styrofoam floats supporting a shoulder-high chicken-wire frame. Moss-green Scotch broom and dirty-yellow canary grass wove in thick all the way around. So natural looking under the trees and behind the flooded corn stubble that the ducks needed X-ray vision to spot him or Charlie. Once they ran the boat inside and closed the brush gate.

But not that morning. Not on Zack's last hunt with his brother for what could be a long while. The sight of that burnt-out blind had made Zack feel like somebody'd crapped in his hip boot. Probably one of those fool demonstrators from opening day with a bottle of jellied gas and a stiffy for spoiling a natural sport.

Now, miles upriver from their blackened wreck, Zack still couldn't get the stench out of his nose. Charcoal, gasoline, and benzene. That's what Charlie had said it smelled like. He should know, since he was the arson investigator for the Sheriff's Department. Talk about unhuntable. They'd have to tow that stinking mess out of the farmer's cornfield.

But Charlie wouldn't be around to help.

Whack. Whack.

Fifteen minutes later, Zack had enough material to put up a temporary blind on the gravel bar. At least they'd have clear shots.

He dropped the cuttings behind a beached log, where he'd set down a thermos and a box of Charlie's jelly-filled heart-cloggers. Flicked his two-way searchlight to *lantern*. The best he could do was put up a hedge of branches and sticks and drape it with long grass. Enough cover to disguise body outlines. Fool a low-flying widgeon or two that might decoy into range.

He staked thick boughs as corner posts, piling up brush, picturing that deputy, Chavez, standing behind it in hunter's camo. She'd still look good. Came off like his big sister, and that was okay, too. Maybe she'd get back to him about applying. Reserve deputy would be cool.

For some reason the skin at the back of his neck went all crawly. He straightened up. Peered into the dark and listened. The feeling he was not alone stayed with him. Except for Charlie going off on his gallivant, there'd been no engine sounds on the river, no running lights for over an hour. He flicked the searchlight to *spot* and sprayed light around. Nothing but moving water and brushy banksides.

Zack took up the Remington Wingmaster he'd propped against the log and cradled the gun in the crook of his left arm—mostly for the comfort it gave him. Still way too early to load up, but . . .

His shoulders twitched. The dark had never bothered him before. It bothered him now.

He pointed the spotlight toward his left, tracing downstream along the heavy overhang. At sixty yards the powerful beam lit up something snug against the bank and making ripples. He angled the beam up a notch and stiffened.

A guy stood in the middle of a low-sided boat that was brown as beef gravy. He shot a glance in Zack's direction, hustling on a parka over what looked like black underwear. Zack lowered the light, figuring he'd just interrupted a call of nature.

He counted to twenty—zip-up time—wondering why the guy hadn't flashed a light to let him and Charlie know the hunting spot was taken. On this river, shooters got cranky when somebody parked a boat within a duck's call of their setup.

Zack decided to bluff. Act like he had first claim. He put the light back on the guy and yelled, "Hey, Mister. Can't you see our decoys? We been set up here since four AM."

A tiny flame sparked to life. Johnny-come-lately took his time lighting up a cigar or something. It crossed Zack's mind that a really pissed-off hunter might resort to arson. He pushed the thought into the back of his head.

The hunter crouched in his boat, came up with a pair of decoys, and waggled them in the air. Zack cursed under his breath. *Shit. The guy's gonna say he was here first. So he's got dekes. Why the hell didn't he set them out in the first place?*

Zack's final hunt with Charlie had just turned into two hip boots full.

The other hunter started his outboard and put the boat in motion. For a second, Zack thought the guy was taking off. No such luck. The gravy-colored boat made a sharp turn and swung up into Needle Island's inside channel. Zack ran his light over the approaching watercraft. He'd seen that Louisiana-style Go-Devil before, but always from a distance. Heard talk about some hunting guide taking three hundred ducks a season out of a specialty boat like that.

A minute later, the bow was fifteen feet out and even with Zack's left knee. The hunter dropped anchor in the channel and cut the engine. Damned if he didn't plan to stay awhile. In bright light, his cigar looked narrow, but not like the cheroots Zack used to smoke.

The hunter filled out his brown khaki parka with a Hulk Hogan thickness that had Zack thinking he wouldn't want to tangle with him in an alley. Instead of Hulk's or Zack's own blond horseshoe 'stache, the guy's face was a bristle of ginger, poking out like frayed fishing line. Not more than forty, his eyes looked older. The coarse skin on his face and scar tissue across his nose said he'd been through rough times. Having never seen the man up close, Zack couldn't help staring at his cold-weather snowcap, flaps up, tie strings trailing.

Looking colorful must be part of a hunting guide's job description.

The visitor pointed using the cigar. "Hey, ace. Mind taking that spot outa my eyes?"

Embarrassed, Zack thumbed the button over to *lantern* and set the light on the log. The sweet, woody scent teased at his nostrils. "You the guide used to hunt that island blind downriver from Salem? Still takin' rich dudes out at four hundred a pop?"

"Not anymore."

Smoke seeped out the corners of the guide's mouth.

"Giant pain in the ass, telling the same old jokes." More smoke. "Making nice all the time with stuffed-shirt lawyers and Silicon Valley CEOs." *Puff.*

It seemed like words had to rattle around in the guy's head before he could string them together. "Chasin' wounded birds some yahoo jumped the gun on." He studied the end of the narrow cigar. Live ashes sizzled when he tipped them into the water. "Nope. Tweety Bates hunts for himself. Hunting that counts." A flick of his middle finger and the stub spiraled into the darkness, dying with a hiss.

Zack scratched at the side of his jaw. "Yeah well, uh, Tweety?" His tongue tripped over the notion of a big strong hunting guide named after a cartoon character. "We're already set up here. My brother's gonna be back pretty soon, and—"

"You know you're losing dekes?"

"Whaddaya mean?"

Zack's breath fogged the silence hanging in the air. He started to ask again and thought better. Some people weren't meant to be hurried. He shifted his shotgun to his other arm and waited.

The ex-guide scooped up a pair of brown-headed decoys by the necks, maybe the pintails he'd shaken at Zack from downriver. He tipped the decoys upward, showing their white bellies and ownership IDs—thanks to Magic Marker. "I'm guessing you are Zack L." An easy toss and the decoys landed at Zack's feet with hollow-sounding clunks.

"Yeah, but how in the hell . . . ?" Zack jerked a nod out toward his spread. "I got one-pound weights on all my decoy cords."

"Take a look at the string ends."

Zack leaned his Remington against the log, picked up an anchor cord. Sheared a foot below the belly of the decoy. Something had come along and clipped those lines.

Zack stared out into the predawn murk, down to where the river seemed to swallow its banks and fall off the edge of the world. Where he and Charlie had abandoned a set of scorched pontoons and melted chicken wire. He snatched up his Q-Beam, switched back to *spot*, and fanned the light across his decoy set. Fog was starting to form, but he could see that the outermost decoys—all those magnum mallards and pintails he and Charlie had set out—were MIA.

He pushed back his stocking hat and scratched his suddenly itchy scalp. Was this Tweety playing him? Hunters needed other hunters to keep ducks moving around. But they got pissy when somebody hunted close by. Nah. The guy seemed friendly enough, for a lone wolf. And he'd done Zack a favor, returning the pintails.

He switched back to *lantern*. "Undercurrent might've rolled a sinker log downstream. Carried those decoy anchor lines with it."

"Not likely." A yellow-and-black cigar tin appeared from the ex-guide's parka. Cohibas. Zack licked his lips, wondering about this chain smoker's Cuban connections. Fire flared from a brass-crested lighter, pitted with use. Tweety talked around draw-ins. "Not unless that log"—*puff, puff*—"had knife blades for limbs."

Right. Clean-cut ends ruled out that notion. Zack shook his head in exasperation. "This season's turnin' out to be fuckin' weird."

"That isn't the large of it. Fewer decent hunters, these days." The ex-guide clicked the ancient Zippo shut and stuffed it into a coat pocket. "Seen it all before, ace. This river's gettin' infiltrated."

Zack barked a nervous laugh. "Who by, bunny-hugging protesters?"

Tweety pulled the anchor up and gave him a sharp look that said he was dead serious. "Them protesters are tricky, too, boy." He grunted out something else as he cranked on the outboard. "Them and . . ." The motor coughed to life.

What'd he said? *Them and duck turds?* And now it was *boy?* Zack liked *ace* better.

From far upriver, a high-pitched buzz signaled Charlie was on his way back.

"You have a decent hunt," Tweety called out, his boat drifting. When he'd made deeper water, he kicked the outboard in gear and shouted around the cigar clenched in his teeth. Zack caught the words that never made sense. "Keep yer eyes peeled."

For what, duck turds? Zack gave the corner of his mustache a thoughtful chewing as he watched the guide dodge decoys and angle downstream.

Darkness and a building mist swallowed Tweety and his Go-Devil.

Talk about odd ducks.

10

Early-morning rain pelted the ground outside the half-basement office of Sheriff Gus Grice, turning the landscape beside the courthouse annex into a miniature land of ten thousand lakes. A squirrel huddled at eye level on the inset window ledge, riding out the downpour. Gus tapped the glass. The tree-rat perked up but stayed put. Gus couldn't blame it for seeking shelter in a storm predicted to ruin the whole weekend. Even the Farmers' Almanac forecast a wet winter for Oregon.

Winter, hell. Try October.

He sent out a silent prayer in the direction of those ten thousand lakes, hoping one of Minnesota's breeding ponds for oversize mosquitoes would swamp Charlie Lukovsky. Or better, inject Nile fever into his defecting ass. Eight thirty, according to Gus's desk clock. Schenkel should've been here a half hour ago.

Gus had deliberately kept Chavez waiting outside his office. Both would get the same earful, a fitting kickoff for her temp assignment to Investigations.

A knock rattled the glass-paned door, timed with its opening. Annie breezed in and dropped a rubber-banded wad of mail onto his in-box. "Mostly junk today, except that interesting one . . . from back east?"

Gus's silent gaze met hers, until she turned away.

Annie never flounced, but her retreating walk was a pleasure. She had the door open again before Gus found words. "Oh, uh, thanks, Annie. Schenkel here yet?"

She paused. "Here early and gone. Got a call on a floater and hitched up the patrol boat. Said to go ahead without him." She slipped through the doorway, then ducked her head back in. "Chavez's been waiting a long time. Can I tell her to come in?"

"Not yet." Barely hearing the door shut, Gus was in motion toward his desk. In particular, toward a gray envelope in the bundled mail. He plucked it up, tore off one end, and shook it over his desk blotter.

"Hot damn." Now he could really cover his tracks.

He started to tear up the envelope when a piece of paper fluttered out. The note from Bannock included a series of digits and instructions so terse, a chill settled into the base of Gus's skull: *Never call Little Creek. Use this number. Nightly progress updates at 2200 hours.*

His attention settled on those block-lettered words. The coldness spread, wrapping around his neck as if he'd strapped on a dog collar. And a leash that stretched clear from Virginia.

But then, three thousand miles left a pile of wiggle room. At that warming thought, Gus shook off the shivers.

Glancing out the window, he scooped up the items, clapped on his rain-protected Stetson, and wedged his frame into a slicker. He had places to be.

* * *

At the rattle of Grice's door, Delia lifted out of a wall chair and tugged down her coat front.

Until a moment ago, she'd been pacing the waiting room space between the communications bay and the sheriff's office door, squeezing the grip-strengthening ball in her pocket, eyeing the name painted on the frosted glass. Musing over what the *L* and the *B* between *Augustus* and *Grice* stood for. *Lizard Breath* ran neck and neck with *Lead Butt*.

She smoothed the outside of her smoke-gray jacket. The extravagance of Italian leather had pushed her credit card balance to the limit, but what the hell. As a newly minted detective, she could afford it. Couldn't she?

The sheriff stormed out of his office, head down and buckling a yellow, calf-length rain slicker. He paid her no notice, moving instead toward Annie. "Back in an hour. Gotta make a ba—uh, quick stop and then get breakfast."

Before he'd cleared the com bay, his dispatcher was off her rolling ergo stool and tugging at his sleeve. "Forget somebody?"

"Huh?" His brows bunched together as he glanced toward Delia. "Ah, for crissake." He turned back, ripping open the fasteners on his raincoat as he approached.

She met him midroom. "You wanted a word?" she asked in the calmest of voices, as if he'd kept her waiting five minutes instead of forty-five.

"A word," he answered, in a half snort. "After that opening-day river fandango?"

She started toward his office, but his hand was out, motioning her to the pair of chairs on the waiting room wall. She settled onto the seat she'd just left. Instead of sitting, Grice set a foot on the seat next to her and leaned over, so close she had to sit back and tilt her head at an awkward angle. He spoke in a low rumble, somewhere between a Rottweiler and a whisper, while poking a thumb into his well-rounded shirtfront.

"The word for what you give me right here, Cha-vez"—as usual, he mispronounced her name, the *Cha* sounding like the first syllable in *chastise*—"is worry." He bent down into her space and shook his head. "No matter where you're assigned—whether it's behind a tavern in Independence or at a protest at the Buena Vista boat ramp—you end up churning my insides. Worse'n a gut fulla hot tamales."

She bristled, drawing in a quick breath. More like rum-soaked tamales. *Lizard Breath* had just won out over *Lead Butt*, by a mile.

Seconds passed. She didn't bite. He straightened and took a step back. She exhaled slowly, realizing it mattered little who'd been assigned to Buena Vista or that someone else had discharged a firearm at that hunting protest. She rammed her hands into her coat pockets, one of them curling around the ever-present rubber ball.

Squeeze and hold.

The line of his mouth was a taut cable. "And the word is that you provided piss-poor backup in a tense situation."

Release and rotate.

She felt her cool melt away. Clearly, he wasn't finished.

"—left a fellow deputy in the lurch, and—"

Cheeks flaming, she leaped to her feet, the swell of her chest inches from the bulge of his belly. "Now hold on. That marine park jam-up was on Castner. My day sheets spell out exactly what hap—"

"Spare me your ass-covering incident log tweaks." His finger jabbed the air an inch from her nose. "It was you who responded late to his backup call." He dropped his foot, jerked his head away, and stared at the potted rubber tree in the corner, as if eye contact offended him. "I'd be waist deep in crap had one of those weekend greenies taken a load of bird shot in the hind end, all because you couldn't work around a few carloads of hunting protesters."

Delia bit her tongue, checking the words she wanted to char his incompetent hide with. "Wait him out," Harvey had advised, a few months into Grice's reign of error as sheriff. When he'd gone from Jekyll in uniform and duty boots to Hyde in poly-suede and Tony Lama snakeskins. He dressed just like a Texas sheriff.

She ground her molars. Wait him out? Bullshit. He might bounce her ass into a patrol car, but she had to defend herself. "You're blowing off key facts. First, Castner was dispatched to Buena Vista as a crowd-control squad of one. Why? Because your patrol division's stretched too thin." The lid was off. She inhaled and went on. "Second, the closest backups were way the hell across the county. Third, nobody got hurt. And fourth, I responded as soon as possible, under the fucking circumstances." The last, she said in a controlled but emphatic voice.

That got a wince from him. She dug her fingers into her thighs, trying not to reveal how much she was shaking. "Now, am I in Investigations or not?"

Annie's communications panel buzzed loudly in the charged silence.

Lizard Breath buried his hands in his coat pockets and stared at the floor, his jaw muscles bulging. His next words came on a slithery softness.

"Just so we're clear, Acting Detective Cha-vez"—he rocked on the balls of his feet—"I'm instructing Schenkel to limit you to class Cs, the white-collar end of his caseload." Head lowered, he anticipated her next question with a sideways glance. "Because I want no excuse for you to draw your goddamn weapon."

His fact-stretching reignited her burn. She opened her mouth to let fly.

"Sheriff." Annie's sharpness overrode her next volley. Delia turned and caught her look of alarm. Way out of character for Annie Mae Cox. "That was Salem Hospital. Harvey's been in an accident. Somehow his truck and boat trailer backed over him down by Yamhill County." Annie's forehead creased with worry. "He's still in surgery."

Delia swallowed, shock constricting her throat. "Aw Jesus, no."

At the same moment, the sheriff wheezed a guttural, "Well I'll be damned." Her gaze locked with his, and she felt a wrench of confusion. While his somber face and drawn-down mouth expressed concern, the glint in his eyes seemed way too cheery. Besides being set against her, did he have it in for Harvey? Or was it something to do with that gray envelope Annie had told her about?

Instead of asking for particulars or saying something like "Let's get to the hospital," Gus Lizard Breath Grice buckled up and headed out, toward the Blue Garden.

11

The instant Delia stepped off the elevator at Salem Hospital, her senses came under assault. The smell of used bandages and fear mingled with the taste of bad memories. They multiplied as she plodded toward Harvey's room, down a corridor banked with gurneys and IV poles. It was the migrant farmworkers' clinic of her nightmares. Only the wooden bench was missing.

The rural medical clinic had smelled the same but was too small to have a waiting room. Uncle Tino and Aunt Matilda had sandwiched her between them, taking turns hugging her shoulders. Too hard. Kissing the top of her head. Too often. Waiting for an ambulance that came too late.

Delia was eight when the farm truck accident took her parents and she and her brother Enrique went to live with relatives. Eighteen when she nearly lost her aunt Matilda to sepsis. At this very same hospital.

And she was twenty-two on her last hospital visit. That was when Enrique dropped the keys to his cherished Super Sport into her hand and hobbled out of the custody unit on crutches, shackled between New Mexico corrections officers.

Hospitals were places where families fell apart and died.

She made for the open doorway of room 333, thanking God the background check Polk County HR had run on her did not extend to family members. No doubt Grice would have found a way to use her brother's incarceration against her.

Delia caught sight of Harvey Schenkel and suppressed a gasp.

"Jesus, Mary, Jos—" Her hand flew to her mouth.

Lying prone on a canted hospital bed, his face was a carpet of scrapes and bruises. Tubes snaked into his nose, now broken. The damage hadn't stopped there. From his neck down, just about every part of his half Dutch, half African, all American frame not in a cast was bandaged or braced.

She leaned against the doorframe, pressing her forehead into the cold metal, choking down the tightness that pulled at the back of her throat. Her heart flooded with a grieflike intensity she hadn't felt since childhood, since her parents' funeral.

What now? Who's got my back? Out of uniform, but on paper-thin ice, she needed Harvey. Here the big man lay, helpless, looking like he'd been hit by a Mack truck.

A nerve twitched inside. She straightened up from the doorframe and forced her eyes to focus. What was she thinking? Hell, he had been run over by a truck. She cast around, looking anywhere but at Harvey, struggling to shed the guilt she felt for thinking of herself.

She peeped at him from the doorway, uncertain whether he was even conscious. His balled fist jerked, the thumb punching on something attached to a cord. His head lolled in her direction and he croaked a greeting.

"Heydee there, Dee-Dee." Good. Using the family nickname she'd told him about meant he was somewhat lucid.

His eyes glazed as she stepped to the bed and gave a gentle squeeze on the only one of his coffee-colored limbs that seemed undamaged. "Geez, Harv."

He winced. Her hand sprung up as if from a hot stove. She blinked back the rising moisture. Though his mouth seemed too swollen to smile, his eyes crinkled. He spoke with a stretched-out tempo, his voice wavering in a medicated lilt.

"Boo-boo. Old Harv got a boo-boo."

"In a lot of pain, huh?" His eyes went out of focus.

"Not ri-ight now-w-w."

She glanced toward the hallway, thinking she should come back later. As if mind reading, he rested a hand on her arm, his fingers dead cold. "It's okay-y. Always wanna talk to Dee-Dee."

She pulled a molded plastic chair close to the bed and sat in a forward lean, fingers clasping and unclasping between her knees. Harv's eyes rolled toward the left, looking up behind her.

"Dead cow-w."

She frowned. Okay, this was already too weird. "What? A cow got hit, too?"

Lifting the self-medicator, he waggled it toward the far wall. "Dead cow-w."

Confused, she shifted around to follow his line of sight. A double wall sconce had one light burned out. She went with the flow. "Oh, right Harv. That cow sure is dead. But the other one is still mooing." He cracked a one-sided smile and grimaced, making *her* wince.

Desperate to stay upbeat, she nodded at the coppery-gray fuzz spilling over gauze that circled his head like a melting ice cream cone.

"Man, that thing wrapped around your head makes you look like a Ben and Jerry special."

"Wha' flavor, Rocky Road?"

"No, Orange Man Bad."

The Iraqi vet wheezed out a laugh that ended in a pained expression. She sat back.

"Damn. Sorry, Harv." He managed a wave-off and she breathed a little easier. "What the hell happened, anyway?"

He said nothing. His upper eyelids lowered to half-mast. She tried a prompt.

"The Yamhill deputy said he'd spotted your truck and trailer, headlight deep in the Willamette, with the county's search-and-rescue boat wrecked. Said the current took it downstream and wrapped it around a piling."

"No mer-gen-cee."

Delia frowned. "It sure as hell was. The EMTs had to dig you out before they could put you on a stretcher. If it wasn't for the thick river mud at the bottom of that boat ramp, you and the truck would've been toast."

"No. No farking mer-gen-cee." She cocked her head, trying to understand. Harv rolled his eyes upward in exasperation. His one free hand waved in a circle at the wrist. "Crankety-crank . . . whoopsy-daisy . . . ka-whump."

She followed his gaze toward the ceiling, wondering if they'd looped back into the dead-cow conversation. Saliva dribbled out the corner of his mouth as he sighed with effort, then appeared to give up.

Delia pulled a tissue from a box and dabbed at his chin, his hazy words drifting in her head like dust balls. Maybe his truck's gear had slipped out of park, or he forgot to set the—

"Harv, did you mean the emergency brake?"

Harvey's lids had closed. An air bubble formed between his lips and popped soundlessly. She slumped back into the chair to wait. It wasn't like him to forget to set a brake. Not Mr. Careful.

She rapped her knuckles on her knees, assaying the damage. People who got banged up in accidents seemed worse off than they were. But Harvey looked as bad as she'd seen—out-of-commission bad. And here they came, trooping back: her own how-fucked-am-I questions just wouldn't stay tamped down.

Like Annie, Harvey was family. Not by blood—a kindred spirit who got her and she got him. Gut check? He'd kept her on track. But now? How would she make the shift into Investigations without Harvey? Without derailing herself?

Earlier that morning, she'd scanned the roster of active investigations and found a substantial backlog. Nothing major was brewing aside from the human remains that had turned up just inside Yamhill County jurisdiction. The hunter who had gone missing was a Polk County resident. His death would likely be ruled accidental drowning. Case closed, like the Gatlins.

Oh yeah, she could work off the case notes, manage for a while, but—

A nurse bopped in. "Sorry. Time to take care of business—fluids, meds check, and such."

Delia headed for the waiting room thinking about how Harvey finessed the sheriff with ease. How Grice's sour face alone could set her off. And how that friction, minus Harvey as a buffer, could put her in deep shit.

* * *

On Delia's return trip that afternoon, a gray-haired man in a knee-length white coat walked out of Harvey's room and disappeared into the next. She continued to slow-step. Key questions for a doctor had been answered on her initial visit to the room. Polk County's senior detective wouldn't be back on the job anytime soon.

While leafing through her fill of waiting room mags, Delia had resigned herself that Grice would find a way to bounce her out of Investigations and back into a patrol unit. She could almost hear the creak of her old duty belt, feel the daily groove it rode into the flesh on her hips. Familiar territory, but could she take six more months of running property checks, refereeing domestic squabbles, and busting reoffenders paroled through a revolving-door system? Weeks of uniformed boredom, sprinkled with seconds of heart-pounding terror?

Three hours had done wonders. Harvey was sitting up and looking sharper. The nurse was long gone.

"Ah, back from Purple Haze–ville, I see. How you feeling, Harv?"

He shrugged the shoulder that wasn't in a cast. "Like that comic strip caveman after the first stone wheel rolled over him. Thor sore." His eyes motioned toward the chair beside his bed. She sat and leaned toward him, a rolled-up *People* magazine still clutched in her hand.

"Harv, did you see anybody else around that boat ramp? Anything out of place?"

"Uh-uh." His head tilted. "Thinking on it, you don't see many kay-akers this time of year. But he'd paddled off." She made a mental note: *Ask the Yamhill deps to check the cab. That brake. Dust for prints.*

Despite the ruin in Harvey's face, he'd put on a work frown. "Anyway, wanna talk shop?" His voice was an echo of the old, healthy-as-a-Clydesdale Harvey.

"It can wait."

He shook his head. "Too much goin' on." His brows bunched. "Sorry I left you hanging this morning."

Delia shrugged, quoting one of his fortune-cookie wisdoms: "Cop with hot tip burns rubber to crime scene. Pokes in stinkometer before shit cools."

Harvey sniggered with obvious pleasure. "Yeah well, that Falls City hunter has to be colder'n a brass suppository. If he still has a colon to insert one into. Better follow up with Yamhill on those remains, huh?"

"Already on it. I meet with their ME tomorrow—if I'm still acting detective."

He glanced toward the hallway. "Anybody else around? Annie, maybe?"

"She's coming as soon as she can arrange a dispatch fill-in." She stared at the floor. "No doubt the sheriff will have me back in a patrol car in a blink. So he can start over."

Harvey touched the back of her hand, and she looked up. "Not gonna happen, Dee-Dee. Grice has burned so many personnel bridges, nobody qualified will touch our investigative unit with a forty-foot flagpole. Especially on short-term assignment. County commissioners won't budge on their hiring freeze, either—not while they're reviewing his expenditures."

He continued to stare into her eyes. In that pregnant silence, it dawned on her where the conversation was headed. She sat up straight and studied Harvey's battered features. "So that leaves . . . ?"

"You, Dee-Dee."

She tensed, shifting in her chair. "Me? Solo in Investigations? Oh hell, no."

"Oh hell, yes." Through his distorted features, Harvey managed to fake an indignant pout. "But, Acting Senior Detective, cane or crutches, I'm coming back. Maybe not as far as I wanted, but back I'll be."

"Damn straight, Harv."

Her body language must have telegraphed the panic inside her. "I know this is patently unfair, Dee-Dee. You deserve to be brought along step-by-step instead of having the whole caseload dumped in your lap. Think of it as the chance to stretch your legs, put that do-right obsession of yours to a real test. Yeah, that's it: Senior Detective Delia Do-Right."

"Oh, har-har, Harv." Her leg danced a nervous bop.

"Seriously, it's KOKO time for both of us."

"Cocoa?" Two inside of a minute? She wondered how much of his meds had worn off.

"Short for *keep on keepin' on*. Martin Luther King borrowed it from the Salvation Army. You're stubborn enough to get really good at KOKO."

"Thanks, I think?"

Despite them being alone in the room, Harvey lowered his voice. "Grice has himself between a boulder and a rock crusher. Talk to Annie."

"Have been. We're looking into why he's acting so close to the vest lately."

"He's bound to be uptight. After the mess he's made, they're sure to elect a reformer, somebody who'll turn the Sheriff's Department around."

"I don't know . . ."

Her hesitation wasn't over the county's white shirts and black skirts—staunch Republicans all—concluding their boy was a screw-up, or concern that they would actually do anything. No. It was her getting bulldozed.

"Harv, you know Grice can barely stand to talk to me, let alone sit through case reviews. Even if he is replaced, the switch won't come soon." She popped up and paced. Three steps put her under the TV monitor, three back to bedside. "That's months of lame-duck revenge. If he knows he's on borrowed time—"

"Ah, but Grice believes he's still got a shot."

"What if he doesn't? What's to stop him from sabotaging cases?"

"Perry Barsch. He's had it with Grice. Wants badly to keep in a simpatico sheriff, so he'll back my recommendations over the interim."

"Sim . . . huh? You, a Republican pol? I thought sheriffs were nonpartisan."

Harvey tilted his head, the corners of his mouth drooping, shrug-wise. "I prefer Centrist."

Delia frowned. "How'd you manage to get Perry on your side?"

Harvey Groucho'd his brows. "Haven't kept my Second Amendment powder dry for nothing. Got him into my Set Wings Hunt Club. Grice will think twice before he tries to step on your neck. Just remember KOKO and you'll own the senior detective slot, assuming I win the election."

"I can still tap you for advice? I mean, when—"

"Ah damn it to hell, Harvey."

That came from Annie at the hospital room door, looking like she was trying to swallow her knuckles. Tears welling, she rushed in.

"Couldn't get away," she said. "Got here soon as I could."

Delia backed out of her path as Annie fell across the hospital bed, bending far over to dispense a hug—a hefty, clearly heartfelt embrace.

Harvey didn't flinch.

12

A car honked impatiently on the far side of the Willamette. Packy McFarley scanned upriver from inside the Buena Vista ferry's wheelhouse, thankful for a day with no fog and few rainsqualls. Spotting nothing adrift—no prop-tangling limbs, no monster logs barreling downstream—he kissed the crucifix on the rosary hung from a window latch, touched a snapshot of himself from his bantamweight boxing days, and set his shore-powered vessel in motion. The prop shafts rumbled and four electric motors whined. The upriver guide cable bowed, and one of the thin cords connecting his boat to each shore lagged in a low droop, first dipping into the water, then skipping across the backwash of yellow foam. Only Packy's wife knew how much the river ate at his nerves.

A week to go. Seven more days of high-water crossings and back-rev landings before the county ferry service shut him down due to rising water. Couldn't come too soon.

Packy respected the force that slid beneath the hull. Like him, the river could pack a punch. Twenty-seven years captaining ferryboats had taught him why the local Indians had worshiped the godlike powers of the river. Buena Vista had not broken loose. Yet. One nightmarish, cable-busting ride downriver in another ferry had taken what was left of Packy's youth and rooted that fear deep in his bones. Two years, then done with the river.

70

The current was really rolling today. Strong enough that he angled the boat upstream to keep her on course.

He shifted his glance upriver, keeping a close eye on the loop of coated coaxial cable that sagged farther underwater the closer his ferry came to the top of her upstream arc. God knew that connector made for a nothing lifeline. Three days back, he'd had a devil of a time keeping a snagged fir bough from swinging in under the west-end forward drive. Thank God it had broken free and slipped around the stern. Staying safe meant keeping a sharp lookout for anything the river tried to sneak under his nose.

The swing mark was a piece of red canvas wired onto the main cable high overhead, signaling halfway. As it slid past, he held his breath. A minute more and he'd ease off the upstream slant and square the bow with the landing ramp on the Marion County side.

A barely detectable shudder vibrated up through the soles of his shoes, translating into the slightest change in the ferry's course. In nearly three decades, Packy's senses had become part of the machinery, prompting him to zero in on the drag source.

"Good Lord, not again."

Normally a curving U, the guide cable now cut a deep V that bottomed out well below the river's surface. No limbs or branches, so the obstruction had to be something waterlogged. The roots of an old cottonwood?

Packy cranked the wheel and reversed the engines, swinging the ass-end of his ungainly craft upriver. He slacked off on the power and the boat inched downstream, pulling the guideline taut. The cable rose and the underwater blockage surfaced.

Packy's spine went icy stiff. The lump he first took for a bare tree trunk or stump was clothed in hunter's camouflage.

River water backed up on the object, peeling away fabric from patches of stark white—a bloated belly, a puffy face beneath a balding scalp. For Packy, the impossible position of the body was the heart-stopper. Its spine and torso bent sharply backward, doubled over the cable like a wet mop. Arms and legs, palms and heels dangled together, dancing a Pinocchio jig, the surging current acting as puppet master.

* * *

Delia shook water off her rain slicker and hung it on the wall beneath the staircase that connected the old courthouse with the sheriff's annex—just as Grice was coming down.

"Where's Cha-vez? She was supposed to be here at ten." His shout seemed directed at all personnel in the duty room.

"Right here," she shouted back. His head hunched into his neck as he wheeled on her.

"Jeezum. Don't sneak up on a man." His foot landed hard, slipping off the last step with a *phwap*.

She came around the banister and matched his pace toward the com desk. "My car died this morning and I had to get my brother's out of storage. What's got you so skittish, Sheriff?"

"Nothing. Never mind," he said. "You just better be good and ready to hit the ground running, 'cause we got a probable homicide."

"That makes two."

He stopped. "Two . . . you sure?" His pale eyes took on a light that hinted excitement. Off-kilter with the news. Almost gleeful.

"Pretty sure," she answered. "I just got back from the Yamhill County ME on that floater Harvey had been on his way to investigate. More like a headless hung-upper. Nine months in the water, going by the decomp."

"What makes you think it was homicide? And why should a Yamhill body concern us?"

"A detached finger, for starters. Harvey's desk file on last year's missing Falls City hunter ties the deceased to our county."

The sheriff glanced upward, as if stargazing indoors. He shook his head. "Mighty cold case when we have a red-hot one at Buena Vista."

"Oh, and by the way," she added, as they veered toward his office. "Harvey will be out longer than we thought. More surgery coming up."

"Sorry to hear that. What about his accident?"

"Maybe no accident. I spoke with the Yamhill deputy who investigated. Harvey's F-350's emergency brake tested A-OK. He was adamant he'd set it."

"Suspects?"

"Next to none. He noticed a kayaker hovering upstream when he backed down the ramp. Gave me a rough description. No bow numbers on a kayak. Still, I talked the Yamhill dep into lifting door and cab prints off Harvey's rig."

Grice paused, unlocking his office door. "Leave it for now."

She waited, a touch of wishful unease creeping into her thoughts. Did she imagine it, or was he just a tad more civil? He'd just come down from a meeting with the county biggies and she'd read bad news all over his face. Did he think he could make hay with a high-profile murder investigation?

"I want hourly updates on that probable homicide. Hourly, Cha-vez."

He stepped in and shut the door on her.

Delia turned back toward her slicker, cautioning herself not to be fooled. What was that old saw? *The more things change, the more they stay the same.*

* * *

Delia rode the clutch on Enrique's '67 Camaro, braking her "borrowed" ride to a stop above Buena Vista Ferry, inches from Craig Castner's duty brogans.

Her fifteen-year-old Pontiac had died earlier that morning. After telling the Yamhill ME she'd be late for their meeting, she'd hiked home for her brother's pride and joy, which she kept stored in her garage. When she'd gone to update Grice, she had parked the convertible an inconspicuous two blocks away. Why? Smirks like Castner was giving it right now.

Four hundred forty horses rocked the frame at a galloping idle as she rolled the window down and braced for the inevitable. He didn't disappoint.

"Wow. Nice flame job. Will Cheech be joining you?" Thumbs in his utility belt, her least favorite coworker stood before a police tape barricade flanked with road flares.

She mustered a pitying smile. "That the best you've got?"

His smug expression didn't waver. "Just itching to see you bounce that cholo-mobile off the pavement."

Still smiling, Delia shook her head. "Misinformed, as usual, Craig. This is a classic muscle car, not a barrio lowrider." In no mood for more of his crap, she nodded toward the driveway off to their right. "In the marine park?" The 911 message on her screen was short on details, only the location and *body recovered from the Willamette, possible homicide.*

Castner unhooked one of his thumbs from his belt and motioned down the blockaded road. "Nope. On the ferry."

"Of course it is."

"What?"

"Never mind. Did you call for the ME?"

He made a face. "Now what do you think?" Then he hawked and spat to the side. "Better not fuck this up, Hot Rod. The ferry pilot who found the stiff is down there and waiting. Surly little rooster. Name's McFarley, and he doesn't—"

Delia closed her window on Castner, her cheeks prickling with irritation—mostly at herself for feeling embarrassed about her ride. She stared ahead, waiting for him to scoot back the plastic barrier horses, hating the rumbling, chassis-shaking mill that powered her jailbird brother's Super Sport.

She geared the Hurst speed-shifter into first, feathered the gas, and eased out the clutch. Rear tires chirped and Enrique's supercharged bomb lurched forward, every start a prelude to a drag race. Delia blew out a puff of air. "What the hell. Might as well act the part." She thundered past Castner, feeling immature but satisfied at having flipped him off.

The docked ferry loomed over a slight rise. The far end of the four-car barge slanted downstream, bent by an angry brown current. Delia cut the engine and rolled to a stop short of the steel on-ramp. Clutching the religious symbol at her neck, she swallowed on an acid taste that climbed her throat every time she got close to that damned river.

Flashing lights went off in her rearview. Castner had reset the roadblock at the top of the hill and repositioned his patrol car behind it. To better eyeball the proceedings and report back, she bet. She stopped twisting the crucifix on its chain and let it fall against her collarbone. Her other hand found the door handle. She refused to be trapped between a hard-ass and a wet place.

Delia figured Castner was wondering why she hadn't driven onto the ferry. Well, why hadn't she? Truth be told, she wouldn't drive across a Willamette River bridge if she could get around it, let alone onto a hunk of iron that was barely afloat.

Her thing had a name. Potamophobia: fear of rivers or running water. She knew exactly what she had; even studied it in college. Knew by heart the mumbo-jumbo for fighting it: Face fear head on. Don't let it paralyze you. Put fear into perspective—what it robs from your life. Like, your family?

She'd found a simpler way. Avoid rivers altogether.

No avoiding this time. Not the memories, either. Those newspaper photos were burned into her brain. A migrant farm truck upended in the Pudding River. The blue tarps draped over her parents. That mud-brown stream meandering off, satisfied at its theft.

Instead of being given by Delia's parents, her quinceañera had been put on by an aunt and uncle. Beautiful but not the same. Nothing had been the same.

Get on with it, Chavez. Step out, shut the car door, breathe.

She ignored the nauseating odor of riverbank rot, retrieved her evidence kit from the trunk, and concentrated on the ferry ramp—its two-car width, the welded metal sturdiness. Head down, she trudged upward.

"Hope you're here to get this dead guy off my boat."

She tracked a voice that could hammer tacks over to a forty-something man standing with his backside against the ferry's blue-and-white pilothouse. The boat pilot, she assumed, unfolded his arms, uncrossed his ankles, straightened up to a whole five foot two in his peacoat, and strutted toward a tarpaulin-draped mound. A red-tipped stocking foot poked out from one corner.

She advanced slowly, taking in details, doing her best to tune out any movement past the plate iron she walked across. From the corner of her eye, watery mouths opened and closed as they swirled past the empty car deck. One eddy sucked noisily at the surface—a river hungry for more victims.

They met at the tarp, the shrimp-size boat captain's glance traveling up and down, then between her and the parked car at the bank. "You are a detective, aren't you?"

She set the kit down, flipped open then pocketed her new ID in a recently practiced motion. "Chavez. Polk County Sheriff's."

"McFarley, Marion County Ferries."

She shook his ice-cold hand and surveyed the empty car deck, noting drag marks through puddle depressions on the welded metal deck. "You moved the body?"

McFarley nodded, motioning toward the ferry's upstream corner where the water trail ended, or rather, began. "Draped over that cable like a limp blanket on a clothesline." He shrugged, anticipating her why question. "Afraid the uh—corpse—would wash downstream, so I gaffed it by the coat and hauled it onboard. Docked my vessel and called 911." Again, he eyed her.

Though she was accustomed to men staring, she still buttoned her coat. Crouching beside the green plastic cover, she removed and snapped on black surgicals. McFarley's rubber-soled work shoes stayed planted in the corner of her vision. She shot him a look. "I'll let you know when I have questions." Mr. Roving Eyes wandered off. She peeled back the tarpaulin.

Fully clothed, except for missing waders—suspender fragments crisscrossed at the shoulders—the body looked as if it had been in the water awhile. Sharp-angled lids framed brownish milky eyes, indicating the dark-haired man may have been of mixed ancestry.

A massive, X-shaped throat puncture was the obvious physical insult. After photographing the body from all angles, she knelt and eased the man's head upward, discovering a larger exit wound, also four-sided but jagged and torn. Fleshy material hung down the back of the neck, suggesting a force powerful enough to punch severed larynx rings and pieces of vertebrae backward and out the rear lesion. The weapon that killed the man had been driven through the neck and later retrieved, probably by yanking the thing out the back. No mere knife blade had inflicted this damage. By the wound's position, the crushed voice box and sliced arteries, she figured the victim had choked or drowned on his own blood.

Searching his pockets for ID, she withdrew a lanyard with a tube-shaped wooden object attached—a duck call. Eight letters had been burned into the wooden barrel: *H. T. Snyder.*

A siren wailed in the distance. Back in a crouch, Delia crab-walked around the body, scrutinizing what was visible. The man's left arm lay crooked beneath the zipped hunting coat. The siren grew louder. She lifted the soggy material, slid the hand out, and instantly let go.

"Ah shit."

She gazed up the road at the approaching ME van, overcome with the need to fixate on a less jarring, more routine image. Lights flashed. Red, blue, white. But the pearly shine of a bared knucklebone where a pointing finger should be—and what that might mean—stayed with her.

The siren cut off midwail.

* * *

The Blue Garden had seen better days. And now new life. Back in the lounge, mainly, where Delia had made more than a few collars. Scooting across Main from the Dallas, Oregon, courthouse, she cringed at the restaurant sign's daytime shabbiness compared with the nighttime brilliance of royal-blue neon.

Grice had left a note for her to come find him as soon as she'd finished processing the crime scene that wasn't. Who knew where the murder had actually happened? Two miles upriver? Twenty? None of the hunters or vehicle drivers she'd questioned in the area had seen anything.

She pushed between the thick glass doors, cased the patrons at the candy counter and fifties-style soda fountain down the left side, then headed over to Grice's hangout in the bank of time-worn hardwood booths. A waitress with a straw-colored wig stood by while he slipped something inside his coat and gestured toward the chalked-up luncheon special—clearly why the perfume of onion rings hung in the air. She left and Delia took the seat opposite him, releasing her grip on the Crush Ball and withdrawing her hand from the pocket of her jacket.

He said nothing, stirred his coffee, and eyed her Italian leather, like she should be in uniform. Still, his silence seemed an improvement of sorts.

"Sheriff, I just picked up your message. It took a while to wrap up—"

"I know how long you took." He swigged deeply, as if something had cooled the black coffee.

Yeah, you do, Delia thought, a faint boozy pong drifting past her nostrils. Castner had already updated him on her progress at Buena Vista.

Still wired from the morning—the good, the bad, and the gruesome—she tugged at her sleeves under the table. "Definite homicide, Sheriff, a real freaker. The ME—"

"Hold off." Gus peeked around the corner. The booth behind was still vacant. "Lower your voice." She skimmed the room, wanting to ask why even meet here, but knowing the Blue Garden functioned like an informal rotary for the local business crowd. His kind of place for rubbing elbows with supporters. Deal-making, too.

"I already got most of the particulars." Castner again. So she wasn't here for a case debriefing. "First off, let's set things straight—"

Delia flipped her hands in a shushing-him-back motion and nodded to the left. The waitress arrived with his special. It had to be a dish-up-and-serve.

"Thanks, Mae." He turned the plate, inspecting the meaty bounty.

Mae also set down a menu and water in front of Delia, who averted her sight from Grice's sauce-smothered, onion ring–piled concoction and up to the waitress's big-tip smile.

"And what can I get you, hon?"

Grice put a thumb on the menu and slid it toward the waitress. "Take it. She'll be leaving soon." Yep, she thought. The old Grice was still there.

Mae scooped up the menu. Delia's gaze following her retreat, wondering if salad was the only vegan option. She started to call Mae back when Grice dropped something on the table that made a loud clunk—a mobile communication unit the size and thickness of a Belgian waffle. His forearms surrounded his lunch and he dug in.

She sat back and stared at the rugged phone.

"Military? Thanks, but I use an iPhone."

"Not on this case." He folded then shoved a crusty ring into his mouth, chewing as he talked. "Minimizes eavesdropping."

"When did the department acquire these?"

"It didn't; I did. This one's not just military grade but military secure. Locked in to call my number and one other. Annie's, but only in an emergency and you can't get me."

"Why the extra security?"

"Because I don't know how big this case is or where it's going, and neither do you," he said between last-bite cleanups. "Trust me, you'll need that security." He pushed the plate aside. "Until further notice, you're replacing Harvey, but at Detective One pay grade. Two-a-day debriefings, eight and four, always in my office. You get called out"—he reached over and tapped the Ulefone's sturdy case—"you get on this cell straightaway. You uncover new information—any at all—I'm the first to hear."

He leaned in. "Understood?"

More than he figured she did. Military tie-ins, secure phone, "trust me." *Need any more alarm bells, Chavez?*

She crossed her arms, her lips tight together, barely opening after a measured delay. "Still on C felonies? Property crimes only?"

"What?"

She lowered her voice. "Yesterday morning, you restricted me to the not-so-lily-whites in Harvey's caseload. Now, a looming murder investigation tops that list."

Grice made a wave-off motion. "Oh, yeah. Yeah, that comes first."

"Big overtime allotment in your budget?"

His head tilted, one eye narrowing. "You damn well know there's none."

"You plan on sharing the load? Fieldwork, too?"

Grice sat back, giving her the stare. She could take his pulse visually, at both temples. "It's an election year. What're you getting at?"

"So. I'm in charge of an investigative division consisting of me, and I'm staring at a list of actives that'd choke a Clydesdale"—to use one of his Texasisms. She flattened her hands on the table. "In the same breath you dictate a shitload of debriefings, knowing full well field time breaks cases. You can't have it both ways, Sheriff."

He looked around and hissed at her. "Keep your voice down." Grice didn't embarrass easily, but she could see the flush now, mainly because she was right and knew the spot he was in. Her message was clear. It didn't pay to underestimate her.

He took a couple of deep breaths, and the redness drained from his face. "Okay, granted, the situation's changed." His eyes narrowed into a thoughtful squint, but he wasn't all that good at pretending. "I have an idea that'll lighten your load."

She leaned forward, saying nothing, looking unconvinced.

"Granted, you're going to need, uh, flexibility. Also, whatever resources I can scrape up. That's provided this murder case stays all ours, jurisdiction-wise."

She shook her head, wondering why the cave, why *all ours*. "Looks like it's joint, since the ferry's run by Marion County. God knows we can use an assist from their investigative division, especially since we no longer have river patrol capability and they do. I could get in touch—"

"Never mind that. Did the Staties or Marion County tumble to it yet?"

She frowned. "Tumble? Uh, well no. McFarley, the ferryman, lives in Buena Vista, so he docked on our side of the river and called us. But we still need to notify—"

"Good, good. Let's keep it Polk County for now."

"Sheriff, you just said we need resources."

"And I've got them. Most of the cases on Harvey's list are in the Dallas area, right?"

Her moment of hesitation ended with a guarded nod. "Mostly. Here and around West Salem." His shift in direction was too easy. Too quick. "Why?"

"All those actives. Mainly misdemeanors, Class Cs or unclassified felonies, right?"

"For the most part."

"How many major felonies or violent crimes?"

"Aside from the ferry homicide and Harvey's truck running over him—which is damned suspicious—a handful. Oh, and I'm betting there's a link with the Yamhill body find."

"Perfect. Now head back and pull the files on everything except for those three, anything within ten miles of Dallas, Oregon, and West Salem city limits."

Her frown deepened. "What're you going to do?"

His smirk told her Grice was in his element.

"Call in a few chits."

Yep, she thought. Way too easy.

81

13

Reaching the last on her list of questions, Delia dropped her foot from the pickup's step rail. The four hunters inside the crew cab had their windows rolled down, the one with a wispy chin beard leaning out and grinning, watching her draw from her jacket three finger-worn photos.

"Have you seen any sign of these?" She passed around the marketing renditions of Ham Tran Snyder's Starcraft boat, Isuzu pickup, and Calkins trailer. From Ham's duck call moniker, she'd easily recovered driver's license, auto, boat, and trailer numbers. "Anything like them? Maybe an abandoned boat hung up somewhere on the riverbanks?"

The driver asked, "Who'd hunt outa that red-and-white piece of shit?" and got back hearty laughs.

Chin Whiskers handed the photos back. "Ain't seen nothin' like those, ma'am. You, Cletus? You, Norm?"

"Nope."

"Uh-uh."

"We gotta be goin'," said the driver.

Delia took down license names and addresses, then passed out four PCSD cards, saying, "Call if you see something out of the ordinary."

Chin Whiskers finger-flicked his card. "I'd call, even if I don't."

Delia shot him her give-me-a-break look. "Have a nice day."

They drove off from Riverview Marine Park, their trailered boat spewing dirty river water from its unplugged interior.

Like the other 142 she'd questioned coming off the river over several days, these hunters had given her little to go on. She got in the Camaro and sat, tapping on the steering wheel, thinking back on those detective stories she'd read as a child. The board games she used to play with her aunt and uncle and Enrique. Clue and Mr. Boddy had gone far to inspire her.

But this was no Colonel Mustard in the parlor. No tidy little cozy mystery. It was a clueless, leadless mess. Her case going nowhere, frustration was mounting. She keyed the ignition, then killed the motor.

A grizzled-looking guy who stood at the far end of the marine park in solid mud-brown hunting clothes had caught her attention. He was doing what she'd done for the past week: moving from parked rig to parked rig, taking down truck and boat trailer license numbers.

She got out and strode toward him. "Hey, Mister."

He pivoted toward her, yanked something from his mouth, and tossed it down. Without hesitation, he took off on a trot, down toward the far woods at the waterline.

"Hold on." She broke into a trot. Seventy yards away, he sped up to a full-out run and disappeared behind the trees. By the time she got there, sounds of an outboard motor racing around a bend reached her ears.

She turned back and traced along his path, speculating. Could the guy be an antihunter? Someone else? When he'd swiveled toward her, she'd caught an impression of something black covering his chest and neck. Too thick and shiny for underwear.

Reaching the empty boat trailer where he'd last stood, she froze, then knelt.

"Well, well . . . An actual clue to bag?" The gold-banded clue smoldered on the pavement.

*　*　*

The next day, Delia rolled up to a pump at Independence, Oregon's twenty-four-hour Octane Stop, wondering what in the world possessed hunters to scramble out to a river before four AM just to bang away at creatures who wouldn't hurt a fly. Well, maybe they'd eat it. She didn't know what ducks ate, or anything about hunting. One reason she was here, sitting under the yellow glare of sodium lights, hours before the sun came up. The other was to interview more hunters—so far, 146—who saw, heard, spoke no evil.

She opened her window and killed the ignition. *Tink-tink* went the motor. *Think-think*, it said, bringing to mind Harvey's old *think like a killer* saw. Except her version took it one step better: *Outthink a killer, catch a killer.* To do that, she had to immerse herself in the crime, its victim, the scene, the evidence gathering.

Exactly her problem.

Focusing on the most recent case, she knew who the victim was and how he was killed, but that was about it. For a crime scene, she had a nasty, meandering, miles-long river. In rapid motion, constantly washing evidence away. A river she wasn't about to set foot on, for sure not in some wobbly boat. To Delia, the crime scene was an alien, hostile world where even the victims packed weapons, where she could not just walk out and canvass a neighborhood.

"High-test?" The acne-faced attendant looked sleepier than she felt.

"Highest you've got."

He ran and returned her card to her. "Figured. Lotta compression under that hood," he said, as he started the pump and sauntered off. Yawning, she checked her watch and thought over the choice she'd made.

After she'd reread Armstrong and Erskin's *Water-Related Death Investigation*, realizing she had virtually nothing to go on, a conclusion had gelled—she desperately needed a hunter SME. Police and writers used subject matter experts all the time, and Grice's in-house tether did not keep her from carrying out *in-depth civilian interrogation*—what she'd call it in her reports.

So who'd make a good, unpaid SME? Harvey hunted, but was due for more surgery. Castner hunted only big game, and Delia considered him expert at nothing. The rest of the county deputies were stretched to breaking. Charlie Lukovsky was out of here but had given her a lead, describing him as "the best goddamned waterfowl hunter on the river."

The gas nozzle clicked off. No attendant appeared.

She'd left messages for her SME prospect, got no callbacks, and buzzed Charlie again. He was driving a U-Haul to Minnesota but told her the good bets were either at the prospect's favorite launch point or here at his prehunt pit stop. She'd picked here.

Delia opened her door and got out, tempted to commit an Oregon no-no—finish pumping her own gas—when a red pickup towing a small boat wheeled in. She recognized the driver but not the young passenger.

Zack Lukovsky left his truck and strolled up, eyeing her convertible from fender to fender, his mouth shaping a silent whistle.

"'Lo, Detective. Heard you took Charlie's spot."

She shrugged, relieved he hadn't brought up applying for deputy sheriff. "Something in between. His desk's still open. Your brother said you were an expert at duck hunting on the Willamette River."

"He did?" It seemed to take him back a second.

"That's why I'm here," she answered. "Two bodies turned up on the river, and—"

"Hunters? Drowned?"

"Can't go into it, but I suspect foul play. Zack, I'm looking for someone to bring me up to speed on river hunting and hunters. Their equipment. The hunting culture. How they deal with antihunters. Can you do that?"

His head tilted in a deliberating way. The frown on his brows lifted and his expression seemed to lighten.

"I guess I can all right." He motioned back toward his truck. "Fact is, you can start right now. Me and my Gonzaga U cousin's headed for the river. I'll dig out an extra life vest, and you can—"

"Hold on." Her hands flew up, but she stopped herself from taking a step back. "No can do—uh—not this morning. No. What I want is a sit-down interview where you supply details on what I need to know. How best to talk with hunters, ways to get at what I'm looking for. The no-snitch code they seem to follow." She paused a moment, slowing her speech. "See how that goes, then talk about next steps."

The attendant returned, did his thing, and disappeared inside.

Zack pulled at a corner of his mustache. "Good enough. Where and when?"

Relieved, Delia handed him one of her PCSD cards. "Call when you're done hunting."

*   *   *

In near pitch river darkness, Zack Lukovsky lowered his stocking mask over his face, yanked the outboard motor to life, and levered the gearshift ahead.

"Kenny, sit down before you fall down."

Fair warning. Standing with a boot heel against the frost-coated boat transom, Zack hand-throttled the old fifteen-horse Johnson with a vicious twist. The little Jon boat lurched out from the launch dock.

Caught in a four AM yawn, his cousin, Kenneth Lukovsky, tumbled backward onto a pile of decoys with a *ka-wump*. The Q-Beam he clutched blazed a column of spotlit glitter straight up into the icy mist.

Zack snorted, squelching a laugh. He'd needed that. Helping his brother Charlie load furniture into a U-Haul and watching him drive down the road had filled Zack's heart with lead.

But the thing with the detective sounded interesting. More interesting than Kenny, if he'd gotten her to come along. Funny, she'd never said a thing about deputy training.

Grumbling, Kenneth—his Joe College cousin preferred *Kenneth*, so Zack called him *Kenny*—worked his way off the decoy pile and onto the bow seat and glommed onto the side railings as if he wanted to draw them over him like a blanket. Lesson learned.

Zack aimed the metal twelve-footer's bow into fast current, but not too far out from his landmarks. He'd done enough predawn runs up the Willamette to know how thick air played tricks, made a boater think he was where he wasn't.

Two-thirds throttle was plenty. Even now, silt-colored water splashed over the bow like slopped coffee. He glanced back toward the marine park's fading streetlamps, relieved to see no glowing backup lights. No big-ass trailer launching a big-ass boat for a hairy-ass run past them to the best hunting spot.

Up front, Kenneth kept a mittened hand glued to the boat side while he retrieved the spotlight from the decoy pile. Wherever he played the Q-Beam, the shore brush glistened with a white coating. The first hard frost of the fall.

"Kenny, do like I told you. Shine that light out front and low on the water."

"I can't see a thing, Zack. What am I supposed to be looking for?"

Making fair headway, Zack had to shout over the engine's steady buzz. "You'll know when it comes at us."

"What?" Kenneth twisted halfway forward. He sprayed the beam around, but up high so that a wall of blinding light bounced back off the fog. "When what comes at us?"

Zack jerked his free hand from a coat pocket and made a lowering gesture. "On the river, Kenny. On the fuckin' river."

A three-day rainstorm, followed by a sharp temperature drop, had bumped the Willamette up near flood stage and made for a frigid boat ride. Fog was good for duck hunting. High water was another story. A guy never knew what castoffs nature might float at him.

Kenneth turned full ahead and angled the beam lower. Better, but the powerful beam still reflected back more sparkling whiteness than it penetrated. Thirty feet didn't allow much zig time.

Zack's eyes never left the river as he held up the bottom part of his ski mask to spit sideways and discard an overworked cud of Red Man. Resetting the mask, he squinted past the Gonzaga Bulldogs stocking hat riding low over Kenneth's stringy brown hair. Out into that band of gray mush between air and river.

His pansy-ass cousin was here only because Zack had promised his mom and Charlie not to go hunting alone on the Willamette.

He jigged the tiller and skated around a boil-up marking one of several well-known snag piles. Back on track and into a fairly safe stretch of river, he watched Kenneth tug at the tightening straps on his life jacket, the spotlight's cone of safety meandering every which way but out front, where it should be. Zack tried to picture his cousin helping in a crunch situation. Yeah, like that would happen.

Crooking a knee over the tiller, he was about to finger a second tobacco pinch inside his lower lip when Kenneth's spotlight picked up a dark stain out front. They overtook the discolored water. In a blink, the patch had swelled to a lump thirty feet across and several feet thick.

Zack dropped the can of Red Man, grabbed for the tiller, and bellowed at his cousin.

"Hang on."

They hit with a thump and sailed over a monster log. The little Johnson screamed, its prop slicing air instead of water. For a split second, Zack saw Kenneth free-float above his seat. Then the hull pancaked with a sickening *whump*. Zack's bent legs absorbed the landing shock and the outboard dug in, droning along as if nothing had happened. Up front, Kenneth was hunched forward. Head sunk between his shoulders, he gripped the boat sides like he'd just survived a Tornado ride at Six Flags.

Zack powered down and let the hackles settle on the back of his neck, watching his cousin scuttle backward onto the boat floor, his legs wedged against the side ribbing. Elbows on the bow seat in front of him, Kenneth sprayed light around, muttering *ohmigod*s for all he was worth.

Another lesson learned, the hard way. Zack waited for his heart to stop banging against his ribs before throttling up. Slower this time. No need to hurry.

Frozen in place and lighthousing the river, his cousin mouthed something over one shoulder. Zack made him repeat it.

"Huh? You say somethin', Kenny?" Nothing like bluster to cover his screw-up.

Kenneth found his voice. "I said this is way too weird. What did we run over, anyway?"

His composure back, Zack couldn't pass up the opportunity to get in a dig. "Felt like a BMFL."

"A B-M-what?"

"Big motherfucking log. Sometimes they drift downriver after heavy rainstorms. No BFD."

"Zack, we gotta go back. This is insane. I—I can't swim." Kenneth's stocking hat rubbed back and forth against the rim of his collar. "How you call this fun I'll never know."

Charlie would know. It's what Zack and his brother had done for years. Running the river on pitch-black mornings was special. Kept a guy on his toes, and brothers close. But Charlie had flown the coop, and now Kenneth sat in Zack's boat. Like one sack of decoys too many.

"Ah, come on, ya wuss. That little speed bump was a fluke. Hell, we're over halfway to Black Dog now. If you don't crap your pants before we get there, you might just have a good time. I'll show you some fun shootin'."

"Oh boy, can't wait." Kenneth rolled onto his side and fixed a pasty-faced gaze back toward Zack. "Why couldn't we have slept in? Had a nice breakfast, then come out here about ten or so, when we can actually see?"

"Kenny, I told you. Have to beat the competition to a special place if we want to get in a decent hunt." And Black Dog Slough wasn't just any old backwater. It was a duck hunter's glory hole, even before the field puddles froze up and channeled migrating ducks down onto the river. "We'll be there in no time."

"Hey, Zack." Kenneth was staring at the river behind their wake. "Is that the sun coming up?"

"At four AM? Don't think so, Kenny." Snapping a look over his shoulder, Zack glimpsed a yellow-white glob cutting through the inky gray. "Damn, somebody's tryin' to beat us upriver." He gauged the approaching light as it sharpened into a disk, the tight beam bouncing off one bank, then the other. "Shit. They're comin' on fast. Prob'ly that sumbitch Tweety and his Go-Devil."

"Who?"

Zack coaxed the flat-bottom craft up toward planing speed, shifting his weight as far forward as the tiller extension allowed. "Scrunch into the bow, Kenny." Adrenaline thrill pumped through his veins as he squeezed out the last drop of boat speed, his earlier scare a dull memory. The outboard burred in tune with his anger. No way was he getting beat out.

Kenny ducked low when the splintered end of a floating oak limb scraped past, just missing the side of his head. Disregarding the danger, Zack kept the Johnson full out and leaned into the wind, as if willpower added horsepower. Needle Island's lower end showed, a blur of flooded woods. Not far above lay the inlet to Black Dog.

In no time, a converted metal bass boat, its open bow piled with decoy bags, overtook Zack and his cousin.

Four hunters blew on past, raising one-finger salutes, laughing and yelling in unison. "Loo-hoo-sers!"

They disappeared into the darkness ahead. Zack yanked the Johnson's kill switch and threw down his gloves, bobbing his head on each word out of his mouth. "Son. Of. A. Bitch. Man, those guys are nuts, goin' that fast out here."

He let his boat slide back downstream, rocking in the wake of the faster vessel, the fading rumble of its monster outboard grinding defeat into his ears.

"Well, so much for choice hunting." He shaded his eyes when Kenneth wriggled around, flashing the powerful light in his direction.

"So, we can go home now, right, Zack?"

"Kenny, point that goddamn light someplace besides my face."

Peeling the ski mask up over his forehead, Zack gazed downriver for a long count. "I guess we can try back at the Santiam, or—"

A screech, paired with a loud bang, cut him off. A misty hush settled over the river as shivers drilled down his spine.

Zack and Kenneth locked eyes.

"Did those guys run into something, Zack?"

"Yeah, something. But that didn't sound like no BMFL."

14

Delia parked the Camaro in a police slot, snatched up her portable Toughbook, and hustled toward the hospital's emergency entrance. The cherry-red Apache and boat trailer sat close by.

Barely an hour earlier, Zack's garbled call to her had come over the roar of an outboard engine. Something about a boat crash, then a "Hell yes" to her question about 911, then that he could see the EMT unit waiting on the Marion County side of the river. The last words she understood before his phone cut out midshout were that he was bringing back four "ice pops" he'd fished off an island. A few minutes later, her call to the 911 dispatcher had confirmed the EMT unit was en route to Salem Hospital with four severely hypothermic boaters. At a sub level, her suspicion was that these off-kilter river incidents—overactive protesters, sabotaged hunting blinds, slashed boat trailer tires, and now a wrecked boat—were either tied in with or provided cover for the killings.

Just past the ER reception desk, she spotted Zack and the college-age kid she'd seen with him—the only ones wearing heavy camouflage coats and hip boots, and looking like they belonged out in nature's bounty.

Delia took the empty chair beside Zack. "What happened?"

He flipped a hand up. "Battery died."

"No, the boat crash."

The youth in the blue, red, and white Bulldogs hat peered around Zack. "I told him we had no business being out there."

91

"Sit back, Kenny." Zack jabbed a thumb to his left. "My cousin." He took a deep breath and started in.

"Four idiots ran past us, goin' upriver like bats in the fog, and hit something creepy."

"A log?"

"Worse."

"He meant something very aberrant."

"Whatever, Kenny. Somethin' that can rip off the bottom unit of a two-hundred-horse Mercury outboard and flip over a twenty-footer sure don't belong in a river." He jerked his thumb toward the end of the hallway. "Talk to the Iraq vet runnin' that boat. Soon as he thaws out."

She opened her Toughbook, waited a moment, and took down names. Berlson had been driving the boat, according to Zack. She looked up. "You two picked all four off an island farther upstream? How'd they get there? Swim?"

Zack shook his head. "Crazy thing was, them and the boat they clung to shoulda drifted downriver. 'Cept those yahoos were already on that island logjam when we made it upriver. You gotta hear it from Berlson to believe it, Detective."

"That how you saw it, Kenny?" she asked, entering more notes.

"Pretty much what Zack said. But he'll have to go back upriver for the decoy bags I had to unload. Otherwise, those guys would've swamped our boat. Us with it."

"Anything else?"

"Kenny did a heckuva job, helping out on the river. Make sure he gets recognized for it." With that last from Zack, her regard for him climbed a notch or two.

She closed the book and stood. "I need to interview your ice pops, but can you stick around?"

"Hafta drop Kenny off at Greyhound. If it's about those, uh, hunters you found, I can come back." Kenny showed no sign Zack had leaked anything to him. One more notch.

She glanced at her watch. "Creekside Dining in one hour? It's in Building D." He nodded, and she headed down a hallway flanked by a series of ER bays.

A nursing assistant pointed her toward an open bay where a balding man lay cocooned in a forced-air warming blanket. "Roger Berlson?"

"That's me." His voice was steady and he wasn't shivering, so she proceeded.

"I'm Detective Delia Chavez, here to ask some questions about your boat getting wrecked."

"Fire away."

Scooting a chair closer to the bed, she woke the Toughbook. "Let's start with a rundown of events beginning with when and where you launched your boat."

As he gave his account, Delia entered details of a boat race in a foggy darkness, all of it sending chills down her spine.

Duck hunters.

On the latest entry, her fingers froze over the keyboard. "Wait. In the beam of your spotlight? Sparkly what?"

"Yeah, like a row of diamond dust out front, just before the boat flipped. Damn glad we had on life jackets." A change in MO? she wondered.

"Your rescuers said you should have drifted downstream. How did you get upriver to that island?"

"Damnedest thing." His arms flew out, gesturing. "We're all in the water, hanging on to my upturned boat, when we get floodlit."

"By what?"

"Well, see, I was Navy, boatswain's mate, during Iraqi Freedom, and I know an assault ribbie when I see one." She canted her head, and he clarified. "Rigid-hull inflatable. That big Zodiac circled us with its light rack blazing. We yelled for help but got no answer. Then somebody hooked a line onto our boat and towed us into shallow water at the end of that island."

"Intending to rescue you," she offered.

Berlson snorted. "Half-assed, if that. Dropped the towline and powered out of there. If those other hunters hadn't come along . . ."

"How many in the Zodiac?'

"One guy. A six-foot shadow. He stayed behind the lights, so I can't tell you what he looked like."

"Anything else? What the man wore?" she asked, noting down the last items Berlson gave her.

"Not a hunter. Long coat, brimmed hat."

She glanced up, recall kicking in. "Boat markings?" Could this boat crash have something to do with Grice acting cagey over a fugitive warrant?

"Couldn't see numbers. A weird up-down camouflage pattern ran along the sides. Check with my buddies."

"Next on my list," she said, noting a reminder before saving what she had and bagging the computer. Standing, she paused. "One more question. Have you had any run-ins with antihunting groups? Maybe putting your boat in during the opening-day protest?"

He fiddled with the patient control, raising then lowering the bed angle. There it was, that clamshelling hunters did with cops. Her, anyway.

"Nah. We were nowhere near Buena Vista."

"Okay, thanks for your help." She shook his hand, this time making a mental note. She hadn't mentioned where the protest had taken place, but he could've heard it in the news. "And thank you for your service."

* * *

Finished interviewing three more hot-air-blanketed hunters who'd echoed Berlson's story, Delia bought a salad at Creekside Dining and took a corner table. Hospital dining might've changed, but they were still hospitals. While she ate, a flight of questions circled for a landing inside her head.

Who was the guy in the Zodiac, and did he have a peg leg? How many more booby traps had he set? Was that how Ham Tran and the dead hunter found in Yamhill County had been stopped before being killed? If so, why had the guy halfway rescued his latest victims?

Pushing aside the kale with her fork, she let her mind wander into uncharted territory. Was all of this some form of ultimate protest against the killing of animals? Certainly not against the taking of human life.

Her pocket vibrated. Not her personal phone, the one Grice had given her. Shit. She hadn't given him an update since the Blue Garden.

"Where are you and why haven't you updated me on your investigation?" Highway sounds. Grice was driving somewhere.

"Salem Hospital. Just finished interviewing four hunters who got their boat swamped under suspicious circumstance. I'm pulling together the details now, but I still need to run boat IDs, several truck and trailer plate numbers."

She gave him a thumbnail sketch of what she'd learned from the four hunters.

"What's that got to do with the homicide case?"

"A potential suspect? Also, there's a connection we're missing, maybe with the antihunting set. And there's other elements. Appears that boat was deliberately wrecked by someone in a big Zodiac. Someone I might have seen before."

"Enough for now. Just pulled into Marion County Sheriff's for a meeting. Oh, and you've been on marine patrols, right? Operated large boats?"

"No." Electricity or something like it charged through her brain. "Never been on one."

"Marine patrol? Or large boat?"

"Any boat." Her heart galloped. "All my duty tours have been on dry land."

"Until now. Better find somebody to show you the ropes." She winced at the slam of his car door. "I'm about to twist Sheriff Chop

95

Tellson's arm for a loaner to replace the boat Harvey Schenkel put out of commission."

He rang off.

For a while, the phone seemed stuck to her ear.

＊　＊　＊

By the time Zack Lukovsky strolled up to Delia's Creekside table, she'd calmed her nerves with a scroll through her case notes. She'd marked *SME* beside items he might help with, except for the last item, hoping to God she wouldn't need boat training.

He sat across from her, one leg stretched out to the side. The stocking face mask and hip boots were gone, replaced by straw-blond hat hair and mud-toned outdoor boots.

"Thanks for agreeing to help, Zack."

He leaned over the table, speaking barely above a whisper. "Foul play, you said. Like murder?"

She nodded. "First off, what goes between us—I mean everything—you keep to yourself."

"No problem," he answered, an eagerness in his voice. "What d'you need?"

"Where would I look for these?" She handed him printouts, tapping on the photos and IDs. "An Isuzu pickup and a Calkins trailer with these plate numbers, and a Starcraft boat with this bow number." From Ham's duck call moniker she'd easily gotten the rest, pulling stock ad photos off the Internet. "I've canvassed the county boat launches and asked everyone loading up whether they've seen the Starcraft."

He pulled at a corner of his mustache, turning the photos around, then pointing at the Isuzu. "Some farmers let hunters launch from irrigation pipe lanes. I'll scope out the ones I know of." He pointed to the boat pictured in red and white. "No duck hunter would leave it that color, probably spray on flat army tan or camo tones."

He gathered in the photos, his head shaking. "I'll ask around. Keep my eyes open, but it's been a while back. That boat could've drifted clear into the ocean, or been rain-sunk. Might've been weighted down with rocks."

"I appreciate your willingness to do this, Zack." She stood, shouldering her computer bag.

"That it?" he asked, getting up, too.

"For today." No need to signal this was a test.

*   *   *

An hour later, Gus rolled out of Marion County Sheriff's, heading for the Salem-Dallas Highway, last mission not accomplished. His meeting with Chop Tellson, an enforcement division commander at Marion County, had not gone well. No boat loan from the marine patrol. The SOB had whined he had every unit tied up after all the rain and flooding and shitty weather. Ole Choppy'd almost acted like he didn't want to be seen with Gus.

The fog had lifted to a low overcast. He skirted around West Salem and was well into Polk County when his cell phone buzzed.

"Grice here."

"The Bastard. Tell me you have a fix on him." Bannock's words dribbled off a thick tongue, sounding like so much mush.

"What I have, John, is a whole lotta questions about this maverick operator of yours."

"Meaning you don't have a fix on Bastida."

"Meaning I'm worried. About just how far the cheese has slipped off his cracker."

A pause. A sound like liquid poured from a bottle traveled over the line. "I'm losing patience, Grice. Already told you he's obsessed with this personal vendetta thing."

"Against hunters?"

Bannock didn't seem surprised. The long silence confirmed Gus was on track.

"Listen, John, we've got an assault boat running up and down the Willamette like it's the damned Amazon. And now casualties are turning up, two dead hunters that we know of. Time to can the need-to-know military bullshit and detail out exactly what kind of black-ops freak I'm up against. Otherwise, I'm tempted to pull the plug on this deal."

"The *hell* you say." A crashing noise pummeled Gus's phone ear, then another that sounded like wood splintering. "No goddamned plug-pulling, you motherfucking turd. The fucking plug stays put."

In the relative quiet that followed, Gus released a silent whistle, mighty glad the naval officer was three thousand miles away. Damned sorry he'd used up what Bannock had sent him.

"Okay, John. But you're going to have to up the ante to keep us looking."

Gus held the phone away from his ear and waited.

He'd come around. Gus was out here and Bannock was *way* back there.

15

Delia entered the next morning's debriefing with the sheriff prepared to argue for outside resources. In addition to a preliminary report on Harvey's "accident," she'd armed herself with a rudimentary murder book that revealed glaring holes. She intended to make the case that collaboration with a larger agency, such as OSP's Criminal Investigations Division, was necessary to fill those holes.

Grice's office-door greeting and broad smile—all teeth, no gums—had thrown her off-balance. He'd ushered her to one of two leather wingbacks flanking his desk, then plied her with freshly brewed Kona. "Pure estate peaberry," he'd crowed. "Not that ten-percent-blend crap you get in stateside stores." She didn't know peaberry from pee-holes in the snow, but found herself into her second refill of really great coffee as she waited to answer his questions. Grice drained his reloaded "Hula Babe" mug while paging through the material on Harvey.

He flipped her report over and pushed it aside, no questions asked, then opened the murder book, skim-reading while Delia summed up what few case developments there were. She led off with the Polk County ME's confirmation that Ham Tran Snyder's death was the result of an ultra-sharp four-sided projectile, shot or driven into his neck, then retrieved by pulling it the rest of the way through. She made particular note of Ham's severed index finger before moving on to the second autopsy she'd witnessed that week.

"A six- to eight-month window on time of death?" Grice grumbled. "No chance it wasn't more recent? August, maybe?"

Delia nodded at the Yamhill County ME's photos depicting partial remains. "Likely the Falls City hunter who went missing last season. The Yamhill coroner's findings came from a badly decomposed torso, lower jaw, and not much neck to speak of." She omitted the part about leaving her lunch in the drain beneath the morgue table. "The coroner's waiting on dental records. Legs and arms were mostly intact. What stopped me was the index finger cropped off the guy's right hand."

"Cut. Not rotted off?" Grice tilted his head back, scrutinizing her from narrowed eyes.

She answered with a solemn nod. "Same knucklebone markings as for Snyder, same torn edges on the flesh. Done with a serrated knife." She blew air up toward her eyebrows and shook her head at the implication. "Kind of a leap, with everything else happening on that river, and going on a body count of two, but I'm thinking we've—"

"Got a nutcase out there who's not finished." Getting caught up with her thinking had prompted him to set aside whatever had been making him drag his feet.

She took a last sip. It was time to make her case. "Sheriff, this investigation is on the verge of snowballing. Way I see it, we don't have a choice except to collaborate with—"

"Damn the budget." Grice slapped the desktop so hard she jumped, slopping tepid Kona onto her merino-wool slacks. "You need help and I'm gonna bring it." He thumbed the com button on his desk phone. "Annie, remember that ex–Coast Guard search-and-rescue guy, swung by last month? The one pitching a county co-op scheme to contract out his jet boat?"

"Oh, let me think now." Annie's sultry tone made Delia glance up from daubing at the coffee spill. "Pinch-me blue eyes, sandy-blond hair. Pair of shoulders filling your office doorway. But didn't you just talk—"

"Yeah, yeah, that's the one. See if you can rein in your hormones long enough to find his card." Waiting, Grice cupped the side of his mouth as if somebody else might overhear him. "Tellson put the kibosh on a patrol boat loan, but I've ginned up a better option."

The squeak of chair rollers came back over the speaker. "Right here in a special corner of my cork board. Jerzy Matusik."

"Ring him and transfer it in."

Grice switched to phone receiver, pulled out a drawer for a foot-rest, and settled back into his swivel. He stared at the ceiling, clearly not interested in Delia's input on the "help" he was about to recruit for her case.

The tightly balled napkin she flicked at his wastebasket missed by a mile. She stayed seated, rattled by the image of her clinging to a jet boat—whatever that was—piloted by this Matusik guy. "Sheriff, we're better off hooking up with an established water patrol unit—Oregon State Police or Marion County." Far better off. Their guys would do the water work and she'd keep her feet dry.

"Nope. Like I said, this investigation stays inside our jurisdiction and solely under my direction."

"This Coast Guard guy. Does he have any law enforcement training or experience? Any at all?"

Dismissed with a shrug. "He's got a boat, an expensive piece of equipment that's no longer in our inventory, thanks to Schenkel's carelessness. Also, we need Matu—"

"Carelessness?" Ears prickling with heat, she hammered the mug down onto Grice's desk. "That's what you think put Harvey in the hospital? Guess you missed the part where they lifted a set of partials from the truck's brake handle. Matched the prints and rap sheet on a guy named Moon—"

Bang, bang, bang.

Grice gaveled his desktop with the phone receiver. The old Grice, barely skin deep.

"You are in my office." He pointed the phone at her. "When you're in my office and I'm talking, please show the courtesy not to interrupt."

Delia sat back, folded her arms, and fumed. Her report spoke for itself, if he'd read it. Harvey could not have launched without setting the truck's emergency brake, and there was no sign of mechanical failure. Also, Harvey had mentioned a boater in the vicinity around the time of the accident.

The color in Grice's face subsided. "As I was about to say, Matusik's got the chops. Coast Guard and more. He's dive-rated, qualifying in and performing air-sea rescues. Served a tour with a tactical pilot recovery unit in the Iraq invasion. Besides, the guy grew up fishing and hunting on the Willamette River. Knows it like the back of his hand. What's more, he's affordable."

Delia unfolded her arms. Grice and this local yokel had already talked money. "So, no law enforcement training or experience whatsoever? Sheriff, I don't get it."

"That's obvious, especially the elements driving this investigation. First, you've got hunters—two dead ones with protesters out there wishing more would die. Next you have its watery underpinnings."

She stiffened. "By watery, you mean the river. So far, I've canvassed every boat launch and dock in the county. Questioned over a hundred and forty hunters, boaters, kayakers, lookie-loos, antihunting groups, you name it."

"And produced no leads, no suspects, not even prospects. Correct me if I'm wrong, but you have not been on the Willamette, not investigated where the killings took place."

There it was again. "Sheriff, that crime scene has forty miles of brushy, wooded riverbank. Between those shores, a fast-moving current over a hundred and fifty yards wide that destroys any sign of criminality in minutes"—she couldn't stop the heat from creeping up inside—"and fucking hard to do with no boat."

Delia winced. She should *not* have said that.

"Exactly my point."

A phone line lit up. He punched a button and put the receiver back to his ear. "This is Polk County sheriff Gus Grice. Who's this?" His mouth twitched at one corner. "Well, don't you have a Jerzy Matusik running a dive school out of your marina?" His wiry brows knit. "No-o, he's not wanted. Is he there?" Delia chewed at the edge of her lip. "Okay then, have him phone me when he brings his dive class back to the dock." He left a callback number, hung up, and faced her, sighing dramatically.

"Young woman, in the time since Schenkel was hospitalized and I handed you this career-making case, I have let you run around in your hot rod and rack up extra clock hours pursuing leads that may not even pertain to this case. I've signed off on all your mileage claims. Also—no small thing—I've gone to great lengths to relieve your case-load. And what've I got from you? A fledgling start on a murder book and speculation that a serial pattern exists. Well, I'm inclined to agree on that speculation, and it's time to ramp up this investigation."

He sat back. "Now where was I? Hunters, river—"

"Military?" she filled in. He stared at her, a second too long, and she went for it. "Rumor has it a naval officer's been in contact—"

"He did give me a call, yes." By Annie's count, five calls, plus the mailings. "It was on another matter." Grice fidgeted with the pen on his desk. "Nothing to do with this case. But you *have* brought up that third element—military." Delia drew her chin back inquisitively. A diversion tactic? "Among other things, your account of the Zodiac and those rescued hunters prompted me to bring in Matusik."

Shit. Delia swallowed at the sourness in her mouth. Maybe it was the aftertaste of getting outmaneuvered, or that her maneuvering hadn't mattered one iota. Or was it just the growing need to pee? That coffee was really perking through her system. Either way, she had to reset.

She got up and returned her empty mug to Grice's coffee alcove, thinking about her failure to uncover much of anything useful, ignoring the eyes she felt appraising her backside.

Outside, the rain beat against the basement window.

Given time and enough leeway, she'd make up that ground. But his insistence on hiring this Matusik character was the puzzler. So a hunter and his buddies got partially rescued by a boat they could've mistaken for something else. She saw plenty of other avenues to investigate.

She turned around and leaned against the counter. "Granted, both of our victims were hunters, both were found on the same river where all kinds of weird activity has gone on . . ."

"Your point is?"

"Most of the guys—and one woman I questioned—hunt in groups or pairs." She shrugged with her mouth. "There could have been a dispute that ended in bloodshed and a dumped body. And Lord knows, there are extremists among those antihunting groups. Several hunters mentioned a kayaker that hovered around out there."

Delia cocked her head. "But now you're narrowing the case down to this military angle, based on what, that veteran's flashback to the Iraq war? And what else? Missing fingers? Last I heard, the Pentagon frowns on soldiers running around cutting off enemy body parts for souvenirs."

"Soldiers are Army."

"Oka-a-ay. I'm still not following. Unless there's something more . . ." She let the words hang like a fishhook.

Grice didn't bite.

"I'm basing my decision on that vet's description and experience. Trust me, Cha-vez, it takes one to know one." The sheriff stood. "I'm ex-Navy." He picked up his Hula Babe mug, came around the desk and approached her. "Having time on the pond—Southern Command— I'd bet my sweet patoot against an ace-high straight the killer we're after has experience in special operations."

She made room, catching a whiff of something other than coffee on his breath as he ran water into the mug before hanging it on a rack.

"That's why we need somebody who acts and thinks with military logic, a trait you'll grow to appreciate. More important, Matusik's outfitted to help you take this case to the scenes of the crimes, which you seem anxious to palm off on others."

Delia's gaze had drifted past him. Out the window where the drenching rain threatened to turn the parking lot, the courthouse lawn, the whole world into a river of water.

"Still my case, right?"

He paused, then nodded.

"Well. I'm running checks on this guy."

* * *

104

She booked it for the women's restroom, barely noticing that Darrell, Annie's new dispatch intern, had replaced her at the com desk.

Minutes later and much relieved, Delia emerged from the second of two marble-partitioned stalls and found Annie had hiked herself onto the counter to the right of the washbasin. Her crossed ankles swung in a lazy circle as she popped her chewing gum.

"Phone message in your box."

"Zack Lukovsky. Charlie's brother, right?"

Annie nodded. "Said he found the Isuzu and gave directions."

"Well, that's something. Means I'm out for this afternoon."

"When'll he be here?"

Delia stepped to the basin, knowing Annie didn't mean Zack. She adjusted the water temperature and pumped a dollop of soap. Despite a lingering tincture of urinal, the refurbished former men's room had become their testosterone-free haven. "Who?"

"That blond Coastie with the sexy Polish name. Coming to guard my shores, if I play my cards right." Delia smiled, thinking back to before they could even talk like this.

She and Annie hadn't always been close. That was on Delia, who'd kept her distance, despite the dispatcher being one of the more intriguing persons she'd known. During high school, Aunt Matilda's constant admonishment against Delia having anything to do with *chicas flojas*—loose girls—had done its damage.

So what had brought Delia around? Target practice. She'd happened across Annie and her hot-pink home-protection semiauto at Salt Creek Rifle and Pistol Club—kicking up dirt all around the target paper. After watching Delia put four of five cowboy loads in the bull's eye with her chunky .44, Annie had asked her for pointers. She'd shown Annie the power isosceles stance and support-hand placement. Afterward, Annie was at least hitting targets. Several shooting meet-ups later, they'd become fast friends, and it dawned on Delia how the woman had pulled a Ben Franklin on her—find something your "unfriendly" is good at and ask her for help.

"What about Harvey?" Delia asked, with feigned innocence.

Annie stopped chewing. "What about Harvey?" She shrugged. "He's, you know, home alone now. I'm helping him convalesce, okay? Making sure he eats right."

"Hope he's feeling loads better." Delia yanked paper towels from the dispenser. Having Annie off-balance for a change, she squinted at her friend's jumble of curls. "Bad hair day, Cox?"

"Huh?"

"Kinda mashed down on one side."

Annie fluffed reflexively, exposing her ear in the process. Delia clucked her tongue. "Guess the keyhole imprint's faded already."

Annie put on a look of mock affront. "Well, Miss Smarty Sleuth, I don't listen at office doors. Just put two and two together from the sheriff calling Matusik again." She double-popped her gum. "So? When does the big guy get here?"

Delia balled the paper and swished it into the far wastebasket. "Maybe never, if I can help it." She performed the briefest of mirror checks, tucking a loose strand behind her ear. "Your prospective boy toy seems more burden than blessing—an outsider with no law enforcement creds."

"Then why does the sheriff want to hire that gorgeous guy?"

"Besides the fact your 'gorgeous guy' works dirt cheap? Good question."

"Well, with Harvey out and these murders, and now the boating mishaps, you need—"

"Wait. Mishaps?" Delia asked. "As in more than one?"

Annie confirmed with a grim face as she slid off the counter. "Castner radioed in from Buena Vista Marine Park. Two hunters paddled back to the launch ramp with a mangled motor on a swamped boat. They swore up and down some weird obstruction yanked the back end under the river, then let go, shearing off the prop. Which makes my point: you need to take any kind of help Grice gives you. Especially somebody who knows his way around the outdoors."

Delia swallowed and said nothing. By *outdoors*, Annie meant that assbite river.

* * *

The little blue Isuzu's plates matched Delia's notes, as did the attached Calkins trailer.

Zack had met her where the farm lane butted against the highway. He'd driven her to Ham's pickup in his own truck, along the lane that ran beside an irrigation feeder pipeline and stopped down at the river. An electric pump sat in silence under the chill November rain. Behind the trailer, a makeshift ramp sloped into the water. Delia kept her eyes averted.

They both got out and together walked a ground perimeter around the vehicle. With everything rain-washed, nothing stood out. Facing uphill, the pickup was locked and waiting, revealing an empty truck bed and nothing scratched or broken. No sign of vehicular trauma.

"I checked all the surfaces," Zack said. "A few mud spatters. That's it."

He meant no blood. Of course not. It wasn't the crime scene. No such lab technician's luck.

Peering in, the truck cab appeared clean to Delia. A full canvas bag occupied the passenger's bucket seat. "What are those flat bird heads sticking out?"

"Goose silhouettes, maybe seventy or eighty. You're dead hunter must've field-hunted, too."

Delia straightened up. "I forgot to thank you for finding the truck. Any luck on the boat?"

He shook his head. "Been slow-trolling the riverbank brush and sloughs upstream of the ferry. My guess? That Starcraft's long gone."

She blew out a puff of air. Unless the county motor pool techs found something, she was looking at another snuffed lead. There *was* one takeaway.

"Zack, am I looking at this right? That this hunter went out by himself?" If Ham did hunt single, it suggested the killer preyed on lone targets. In a way, it made sense—one shotgun to contend with compared to three or four.

"Think so, Detective. Only one guy fit in this little truck, and we didn't find any other tire tracks."

"Well, that's something." She pulled out her iPhone. "Zack, I need to get back. You okay with guiding the county tow truck down here?"

* * *

"Told you our boy was clean."

Sitting in Harvey's cubicle that afternoon, Delia stiffened at the pooh-poohing tone in the sheriff's voice, but checked an urge to blank the computer screen she'd parked in front of. A glance at the floor beneath her chair confirmed Grice's Tony Lama snakeskins jutted well into the space, giving him a bird's-eye view of her work. For a big man, he moved like he wore felt slippers.

She'd gotten nil results, running Jerzy Matusik's name through crime databases. Paper records yielded little—an open-container hassle back in high school, but no conviction. Was an outstanding wants-and-warrants sheet or a dishonorable discharge too much to ask? His Enlisted Field Service Record had lines and paragraphs redacted. Something wasn't right about the guy. Or how Grice insisted on using him.

She swiveled in her chair, noticing the sheriff had written something on the cover of the portfolio he clutched. Her murder book. "Our boy separated from the military on a general discharge. Why?"

He shrugged. "Doesn't mean a damned thing. So long as his discharge classification was not 'dishonorable' or 'other than honorable,' I'm okay with it."

She rapped a knuckle against the monitor's glass facing. "I'm wondering how he'd explain these inked-over paragraphs at the end of his service record."

Grice bent forward, squinted at the screen, then straightened up, shaking his head. "SOP for a combat operation."

She shot him a questioning glance. "Combat?"

"Iraqi Freedom. It's likely Matusik was in on the early invasion stuff with the Navy." He looked at his watch. "That all you got?"

"Sheriff, I'm just exercising due diligence—"

He thumped the cubical frame, kicking dust into the air. "No more stalling. I have to put off the media, now. Give them something. So I'm announcing we have persons of interest—"

"Like who?" she asked, throwing her hands up. "The ferryboat driver? Some antihunting wing nut with a taste for finger stew?"

"—and I'm telling them I've formed a special team."

"Team? What team?"

"Get used to having Matusik as your interim partner. First off, work up a new canvass-and-search plan for me to approve. You will use him to move this investigation forward. Period."

He plopped the murder book onto her lap and pounded away toward his office. No felt slippers this time.

Pinching the bridge of her nose, Delia read the title Grice had added to the cover and choked back a knee-jerk guffaw. Then she let go with a gut laugh bordering on mental. Using a tangerine Sharpie and bold strokes, her one-upping boss had printed and double-underlined *The Argonaut Case*.

Inside the cover, Grice had attached a stickum note for her, written in block letters: *MEET ASAP WITH MATUSIK—RUN EQUIPMENT CHECK.*

Delia stifled another round of convulsions. Whatever the sheriff meant, she knew what Annie would make of that.

16

SIX WEEKS INTO WATERFOWL SEASON

Delia's meeting with Jerzy Matusik was put off until students in his dive class were certified. By then, the sheriff was fit to be tied, insisting she catch up with his new hire at a backwater restaurant near Salem. Never mind it was Thanksgiving morning and she'd miss helping Aunt Matilda make tamales stuffed with turkey and spiced with gossip on the relatives.

Even in fog, nobody driving down River Road South missed the Flapjack Corral. Its neon-rimmed sign featured farm livestock in tutus, merrily dancing along a wood rail fence. Below that, *Laissez les bons temps rouler* was written in artful scroll.

Delia swerved into a parking lot so full of pickups it could have passed for a truck seizure auction. She backed her brother's Super Sport into a space opposite the bared-teeth grille of a yellow Hummer. Attached was a strapping big boat on a tandem-wheel trailer. Matusik's "equipment," she surmised.

In the quiet of a stilled engine, she repositioned the mirror and angled her head to check the French braid she'd coiled into a seashell bun. Scrunching her face, she removed Mama's heirloom comb, and her duty braid fell free. Leave the primping to Annie; this was business. To get her head right, Delia concentrated on why she was there.

The sheriff had demanded she "deploy" Matusik by next morning, leaving her only a breakfast meeting to scratch beneath the ink

110

of those redacted paragraphs in his service jacket. One day to size up his capabilities—whether he'd do her investigation any good. Given a pass, she could start him canvassing by proxy what amounted to a forty-mile-long crime scene. Because no way was she setting foot in that boat or going on that river.

Overcome by a sensation of being watched from behind, she re-aimed the mirror and picked out a blurry image through the yellow vehicle's reflecting windshield. Two brown eyes and a hockey-puck nose, a pink tongue lolling beneath. A large, light-colored dog waited patiently behind the steering wheel as if ready and able to chauffeur its master anywhere. Delia snickered, grabbing her bag and getting out of the car. Likely Rover was just waiting for a greasy treat.

As she made a pass around the Hummer-boat combo, Rover reeled in his tongue but stayed quiet, watching her survey the vehicle's contents. The back seat held one suitcase and a duffel bag. The rest of the inside was crammed with assorted scuba gear, including several wet suits. She knew nothing about boats, so the walk around it was perfunctory.

With the sheriff's mandate for an equipment check satisfied, she headed for the restaurant. Pushing open the heavy plank door, she was taken aback by a pungent clash of sausage gravy, buttermilk biscuits, and charred bacon. A carnivore's idea of heaven.

For a Thanksgiving morning, the place was noisy with hunters, enthusiastic pig eaters, and waitresses scurrying in and out of a kitchen door, bearing platter-laden trays.

The lobby sign said, *Don't just stand there! Park it!* She headed in.

Booths lined the sides of an aisle that hooked left at a pony wall. It was latticed with fake climbing ivy and blocked her view of the back. Except for a clutch of white-haired ladies, most of the patrons looked to be charter members of the ball-cap-and-field-jacket clan.

Delia made it to the ivy when her feet stalled. "*Híjole*," she hissed, on a steep intake of breath. For once Annie hadn't exaggerated. Mesmerized, she stood there, taking in the suave-looking Anglo seated at a back table and framed by a corner window. The misty river barely registered beyond those squared shoulders.

If that man was Jerzy Matusik, he was gorgeous. Although his slightly shaggy head was bent over a map, his even features stood out. Not the body-builder physique she'd imagined. More like what's-his-name. That new actor Viggo something, only not so rugged. And taller. And blonder. And tanner, and . . . *Stop it now. Get a grip.*

She adjusted the bag on her shoulder, telling her legs to get moving.

Her legs were about to follow through when he looked up and their eyes met. Her hand had a mind of its own, leaping to the base of her throat. She faked a lame glance around, then back to him, open mouth now closed, then into a grin. With that jaw, he could've modeled for Michelangelo, smiled for Da Vinci. Feeling schoolgirl stupid, she yanked her hand down, stuffed it in a coat pocket, and strode up to his table.

"Jerzy Matusik? I'm Detective Delia Chavez."

The man's six-foot-plus frame rose abruptly, tipping a glass of water and splashing it across the front of his chinos at the most strategic location. He followed with reflexive swipes that only spread the wetness.

"Shit. Sorry. Yeah, I'm him. He."

So much for suave. She grabbed for napkins and helped dam the water at the edge of the table, choking back a laugh. Once they'd pushed the map aside and sopped up most of the wetness, she shook his moist hand and sat opposite him.

"That your chauffeur in the yellow Hummer?"

"Chauffeur?" Looking into his deep water-blue eyes, she had a fleeting sensation of being adrift and beyond sight of land. "Oh, Beezer. Jumped in the front seat, huh?"

She nodded in recovery. "Retriever?"

"Well, his mama was a purebred Lab and his daddy was . . . clever."

She covered her mouth and stifled a guffaw. Whatever was hidden in his past, Matusik seemed to have a certain comic charm.

"Why *Beezer*?"

"You must've seen that polar-bear nose on your walk-by. What else fits?" He smiled crookedly, shifting around in his seat. Inside, she commiserated. Clammy underwear was the pits.

Enough small talk. She decided to take a side route, see if Matusik might volunteer something about the service record blanks. "Besides tanks and fins, I noticed a pile of wet suits in your vehicle. Ever dive in strong undertows? River current?"

"Yeah. Coast Guard and some volunteer rescue assistance on the Snohomish River. But I wear a dry suit as a matter of course on winter boat runs. Best insulation going when the wind blows past you at forty or more."

She frowned to herself. Maybe it explained that hunter's getup at the Octane Stop. She tried to question a man named Bates but he'd driven off in a hurry. No boat or trailer, just rows of five-gallon jerricans rack-mounted behind his old Jeep. Said he hadn't seen anything out of the ordinary.

Delia was set to bring up the Adriatic when a well-rounded waitress with a teased mullet stopped beside their table. She balanced a large serving tray as if it were an extension of her arm. "Jerzy Matusik, you heart-stopper, you. Where you been, *cher*?"

He grinned, color spots showing over his cheekbones. "Here and there. Back in the Valley now. You look good as ever, Pixie."

"Aw, you're sweet, hon. Be right back." The waitress hustled off, stopping at another table.

Matusik ticked his head toward the woman. "Pixie's a transplanted Cajun. Bought into the place and added some real zingers to the menu. Couscous, bread pudding pancakes. Sometimes even smoked frog legs. Used to feed up Dad and me after our duck-hunting trips."

Frog legs. Delia held off from wrinkling her nose. Leaning forward, she set her forearms on the table and said the first thing that came to mind.

"Matusik. Polish, right?" She winced inside. No take-backs on stupid.

He just smiled. "Dad immigrated here and set up his medical practice in Silverton. I grew up hearing every 'dumb Polack' joke in the book. Learning they weren't worth fighting over. You're Latina, right? I imagine you've had similar experiences."

"Many." He was and wasn't hard to read, she thought. Fairly forth-right but holding back. All business? She couldn't be sure. Interested? *Stop that.*

Glancing outside, he rubbed the back of his wrist under the cleft in his chin. "Saw you give my boat the once-over. What say we put it in the water after we're done here?"

Delia stiffened. Sat back, shaking her head. "Look, I don't know boats from beehives. Yours has a front and a back and no holes in the bottom that I could see." Time had not muted her memory or the nau-sea of just walking onto a docked ferry. "To be honest, I have never ridden in a boat and don't intend to." His smile disappeared when she tapped a subject-changing finger on the table. "I am here to decide whether you will be a help or hindrance to my homicide investigation, and then—"

"Homicide?" His eyes got wider. And bluer. "Hey, I contracted with Sheriff Grice to scout the Willamette, help your department get a fix on some whacked-out military fugitive. Well, not him, per se—where he operates from. You mean he's killed somebody?"

"There've been two murders. No solid suspects, but I'll get to that." She brushed her napkin-wrapped tableware aside. "Back up a second. You said *fugitive*."

Matusik nodded. "If I heard right, Bastida's on the U.S. Marshals wanted list."

Delia leaned toward him. "Grice named this 'fugitive'?"

"Robert Bastida." He followed with a dismissive hand flip. "The Navy confirmed it was a trumped-up identity. They don't know who he is for sure."

"The Navy." Heat rimmed the tips of Delia's ears as she flashed back on the sheriff pontificating from behind his desk. Taking her in with his powers of deduction.

"Did Grice say who in the Navy?"

"No, but when we got to trading stories about the Service, I gath-ered he used to be in close contact with Central American antidrug operations."

Trading stories. She wouldn't mind hearing a straight story for a change, including Matusik's abbreviated tour in Iraq. But it was Grice holding back on her, snowing her with "hunches" about an ex–special ops killer, pushing the military angle, that set her teeth grinding. She and Annie had wondered if he had some kind of side game going. It felt right, down deep. Then Matusik was part of it. Well, maybe only a pawn. Or here just to distract.

And doing a good job of it. Already she'd missed part of what he'd said, rattling the map open and thrusting it in front of her. Something like, "Still need to find the guy, right? Well, I'm ready and available. Anytime except Wednesday evenings."

The satellite map featured a greenish ribbon of water snaking down toward her chest. It gave a vulture's-eye view of the river sliding past somewhere outside their window. She liked paper maps, too. No batteries to run out. A yellow Ticonderoga number-four in his grip, Matusik bent over the map, underlining notations he must have made earlier. "So, here's my take on this action. The search plan I ran past the sheriff includes locations I've pinpointed where I think—"

"O-o-okay, I'm stopping this right here." She aimed a gimme gesture at the pencil.

A quizzical look passed over Matusik's face, but he handed it over. She set the pencil aside, rolled up the map, and stuffed it into its pouch. With the deck cleared, she clasped her hands on the table and let a long silence reverse the cart with the horse.

"Now, I need to get a few things straight." She made it a point to speak in low, even tones. "Let me clue you in. First, this is a criminal investigation, not a search operation. Second, I don't know why you left the Coast Guard or Navy or whatever, but you are now a civilian with zero law enforcement training." A burgundy undercoating darkened the tan in his face. She didn't let it slow her down. "And third, as acting senior detective, I run this investigation."

Pixie dropped by and rested the palm of her hand on the table. "I know what Jerzy wants. Hon, what can I fetch you?"

Delia glanced up, her mouth tight with irritation. "Coffee's fine."

"Oh *chèr*, you don't need to be on no diet. How 'bout I tempt you with our lite special, café au lait and a plate of sugar-powdered beignets?"

Lite? Bathed in Pixie's infectious don't-worry-be-happy warmth, Delia felt compelled to smile back.

"Sounds very Louisiana, but no, just the coffee. Black." She waited in silence until Pixie disappeared around the pony wall before fixing her attention back on Matusik. "Have I made myself clear?"

"As a rock and a hard place." His gaze was locked onto something outside the window.

"What do you mean by that?" Those ocean-blues tracked back on her. She saw no annoyance or impatience in them. No deceit. His distress seemed genuine. He leaned closer, patting the table with the flat of his palms, fingers inches short of hers.

"See, I'm fine with you running things. Problem is, the sheriff was specific about what I need to get done. Mainly, carry out river recon runs until I find out where this guy goes home to roost, and without him tumbling to it. Also, I'm to keep Grice constantly in the loop." Those broad, fabric-stretching shoulders rose and fell in a whatcha-gonna-do sort of shrug. "In short, he was clear about me answering to him."

She sat back and folded her arms, chewing pensively at her lower lip. Was this the same old crap? Was Grice just setting up a male buffer zone between them? Or was his side game somehow yoked to his black-ops-killer theory? Probably both. Matusik appeared truthful about his situation, and that was a good sign.

"Sounds like what you and I have here is an old fashioned standoff."

He laughed. "Sure looks like we do. Rapiers? *Pistolas* at thirty paces?"

Delia started to chortle, then clamped her mouth shut. What did she have to laugh about? Between the sheriff's side-gaming and

Matusik's charm offensive, she hadn't learned a damned thing about those inked-over paragraphs in his service record.

*   *   *

Not gonna happen in this heavy fog. Not on this river. Zack's patience needle sank into the doubt zone. He shook the blood rush from his ears and nudged his hunting partner. "Hey, Charlie, we been standin' behind this boat blind, staring at nothin' but gray, for most of the morning. Whaddaya think?"

His brother had flown in for Thanksgiving, and Zack had sunk his hopes into a decent hunt on the Willamette. One that might tip the scale on Charlie moving back, if he was reading him right. But would the local wildlife cooperate? A single flight? A pair of mallards? A lone teal, maybe? No such luck.

Narrow by nature, Charlie's dark eyes tightened to impish slits. "All right, I'll give it a shot." He spread the sides of his mouth, using his pinkie and pointing finger. His chest swelled.

"No, I didn't mean do your lame-ass—"

"*Fweet-fweet-fweet.* Here, ducky, ducky!" Charlie's booming clown call bounced around the socked-in backwater as he took in more air.

Grinning, Zack pawed the Desert Storm boonie off Charlie's head and mashed it into his puss, muffling a repeat performance. "Ah, shut the fuck up. We'll hang around for another thirty. See if anything drops in on us."

Charlie swatted the hat against his thigh and settled the boonie back onto his shiny dome. "Man, here I am, takin' red-eyes both ways just to spend time with my little bro. Does he respect my hunting acumen? My calling skills? Hel-l-l no."

Zack let that one go. They both knew who the real caller was in this family. If ever they had ducks to call.

Charlie seemed to lapse back into his own thoughts. So did Zack.

A dead quiet pressed down on them, slowing time and motion. Only leaves and sticks floated downstream into the little slough.

Anchored decoys, barely twenty yards away, fuzzed in and out of sight. Those and the hazy, come-and-go shapes farther out that Zack formed with his mind's eye and lost in a blink.

Standing in a boat for hours tied up against a willow bank in chowder-thick fog, a guy started to imagine things. The crazy shit he'd seen and heard on the river these past weeks didn't help matters. Torn-up boats. Antihunting nuts out burning blinds and cutting decoys loose.

And then there was that goofball Grundy, yammering about a scuba-diving bogyman when Charlie and Zack had stopped to pick up doughnuts at the Octane Stop. What was up with that?

His flat-bottom Weld-Craft lurched—Charlie shifting weight. Zack steadied the collapsible blind he'd mounted around the boat's topside and waited for aftershocks. When his brother moved, every thing moved.

"Fifteen going on twenty, Zack. Still no bird action."

"Not so much as a stray widgeon."

The boat shuddered again. Charlie, scratching. "Seems like we're the only ones out here, haired or feathered."

"Looking that way." Nine times out of ten, a thick mist meant great hunting. All this fog had done for Zack was clam his skin like wet leather. "What say we give it five more and—"

"Mark."

His brother's whispered signal pumped a charge of adrenaline through Zack. Both of them automatically lowered into a crouch behind the blind. Fast wings beat high promise overhead. Zack hated getting skunked, almost as much as Charlie.

Keeping his face down, Zack fumbled for one of the duck calls hanging from his neck. It was great seeing Charlie fired up and grabbing for his Browning over-and-under.

"Give 'em a highball. So they know their buddies are down here."

Zack put the mallard tone to his lips and filled his cheeks with air. Starting at *frantic hen*, he followed the high note with a series of quacks that dropped in pitch and loudness, ending with *fat-bellied feeder*. Unseen wings whistled close overhead in the gray.

They faded to nothing.

Charlie straightened, still craning his head. "Try your come-back call."

Zack took another breath, blew a long, forlorn note—his version of a lovesick hen mallard. He waited, listening. The stillness dropped back in. He drew breath for another try, then held off, not knowing why but relieved that the flight had moved on. That Charlie might now be good and ready to collect their decoys and get off the river.

The quiet whoosh of landing splashes filtered back through the heavy mist. The eight or so ducks had set down a good two hundred yards away. Maybe along the gravel bar out by the Santiam River.

Charlie leaned his gun against a seat and shoved an arm inside his waders, scratching at his backside. "Shee-it. We get one flight and they land on the Santiam. Now they'll drift down into the Willamette. What'd you do, blow your stay-the-fuck-away call?"

Zack squinted sideways at his brother's narrow eyes and tight smile, knowing the taunt was bogus. He lifted the lanyard from around his neck and held out the calls.

"Here, bend over and blow 'em an ass-quack."

His brother snickered. "So long as you put it back in your mouth and blow the next call."

"Okay, if the reed ain't burned out by then."

Zack and Charlie shared the stifled, wheezy laugh of duck hunters trying hard not to scare game away.

The day fog closed in tighter than before, framing a world no more than a decoy's toss in any direction. Zack thought about the thing that ate at him. "Ain't heard no Lena and Ole jokes since you showed up on Mom's doorstep."

His brother glanced down at his boot tops. Not a peep.

"Know that other detective? Chavez?" Zack asked, breaking the silence. "She asked me to help her out. I even found that dead hunter's pickup she was looking for."

"That's great, Zack. Stick with it. You never know."

"You gonna stay in Minnesota?"

Charlie sighed, adding to the mist. "Ah, hell. I dunno, Zack. Job's not working out like I thought. I miss Oregon, a lot. Steelhead fishing . . . river hunting . . . all that." He nudged Zack's elbow. "Besides, Minnesota's got some damn cold nights. Soon as I hit the sack, Ginny's got her bare feet glued to my butt. She might as well strap on a pair of TV dinners."

Zack snorted, breathed in a little hope, and waited. He missed Charlie something fierce. And he sure didn't want any more fucked-up hunting trips with his Joe College cousin.

Charlie toed an empty decoy bag. "Sheriff's still too pissed to talk with me, so I met with Harvey Schenkel. You know, my former supervisor? He's recuperating from a truck mishap but thinks he'll run for sheriff. Says I need to bide my time, that Grice is on his way out. If Harvey wins, I could be back by late spring."

Zack punched his brother in the shoulder. "Damn, Charlie. That's fuckin' great. I'll come help you and Ginny with the move. Get you situated here, and we'll go fish the hell out of those high-lake brookies. Later on, there's sea-run cutts on the Siletz, or we—"

"Whoa, whoa. Roll up your fish-and-game calendar there, little bro." Charlie rubbed at his upper arms. "Nothing's for sure, and I don't want to jinx it."

"Won't say another word, Charlie. So long as I know—"

"Shh. Listen." Charlie cupped a bare hand behind his ear. "Hear those quacks?"

Turning down-slough, Zack heard only silence, the same roaring hush he'd been trying to shut out all morning. "Don't hear much of anything. What say we bag it?"

Charlie hiked up his waders and retrieved a pair of near-scorched gloves from in front of their propane boat heater. "Betcha that bunch paddled up this way." Pulling on the gloves, he straddled the shore side of the boat and lowered one booted foot, testing the shallows for bottom. "Think I'll stretch my legs. See if I can jump-shoot a green-head or two."

Unsure why, Zack felt his skin prickle watching his brother lift the other foot over, snatch up the Browning, and ease down into the water. He couldn't shake the notion that river hunting had gotten too risky. "When you move back out here, maybe we should look into one a those duck pond leases over by Baskett Slough. Flyway's shifting, anyway."

Charlie looked up at Zack for a few beats, reading the silent language between brothers. "Tell you what. You collect the dekes, pick me up out on the point of this gravel bar, and we'll jaw about it on the way to Mom's." He gave Zack a two-fingered poke in the knee, his voice climbing an octave. "Load up on summa dat stuffed toikey and gravy, eh, Moe?"

Zack grinned, watching him break through thin shore ice and wade off into the willows. The old Charlie and his stooged-up Curly impressions were back—a damn sight better than that Scandihoovian claptrap he'd been spouting all fall.

Charlie's bulk faded into the fog. Zack called out using his best Three Stooges Moe voice. "Watch yourself. Don't step in any postholes, ya big palooka."

Seconds later, Curly's muffled answer drifted back.

"Nyuk-nyuk-nyuk."

17

On that same morning nine miles downriver, Delia Chavez lingered in the Flapjack Corral, watching Jerzy Matusik struggle to keep his cool. It seemed her last-second preface—"Don't know why you left the Coast Guard or Navy or whatever"—had struck a nerve. From his furtive glances, that glistening forehead in the morning coolness, she inferred he was braced for something.

Not one to disappoint, she cocked an inquisitive eyebrow. "In the Coast Guard you were what, a petty officer?" He sat back, his brows knitted. She waited.

Reprieved by Pixie. The waitress unloaded Matusik's plate of kitchen-sink proportions. For Delia, a cup of steaming brew and powdered pastries. "For you, *chèr*. Coffee with a hint of chicory and beignets. Good as you get at Café du Monde. Don't let Jerzy eat them all."

She glided away while he filled his mouth until his cheeks bulged. A person sure couldn't be expected to answer with a mouthful.

She gave him expectant eyes, reminders she wasn't letting him off the hook.

Several bites later, with him fanning his mouth from the heat of the sausage and spices, Matusik set down his fork. "My rank was E-6—petty officer first class. So how do we work this?"

Her cup stayed on its saucer, her fingers circling the rim. "I'll get to that. First, I want clarification on your service background."

She could almost hear him think *crap*. His arrangement was with the sheriff, not her, and she was going to know who she had been forced to work with.

Delia couldn't stand messiness and made circles around her mouth with her pointing finger, until he realized she meant his mouth. Wiping sauce and powdered sugar off his face, he wadded his napkin and pushed out a sigh.

He started to summarize his search-and-rescue qualifications, and she waved that off. "Oh, no doubt, your Coast Guard background's impressive. I want to know about the last part. That naval assignment in the Persian Gulf. Specifically, why the general discharge?"

"Can't talk about most of it . . ."

She sat back. He was going the classified route? Okay, there was some truth in that, but it was coming across as lame. His glance said he knew it did. She kept her eyes on his—patient but insistent.

"Let's just say I let alcohol cloud my professional judgment. I failed to answer muster, and others paid for it." For a while, he took in the sweep of the river.

She waited. No signs he'd dissembled. No attempt to overexplain.

"You going to say something to the sheriff?"

She shook her head. "Not if you do."

"I will. First thing."

"Finish your breakfast," she said, reaching for a beignet.

They ate in silence.

In the time it took her to finish the pastry, he managed to download a good portion of the Cajun hash, doused with Tabasco. His lips had to be doing a slow burn. When she spoke again, he was in the process of draining what water he'd managed not to spill.

"Let's get down to business." She pushed the dishware aside and lined up her spoon next to the knife. "Before you put that boat on that river"—she nodded to her right—"you need to know the situation. Two murders, one the end of last hunting season, the second a week into the start of this season. Both victims were hunters found on a flooding river that mutilates bodies and drains away evidence at eighty thousand cubic feet per second. In addition, a detective was injured when a boat trailer ran over him, antihunting groups are sabotaging hunting blinds, and someone, possibly a military fugitive with a military-style Zodiac, may be booby-trapping boaters." She took a recovery breath. "It's exasperating."

"I guess," he said, like he meant to say *holy shit*. "How do you know the two deaths are related?"

"Each corpse had an index finger sawed off."

Matusik's Adam's apple did a little bop. "Jeez. Glad you saved that little tidbit until after breakfast."

She showed him a smile drained of humor. "Best-case scenario, the killing is over for this year."

"Worst?"

"The season's young and he's just getting started."

"You think this military fugitive's behind all of it—the murders, the boat-wrecking?"

"Apparently, the sheriff thinks so. If he's assigned you to my investigation, I'll expect you to help sort that out. Right now, I've got a more important job for you." She had his full attention. "Grice wants to downplay the murders with the press and avoid involving other law enforcement agencies." She felt stress lines crease her forehead in her struggle to go along with the sheriff's logic. "Not until I've made progress on the case."

Matusik nodded. "Yeah, he hammered me on that point."

She could feel the furrows deepen. "All the same, it's critical to warn hunters off that river. Tactfully."

He sat back again. Pulled his arms off the table. "That could pose a problem. Duck hunters are a tribe of their own. Hunting's a passion they aren't about to give up. We can alert them, and some will listen. But a lot are going to say, 'Fu—,' uh, 'Forget that.'"

"At minimum they need to be put on the lookout."

"We can try. Might catch up with some at the launches. On the water's best, because they're usually in duck blinds way before sunup."

"On tactics, I want you to handle the blinds while I hit the boat ramps."

He squinted at her. "Better if we double-team."

"Nope. I want a division of labor—you on the river, me covering shore access points." She stood and opened her purse "Ready?"

Matusik reached into his back pants pocket. "Shit, left my wallet at my dad's house." He grinned sheepishly. Delia wasn't amused, fishing bills out of her bag.

"Don't let this be a habit. No driver's license, I suppose." She moved toward the front of the restaurant, him close behind. "Consider yourself lucky I'm off traffic patrol."

On her pass by an empty, dish-cluttered table, she grabbed up an unused napkin, captured a partially eaten sausage link, and handed it to him. "Bet someone's expecting a treat."

As soon as they stepped outside, even under the gray overcast she felt him studying her in profile. Not in a creepy-pervy way. Like he was at a loss for words, seeing her in a different light.

When they reached his Hummer, Matusik raised the sausage like a finger extension. His yellow Lab mix wedged its big snout through the narrow window opening and gave out a fetching whine. A sucker for dogs and cats, Delia took back the sausage and offered it to the twitching muzzle. Beezer inhaled the snack and slurped her fingers for good measure.

"You have a natural way with dogs," Jerzy said, making his way around to the driver's side.

"I'm attracted by their honesty," she replied.

* * *

Years ago, Zack had accepted getting skunked as part of the ups and downs of hunting on the Willamette. He knew when nothing was going to happen, duckwise. When to lower the blind, untie the boat, and paddle out to pick up decoys.

After the sloshing of Charlie's boots had died away, a fog hush clamped down on Zack's ears with the force of a headlock. So hush he welcomed any kind of noise, even if he made it. Like splashing water when he drained the hollow keels of his dekes, the clunk of lead weights against plastic mallard or pintail bodies, winding up anchor cord. The imagined calls from Charlie to get a move on. Come pick him up, already.

Decoy bags filled faster thinking about good stuff. Like a Christmas present for his brother. Something extra special this year. Maybe he'd spring for a Lamiglas blank and wrap Charlie a new fly rod. Custom-shaped cork grip, titanium carbide snake guides, the whole shebang.

A V-shaped wave cut the surface in front of him, heading upstream toward the entrance to the slough. Out where Charlie had gone. Watching that ripple, Zack felt the jimjams squirm up between his shoulder blades. He shook water out of a decoy's keel, reminded again of Grundy's gas station jawboning. How some kind of eco-freak frogman had scared the shit out of him. Kept repeating that he wouldn't be running the Willamette anytime soon.

The ripple disappeared in the mist. Zack told himself it was just another one of those damned nutria. He kept on winding anchor line and stuffing decoys into mesh net bags—much faster than before.

He packed the last fake pintail into a bag and checked his watch. Charlie should've scared that flock off the water by now. Time to motor on up there.

He was bent low, stowing the paddle, when shots boomed out, one on top of the other. Then came splashes. Loud ones. But not like birds launching off the water.

He ticked his head to the side, listening. Wondering why the splashes had come after the shots.

Had Charlie fallen in again? Nah, he'd yell his head off. One time, his brother had squatted down on a log to shoot under some branches. The recoil knocked him backward into three feet of slough water. Funniest damn thing Zack had ever seen. Laughed his ass off watching Charlie feel around in the mud for that old Browning twelve.

Not so funny now, not in thirty-degree weather.

The little Johnson coughed to a start on Zack's first yank. He throttled up and aimed the bow toward the mouth of the slough.

Zack kept the outboard cranked until the shore brush on his left thinned to bare gravel. The fog started to lift, too. Above, a creamy disk showed through, only to slide back into hiding. He felt like he was coasting through a fuzzy dream.

About where Charlie should be, Zack cut to a slow troll. For a second, he thought he'd glimpsed a hazy form. His boat was overloaded with decoys or he'd stand when he called out.

"You shoot any ducks?"

Ducks echoed back. Zack waited a few heartbeats. Whatever he'd seen was gone.

"Charlie? Where you at?"

At repeated itself. The answer he expected didn't come. His mouth went dry. *Oh Christ. Maybe Charlie did fall in.*

The fog climbed into the treetops. He could see out to the Santiam where the low mound of boulders and sand dropped off into heavy current. No sign of Charlie. The whole gravel bar was empty. No sounds except for the river, but he sensed he wasn't alone.

He throttled up and moved on, scanning the agitated water past the slough's intake, hoping to spot a pair of flailing arms, or maybe a bobbing head out in the current. A disturbance broke surface. Bubbles, clusters of them, spaced ten feet apart and coming at him. Grundy's early-morning prattle bubbled up, too—*Son of a bitch swum in from behind. Had me tits up and suckin' river water.*

A scalp-tingling *look out!* raced from Zack's brain into his tiller arm. His hand wrenched the throttle full up. The light boat shot ahead, out of the slough and into the Santiam chop.

At midriver and into calmer water, he eased off on the gas, took a breath, and threw a glance over his shoulder. The bubbles were nowhere in sight. Zack swallowed his heart back down his throat and scanned the water downstream.

Something in an eddy caught his eye. A hump of camouflage material, puffed up with captured air, turned slowly in the swirl of current. Along with something smaller. Rounder. Zack felt the blood drain from his face.

He steered toward the slow-moving water. Zack wasn't big on church, but he prayed now.

"Don't let it be Charlie. Christ, please don't let it be Charlie."

His boat closed in. The Desert Storm boonie floated past, nestled inside a patch of yellow-white detergent foam. Standard stuff on rivers these days.

Maybe it was the jitters. Eye tricks might give that froth a tint. He steered wide. The edges stayed pink.

"Oh God. God, oh God."

The boat coasted past the hat, and Zack collapsed into a slump, gasping for air as if someone had punched him in the gut. The untended tiller handle vibrated to the left and banged against the metal boat side with each chug of the engine. The Jon boat circled clockwise around the floating lump. He felt frozen in place, afraid to look.

A shred of hope pushed at him. He had to be sure. Wiping at the corners of his eyes, Zack struggled out of a daze. Maybe it was some drowned fisherman.

He straightened course and came alongside the lower end of the ballooned-up coat. He made out a collar, then sleeves, dangling down into the depths. Maybe it was empty.

His hands shook so bad he yanked his gloves off with his teeth. He lunged sideways, latching on to the stiff fabric. The bobbing mass balked at being turned over. He spotted a slit across the shoulder seam. No, more like a razor slice. Leaning far out, Zack used the opening to gain leverage and pulled. This time he succeeded.

And wished he hadn't.

Mouth open, Charlie's head lolled back like it had come unhinged. Trapped air burbled from his coat front. His body started to sink, but not fast enough. Zack's eyes filled with horror at the second opening below his brother's chin. A gaping, red-raw crescent moon stretched from ear to ear.

Zack recoiled, letting go of the coat. The gorge of morning snacks rocketed up his throat as his brother's body disappeared into the swirling gray-brown murk. He spewed lumps of Charlie's jelly rolls over boat and water. He kept on spewing until his stomach touched his backbone. Until he had nothing left.

Done puking, he wiped his mouth with his sleeve and cast around. The roaring hush poured down over his head like an emptied bucket.

18

Saturday vigil hours were nearly over when Delia drove up the hill past Saint Fyodor's, cut into the overflow lot, and stashed her hot rod loaner in a corner slot. It seemed tacky to park her brother's gaudy ride anywhere close to the eye-catching but simple chapel with its burnished metal onion dome and natural wood siding—a picture postcard from the old country.

From Russia with love, she thought as she got out and shrugged on a smoke-gray lambskin blazer—the closest she had to mourning attire.

She'd come to pay respects to the Lukovsky family; also, to catch up with Charlie's younger brother. Tell him she'd lost a brother, too. That she would not stop until his brother's killer was in custody. Or dead. A somewhat empty promise, she thought. What with the rising river inundating the lower Santiam, where Charlie had been killed.

The last rays of winter sun played off the church cupola, turning its copper shingles into molten drops as she approached the front driveway. She'd slip inside and do some praying or chanting, or whatever was orthodox, and if possible avoid an open-casket viewing. No artful concealment of Charlie's wound could erase the image of him lying on the ME's table, ash white, gashed from ear to ear.

She was halfway up a set of railroad ties dug into the hillside for steps when the sheriff's unmarked Interceptor wheeled into the church driveway and stopped below her. Grice rolled the window down, shouted her name, and motioned her toward him.

Reversing her steps, she made for the sheriff's car and peered in his open passenger window.

"Evening, Sheriff."

"Think I'm a fool, Cha-vez?" He flapped his hand up toward the church. "Think I don't know you sent Shiftless in to twist my cojones?"

The heat rose in her cheeks. She spoke in an even, hope-you-don't tone of voice. "Coming in, Sheriff?"

He tipped his mouse-gray Stetson back on his head. "Just because three kills qualifies as a serial homicide case and the last was a cop, you think we're going to turn over a major investigation to the Staties? Well, I'm here to tell you nothing's changed."

"I heard Zack lipped off and you kicked him out of your office." She forced her voice to stay even, if intense. "Charlie and his family deserve the respect of *every* PCSD staff member."

"I know exactly what's deserved, Cha-vez. Yes, I'll be at Restlawn tomorrow, leading the ceremonial procession in full dress uniform. 'Cause Charlie Lukovsky once worked for Polk County, and I hate seeing any law officer get killed. I'm sure you're aware that when Lukovsky quit on me, he left us in a helluva lurch." If Grice could grow a handlebar mustache, no doubt he'd be twirling one end. "Still, Charlie was one of ours. We'll honor him by not going off half-cocked, by keeping this investigation solely ours. It stays locked down tighter than a banker's heart. *Comprende*?"

She *comprende*'d. Grice's ass-backwards logic seemed all about protecting his side thing, whatever that was.

In law enforcement work, kudos came *after* a criminal was apprehended. So why put all this energy into locating a fugitive only to back off once they found the guy? She'd done joint response drills with OSP's SWAT unit, and so had Grice. Why not bring in a team when the time came to make the bust? Was Grice's side thing tied to this case? Not even kudos related?

"You hearing me, Chavez?"

She matched his stare with one of her own. "Better than you think."

His eyes narrowed. "What was that?"

"If you're not coming in, why even stop here?" *Don't bait him, Delia. Don't.*

Grice reset his hat. "I'm on my way to Albany PD, see if I can palm off that barn arson case of yours. Which brings up the second reason. Making sure you're making full use of Matusik and his boat."

"Not fully."

"Why the hell not?"

Delia cocked her thumb toward the church. "Besides the obvious? I need something more from you."

"More? Jesus. I'm whittling your caseload down to one; I got you a boat and a river-savvy boat driver to team with. What else?"

"I want what you've been holding back on Robert Bastida."

Behind the wheel of his Dodge cruiser, old Lizard Breath looked away from her, his tongue darting about. Scouring the dryness off his lips, she figured.

"Get in."

She complied.

The motor stayed at idle, but Grice's expression told her his brain-wheels were doing ninety. Stewing over the truth? Thinking up a story to pass the sniff test?

She waited, watching him peruse the churchyard. The empty cars in the parking lot. The oncoming darkness.

His eyes narrowed. Quick as a snap decision, he reached over the seat back and brought forward a rubber-banded roll of paper. He tapped the tube against his thigh for a moment, then handed it to her.

"Planned to brief you anyway—an add-on project that got dumped in my lap." He switched on the dome light.

Add-on? she wondered, turning the tube over in her hands. More evasion?

She slipped off the rubber band and unfurled two pages, one a federal marshal's fugitive circular and the other a diagram for a military-style boat. The cut of it seemed familiar. She skimmed the circular on Gunner's Mate Robert Bastida, noting a litany of warrant charges:

desertion while on deployment, larceny of U.S. government property, reckless endangerment of a military operation, attempted homicide. The last and most relevant gave her pause. She tried to imagine
how a naval specialist trained to kill silently, quickly, and efficiently
had earned a botched homicide charge. A photo at the bottom stuck
with her. The head shot was marred from a dirty fax machine, but
the faintly distracting image had her struggling to process what Grice
was telling her.

"Don't pay that old circular much attention. Bastida's an alias.
Nobody in his home state knew anything useful. But he's our guy."

Grice leaned toward her, the springs of the bench seat creaking.
"Keep this on the q.t. I'm not allowed to go into details, but a certain naval unit in Virginia has requested assistance in locating this
fugitive's base of operations." He shrugged. "As for his arrest, well . . .
when the time comes, I'm prepared to bring in, let's say, specialized
resources."

"Yeah, but—if he's our killer—"

"Look, the Navy wants him back in the worst way. In my book, the
Navy takes precedence."

"Over a murder investigation?"

"In this instance, yes. Bastida's a genuine badass and a major head
case, but that's the tip of the iceberg."

"I don't understand."

"Simple. Whatever he's got, they're desperate to locate and recover
themselves."

"What? Did he steal something top secret?" She threw in the next,
half in jest. "Some kind of advanced weaponry?"

In the span of a second or two, Grice's eyes widened then narrowed, then took on a glint, as if her notion had merit. "Come to think
on it, you might've just hit the nail. They were cagey about what the
thing was, but special-ops groups routinely test experimental stuff."

She tongued the inside of her mouth, rolling the idea around. "So,
that's the larceny. Maybe. But where did he earn the reckless endangerment, assault, and attempted-homicide charges?"

The sheriff made a guttural throat noise. "Uh, down in Colombia, I assume. Where he wrecked a counterdrug operation and bailed on his unit."

"Jesus, was that before or after he stole the ray gun or light saber, or whatever?"

Grice thumped the wheel so hard it startled her. "Don't joke, god-dammit. I already told you, no particulars." He picked up and reset his hat on his head, took a breath. "I didn't bargain for complications. But we have a good shot at wrapping up this wrinkle and our investigation. The sooner you and Matusik get your asses in gear and get on that river, the better our chances."

The sheriff switched off the dome light. His foot pressed on the brake pedal and he dropped the gearshift into drive. "You're a detective and I'm late. You know everything I can tell you about the suspect, so go detect." Delia stepped out, the curling pages still in her hand.

She barely had the door shut when gravel spun from the Interceptor's wheels.

Go detect, he'd said. Fucking A, she would. Especially this "add-on."

19

Delia couldn't have missed Matusik's buttercup-yellow Hummer if she'd tried. Backed down the launch ramp at West Salem's Wallace Marine Park, it stood out like a beached sunfish.

By the time she'd swung off the Salem-Dallas Highway, found the right surface street, and driven into Wallace's parking area, he'd launched, locked up, and roared off in that topless silver-and-blue jet boat. She barely had time to focus her long-range 25 × 70s, first on the back end, emblazoned with the name *Jackie*, next on the bow ornament with the flapping ears—Beezer. His dog, whom she'd met and instantly liked. *Jackie* had her puzzled. Current girlfriend? Old flame?

That twenty-something-foot Duckworth could paddle right along. If Delia wanted to keep him under observation, she'd have to scramble. Dropping the SkyMaster binocs, she cut a tight circle, exited the park, and accelerated back onto Highway 22 toward Dallas. Fortunately, the road paralleled the Willamette for several miles upriver.

Yes, she and Grice's hired boat driver *had* reached an understanding at the Flapjack Corral. Good in itself, but to Delia, understandings backed by observed compliance were golden. The troubling piece remained Grice's fixation on *place*—locating a military fugitive's top-secret-laden hideout, when her investigation should be about *person*—finding out who was doing in hunters. Besides, the detective's itch inside needed scratching. Was Matusik following her instructions? Or was he on the river only to search for that elusive place? So after the law enforcement funeral procession, she'd made her apologies to

Charlie's family, taken early leave from the reception and mercy meal, and set about tailing Matusik.

Eola Inn was in sight when the jet boat slowed on the river, curled in toward the west bank, and disappeared behind the gentle rise the inn was built on. Delia recalled that Rickreall Creek entered somewhere beyond the restaurant's picture-window view of the Willamette River. She hooked left off the highway and onto Willamette Street, passed by chainsaw sculptures of bears and eagles, and pulled over next to a clearing in the tree line that afforded her views of the creek mouth and beyond. A minute later, Matusik's boat cruised past the Salem Yacht & Boat Club—mainly a sand peninsula now under winter river water. She trained the SkyMaster on the jet boat as it coasted into one of four small slough openings. Ducks circled above, then sailed off.

It wasn't until Matusik neared the end of the slough that she saw movement beyond and zoomed in on a parked watercraft looking for all the world like a floating brush clump against the backdrop of flooded trees. A half-dozen ducks bobbed on the water's surface. Not dead, but not going anywhere. What else but decoys? Zack had given her a rudimentary rundown on migratory bird hunting, not so much on why it appealed to anyone. Duck tamales? ¡Puaj!

The cloud cover had let the sun burn through, then closed in, settling a thin, dirty mist over the river. She couldn't see the face of the person moving behind the brush, just his flappy-eared hat and mud-brown hunting clothes. Matusik's boat slowed to a stop with the decoys between him and the brush boat. From her perspective, he seemed to be jawing with the man inside it. An encouraging sign.

At first light, she'd sent him off with warnings for anyone on the river who'd listen. She'd also given him a question list intended to provoke leads on the three Willamette River killings. When he looked at her funny, she'd explained she had a funeral to attend.

And now? To her surprise, Matusik maneuvered his boat back into the flooded trees and out of sight, then emerged wading toward the brush boat with Beezer dog-paddling beside him. She adjusted the SkyMaster and zoomed in closer as they scrambled into the brush boat. Was he goofing off or planning on interrogating this hunter?

Flappy Hat seemed to know Matusik, clapping him on the back after both reacted to a water baptism by the dog as he shook his fur between them. She wished she could've tapped into the cell phone she'd loaned Matusik, but in Oregon, recording face-to-face communications required the consent of both parties.

Several minutes passed where Flappy Hat lit and smoked down a cigar and they talked. The conversation was interrupted by a flight of ducks with green heads. When she again trained the binocs on the brush boat, the hunter and Matusik had disappeared behind the brush. The only movement was the vertical twin barrels of a shotgun that seemed to trade places.

When the four ducks cupped their wings and settled over the decoys, she was surprised to see Matusik rise up and fire, the large-bore boom of the shotgun reaching her ears shortly after feathers floated down. All four ducks were now in full flight. Matusik shot again. More feathers filled the air in front of the boat, but the green-headed birds made their escape. Flappy Hat was up and slapping a hand onto what looked to be a storage lid in the front of the boat, his shoulders shaking as if he were having a hearty laugh.

So, she thought, lowering the glasses. Matusik *was* a big goof-off.

After several minutes, he and Beezer took their leave and returned to the jet boat. Delia lowered the SkyMaster, picked up her iPhone, and touch-tapped the only new entry in her contact list. Matusik's boat had entered the Willamette when he picked up.

"Having a good time?" she asked.

"What? Yeah, uh, just finished talking with my fourteenth on the river today. They're a pretty closed-mouth bunch, and nobody seems ready to give up hunting. The only leads they gave me were on damaged blinds and slashed boat trailer tires. Done by 'animal rights jack-offs,' according to one group of hunters."

"Tell me about the fourteenth."

"Tweety Bates? Okay, yeah. He used to guide back in the heyday of river hunting. Took my dad and I out on slow days. He's sort of a river hermit, and I figured if anybody saw or knew something, he would. Tweety's always been colorful, but he's not the same these days. He quit guiding after he lost his dog, Trudy. Some kind of accident, I gathered."

"So you were banging away down there for old times' sake?"

Long pause at the other end. Then, "How'd you . . . You have me under surveillance?"

She could almost feel him look over his shoulders. "The funeral was over, and I wanted to see how you work."

"Through what, binoculars? If you're wondering, I'm sticking to our arrangement. Why not just come out on the river with me?" His voice didn't sound accusative—more like disappointed. "You'd certainly loosen more tongues than I ever could." She wasn't sure which way to take that. Decided to let it slide, along with the boat ride offer.

"Back to this . . . Tweety, is it? As in Tweety Pie and Sylvester cartoons?"

"Likely from the widgeon whistle he favors over mallard calls."

"And what did you learn from your 'hunters' bonding moment?'" His boat coasted out of sight. She made no move to start the car.

"Not a whole lot. He's still colorful, and a prankster, foisting that shotgun on me with feather loads instead of steel pellets. Yelling, 'Take 'em,' then laughing his ass off when I filled the sky with duck down."

"Has he seen anything? An empty Starcraft? That Zodiac?"

"No, but he's sure got his opinions."

"About?"

"Protesters, Portlanders who think they're decent hunters, you name it. In fact, he had names for them all: Bird Worshipers, Concentrics, Hunturds."

"What's a Concentric?"

"Perfect asshole. Tweety talked about one that scoots up and down the river in a sea-green kayak. Scares off ducks looking to land in somebody's decoy setup."

"And a Hunturd?"

"Not sure. Said they were coming out of the woodwork. Told me to keep out of their way. I left him one of your cards in case he runs across anything we can actually use."

"Hang on." Delia had an incoming call. She tapped *hold call* and answered, noted down the information, and returned to Matusik.

"There's been a development. Meet me at Buena Vista Marine Park."

"Is this development upriver from my position? I'm low on fuel."

"Looks that way. Oh, and you might need . . . like a grapple."

"I've got a telescoping boathook in my Hummer. I have to pull out, gas up, and relaunch anyway."

"Independence in forty." She had her finger on the red *off* icon, recalled his little shooting exhibition, and couldn't resist.

"Oh, Matusik?"

"Yeah?'

"If I get in a shots-fired situation, remind me not to use you for my backup."

"Very funny."

20

"Are you certain there was a body inside those waders?"

Still in full funeral uniform, standing astride a water rivulet on the downslope of Buena Vista's launch ramp, Delia bent low and peered inside the rear left door of Castner's patrol unit. She ignored the light rain and kept her eyes trained on Elmer Grundy, the twitching man-wreck Craig had poured into his back seat barely an hour ago. Better outside and slightly damp, she thought, than inside and overwhelmed by Grundy's breath rot.

Going by his amber teeth and jerky limbs, his eyes in constant motion and the borderline paranoia of his ramblings, Grundy was a meth-head. Still, his account of a dead hunter on the lower Santiam River seemed credible, considering the strip of ripped chest wader she'd found impaled on an anchor fluke of Grundy's beached fishing boat. His other story, about a knife-wielding underwater swimmer running him off the Willamette weeks earlier, could easily have been a tweaker's hallucination. Said he'd sworn off hunting, unless they caught the guy.

"Good God, do I wish it weren't true," Grundy answered, digging at an armpit as if something with six legs had burrowed there. "Wish to hell I hadn't fucked up and drifted below my takeout spot." Scratch, scratch. "Wish I hadn't pried that boot leg out of the water and felt the squish of dead meat inside." His chest quivered, then seemed to sink into his backbone.

Up front, Castner paid them no attention, tapping away at his dashboard computer. She uncoiled and scanned the screen on her

Toughbook. Her typed directions held enough detail that Matusik could run his boat up the Santiam. Locate the downed log where Grundy's pontoon boat had supposedly gotten hung up by somebody else's snagged boots. At least confirm whether this tweaker was round the bend or right on. Tweakers weren't to be believed sight unseen.

"Depending on what we find, we may need you at the sheriff's office." She showed Grundy the screen page where she'd inputted his ID particulars. "You'll be here this afternoon?"

"Yeah. Riding herd on my girlfriend's rug rats. But first I need to get to my rig so I can drive back here and load my CatcherCraft."

"Deputy Castner should be able to drop you off, right, Deputy?"

"That's me," he grumbled, "a chauffeur in uniform." Since her promotion, Castner had shifted from blatant antagonist to passive-aggressive. She took both with a grain of salt.

Edging ahead, she motioned for him to roll down. The window opened a crack. Not caring whether Grundy heard or not, she hissed through her teeth, "Follow this guy back to his girlfriend's and check on those kids. Make sure they look clean and fed."

"Wipe their butts, too?"

"Just do it, okay?"

Shutting the rear door, she stepped back. Castner hit reverse and spun the tires, jammed the gear stick into drive, and roared off. She checked her watch. Twenty minutes to get to the Octane Stop.

* * *

Already late for a meet-up with Matusik, Delia skidded the Camaro onto Route 51 and accelerated into pounding rain. She boosted wiper speed and slowed. Within seconds, the Camaro's soft-top had developed a leak. To avoid a waterfall, she scrunched to her right. Steering one-handed, she traded wet uniform for dry leather jacket. Last, she shucked the soggy brown tie, convinced she must have some kind of water magnet implanted in her chest.

The rain let up six miles on, and she cracked her window. Coming into Independence, Oregon, she spotted Jerzy Matusik's yellow

141

Hummer and trailered jet boat at the low-roofed Octane Stop. Matusik was inside the boat, crouching near its back end. He straightened briefly and waved.

She cut a U-ey and rolled in behind the boat. Getting out, she remembered it had been christened *Jackie*. Again she wondered, old flame or current one?

A sharp bark greeted her approach. Beezer alternated between turning backseat circles and wedging his blocky head out the Hummer's window.

Jackie's rear-deck cowling was propped open beside the man, giving Delia a view of the power plant. Corvette. Fuel-injected. Twin-turbo kit. Impressive.

As Matusik knelt in *Jackie*'s cockpit and checked the connections, his khakis were stretched tighter than tree bark. Also impressive.

He peeked at her from under one arm and smiled. She glanced away as a station attendant finished pumping high-test. He handed up a receipt and left. Matusik casually stuffed it into a shirt pocket as he reached for something below her line of sight.

"So, what's up, Detective?"

"Shitty gas you're running through that rat motor." She estimated the big-block Chevy had to corral over six hundred ponies under those stainless-steel head covers.

"You could be right." He sank an oil stick back into the engine, stood, and reached out a hand. "How about coming aboard for a closer look?"

She glanced at her watch. "Not the boaty type. You about ready? A fisherman named Grundy says there's a body on the Santiam. I want you to run up there and check it out."

Matusik closed the engine housing, his gaze trailing back toward her vacant Camaro. "The guy's not going with us?"

"With you? No. He was pretty wigged out. Said no way he'd go anywhere near what he'd seen."

Matusik climbed down from the boat and stood facing her. "So it's on us to locate this body?"

She jammed her fists into her coat pockets, one hand curling around the ever-present grip-strengthening ball. "No again. It's on you to do the locating."

He leaned in, those narrowed, pepper-flecked blue eyes searching hers. "That how it's done in your shop?"

Somewhere in the back of her head, she heard tsk-tsking. Knew Harvey would've ripped on up that river without a second thought. The fingernails of her left hand dug into hard rubber as she walked away. Stopped at the drip line of the roof, turned and came back, squeezing the life out of the ball in her pocket.

"Look, Matusik, the guy's a—"

"Jerzy. Please."

"Okay. Jerzy. This, uh, Grundy is several flakes shy of a snowball. It's likely you won't even find a body."

Matusik nodded. "Say I do find one. Then what?"

Instead of answering, she stepped over to the Hummer, where Beezer's head poked out a window. She scratched under his ear. He licked the inside of her wrist. There was no way around this fucking boat ride. That damn thing had better have a self-inflating life raft, or water wings, or something.

Letting out a ragged sigh, she came back and faced the man. And her fate.

"Who's Jackie?"

* * *

Jackie wasn't a girlfriend. Learning that had cost Delia a quick retreat to the Camaro, covering for the flush in her face, fueled by the deep-down feeling Jerzy had read her mind. Of course he'd have named his boat after Jacqueline Matusik, a mother who'd given him strength, loved boating, and died too soon.

Delia led his Hummer and boat out of the Octane Stop and toward Riverview Park, her thoughts immersed in the sadness behind his explanation.

The river dropped into view. Her gut roiled.

Distraction over.

The greenish-brown water looked heavy with silt and higher than just an hour ago. Beastlike currents swirled past the park's launch ramp, prowling the banks for anything loose and unsuspecting.

At the head of the ramp, Jerzy had already swung around and aligned his trailer for the back-down. He rushed around the boat, loosening and stowing straps. He seemed in a god-awful hurry.

Why? Before she changed her mind? Her body tensed. She'd made the decision. No backing down. Except for the boat.

She drove to a parking spot close to the bank. "It's just a big old river," she told herself as she strode down to the mud-caked edge of the ramp and stopped. And waited for the wave of nausea to die down. Keeping her head level helped.

A blur passed on her left—Jerzy, backing his rig into the water, stopping when the current churned over the trailer's wheel wells. His boat rocked as she swallowed on the acid taste in her throat, attaching her gaze to the row of far trees, the fields, the faraway hills. Anything not wet and moving. Not chewing at the mud-coated concrete.

Now he was out, doing boat stuff right beside her.

Stay steady, Chavez. Look straight ahead. No self-respecting cop pukes on her boat driver.

"Hold this."

She felt something damp and ropelike stuffed into her hand. Her gaze riveted on the far shore, she dearly wished for blinders. He unhooked something else, shoved on *Jackie*'s bow, and disappeared.

The Hummer's door slammed. Its engine revved, and water sloshed as the empty trailer rolled up past her. Delia swallowed back more bile. She registered a free-floating boat out front at the instant a strong wrench snapped her arm out straight.

The damp rope in her grip was a boat line, grown taut from a couple thousand pounds of riverboat tugging at the other end. Jesus. The man had left half his assets in her hands. And the Willamette wanted to steal them from her. As if it hadn't stolen enough.

"You slimy son-of-a-bitch." The adrenaline of old anger flooded her system. Nerves hummed. Arm and stomach muscles tightened, smothering the queasiness. "Oh no, you don't."

Delia clamped a tug-of-war grip on the line and reared back on the rope. The river surged past. Under the added strain, she gave way and almost fell. But refused to let go. Now in water to her calves, she set her feet, struggling to hold on. Pulling hard.

Slowly, she got back inches, then more, then feet, hand over hand. Jackie's bow nosed in past Delia's hip, the railing within reach. She latched onto the watercraft, huffing and puffing, thanking herself for keeping up with her gym workouts. Thanking the strengthening ball regimen, too.

She had won. A small thing, but it felt great to hear *Jackie*'s bow scrape dry land. Okay, soggy mud.

Better yet, it got her past the nausea.

She turned toward the slap of big feet on pavement. Jerzy, back from his parked vehicle.

"Quite a tussle, isn't she? Sorry about that; should've warned you."

She handed him the boat line. "You should have. Beezer?"

"Better he stays in the Hummer for this trip," he said, clambering onto *Jackie*'s bow deck. He produced life vests from a compartment and handed one down. "Coast Guard offshore jacket. Good as they come."

She took the vest and turned the puffy orange material over in her hands, a slightly altered flight attendant spiel running through her head—*In the event of a water landing, strap this on, bend over, and kiss your ass good-bye.* "Oka-a-ay, ri-i-ight."

"I know a ride up the Willamette doesn't exactly thrill you, Detective."

Delia blinked, realizing she'd spoken out loud. She peered at him, then back at the vest. "Like I said, not a fan of moving water."

Holding up the flotation jacket by its shoulder webbing, she figured out what part of her went where, stepped into the two loops of fabric that seemed to go underneath, and slipped her arms through the appropriate holes.

He jumped down and slid the bow farther up the launch apron. "*Jackie*'s very stable. Built for lumpy water. Safe as they come."

"Whatever." Delia struggled with the front of the vest. "How do I get this damned thing fastened?"

"Let's have a look." He stepped in close. Crouching, he bent sideways at the hips. "Thigh straps are about right." Then he rose slowly, his hair smelling of rain forest and red cedar. "Need to loosen the chest straps a bit." He was efficient, careful to touch the material and not her. "See? Clip-buckles in front. All set to go?"

"Everything's just ducky."

"Great." Without waiting, he vaulted over the railing, arm-boosted her up, and motioned toward one of two seats behind the consoles at midboat. His seat, a sort of elevated captain's chair, was bolted down behind a steering wheel and a nest of controls. Delia shuffled her way along the rocking center aisle, convinced an alien abduction would not seem half as unnerving.

She'd barely settled into the passenger's seat when a gear shudder and throaty engine rumble had her searching for a seat belt. Apparently, boats didn't come so equipped. An earthy slither and dry land fell away. A backing turn and the aggravated water took them downstream. Another gear clunk, an engine grumble, and they plowed upstream at a slow churn. Helping her get used to being on the river, she guessed.

Lotsa luck with that.

Still gripping the chair, she swiveled sideways and canvassed the boat's interior. Spare. Uncarpeted. Water sloshing over the floor of the boat. Gallons of it.

"Hey. Captain. Is that rainwater, or is the river coming in?"

He followed her point toward the back end. "Uh-oh."

The hair at the nape of her neck stiffened. "What do you mean, *uh-oh*?" Next came a rush of unspoken thoughts: *We're taking on water? We're sinking? Get me the hell back to shore!*

He flipped a switch. "No worry. Happens now and then." Something gurgled and a stream gushed from the side of the boat. "Forgot to put the drain plug back in. You take the wheel." He jumped up and lurched rearward, leaving *Jackie* driverless.

"Me? You're kidding." Dumbfounded, Delia darted glances between the empty chair on her right and the crouched man feeling for something down in the dirty influx.

He answered without looking up. "No kidding, Detective. And shove the throttle ahead. We need to get up to planing speed. Run the rest of this water out before I reinsert the plug."

Delia scrambled into the captain's chair, latching on to the steering wheel as if it were the safety bar on a roller coaster. "Where's the throttle? What's planing speed?"

"Just press forward on that black-knobbed lever. Keep pushing until the bow lies down and we're running on top of the water. Half ahead should do it. There you are, you little rascal."

A darting glance backward found him splayed on his stomach over Jackie's back end, holding something not much larger than a wine bottle stopper.

She eased the black knob ahead. The front end lifted. The boat seemed to wallow, so she shoved the lever up toward the halfway mark. The boat leveled out and *Jackie* shot forward, her bow carving swan wings out of the river's surface. A counterclockwise nudge to the wheel and the boat banked leftward. A clockwise turn and *Jackie* skated off to the right, like a speed drift through a highway curve. Another quick look told her Jerzy was still with her and seemed to know what he was up to.

Okay, she could do this.

Delia kept to the middle, getting the feel of the boat, not exactly disliking how the rows of cottonwoods on either bank swished past, how Jackie skimmed the river. The speedometer read thirty and felt like sixty.

Jackie could get up and move.

The level expanse of water was like a broad turnpike sans lanes or center line.

A boat passed, running downstream. A following wave rolled under *Jackie*'s bow and slapped at her underside. *Jackie* didn't seem to notice, not a bounce or even a roll. Jerzy was right about her being a stable boat.

Running up the backbone of the beast was no less ugly, but no more scary than a high-speed chase. Driving *Jackie* helped. Got Delia feeling she could do her fucking job and survive the fucking river.

Five minutes later, Jerzy plopped down into the passenger seat. "Plug's in." She started to get up. "No," he said, "stay where you are. You're doing fine."

She scrunched her bottom back into the seat, but kept an ankle curled around the chair post. They rode without talking, listening to the bass drone of the big Corvette.

Knowing nothing about proper boat etiquette, she searched for something to say.

"Good boat. Some hurry-up in that Vette?"

Jerzy leaned across the aisle, pointed ahead, and grinned. "Fifteen, twenty minutes up to the Santiam confluence. Wanna make it eight or nine?"

Delia chewed at her lower lip. She was out here and probably up a creek. Already survived a hole in the boat, and had gone far beyond scared spitless. River bad, speed good. Why the hell not?

She cut him a glance, making sure he meant what he said.

"That okay?"

"Punch it."

The Willamette stretched out for a good mile or more. She settled the palm of her right hand over the throttle, hesitated for a beat, then rammed it. *Jackie* roared, setting Delia's shoulders back into the chair. RPMs climbed toward six K and the speedometer needle pegged out. They were flying. Nervous as hell, but grinning all the same, she shot a look at Jerzy, who waved his ball cap in circles and yelled, "Yee-haw."

Cap reset, he motioned back with his thumb. "Love the rooster tail."

She glanced over her shoulder, impressed with the whitewater *Jackie* kicked out.

Like a proud set of tail feathers.

* * *

Shy of a quarter mile up into the Santiam, they spotted a downed cottonwood, stretched out into the river just as Grundy had described. And wedged into the upstream fork of a limb, about six inches of moss-green rubber boot toe—possibly the waders Grundy's pontoon boat anchor had torn a piece from. The rest of the solitary bootleg disappeared in the downstream current that dove beneath the thick tree trunk. Chugging slowly ahead, Delia couldn't shake the sensation of a pair of eyes on them, scrutinizing their every move.

"If you point her nose into the current, that'll keep her steady," Jerzy urged, heading for the back of the boat.

She maneuvered *Jackie* into a position just a few feet above the downfall. She managed to hold her in place while he probed under the water with a gaff and tried to free the wading boots from the partially submerged limb. When that didn't work, he instructed her to let *Jackie* drift against the upstream side of the tree. Delia did so and joined him at the back of the boat, her sixth sense still telling her they were being watched.

"Somebody seems interested in what we're doing."

Jerzy squinted at her, then glanced around, shrugging. "Hope he gets an eyeful. Ready for a little river tug-of-war?"

Delia shrugged back, thinking she'd done that at the boat launch. Why not here?

Shoulder to shoulder, they lay on their stomachs and stretched out over the stern. Delia took hold of the visible boot at the ankle and drew it toward her, feeling the thickness of flesh and bone inside rubber. The surging water numbed her hands, then her arms, while Jerzy continued to fish beneath the tree with the hooked pole.

"Got something." Teasing a second boot out from under the log, he grabbed it by the heel, let go of the boat hook, and applied a two-handed grip to the bootleg. "Now pull."

Together they reefed up. And got back resistance. One springy tree limb, coupled with a powerful undertow, had won back what little they'd gained. They tried again. Same result. Again. The same.

"Wait. Keep hold of both boots," Jerzy huffed at her, sitting up and swinging a leg over the side of the boat. From her awkward angle, she could make out only that he'd leaned low and grabbed on to the green limb. He gave it a ferocious, boat-rocking yank, breaking it off with a cracking sound that echoed across the riverbanks.

After a struggle that, for her, entailed slippery grips, broken fingernails, and fleeting glimpses of light reflecting off something glassy on the far bluff, Delia and Jerzy had their catch in the boat—a grisly one. No tree snag could have made that kind of neck gash. Or frozen the bloated expression of horror on the dead man who filled those boots.

21

That night Delia pummeled the steering wheel, laughing her head off as she herded the Camaro toward home and a warm bed. The song title she'd just thought up—"Damage Control Hustle"—was so funny. A perfect little ditty for the shoddy diversion Grice had pulled off after her Santiam body-find.

Time and distance and fatigue had burned all the aggravation away. Dropped her into the late-night zone where everything was funny. Grice was funny. Castner was funny. After a hellish long day, unfunny was funny. Especially the Los Lobos–style rock tune she'd invented to keep from falling asleep on the road:

> *Don't need no damned confession*
> *Don't need no smokin' gun*
> *Just collar a tweaker with no muscle*
> *And do the damage control hustle*

A second verse floated out there in the dark, like so many cartoon-balloon questions that refused to rhyme: *Need to give the media a bone? Keep a lid on a multiple-murder case? Put a damper on a stake-out in a cop-killer manhunt? Arrest somebody. Anybody will do.*

Gravel spanked the wheel wells. Delia shook off the drowsies and corrected for drift on a country road where driveways looked alike. Reach hers and she could close her eyes, and sit there.

Whatever the sheriff's side game, he'd sure as hell kept the play in his court. Trouble was, five hours of interrogation sprinkled with

151

corroborating calls to Elmer Grundy's girlfriend, a hunting acquaintance, and a Colonel Sharps of the Oregon National Guard had convinced Delia Grundy was wrong for those murders. He alibied out on the first three homicides, and was unlikely to have reported the location of the last if he'd done the killing.

Yet at the sheriff's insistence, she'd left the guy in holding, scared half to death over his pending arrest and booking for criminal homicide. Left him there after a shout-down where Grice cut her off. He aimed to use that brain-fried fisherman as a tool—announce he had a suspect in custody to make Bastida drop his guard. Meanwhile, she and Jerzy were to pussyfoot around every river dock and boathouse. And if they found what they were looking for, pull back from apprehending a stone-cold killer, all because that überwarrior might have top-secret weaponry stashed away.

That'll work. Until body number five turns up.

She eased off the gas, wishing for toothpicks to prop her eyelids open.

The more her weary brain gnawed at the sheriff's rationale for slinking around, the more dog-eared it got. Dammit all to hell, she was a full-fledged arm of the law, not a skip-tracer for some bail bondsman.

That had been just before midnight, when Delia's butt was dragging the floor tiles and her brain was mush. Still mush.

Her head dipped and rose. Shaking it off, she braked and spun the wheel. The Camaro lurched right and stopped in her driveway, of all places. She knew it was hers because of the silvery-red cat eyes glowing from her front porch.

So funny.

Killing lights and noisy engine, she sat there aching to close her eyes for a minute. But pet duty howled. She stepped out, feeling shoulder bumps against her calves. Only the tink of chrome exhaust headers and the loose-muffler rattle of Clawed's purr box disturbed the country quiet.

"Hey, cat. How was your day?"

Yeo-yeolph.

Rolph?

She smiled. "Thanks for asking. Mine started as a toilet swirly and ended in a shit storm."

She stumbled toward the house. Halfway to the front door, a motion sensor triggered an outside spotlight. For once her porch was clear of headless gifts.

"Whatsa matter, couldn't find one measly field mouse to draw and quarter?"

Meowlph.

Delia barely had the door unlatched when Clawed wedged inside and disappeared into the kitchen. Crunching sounds fractured the cold stillness as she collapsed onto her IKEA corner sofa and let her eyes go shut. Only then did she notice her body was in motion. Up and down, side to side. Boat motion, a souvenir of her water adventure. The whole house seemed adrift. She opened her eyes to the dark. The pitching and yawing didn't stop. Not funny.

She sat bolt upright. Would it ever stop? Was this the Willamette taking revenge? A warning that it intended to take more? And who was that watcher? She snapped on a table lamp and peered around. Relief seeped in. The room was rock-steady. No high-water mark ran across the framed jungle prints on the far wall; the Santiam didn't gush in at her from the bedroom hallway; the big-leaf floor plant she couldn't identify wasn't in danger of getting carried away on river currents. Only death by neglect.

So what in God's good name had possessed her to tell Grice they needed to stake out the river? Her unspoken proviso was him agreeing to involve Marion and Linn County marine patrols. That was going to be her bid, but he'd nixed the idea. Maybe it was for the good. He might've told her and Jerzy to go ahead, but do it on her own.

Clawed joined her, sprawling across her lap like he owned her.

Chilled, she zipped up her jacket and itemized the damage done to its full-grain, fine Italian leather sleeves when she'd retrieved the body from the Santiam. She winced at the mars and scratches her moistened fingers failed to erase. "Shit. Double shit."

Disappointment settled around her like fog as she slumped back, arms sinking to her sides. Justice was one hell of a goddess to worship. Fickle. Fleeting. Demanding.

Those other notions that kept popping into her head were his fault—Jerzy "Yee-haw" Matusik's. Him and his thundering riverboat. The military reject she'd been ready to resent the hell out of.

Who'd turned out to be capable and likable.

Too likable to trust, to think his sense of justice came anywhere close to hers—born of a thieving river and a thieving man who'd forced her little brother, Roberto, into his boat and guilt forever into her dreams. Stoked by the cruelty she saw and dealt with. Every. Single. Day.

She needed to keep telling herself Matusik was the sheriff's guy. After he'd made a beeline for Grice's office this evening, Annie had said, he'd skated out the door in a hurry. Was their Flapjack Corral understanding still intact? She doubted that. He hadn't so much as popped his head in while she was stuck in interrogation with Grundy. Some fucking partner.

Fucking partner. Oh quit that, Chavez. You're not Annie. Shut your eyes and relax, and forget about him. About it. Just for a minute. Maybe two. Maybe—

* * *

. . . caracha, la cucaracha.

"Uh-uh. Cinch it tighter, Jerzy."

La cucaracha, la cucaracha.

"Wha . . . ?"

Delia opened her eyes and found herself still sprawled on the couch. Fumbling behind her head, Uncle Tino's gift phone clattered onto the hardwood floor. The instant she sat up, Clawed leaped off, leaving traction scratches on her thigh.

"Ouch. Shit." She sat back and rubbed at the soon-to-be welts. Vivid images of entwined boat sex wearing nothing but life vests faded to wisps of vagueness under the harsh lamplight.

154

The phone sang again. She picked up and jabbed *talk*.

"Yeah?"

"Are you dressed? Ready to go?"

Delia blinked, a flush rising into her cheeks. "Who is this?" she snapped. As if she didn't know. It was *him*, upbeat and casual, with a voice that promised a hammock on a tropical beach. "Am I dressed. Damned ballsy, Matusik."

"I meant dressed for the stakeout."

"What the hell are you talking about?"

"What do you mean? Grice said it was your idea."

"Well, yeah. Except my rejected idea was to work up stakeout points using patrol resources from other counties. That would've left us free to respond on their call."

"Huh. I spent most of the night locating and setting up the perfect spot. Grice didn't relay my messages or status updates he wanted? Said he would." If the pause that followed had been any more pregnant, a litter of rabbits would have popped out of the phone.

"Relay? Him? When he's in the bag by eight in the evening?" Typical, Delia thought, rolling the cockroach receiver across her forehead. Co-opt her idea and delegate a guy to run with it. At least Jerzy had contacted her.

"So, should I . . ."

"Yeah, go ahead. Only I call the shots. Understood? I'm leaving Grice a phone reminder to that effect."

"Honest, Delia, if I'd known about his closet drinking, I would've checked in with you, on everything, from where to set up to when we meet . . . especially what to wear. It's going to be a cold, wet one with another rain front coming." More quiet. "You do have a warmer coat than that snazzy leather job, right? Something knee length and waterproof? Boots'd be good. Outdoor boots, not those ankle-high zip-ups."

She got to her feet. "What the hell time is it?"

"Oh-three-hundred on the dot."

"Where arc you?"

"Boat's in the water at Independence. Already prepped a brush cutout we can back her into. Found an island that'll put us in the middle of Willamette boat traffic."

"Geez, don't you sleep?"

"Way too pumped. Stretched out in the Hummer and stared at the dome light for a couple hours." He sounded like a little boy hyped for his first fishing trip.

She shuffled toward the bathroom, hugging the phone between chin and shoulder, stripping off clothing in skips and hops. "I'm there in forty. You'd better have a good heater in that boat."

She hung up under a shower of hot water and misgivings. A river stakeout with a storm coming. How many ways could that go bad?

22

"**B**atten the hatches, Detective. Here comes another one."

Delia broke off surveilling her assigned river quadrant and pulled the hood low on her borrowed poncho just as driving sleet pelted down. Needle stings still got to her chin.

Her other loaner—a Vector two-piece wet suit she'd put on beneath the rain gear and flotation vest—had proved a lifesaver. She had to hand it to Jerzy. He came equipped for rotten weather.

All morning they'd stood in his brush-concealed jet boat. Parked on the upstream point of an island. The bow bucked and swayed under the constant battering of current. Every half hour or so, a gale blew in from the south, each time shrinking visibility to forty yards. Didn't matter much. All they'd spotted was a lone duck hunter, his boat pushed by an ancient-looking outboard. Jerzy called it a mud motor and said it was the ex-guide he knew.

She stooped low and felt for the seat behind her legs. Time to give her back a rest and her eyes some relief from staring upriver.

Relief, hell, screamed a voice inside, following her downward glance. Inches of rain and dirty river water sloshed around her Muck boots, raced down the deck, then back. Gallons of the stuff. No matter the source, water inside a boat was just plain wrong.

Give the river an inch . . .

She straightened up. "Hey, Captain Matusik. We're taking on water again."

He swiveled, peeped at her from inside his own hooded raincoat, a deluge streaming off the bill cap beneath.

She jabbed an accusing finger at the deck. He followed her point but seemed unfazed by the influx.

Jackie's bow gave a sharp lurch, prompting Delia to grab on to the windshield frame. Waves splashed into the forward compartment. Looking back toward the stern, she eyed the anemic stream that pulsed out the right side of the boat. "How about jacking up the flow on that bilge whachamacallit?"

"Pumping full out now. It'll catch up soon as the rain moves on."

"Cross your heart?" That last, she'd mumbled.

"What?"

"Nothing." They dripped together in silence.

As predicted, the rain eased off—from cats and dogs to rats and mice. She could almost make out the tree line on the east bank. By then, her leather gloves were so wet she had to yank them off with her teeth.

His raincoat rotated toward her once more. "Been rethinking this surveillance stuff." He'd been peppering her with questions about the sheriff all morning, not that she hadn't provoked a share of them. "Something's bogus about Grice holding back instead of calling out the cavalry."

"That's why I've made provisions." The hint of alarm in his eyes didn't escape her. "I realize Grice butters your bread and your livelihood's at stake here, but if the sheriff's plan goes wrong and Bastida runs, I'm not about to lose him. Annie's on standby to request assistance from law enforcement patrols up and down the river."

His gaze was fixed out ahead for a while. Then he shrugged. "Getting late. Bastida might not even show."

"But if he does, and push comes to shove, I'm okay with you telling Grice I forced you into a pursuit. Whatever CYA you can think of."

He said nothing.

With the letup in rain came a temperature drop. She started to shiver.

He turned to her. "Pretty cold, huh? Want to give it another thirty and call it a day?" Was that push or shove? she wondered.

He toed the Coleman boat heater closer to her so that it sputtered beneath the grab bar she had draped her gloves over.

"Ever had a po' boy?"

She darted a glance at his straight face. "I hope you're talking about the sandwich."

He grinned. "Well yeah, uh . . ."

"That's French bread stuffed with seafood or meat, right? See, I'm vegan. Trying to be."

He nodded. "Pixie makes 'em at the Corral. Has a garden version."

"Sounds good right about now. Skipped breakfast. Bet I could eat a—"

"Hello."

Jerzy's whispered greeting took her by surprise. So did his persistent tug on her poncho, urging her down on her knees beside him. She followed his nod and peeked out on the river through a hole in *Jackie*'s brush camouflage. Her heart skipped a beat. The poor boy would have to wait.

A large watercraft crept through the remnants of the rainstorm as if parting a tattered gray shroud. It skated downriver a couple stone's throws off to their right. No engine rumbles, no wave disturbance gave it away. If her partner hadn't been on his toes, she wouldn't have tumbled to its presence.

The closer it got, the clearer the stenciled side markings, a brown-skinned creature slithering down the length of the inflatable. The undulating body pattern featured a mottle of greenish-brown splotches. A soot-black tongue forked around the bow. From the top of its head, a marbled amber eye tracked her.

"Supposed to be a python?" Delia whispered.

"Anaconda. Interesting camouflage scheme."

She gave the goose bumps on her skin a stiff rubbing. Armed criminals resisting arrest? A pack of pit bulls on a rampage? Bring 'em on. But snakes, including snake images, were second only to rivers on her list of things to avoid.

Within seconds the watercraft was parallel to their hiding spot. The only break in its low outline was a center console where a lone figure stood at the controls. A long coat flapped around his legs.

Delia tensed. It was the guy with the long coat, the tall one she'd spotted at the opening-day protest. He had the same forward-leaning, chin-jutting profile. Gave off the same intensity vibe, as if searching for something he'd lost.

There it was again. That sense of familiarity chilling her guts.

If Grice was right, this was Robert Bastida, military fugitive and probable multiple-murder suspect. The name meant nothing. Then why was she so rattled?

As if thought-tracking, Bastida's head turned. He stared directly at their position. Delia froze, her breath halting mid-intake. She couldn't make out a face under that wide hat but felt his eyes probe through the brushy jumble. Through her. For a split second, she was positive he knew they were there. Certain their feeble stakeout setup had been blown. She expected to see water erupt from behind the big inflatable's dual outboards. She understood why Jerzy had left Beezer in the Hummer. The big Lab-whodunit combo would've barked his head off.

Nothing happened. Bastida's attention shifted to the river and whatever he searched for. She hoped it wasn't a fifth victim.

Quiet settled over them as the reptile-trimmed boat swam on. A moment more and the cloaking rain had swallowed the Zodiac.

Pinned in place by that lingering sense of being watched back, she found relief in simply breathing again. No sign of a mounted weapon. No super-secret death dispenser. Not even light arms. If Bastida stashed them at home, it was on her and Jerzy to find out where "home" was.

"Damned if our cover didn't work." Jerzy's minor gloating broke through her snake-charmed stupor. Still on her knees, she tipped her head back, let the rain hit her full in the face, and counted to three. Jerzy had thrown on a life vest and was scurrying about, flinging brush off the boat sides, clearly pumped on adrenaline. She got to her feet, nearly tackling him when he made for the controls.

"Hold up. Let Bastida get downstream before you kick over that noisy Vette."

His eyes flashed. He started to say something, then shut his mouth. Resetting his cap, he nodded. "Sorry, brain not engaged. By the time we get the front gate on my brush blind unhitched and the tie-downs loose, he'll be out of hearing."

"Then get at it."

*　*　*

Minutes later and a mile downstream, Delia made out a dark smudge through Jerzy's waterproof binoculars. She tightened the focus. The smudge grew into outboard motor bumps. It was Bastida, coasting toward a bend in the river.

She lowered the glasses. "We're closing on him. Cut the engine."

Jerzy complied. A rushing silence hissed in her ears. The stern swung slowly around. She hadn't figured on *Jackie* presenting her broadside to the current. To anyone taking a notion to glance upstream.

Again she leveled the 10 × 50s. Water roiled downriver, where it had eaten the bank away. The Zodiac was gone.

"*¡Dios!* Bastida probably heard us. Saw us." She lowered the glasses, then raised them.

"You could be right. Way our boat's sideways to him. I could use the electric motor."

"Good. Get it in the water. In case he never looked upstream. The guy's hunting for something. I can feel it."

Jackie wobbled. She glassed the far end of the river as they drifted closer. She made out stands of flooded trees and the tops of willow clumps at the turn. Several river arteries sliced through the congestion.

What can we expect down at that sharp bend?

Jerzy's hushed voice came between labored grunts from the rear of the boat. "That jumble up ahead is Murphy Bar. The summer river hooks east, then loops north again." Glancing to her left, she saw that he'd removed a coverlet stamped with the name *Minn Kota*. He strained to lower a motor into the water. "The winter river cuts side channels across that bar."

The Minn Kota's sleek propeller shaft clicked into place. Back in the captain's chair, he reached under the dash and flipped a switch. *Jackie* straightened and surged forward in electric silence.

Delia motioned downriver. "So where's Bastida likely to show?"

"No telling, but we can run as quiet as he can."

"If that's true, we need to get around this mess. Find a place below and hang back until he shows."

"Aye, aye." Jerzy twisted the dual throttle. Delia watched the dash dial until the arrowhead indicator pegged at ten.

*   *   *

They'd negotiated the large double bend within a matter of minutes and spotted no ready place of concealment. The current sluiced them along a thick band of trees that followed the river's curve back toward the north.

A quarter mile ahead, the wooded bank gave way to open fields. No sign of the Zodiac.

"Well?" She cocked her head at Jerzy, who spread his hands wide.

She twisted around and scanned back the way they came. "My guess, Bastida turned around and scooted upriver." She noticed Jerzy glancing around inside the boat.

"Time for a break while I figure out our next move," she said. "What've you brought?" He switched off the Minn Kota, rummaged in a side panel, and swiveled toward her, a Twinkies fun box in one hand and a thermos in his other. "Coffee? Something to eat?"

Delia shook her head. "Knock yourself out." All she needed was to aggravate the roil in her stomach over losing Bastida. Coffee was tempting, but after six hours in a boat with no facilities, she needed to stay bladder-smart.

Slumping against her seat back, she glared into the last of the trees that glided by. Without headway, *Jackie* slowly reversed ends in the current.

Bastida could've made them after he passed by upriver. Screwed their chances for either the sheriff's or her alternative plan.

A shift in dark-light patterns played across her field of vision: something in the backdrop behind the woods they'd been drifting along. It was water, not bankside. There was another channel behind those narrowing trees.

And moving parallel to them, a large shadow. She sat up.

The tree cover thinned and the shadow took on boat form. For a frozen moment, two watercraft floated in tandem. Past the end of the tree line. Into the merging channels.

The reptile-sided Zodiac faced downriver, its outboards a burble above a whisper. *Jackie*, on the other hand, drifted backward in silence, her V-8 tiger power usurped by a Minnie Mouse electric.

Afraid to turn away for even an instant, Delia felt for Jerzy's rain slicker. A hard tug earned a Twinkie-stuffed "F-f-what?"

She gave his ankle a sharp sideways kick that got him turned around and looking in the same direction.

"Oh, shwit." A Twinkie gobbet hit the water.

Whirring sounds traveled across the seventy feet separating the two boats. Metal covers lifted off the snake boat's lower engine housings, loading the air with the bass thrum of dual motors at idle. A tick later, engine rumbles grew into roars and the large inflatable shot away. Within seconds, all they could make of their quarry was a pair of watery fins cutting downstream.

Delia slapped the suction cup of a portable beacon flasher on Jackie's windshield, switched it on, and pinned Jerzy with a stare. "I'd say the sheriff's plan is blown, wouldn't you?"

Jumping up, he scrambled to the Minn Kota and yanked the motor out of the water.

Push had just met shove.

23

By the time Delia and her stakeout partner caught sight of the rigid-hull inflatable, now a white smear rocketing under the first of Salem's three bridges, the rain was back in their faces. Despite a river chop, he'd rammed *Jackie*'s throttle ahead and kept on palming the knob as if willing her to stay with the sizzling-fast Zodiac.

Every so often, Delia frantically hit the speed-dial on her cell phone, cussing when she got nothing. She tipped it and water dribbled out.

Once more, she tapped at the phone.

"Annie. Thank God. We're in pursuit of a Zodiac, no decal number. Request assistance from Salem to—Annie?" She banged the phone into the palm of her hand, then upended it. Water streamed out.

"*¡Carajo!*" She dropped the waterlogged phone onto the seat and gripped *Jackie*'s left window strut, riding boat bounces in a jockey crouch. "Annie knows what to do." She tossed him a look he no doubt read as hope. not confidence. "She'll get us backup."

"Not from Salem," Jerzy said as they raced under the bridges, him pointing to Wallace Marine Park. The launch ramps and parking lot were as empty as a church on Monday. The next river access for a police boat was miles to the north.

Grim questions streamed through her head. How long before Bastida figured out theirs was the only boat in the chase? Before he decided to hang a Louie and come at them? Or did he have something else in mind?

The glance she stole at Jerzy confirmed he was worried, too. She adjusted the shoulder holster, making sure she could reach the S&W, wishing she'd strapped on her service auto as well, brought a shotgun, too.

The boat they chased had grown from dot to pea size. She cupped her hand to her mouth, yelling across the aisle. "Can't you get more crank out of this rat motor?"

"You're the boss." The throttle was full ahead, so he tweaked the power trim. RPMs nudged into the red. *Jackie*'s speedometer needled up toward sixty before he shouted back. "We're topped out at better than three-five knots. I figure the best he can do is three-oh or three-two."

"Meaning what?"

"If Bastida keeps to the main channel, we could catch up before we have backup. Then what?"

"Just don't lose him."

*   *   *

Ten miles downriver, Delia and Jerzy had closed to within two hundred yards of the Zodiac. Close enough to smell the hundred-plus octane exhaust from those high-performance Mercs. So close she unholstered the short-barreled .44 Mag. She'd left her service Glock in the car. She was one of those cops who'd suffered one automatic weapon jamb too many.

A short way past Wheatland Ferry, the Zodiac dodged left and faded from sight. The rain made it look like it'd melted into the riverbank. Again, no backup boats could be seen putting in the water.

Delia yelled across the center aisle. "Where'd he go?"

She got back a shrug as Jerzy backed off on the throttle.

They rounded a shoal of scrub willow thickets, which she figured had masked Bastida's sneak move. Just beyond, a deep recess sank into the woods.

Her six-two-plus boat operator was up on his toe tips.

At first, all she saw was the flooded willow bar. Then behind that, a deep cleft in the tree line, like so many of the Willamette's dead-end backwaters.

"Is he boxed in?" She rose from her crouch.

"Doubt it. Even so, a loose cannon in a box is never a good thing."

"If not, could he slip out the other end?"

Jackie closed on the willow bar. The main channel broke right, merging with the rest of the river's wide expanse. To the left, she saw the Zodiac's wake had curled into the narrow offshoot that hung tight against the river's west side.

When *Jackie* broke off and started to angle out toward the river's main arm, she reached over and spun the wheel back.

"No, that way," she yelled, pointing toward the backwater, hoping it was a channel.

"Delia, I think that's Grand Island. The inside channel's like a three-mile moat for most of the year."

She motioned with her gun hand, the barrel leveled at the opening. "Don't you dare lose him. Not now."

"It's a minefield down there." He geared the boat into neutral. "Choked with willow thickets, puckerbrush, and crisscrossed logs."

She nodded out toward the main river. "Say we go around. What's to keep that Zodiac from turning back and sprinting out this end?"

His head shook. "I'm just saying. Beating down that slough is crazy."

She leveled a full-strength glare on him, narrowed eyes and all. "Crazy didn't stop our guy, did it?" She kept on staring, arching her brows in a barefaced challenge. "Hell, the day started out *un poco loco* and ran us downriver from there."

He fingered the controls.

She jutted her chin ahead. "So, let's get after him."

He was stalling, reaching around the windshield for something, a spare flotation cushion that he scooted under his rump. *Jackie* clunked into gear.

"Brace yourself." He rammed the throttle ahead.

A mile into the side channel, Delia caught sight of the Zodiac and could tell it was better at dodging the floating junk. Its rounded boat sides dipped low then high, as if running a slalom course. But she figured *Jackie*'s welded hull was tougher. They cut a fast, straight line down that slough—straight, if she didn't count the brutal ups and downs. All they had to do was hang on and close the gap.

The windshield-mounted police flasher strobed crayon blues, reminding Delia to try the cell again—redirect backup. Nothing. She dumped the phone on the seat.

Dusk wasn't far off. That meant any backup might keep to the main channel, running up and down an empty river.

Two hundred yards ahead, the Zodiac jumped skyward, disappearing on the far side of a thick screen of willows spanning the entire back channel. Had he made it? Delia glanced over at Jerzy, seeing no way past but over.

At a hundred yards, they still had room to reverse course. Bump and thump back upstream. Jerzy had a questioning look on his face. In answer, she holstered her weapon and head-motioned downstream.

At eighty she barely made out his shouted warnings as he adjusted his makeshift butt cushion. "More bend in your knees. Grab on tight. It's gonna get hairy."

When she saw Jerzy slide his fingers along the cord running from his life jacket to the engine's kill switch, she kissed her silver crucifix on its chain, tucked it back in, and latched on to the sides of the windshield.

Sixty yards. Her white knuckles looked like Dollar Tree pearls. His too, one hand on the wheel, the other gobbling *Jackie*'s T-grip throttle.

Twenty yards. Willow reeds walloped the hull like rifle cracks as the jet boat hurtled into the blockage. Bowed under strong winter currents, the wall of thickets bent downstream, forming a makeshift launch ramp.

Zero yards. Jackie's deck shoved Delia's heels up near the backs of her thighs. Unburdened, the boat caught air and the engine roared on Jerzy's mistimed backward yank of the throttle. The river boat sailed for a month of Sundays before crashing back down with a landing that jarred her bones. She almost toppled backward when Jerzy gunned the engine. Ahead, the Zodiac was scooting downstream.

"You okay?" she shouted.

He nodded, wincing as he stretched his left leg. "Football knees. I'll pay for it in the morning."

"Then we'd better get him now." She took out the short-barrel for a second time as *Jackie* sprinted down the widening slough. Never mind the lunatic speed or that they were chasing a fugitive from an elite killing force and likely off his nut, who might turn and wipe them out at will.

What the hell. KOKO meet *poco loco*. She noticed Jerzy fine-tuning the power trim again. The RPMs crept into the red zone. A sliver above raging psychotic, she thought.

The wind had quieted some, still whipping the surface into white-caps. Barely two hundred yards out front, the wave-slamming Zodiac showed plenty of open space. Every hull lift meant lost headway, split seconds when the lighter boat's twin props churned air instead of water.

First the Zodiac, then *Jackie* rounded a dogleg in the slough. Dark surface bumps sprouted against a lead-dark horizon. They were low on the water and growing.

Logjams? Likely. Would Bastida double back? Or had the high water given him a way out? Neither one, she hoped.

Jackie had cut the distance by half. Close enough for her to pick up the driver's shift in posture. He looked back at them, then seemed to search the bank off to his left. His arm poked out sideways, as if aiming at something on shore. That crooked-thumb hand position reminded Delia of a channel-surfing couch potato. Another backward glance and the arm dropped. Then he gave them his back and relaxed his stance, as if nobody was chasing him.

"What's that up ahead?" Delia shouted, her attention riveted on a broad curtain of spray that had sprung up just behind the Zodiac. A puzzling moment dissolved into the excitement of the chase.

They kept on closing.

Barely three boat lengths in front of *Jackie*'s bow, she spotted what had caused the surface break: a horizontal sliver of brightness, vibrating just three feet above the water.

Too late to yell, turn, or stop, Delia froze, mesmerized by the approaching glitter. In a flash, she envisioned the carnage on its way— *Jackie*'s low bow driven under that taut silver band, the boat's momentum carrying the cable back with the screech of metal raking across the railing and up over the windshield, toward her waiting throat.

A loud ping and the metal strand beheaded the beacon from its sucker mount, then hung up momentarily against the jutting windshield frame. During that microsecond of delay, Jerzy wedged himself in front of her, the spare life jacket cushioning his forward shoulder. In a wink, the cable swept Delia and Jerzy off their feet and dumped them back over *Jackie*'s stern.

24

Delia surfaced, coughing and sputtering, in the dim evening light. She was in the river. In the fucking river. Though in shock, she took in air to yell, but something jerked her back under, life vest and all.

Fear surged through her as she struggled to hold her breath against her lifelong nemesis, a world of water that rushed over and around, pushing her deeper, as if she were getting towed. The river wanted inside her nose, her mouth, to squeeze into her lungs. Switch reason for terror.

And it was getting there as she squirmed to work free and failed. Was this a river punishment for hating rivers? They'd gotten her family, and this one wanted Delia. Her lungs burned now, insisted on breathing in—air or water.

Drowning was shitty. Mouth clamped shut, she screamed inside, her lungs ramping up to a gallop. *But if the river wins, I won't find Charlie's killer, won't catch the sheriff at what he's up to. Won't learn what Jerzy's really like. Won't—*

Pain.

Not in her lungs. Something had cut into her ankle. Cut through the despair. Mustering strength, she curled forward against the rush of current, walked her hand down her leg to the thing that had sliced through her boot top—the cable that had knocked them out of the boat held her under. Giving the thin wire a vicious yank, she ripped it loose, popped to the surface, and reveled in the sting of chill air.

Still frantic to keep her chin above water, she beat the hell out of every face-slapping wave the Willamette shoved at her. Kicked her legs at a syrupy thickness that wanted to suck her back down again. Fill her lungs with grit and silt and river.

Realizing her thrashing was getting her nowhere, she stopped flailing to see whether the life jacket did its job. Okay, it kept her up.

Then came more shock. The river was taking her somewhere. Not down to the bottom but downstream.

Everything at eye level was in the river's grip and moving with the current. The poncho was gone, wrenched off when she hit the water. Ten feet to her left, the beacon light bobbed along. Half filled and sinking, it still flashed gamely.

Several yards off to her right, *Jackie* floated broadside to the wind. The kill switch must've worked. Though dropping, the light breeze pushed the boat downriver at a faster clip.

Silenced and emptied, *Jackie*'s drifting outline shrunk away.

Jerzy.

Delia stiffened, her heart clenching with the dread of something found then lost in an instant. She pummeled the water, corkscrewing her body one way then the other in the failing light, craning to catch sight of him.

"Jerzy!" She waited a beat. "Jerzy!"

Drawn along under the silent power of an unstoppable force, she strained to hear. Something. Anything. A sign he was still alive. Seconds passed. Nothing. Even the wind had gone quiet.

She cocked an ear upstream. Had she heard a splash?

A lump took shape in the oncoming gloom. She faced upstream, waving, crisscrossing both arms back and forth. A part of the lump moved.

"Jerzy. That you?"

A muffled "me" carried across the dead air. Flutters of relief rippled through her. The wave-back he'd given was a paltry thing. Like hitting the Megabucks pick-six. At least they were on the same trajectory. Shared the same fate.

Floating backward, she cupped her hands and yelled upstream. "Are you all right?"

Again, a single hand-wave. He seemed to be sculling at the water with one arm. The other floated out from his side like an empty sleeve. The cable thing must've bunged up his shoulder.

Thrashing the water to slow her drift, Delia shouted, "Just keep working toward me, and I'll—"

Something hard smacked the back of her head, dunking her face downward, forcing her to expel river water. At nearly the same instant, an object like a highway divider wedged itself between her legs, wishboned her thighs, and laid her out prone underwater. Brain-numbing silence became a breath-holding, roaring, gurgling crush of pressure as the top of her head took the brunt of the current's force.

The object had to be a tree sticking out from one of those snag piles. Its rounded thickness was half submerged and in constant motion. The water pressure would either wrench her over the tree trunk or draw her under the damned thing. Emptied lungs screamed "Over!" as she battled to right herself inside a snarl of thrashing branches and limbs.

Breaking the surface and gulping air, Delia locked ankles beneath the trunk of her seesawing mount and waited out the rise and fall of a current surge. No way would the stinking river tear her off this perch. She might be riding a dunking stool, but Delia Chavez was done letting the Willamette treat her like so much floating garbage.

She'd barely caught her breath when the crackle of a breaking branch pumped more adrenaline through her. It was Jerzy, slightly upstream, toward the end of the tree she rode. A current eddy twirled him in a slo-mo water dance while he seemed to keep time with a knobby branch that had broken off in his good hand.

The river would sweep him on past, down into the darkness, if she didn't make a try for him.

"Grab something," she yelled.

He dropped the useless stick and took hold of another bough in the tangle of branches. It too, bent under the strain of his body. The small limb swung her way, halting his drift. She scooted as far along the smooth-bark tree as she could, reaching out just as the bough he clutched broke off.

Of course, the chain on her crucifix picked that moment to hang up on a snag. Their fingers touched as he spun past the trunk's jagged end.

Yanking the chain loose, she flipped it over a shoulder, then lunged forward and made a last-ditch grab. She felt nylon mesh and clamped down. The sudden strain jolted her from fingertips to brain, sending sparks across the insides of her eyes. The trunk she rode bowed downstream and sank under the surging water.

Delia sat up hacking and coughing but kept her leg-lock on the tree and a death grip on Jerzy's life vest below an armhole, her fingers entwined in its side webbing. He fishtailed on his back, the river current plowing past and over his head. The strain on her grip was tremendous. Somehow she had to get both hands on him, but she couldn't reach out far enough.

She scanned back over her pain-racked shoulder. It only confirmed the obvious: they were way out on a limb, and nearly out of luck.

"Grab this stick." At Jerzy's shout, Delia whipped her head back around and nearly poked herself in the eye on the second branch he'd broken off. Grasping it in his good hand, he thrust it toward her over the back of his head.

Relying on her locked legs for stability, she took hold of his arm extension with her free hand and pulled. Nothing happened, except new pain. Putting her back into it, she gained some. Encouraged, she leaned upriver and gritted her teeth. The water's pressure again pushed her downward. The river surged, sloshing around her neck, then receding. Her muscles cried for release.

She strained harder, reefing on Jerzy's torso, until the back of his head was against her left leg. Close enough. She let go of the branch, grabbed the far armhole of his vest, and heaved. Jerzy's left shoulder blade ground up over the log and her thigh, his left ear not far from her crotch. He dropped his end of the stick, reached backward around her middle, and latched on to the waistband at the rear of her Vector two-piece. His fingers protruded well into slap-you-silly territory, but it allowed her to relax her grip.

Exhausted, she accepted his hoarsely grunted "Sorry about that" and let her upper body collapse forward, her face lolling above his collarbone.

Spent from the dual effort, they puffed like toy locomotives. Neither of them moved or spoke for a while.

He got his voice back first. The only warm thing out there, Jerzy's heaving breath gusted past her ear. "Jesus, Delia. Where'd you . . . get those . . . strong hands?"

She squeezed out an answer between chattering teeth. "Crush Ball gr-grip strengthener." More clicking. "Uncle Tino hands me jars he c-can't open."

Jerzy's chest heaved as they shared a gallows laugh. Though chilled as freezer meat, it felt like her face belonged close to the crook of his neck.

"I believe it. You must—" The tree took another dip and his words choked into sputters.

She sat up, lifting the back of his head until their hobbyhorse cycled upward. "Come on, we have to work our way back before the Willamette turns us into a st-statistic."

In labored rhythm, Delia shimmied a few inches back, scrunched her partner close into her stomach, then repeated the move. Finally, the trunk widened, bowing less as the current eased. A mishmash of limbs kept them from working back farther. She relaxed only after Jerzy managed to wrap a leg around the base of a branching limb.

She checked her old Timex Indiglo. Couldn't believe they'd been in the water fewer than ten minutes. If they weren't found in another twenty—

A wave of uncontrollable shivering broke into that thought, and she hugged Jerzy closer.

Minutes later, a low thrum played on her ears, adding itself to the light patter of rain on the river's surface. The sound faded in and out.

"Delia—"

"Shush." She cocked her head one way, then another.

"Hope you have your trusty forty-four." Still on his back, Jerzy gazed up into her face and she down into his, not liking the implication.

What if it was Bastida? Back to finish the job?

Her .44 was gone. She didn't know when she and the revolver had parted company. Probably when she'd gotten yanked over *Jackie*'s back end. If she and Jerzy survived, the sheriff was going to be super pissed. No doubt he'd make an IA case out of losing her weapon.

The humming and buzzing grew, separating into distinct motor whines.

She grinned at Jerzy. He flashed teeth. The sound had to be coming from Marion or Yamhill County patrol boats.

Delia wished she had a signal light, something brighter than Indiglo blue.

*   *   *

She caught only glimpses of their rescuers. Lights winked past the opening where the slough joined the main river a tantalizing quarter mile away. Flashing blues, whites, reds.

She pinched on the Indiglo and lifted the watch face as high as her leg grip permitted. She waved and shouted, and waved some more. All Jerzy could do was hang on and conserve energy.

The patrol boats never slowed or varied their course. She kept on yelling and waving, until she felt Jerzy's head nudge her thigh.

"Save your breath," he croaked.

The lower end of Grand Island swallowed the lights. All traces of engine noise died away. Darkness and gloom tightened in around the snag pile and the tree trunk they clung to.

She lowered her arm, then her head, burying her nose into the spongy fabric of Jerzy's vest collar, his hair smelling of damp leaves, wet man, and fear. Cold seeped into her bones. Morbid thoughts into her head.

He tipped his chin back, his cheer-up expression inches below her face. "They're bound to check the backwaters."

She couldn't keep the gloomy sarcasm out of her voice. "Before or after we're facedown floaters?"

"Before or after we . . . swim with the fish?" he asked. A one-up game.

Delia warmed to the challenge. "Dance with the crawdads?"

"Wear pine overcoats?"

"Juggle halos?" That one got a breathy chuckle from him.

"Circle the drain?"

"Bait the hook?" she countered.

"Slip the cable?" He was slowing down.

"Win two for the reaper?" Her best and close to final.

His head turned away. If he had to think about it, she had him on the ropes.

He'd fallen silent.

To keep her teeth from chattering, she clamped her mouth shut. Never before had she felt so close to . . . kicking the oxygen habit.

Well, at least she wouldn't die alone.

His head nudged the inside of her leg again.

"We've got company."

From somewhere out beyond, she heard another rhythmic thrumming—a purring, like her cat, only mechanical. She peered into the murk. At first she saw nothing. Jerzy's night eyes must be better than hers. Then she saw movement. An inky outline glided past their mid-channel woodpile. It dodged the branchy end of their little water ride and kept moving upstream.

"It's the Zodiac. It's Bastida." Her glance met Jerzy's, the whites of his eyes echoing her unease. Her hand slipped inside her life vest, reaffirming the shoulder holster's emptiness.

No running lights, of course. The long, dark blob plowed farther up the slough, cross-skated to their right, then drifted back toward them, stern first. Memorizing what features she could identify in the winter twilight—the driver's broad-brimmed hat and tall, slicker-clad frame—it struck her that a horse seemed a better fit than a boat.

A scant ten feet above them, the boat slowed, then held steady in the current. The man who stood beside the control console was a face-less outline backlit by the Zodiac's instrument panel.

Silent and unmoving.

"What's he doing?" On his back and facing downstream, Jerzy saw none of what she saw upstream.

She replied to his muttered question with a muttered answer. "Looking us over."

For the moment, Bastida seemed content to size them up.

Every couple of seconds, he'd reach to his right and tweak the steering, or adjust engine speed. Once, his body shifted to his left, and Delia noticed the silhouette of a riot-style pump shotgun propped against the console. Buckshot seemed a comedown after the grue-some way he'd killed the last four. If he was the killer.

Another bout of shivers made the rounds through her body. Should she feel relief the gun wasn't a crossbow, or some other weapon that shot razor-sharp pointy things?

Was he just taking his time thinking up a new way to finish them off?

Sure as hell wouldn't take much.

Maybe it was the acrid waft of outboard exhaust that acted like smelling salts, but the impulse seized Delia to just get on with it.

Instead of a forceful command, her croaks mimicked a frog with hiccups. "Robert Ba-Bastida, y-you have the r-right to remain silent. Anything you s-say—"

"Oh shit." That came from her partner's mouth by way of interruption.

"—c-can and will be used against you."

A guffaw came from the man in the boat. His arms lowered to his sides. The fingers on the hand nearest the riot gun started flexing.

Delia sat up straighter, again flipping her crucifix chain out of the way. Of what, she wasn't sure. In case she had to dive under the damned tree? Swim for it?

The Zodiac started to scuttle sideways. Bastida was at the controls, resetting the boat's position closer, now a few feet upstream of them. Its position stabilized, he turned his attention back to them.

Again, she felt that unseen glower. Still not word one from the guy.

Some killers could care less about offing a cop. Others balked. She hoped he was one of the others. "Don't do anything stupid. I'm a Polk County Sheriff's detective, and this is my partner."

After all she and Jerzy had been through, *partner* sounded right.

A blinding light forced her to glance away. She squinted back into the flashlight's glare.

Bastida had knelt at the boat's rear corner and was leaning toward them. The light cone briefly skimmed Jerzy's inert form. It zeroed in on her, and she felt her breath catch. The focused beam traveled along her neckline, down the cleft of her chest, where it stopped, then bounced up, retracing its path. On a protective instinct, her free hand rose to her throat, her fingers closing around the chain that draped her shoulder. For a moment she wondered whether Bastida's intimidation by flashlight was some kind of sexual get-off. Or prekilling fetish.

He jumped up, stepped to the controls, and maneuvered the inflatable closer, until the Zodiac's back end rested against an upstream limb of the log they were marooned on. Getting within striking range.

Again, he knelt and leaned toward them. Again, he zeroed the light in on her. Mainly her shoulders and back. Delia stiffened, afraid his confusion was nearly over.

She sensed Jerzy's head lift toward hers, felt his whispered breath in her ear. "Get ready to let go of me. Might divert him."

She blinked, stunned. Let go? After what she'd gone through, hauling him onto this goddamn log in the first place? Her grip tightened around his chest, and she answered him through clicking teeth. "N-no way, José."

Bastida's light was back on her face in eye-dazzling brightness.

"Get that fucking light out of my eyes."

He redirected the beam and sat back on his haunches. But she had a head of steam built up. "Lean over me once more, you son of a bitch, and you'll find out what it's like to choke on river water."

Bastida's hand plunged inside his coat. Unholstering or unsheathing? She'd gone too far. Racked her brain for anything that might throw him off tempo.

"S-so, what's it going to be? Emerson Viper? Ka-Bar Lockback? A serrated blade, right?"

In the gloom, he pulled out an object much smaller than a knife and cupped it in his palm. She fell silent, her pulse pounding in her ears. Delia had no idea what Bastida had there, or why, but when he tilted his hand toward the lighted instrument panel, she noticed something cordlike stretching back inside his coat. He seemed hesitant. Undecided.

Enrique had always said she was ballsy for a *chica. Well, here goes.*

"If you're not going to kill us, how about rescuing us?"

"Jesus, Delia." Down in the crux of her lap, she felt Jerzy's shifting discomfort.

She looked up to see Bastida behind the controls with his back to them, his hand resting on the throttle. All he had to do was punch it and the dual-engine backwash would swamp their half-sunk tree and wash them downriver.

She was surprised when the boat moved quietly away, gliding upstream without so much as a ripple. Nearly swallowed by darkness, the Zodiac arced out and around their backwater snag pile, then coasted downriver. Soon, the muffled thrumming of the outboards died away, leaving Delia and Jerzy as Bastida had found them, clinging to limbs and branches, and to each other.

A grayish moon edged out from behind the overcast. It occurred to Delia that smart-mouthing a serial killer might have gained them a simpler, less bloody death option.

Bastida had decided to leave them out there.

25

Delia didn't dare relax the cramped hands she held her partner with, but she tipped her head and stretched her back, gaining relief from the knots of torture in her shoulders and neck.

Icy starlight pierced the broken clouds above. A raggedy-ass moon glowered down, looking as cold as she felt. Finger-aching cold. Desperate-to-let-go cold.

Straddling the trunk of a moving tree, half in, half out of the water, while hanging on to the life vest of an injured man, had taken its toll. A man losing the struggle to keep his head above the river.

And back came the shakes. Big-time. Backed up by Spanish castanets when she forgot to clamp her mouth shut.

Apart from the nonstop sloshing and gurgling, their neck of the Willamette was so quiet they might as well be up on that moon. No patrol boats. No nothing. Had the river won?

Maybe rescue wasn't in the cards. Maybe everybody, good guys and bad, had pulled up stakes and moved their operation somewhere else. Or called it off until daylight. Left them to fend for themselves and headed home to warm, dry beds.

God, but she'd never complain about her cheap bed again.

For just a moment, she closed her eyes and shut out the river. Sank herself into that saggy mattress, curled up between flannel sheets, and drew the faux down comforter to her chin.

Somewhere between a low murmur and a throbbing rumble, engine sounds bled into Delia's dream, flushing her out of that warm, dry bed. Back into the wet and the cold, and the flesh-numbing river.

Jerzy'd heard them too, his twisting body straining her dicey grip on him.

She followed his moonlit gaze and was struck by confusion.

Beyond the whipsawing end-branches of the tree they clung to, an empty jet boat plodded upstream.

Jackie. Except it didn't sound like her.

Jerzy's boat skirted their personal water hell, heading upriver. When it veered inward, the moon backlit a second boat, lashed to *Jackie*'s far side.

That one had a driver. Bastida. His Zodiac had Jerzy's under tow, but in tandem.

Lines flew off *Jackie*'s stern and bow. Reversed engines burbled as the Zodiac swung a one-eighty, pointed upstream, and accelerated away. Still sideways, *Jackie* free-floated back toward Delia and Jerzy's snag pile.

Tree limbs bent, cracking and popping under the jet boat's weight, which kept coming at them. Powerless except to watch, Delia imagined her right knee pulped like an orange.

Barely a foot shy of her, the boat scraped to an iffy stop. To her surprise, the constant water pressure slacked off. Jackie's hull seemed to serve as a surface dam, diverting current around either end. But for how long?

Freeing a hand, she reached out and felt more than metal in the shadow of the hull—a wooden lattice, fastened over the side of the boat. The gate from Jerzy's stakeout blind. She drew her hand back. Better not to budge. Better just to—

A tug at the back of her pants jerked her out of the fear freeze: Jerzy and his cheeky grip on her waistband.

"I've h-had enough water recreation for one day. Y-you?"

"Yeah. Oh hell yeah."

* * *

Ten energy-sapping minutes later, Delia and Jerzy huddled over a boat heater, her at the edge of *Jackie*'s passenger seat, him on the driver's side. Their knees overlapped in the aisle as they tented a pair of Indian-style wool blankets above their heads, capturing as much heat as possible.

The Coleman had been in the boat before they were raked out of it, but the stack of neatly folded Pendletons was new. Such consideration from a vicious serial killer. So why had he left? Where had he gone?

The lattice gate he'd lashed to *Jackie*'s hull had been the real lifesaver. Without it, she and Jerzy would never have made it into the boat. She flexed her fingers over the glowing dome. The skin behind her knuckles was diamond-pocked, souvenirs from the torture-grip she'd held on the webbing of her partner's life jacket.

"Getting any feeling back in your arm?" she asked.

The overlapping blanket on his side moved up and down. "And then some. Right hand's numb, but it burns like a bitch shoulder to neck. You'll have to run us back up to the Wheatland ramp."

"Sounds like a stinger. We need to get you to a med center."

He nudged her with his knee. "Hey, forgot to say something."

"What?"

"*Muchas gracias.*"

"*De nada.*" She nudged him back. "*Yo también.*"

"Huh?"

"Same here. If you hadn't body-blocked that cable, it would've taken my head off."

"Been thinking about that, wondering how long Bastida's been booby-trapping the river." He rotated the arm of his ailing shoulder and winced. "The guy doesn't act like a fugitive. More like he's on a campaign. I mean, why go to all the trouble? Is he still fighting a war with someone?"

That last got Delia thinking, too, back through all that had happened since the opening-day hunting protest, when she'd first noticed Bastida. There but not there. Watching that merry band of poop-flingers. Shadowing but not engaging hunters. Not at the time, anyway. Then came the escalation: sabotaged hunts, burned duck blinds, hunters overturned in their boats. Bastida could have done any or all of those. Dumping people in the river seemed a specialty. And of course, four murders. All done using stealth-kill tactics. Casualties of a disturbed mind? In a seriously messed up world where duck hunters were fair game but Bastida hunters had to be rescued? Which reminded her. They still had to get off this crappy river.

Trading seats, Delia delayed answering Jerzy's question until she'd retrieved *Jackie*'s kill switch from his life preserver.

"If Bastida's fighting a war, it's with himself."

26

Bundled in a Pendleton blanket, Delia warmed chilled hands between chilled thighs. She sat across from a series of medical intake bays. The ringed curtain opposite her was closed, drawn around an examining table. A thin veneer of privacy isolated Jerzy from the other emergency room alcoves at McMinnville Community Hospital. The attending physician and staff had crowded her out. Their ER was a small department smelling of the usual—plastic tubing and bloody bandages. Alcohol with overtones of puke.

Bernie, a Yamhill County reserve deputy, had transported them here after trailering Jerzy's boat at Wheatland Ferry and stopping by his place for dry clothing. Jerzy'd kept his mouth zipped the whole trip. Probably stewing over the mess she'd made of the stakeout. The danger she'd put him through.

She squirmed on the plastic seating, feeling naked inside borrowed menswear. No way would she put her underwear back on, or a wet suit steeped in river water. Or confront the sheriff in this getup. She thought she'd be okay until tomorrow, if Annie had gotten her phoned-in report transcribed and on Grice's desk.

She hugged the blanket closer, her brain refusing to let go of the aftermath.

She'd found her Smith & Wesson lying on *Jackie*'s deck, right where they'd made their forced exit. The handgun stuck out like a sore thumb, visible to anyone for the taking.

So, not only had Bastida returned their boat and supplied them with a pile of blankets, he'd left the revolver for her to recover. The incident report she'd phoned in explained the unholstered weapon. Giving it up to a prime suspect would've been a final barb for the sheriff to jab into her professional hide. Maybe deserved.

She'd stuck to fundamentals on the incident report. That she and Jerzy had followed Bastida as ordered, until he'd made them. No need to mention her contingency plan to take after him. Her decision to run the inside of Grand Island without backup.

The shivers finally gone, she sloughed off the blanket and sat back.

She hadn't reported on the unexplainable. Bastida's freak-out flashlight inspection. Getting abandoned and then saved by their bushwhacker–slash–voyeur–slash–murder suspect. Nothing about her near-death experience with Jerzy: The shared closeness, when every drawn breath becomes precious. When cold slows the blood flow until the pulse of the partner you're holding on to merges with yours.

A nurse in blue scrubs wheeled in a portable X-ray and reclosed Jerzy's curtain.

Delia jumped up and started pacing the hallway. Not an easy task, shuffling around in Bernie's XXLs, constantly hiking the waistband up over her hips.

She stopped and yanked at the belt. Already on its last notch, the end lolled like a cartoon dog's tongue. The crotch of Bernie's charcoal jeans hung on her at about knee level, and his black-and-white-checkered flannel shirt drooped below that. Draped over her five-ten frame, the getup aped her notions of LA homeboys.

Minutes later, rings slid on metal tubing. She stopped and turned. Nurses left, wheeling equipment away. Jerzy peered around the plastic curtain, a hello-again grin smeared across his face. He was naked from the waist up, except for a cold pack taped over his shoulder. Eyeing his ripped torso, she barely noticed him lifting the damaged right arm, rotating his wrist.

"Doctor says there's no sign of permanent damage. Can't move my fingers yet, but they tingle."

She hustled over to him and pulled up short of an embrace. Jerzy smelled of Tiger Balm. Slightly rivery, too. No sign of blame in his eyes, though. Blinking, she swallowed a walnut-size lump.

He looked her up and down, still grinning. "Nice outfit. Kid Frost stop by?"

Wearing a cholo smirk, she tucked her knuckles under her chin and stuck out her elbows. "*Eh, vato. ¿Qué onda?*" She snatched at her belt, yanking up just in time to keep the pants from dropping to her ankles, both of them laughing. Once her clothing was secured, the worry came back. "Seriously. You going to be okay?"

The ER resident, Dr. Morgan, to whom she'd given her name earlier, stepped in and closed the hanging divider behind him. He motioned for Jerzy to put on a shirt that hung over a chair back—another loaner, except better-fitting. Morgan sat on a stool and took up a medical chart holder.

"You're a relative, Ms. Chavez?"

"Partner. Polk County Sheriff's detective."

"Ah." He flipped through the chart, curling pages over the back of the holder. "He has no bone fractures or torn ligature. Short-term paralysis, but no lasting nerve damage. More like a sports stinger." He looked up. "All in all, you have a resilient partner."

She agreed, only silently, breathing a prayer of thanks for Jerzy's resilience.

Morgan went on. "Hypothermia notwithstanding, the two of you spending that length of time in cold water had its benefits. The ice packs will continue to help reduce the swelling. The injury is not acute, so cold-heat contrast therapy should help with swelling and muscle relaxation." He looked contemplative, tapping the chart against his knee. "It's late, but you could try the OSU sports complex, or—"

"My hot tub's equipped with a Jacuzzi. Will that help?" Delia clamped her mouth shut, surprised at the eagerness in her voice. She shot Jerzy a glance, who looked up from his one-handed button-fumbling with a quizzical smile. Instant heat attacked both of her cheeks.

"Okay, sure. That would be an acceptable option."

"Hey," Jerzy said, "after today, a soak in a hot tub sounds great. I'd say we've earned it."

Aided by the image of them together in her tub, Delia's burn spread down the sides of her neck and over the base of her throat. She stepped in front of Jerzy and helped him finish buttoning, doing her best to ignore the upturned corners of his mouth.

Morgan got up, drew back the curtain, and beckoned to someone as he stepped out. Bernie poked his head in, holding up a jeans jacket. "Doc says you're both good to go. Need a ride to your vehicle?"

Jerzy took the jacket, looking as if he'd never put one on before. "Sure do. But what about my boat?"

"That's been arranged." Delia helped Jerzy into one sleeve and draped the other over his injured shoulder. "Bernie will tow your boat and loaned trailer to the McMinnville impound lot."

Jerzy nodded okay, then threw his good arm up, smacking the palm of his hand into his forehead.

"Beezer. Shit. Bet he's gotta pee so bad his eyes have gone yellow."

* * *

"Sheriff, they've been to hell and back." Annie had Gus's full attention, leaning across his desk that way to make her case. "What say you study the preliminary Chavez dictated over the phone? Then decide whether you have to drag her in here tonight."

It was the cleavage that convinced him. Especially when she reached down and turned back the cover page on the incident summary—almost like she was using those bodacious ta-tas to bring him around to her point of view. If she was, he didn't mind.

"At least give her time to rest up. Say, nine AM tomorrow?"

He got to his feet, torn between prolonging the sight and shooing her out of his office so he could doctor the mug of coffee in his hand.

His dispatcher had stuck to his ass worse than a horsefly on a buckskin, shadowing him into his office, over to his coffee hutch, then back to his desk, trying to explain away the sorry mess Chavez had made of *her* stakeout. It was *her* idea. She should be the one in here, sweating. But, if he wanted to wet his whistle with something besides coffee . . .

Gus took a slurp and winced. Tepid java and no zing. He sighed in surrender. "Nine sharp. I want her in here by nine."

She straightened up and smiled. "I'll let them know."

"While you're at it, tell Cha-vez I want a full report by noon."

He admired the vista of Annie's retreat in those hip-hugging slacks as he made his way back to the coffee hutch. Pausing until the door latched behind her, he emptied the mug into the sink.

Gus refused to drink reheated coffee. He'd take his rum neat.

Back at the desk, he sat and swigged and swallowed. Waited for that rosy buzz to take the edge off. Settle his nerves.

Thing was, he'd spent the whole damn day chasing a string of dead-end motel leads on Bastida, only to learn that Chavez and Matusik might well have stampeded his pot sweetener into skipping out.

Three fingers went down the hatch while Gus skip-read the bare-facts narrative Annie had transcribed from Chavez. He'd get to the hows and whys of her screw-up later. For now, he needed to learn something else. Had Bastida gone upriver, back into Polk County? Or downriver toward Portland, meaning he was on the run?

That directional information dictated whether Gus's situation was salvageable. Whether he could dissuade Bannock from cutting him off. If Bastida had slipped back into Gus's jurisdiction, then maybe Bannock was right. A family-grudge obsession might be what held the fugitive in the area.

Whoever that family turned out to be.

State and county records checks had turned up a handful of Bastidas scattered around Oregon, especially over in Basque sheep-ranching country, but none residing anywhere along the Willamette. Somehow he'd entered the Navy on that alias.

Gus realized he'd glossed over a compacted part of the report: how Chavez and Matusik had lost and retrieved their boat.

He scrutinized the last two pages, stopping once to snigger at a sketchy passage, including Chavez's laughable attempt to place Bastida under arrest. Gus shook his head, thinking aloud. "That woman has a goddamn death wish."

Pay dirt came at the end of her report.

Subject's boat last seen heading south.

Upriver. Gus sighed in relief.

He sat back in his chair and studied the ceiling, searching his memory for clauses in the *Civil Process Manual* dealing with insubordination.

Ah, Chavez. What to do?

The answer made him sit up. When you find you're riding the wrong horse, switch horses.

He took a healthy draw from his mug and mulled over his options. Not many, being so short on patrol staff. Chavez was a cogitator—too thinky and unpredictable. Gus needed somebody cautious to a fault and rock solid.

Rock-headed was close enough. He did have somebody in the department who would follow instructions and not ask questions. Too bad it was his nephew.

Then again, blood was thicker than water.

27

Late that evening, Delia wheeled Enrique's convertible into her driveway and cut the engine. She sat for a moment in the countryside quiet of Monmouth, Oregon, and listened to the all-male duet: dog pants from the back seat and man snores from the passenger side. How Jerzy could sleep folded like a pretzel into a bucket seat, she'd never know.

After Bernie had dropped them off at Riverview Park in Independence, and after Beezer had watered a lamppost until his eyes went back to brown, they decided to take the Camaro to her place for Jerzy's hot tub therapy. Neither had said anything about going back later for the Hummer. Nothing either about picking up his boat from the Yamhill sheriff's impound lot. His shoulder had improved, but they agreed not to push things, to play the rest of the night by ear.

Beezer whined, rousing Jerzy from his catnap.

She opened her car door and stepped out. "Home sweet home."

Jerzy yawned, unfolded, and rolled out of his side. Beezer followed. Both car doors shut with the sound of one. "Great old farmhouse."

Her porch light was on, but Delia fumbled for the right key, embarrassed at feeling so nervous.

"By the way, how's your dog with cats?"

"Oh, he's just a big old pussycat himself."

"Well, Clawed—spelled with a *w* for good reason—is not. So you'd better hang on to Beezer's collar until they get to know . . . Dammit." Working the lock, Delia kicked at the rain-swollen door and forced it open. She switched on lights, relieved to have picked up before leaving that morning.

The high-ceilinged living room was a showcase for her garage-sale budget. Pillow-stuffed rattans flanked a scarred mahogany coffee table. The jungle flora divan looked like it belonged in a Havana hotel lobby, but it suited her. Potted big-leaf tropicals bookended the sofa, an afterthought to soften the Victorian room angles.

Jerzy stepped in ahead of her, keeping Beezer close at his side. "Nice feel. Homey."

"Thanks."

A lump on the back of the divan rose up and yawned, then drooped into a languid, black-and-gray stretch. Beezer sneezed. Clawed's eyes rounded on the dog. In a flash, he was on the floor, humpbacked and stiff-legged.

He closed the distance, able and willing to take on the intruder.

"Holy buckets, what a monster cat." Jerzy bent low and slipped his fingers into the dog's collar.

She rested her hand on the knob, ready if necessary to throw open the front door. "Half Persian, half Maine coon. Been known to ride neighborhood dogs into the next county."

Cat and not-cat sniffed the air, checking each other out. Beezer whined and backed into the closed front door.

Barely two feet away, Clawed showed fang. The Lab's stocky neck stretched tentatively forward, his ample sniffer collecting enemy intelligence. A paw swipe from Clawed and the Lab yipped, drawing his nose in against his chest.

"Maybe your dog should cool it in the Camaro?"

"Let's try this first." Jerzy nudged Beezer with his knee and pushed the flat of his hand down toward the hall rug. "This is Clawed's place. You'd better mind your p's and q's, buddy, or you'll be out in the cold."

The Lab slowly lowered to the floor, his muzzle resting over a front leg as far away as he could get from the cat's scowling puss.

Clawed sat, tail switching, satisfied to post guard in front of the cowed trespasser.

Delia motioned Jerzy toward the kitchen as she switched on the light and headed for the fridge. "Through the sliding door at the back of the house. Tub's sunk into the deck. Just slide the lid off and dial it up."

"Oh, um . . ." An awkward moment had arrived. She looked up from her search for something edible that wasn't yet a host for fungus. "I don't have a man's bathing suit, but the arborvitae hedge around the backyard makes for privacy."

The corners of his mouth curved downward. "After today, soggy briefs feel like a second skin."

Delia laughed, handing him a bowl of hummus and a packet of semi-petrified pita bread.

He backed against a counter, digging into the bowl like a tailgater on game day. She stepped toward her bedroom, desperate to get out of the loaner outfit, but not sure into what.

"Room for two in that tub, right?" Jerzy's mouth couldn't have sounded more stuffed. Still, his invitation sent a tingle through her heart. She kept walking and spoke over her shoulder. "Well, okay. Give me a minute."

Three swimwear changes later, Delia opened the patio door juggling towels, glasses, and bottles, thanking her inner bitch for making her do all those ab crunches and belly roll-ups at Golda's. The triggerfish-blue two-piece she'd opted for had come home with her on her last vacation in La Paz.

She saw no professional issue after what they'd endured. No contradiction either in her fondness for warm seas and white sand beaches, versus the callous, life-sucking river they had just won a round against. Saltwater healed. Rivers killed. And when they didn't, they left deep scars.

She left the door partway open—in case Beezer needed an escape route—and padded across the deck. Conscious of the way chill air could pucker, she kept a beach towel wrapped around her.

Not that the man soaking in her hot tub hadn't already felt or seen most of her.

Delia motioned toward Jerzy, holding the necks of a Diablo Rojo and a Garnacha Blanca. "Red or white?"

His hand came out of the swirling water, waggling that her choice was iffy. "Uh, got anything lighter?" She frowned, setting the glasses down but keeping the bottle.

"Oh, I guess. Sure, probably good that we don't, after the day we've had."

She went back inside and returned with sparkling cider. "I keep it on hand for my aunt Matilda."

After pouring two of the bubblies and handing him one, she tossed the towel and stepped in beside him, settling into a wondrous warmth that made her groan with relief. The small tub's curvature molded them together shoulders to knees. She didn't mind.

Jerzy started to take a taste, stopped, and clinked his glass against hers. "To Detective Delia Chavez: oorah lifesaver."

She snorted. "You can drop that in the dumb-luck box. If Bastida hadn't brought back your boat, we'd be floaters for sure, sliding over Willamette Falls about now."

He nodded. "When that Zodiac crept back upriver, I figured we were dead meat. Especially the way he'd hovered over us before, inspecting his handiwork. Something had changed his mind. Any notions on what that might be?"

She took a sip and smiled, batting her eyes. "I look hot when I'm wet?"

Jerzy took a swallow, grinning. "Definitely would change my mind." His smile melted away. Their faces were inches apart now, her eyes locked on to his.

It was a sideways kiss, since both clutched glasses and she still had the bottle. Contact was mouth-to-mouth only. Warm, tender, apple tangy. Too soon over.

Jerzy had broken off first, his back settling against the staves. She set the half-empty bottle afloat after pouring, polishing off another glass and recapping. She now wished it'd had some kind of kick to it. Confused, she put her glass aside and debated getting out. Maybe his hurt shoulder bothered him too much.

She moved away, crossing her arms over her chest, staring into the water. Second thoughts about what he'd gotten himself into? About her?

Setting his own glass aside, he shifted around and looked straight at her. "Will my being here bring trouble for you? I mean, complications with the sheriff?"

"No more than usual." She studied his face and saw genuine concern. "Thanks for asking, but *what* I do off the clock, and who I do *what* with, is my business." She sidled back, closer to him. "Truth is, I'm a permanent resident on Grice's shit list, no matter what. So I might as well do *what*."

"Well, in that case . . ." With his cheesy grin, he pushed the bottle toward the far side, then continued his smooth move with a theatrical yawn and a movie make-out stretch, ending with his arm behind her head and across her shoulders. Apparently, that injured arm had made a rapid recovery.

Smiling to herself, she played along and nestled in against his chest.

Neither spoke for a long while. Long enough that her eyelids started to lower on their own. The rise and fall of his chest against her cheek slowed. The Jacuzzi warbled a bubbly, drowsy lullaby. The poor guy was wiped. He couldn't even . . .

* * *

Delia swam out of a foggy drowse, opening her eyes to a bobbing bottle and the sensation of her cheek resting against a warm chest. When she lifted her head, Jerzy slowly removed his arm from around her shoulder, rubbing at his bicep.

"Go away, Beez." He'd awakened first, apparently by the dog lapping at his ear.

Beezer complied, flopping down with a groan some distance from the hot tub while Jerzy rubbed at his upper arm. "Seems like we nodded off."

"Seems so. How's your shoulder?"

"Arm tingles and the joint's stiff, but better."

Sitting up, she scrunched around and leaned in close, giving his shoulder a light finger massage. "Looks like Clawed and Beezer reached a truce." She nodded back across the bubbling hot tub, where her tail-swishing cat lay sprawled atop her beach towel.

His eyes shifted in that direction, then back on her, as if he'd just noticed her swimwear. "Maybe decided to be friends?"

Somewhere under a sky full of stars and up on a far ridge, an owl hooted. A love call? she wondered.

"Hear that owl? He sounds lonesome."

"He?" she asked, her fingers traveling downward, kneading his bicep. Finished, she linked her arm inside his.

"Felt great," he said, flexing his hand underwater. The hairs on his forearm barely brushed her thigh, sending prickles up into her chest, a flush that spread over the base of her throat. "Just what I needed." His eyes locked with hers. "Thanks. Catnap did wonders. For both of us, I guess."

She lifted her hand, showing the wrinkled undersides of her fingers. "Prune skin, though."

"Me, too." He held his palm up against hers to compare. Their fingers entwined and she drew him close. Her lips moved warmly across his, searching out and finding the sweet spot, then settling in. After a while she broke off but kept in close, inviting with her eyes. Jerzy accepted with a full-press embrace and a hungry kiss. She shut her eyes this time, putting more passion into the moment than she could have done even an hour ago. More than she remembered feeling, maybe ever.

Their third kiss was supercharged, an exploratory dance of tongue tips that percolated her blood. Suddenly, she drew back and studied his face, weighing. Deciding. The wall lights of the tub ebbed and flowed, reshaped by the constant water movement.

When she got to yes, it came on a snicker at his obvious confusion. "What's so funny?"

"You know what's ridiculous? Wearing this suit in my own hot tub, way out in the country with only the stars to see."

"Well, not just the stars."

Her smile widened, giving him her version of a Cheshire grin and a challenging arch to her eyebrow. "I will if you will."

His hands dove underwater, thumbs at the sides of his waistband, as she reached behind and unhooked. "On three. One—"

The water erupted in front as she sent her blue top sailing into the darkness.

As expected, the change in view distracted the poor guy so badly he fumbled his take-off. She already had her thumbs inside the bottoms when he protested.

"Cheater. Don't the disabled get a head start?"

Laughing, Delia shifted over on one haunch. "Not when I have more to take off."

Above water, his grin matched hers. Down under, he was shoving frantically at the waistband. Overcoming the last obstacle—in front, no less—his shorts launched skyward. But not before her bottoms cleared the water.

She gave out a victory whoop, then a laughing guffaw, pointing up to where his tossed article of clothing had caught on the top of an arborvitae. He laughed with her, watching the longest frond sag under the strain of its soggy hangings.

The lower the droop, the more breathless she got, hooking her arm inside the crook of his elbow, squeezing it to her breast in delight as the tall shrub bent like a harp. The branch sprang back and the skivvs came down beside Clawed with a plop. The big cat sprang sideways and strutted off in a huff, his tail switching.

Delia's shoulder heaves brought on a series of gasps. Catching her breath, she wiped at her eyes. "Oh boy, can't get more romantic than this."

"Who knows. Maybe if we try harder . . ." His Bradley Cooper blues glittered with more than mirth.

"Close your eyes," she said, realizing she'd wanted to be naked with him ever since she'd hauled him into her lap on that river snag pile.

"Do I have to?"

"Yes."

He did. Her heart pounded as she looked him in the face, lightly skimming her hands across the curves of his chest and down his sides, over his taut stomach, then lower—ever the detective, probing for clues about what he really felt. Thought.

Eyes still closed, his arms encircled her, the fingers of both hands meeting in the cleft of her back, traveling up between her shoulder blades, making her shudder with anticipation. She dove in and kissed him hard, craving to be above him. On him. Heart against heart.

His hands tripped down the sides of her body, helping glide her over him, her legs scissoring his. Mouth on mouth, he drew the rest of her in close, gasping when she touched down on his thighs. His eyes were now fully open in their shared sensation.

The water burbled, the stars twinkled, and the kiss went on and on.

28

Augustus Grice was a morning man. Did his best thinking over breakfast at the Blue Garden. At seven AM his brain box just plain worked right—especially with some added lubrication, making restaurant coffee stay down better. Same for the lump of misgivings he had about elevating his nephew to Investigations.

The night before, when Gus had asked Craig Castner how badly he wanted off patrol duty, he bit like a bullhead on a doughball. Joked, "Who do I have to kill?"

Now Gus dearly hoped he wouldn't regret bringing Craig in on his deal, even partway. But like Mama used to say, "Risk nothin', get nothin'."

He'd finished dappling a platter of biscuits and gravy with hot sauce when Next-to-Nothin' rapped on the outside of the restaurant's window. Craig pointed to himself, then at the empty booth space.

Without so much as a nod, Gus picked up a fork and inspected it for cleanliness. Corralling the big plate inside his forearms, he dove in and crammed his mouth.

Chill air from the open door rustled around Gus's ankles. Craig trod across the yellowed linoleum, plucking at the seat of his regulation browns. "Man," he said. "Don'tcha hate leavin' shower soap between your balls and your butt crack?"

Gus dropped his utensil onto his plate and sat back, wiping at his mouth. "You'd better have something good for me."

His nephew waved off the waitress, eyes jerking around as if scanning for eavesdroppers. "Okay, Gus. I found out what happened after Chavez's river fiasco. Just like you wanted."

Gus squinted across the table. "Last time I checked, Deputy Castner, I was sheriff."

"Geez, sorry. Sheriff." He yanked a notebook out of a coat pocket, flipped a few pages and closed it, pulling his detective face back together. "Well, your instincts were right. Chavez mishandled that whole stakeout and pursuit deal. What backup she'd called in had only the lower Willamette sealed off. Different story upstream. Marion County had only one boat on the water. 'Course those cell phones we're issued are pieces of—"

Gus slapped the table, making his nephew jump. "Damn, son. We know all that. Question is, did anybody see anything afterward?"

"Sure did, Sheriff." Craig fumbled through the pages again, moving his lips as he read. "An hour after Chavez last reported sighting the Zodiac, Sergeant Dan Baxter and another deputy gave chase to a rigid-hull inflatable that eluded them in heavy fog."

"That's him. What did you tell them about Bastida?"

"Not a goddamn thing. You'd be proud of me, Sheriff."

Gus pushed his breakfast aside and leaned in. "Where was that Zodiac when they lost it?"

"Upriver from Salem. Almost to Eola Bend. Baxter swore neither one of them heard that big ribbie slip past. Figured it musta been running on some kind of electric trolling motor. He happened to sweep his spotlight over to the far bank and lit up the side of a hull painted like a damned python. Said the boat cranked up a pair of big outboards and scooted. A four-hour search turned up zip."

"Sound baffles, no electric motor." Gus inspected his cuticles.

"Sound what?"

"Naval special boat units, deployed on night insertions and river operations, had their outboards retrofitted for ultra-quiet running. Saw it done when I was in the Navy. Our guy has quite the past."

Craig blinked, wide-eyed again. "You? In the Navy?"

Gus had lost touch with his sister when he'd gotten run off the ranch in Texas. Even after she'd reached out, he'd kept her and his nephew at arm's length.

He sat back and patted the sides of his belly. "Didn't always have this bumper guard, son. Six years in Colombia wearing an SP armband. Chased señoritas like a whore hound, cracked drunken sailors' skulls, and rubbed elbows with DEA agents. Navy SEAL units, too."

Enjoying his nephew's astonished look, Gus pulled a silver pick from a tiny case and had a go at the spaces between his teeth. "Developed a nose in that jungle air. Smell of cocaine flowing downriver, greenbacks motoring up." He leaned forward and spoke quietly. "Only part of the take got to Cartel del Costa Norte."

He could almost picture the rusty wheels of understanding grind away behind his nephew's smile. He leveled the toothpick at him. "And you know something? I've got that scent again. From the second one, anyway."

Gus worked the toothpick awhile before wiping the tip on his napkin and stowing it away. "What about Matusik's boat? You check it out like I asked?"

Craig's head tilted. "Scraped up, but serviceable. Why?" A pained look slid over his face. "Tell me you're not sending Chavez and that Polack back onto the river."

"What's it to you?"

Craig licked his lips. "Nothing, but I—" The waitress shuffled by.

"Lean in real close and I'll whisper what I have in mind."

After he listened, Craig's brows joined above his nose. Sighing deeply, Gus spelled it out.

*   *   *

At nine AM, Delia entered the courthouse basement and sauntered over to the com bay, sore in places that hadn't been sore for a long while yet feeling like she could walk on air. Earlier, she'd left Jerzy off at the Hummer, so she had only a few moments to chat with Annie.

The morning-after smile she'd worked up to tantalize her friend melted away as she saw Annie's intern, Darrell, manning the com bay.

She'd barely noticed Castner lounging outside the sheriff's office, her thoughts drifting back to the night before. When she and Jerzy had become different people. How, in the span of days, he'd calmly invaded her life, her everyday thoughts. How his mere presence seemed to fill a gaping empty space.

She drifted toward the counter's rear opening.

"Ms. Cox'll be back in a few?" Darrell said. "My, don't you look cheerful this morning?"

Delia's gaze shifted back to him and found he had swiveled around and was peering at her, the corners of his mouth in an upward creep. She glanced away, squelching a blush. Annie *would* pick a fellow gossip hound to intern with her.

"Yeah, uh, tell Annie I'll catch her later, after I—"

The intern sat up, his eyes aglitter. She felt a presence on her left.

"Hey, Darrell. What's crackalackin'?" Jerzy grinned at both of them, nudging her elbow, nodding toward the sheriff's office. "Ready to see the man, Detective?"

As they turned away, Darrell fluttered a hand. "Oh, ah Jerzy? Mr. Matusik? The sheriff would like you to wait outside?" He gestured toward the waiting room. "With Deputy Castner?"

Uh-oh. "Annie gave my report to the sheriff, right?"

Darrell threw Delia an answering shrug. "She didn't say?"

During that solo walk past Castner's smirk and into the sheriff's office, Delia's feet were definitely back on the floor.

* * *

Standing front and center at Grice's desk, she breathed a smidgeon easier. Annie had come through. Those marked-up pages corralled inside his thick forearms had to be her account of yesterday's stakeout and river chase.

Old Lizard Breath hadn't gotten up or looked up or acknowledged her, except for a shushing gesture when she tried to speak. She stood because there was no place to sit. The armchairs normally fronting his desk had been pushed against a table at the far wall.

Grice sat up and slid the pages off to one side, uncovering the Polk County Sheriff's policies and procedures manual that had lain beneath her report. Without looking up, he opened the manual, spun it around, and shoved it across the desk.

"Please read aloud regulation three-dash-three-oh-four."

She picked up the manual and wedged its spine into the crook of her arm. Another dressing-down, a demotion maybe. But she wasn't giving him the satisfaction of seeing her shake.

"Sheriff, I know policy and procedures by heart—"

He thumped the desk pad with the flat of his hand. "Read it."

"'Members of the department shall promptly obey lawful orders from their supervisor.'"

"Am I or am I not your supervisor?"

"Of course you are. That cell phone crapped out, so I made a judgment call to—"

"Well then, what part of my instructions to 'tail only and not to pursue' were unclear or unlawful?"

"None, but Bastida forced our hand when he sidetracked on us, and we—"

"So, you did a lousy job of tailing that resulted in your countermanding my orders."

She slammed the covers together and dumped the manual back on his desk. "We were on a river, not a goddamn highway where you can hang back in traffic."

Grice stood up and leaned forward, his knuckles sinking into the desk pad. "You still don't get it, Cha-vez. That's gross insubordination. Your reckless actions unduly alerted the subject, thereby placing the entire investigation in jeopardy."

"You read my report. The subject left me no choice. Sheriff, you're building a mountain out of a—"

"Your insubordination, on top of your incompetence, leaves me no choice. You are hereby suspended from duty. I'm filing for your dismissal."

Delia took a step backward, his last words a punch to the gut.

"I'm let go? Fired?" She spread her arms wide in exasperation. "Because of a guy who outmaneuvered everybody on the river? Because we got suckered into a situation nobody could have predicted?"

He sat back down, clicked a ballpoint pen, and started writing on a notepad. "We're done here. Leave your weapon and ID with me. And don't slam the door on your way out."

"I'll turn over my service automatic but the handgun is mine. Bought and paid for."

"You have a valid concealed carry?"

This time, Delia failed at hiding the shakes as she placed her badge wallet on a corner of his desk and shook out the folded carry permit. He waved it off with a glance.

Her brain in full stun mode, she knew she had to leave him with something to think about.

"I'm onto your side game, Grice. You and me? We're not done. Not by a long shot."

Delia left his office door wide open, taking with her a small consolation. Her threat had kindled a flicker of fear in his pond-water eyes.

*   *   *

"Delia, what the devil's going on?" Jerzy grabbed her arm and spun her toward him. "Castner says he's taking over the case. That I'm working under him now."

Time crawled. Her mind hazed over and her gaze drifted around the anteroom. Toward Craig Castner, who took forever doubling over Jerzy's river map. Stuffing its waterproof pouch into a coat pocket.

"We're up to bat, Matusik." Things sped up. Castner was out of his chair and trucking toward Grice's still-open door.

Jerzy's head swiveled toward the sheriff's office, then back to her. "Christ, what an outfit you work for."

"Correction, worked for." Folding her arms over her chest, she ginned up a gallows smile. "You'd better get in there. Got to keep

Beezer in kibbles. You don't want the bank coming after your boat." She searched his eyes. "Do you?"

He didn't budge. She reached over and touched his wrist. "I'm all right with it, really. Do your job and we'll come out of this together."

His eyes stayed locked on hers. She laid the palm of her hand against his chest, lingered for a moment, then gave him a firm shove. "Go. We'll be okay."

"Matusik. Get your ass in here," the sheriff yelled. "And shut the door behind you."

"Hang back in parking, okay? I'll meet you at your car." Jerzy said this backing away, making a sit-tight gesture.

She nodded, indicating she would, and he turned and stalked into Grice's office. Instead of the jamb-rattling bang she half expected, the door eased shut behind him.

* * *

When Matusik hung back at the closed door, Gus didn't react. He and Castner stayed bent over the map at his office table, even when he felt a pointed tap on the shoulder. He didn't have to ask Dr. Ruth to know Matusik had provided Chavez with more than water-taxi service. The two of them had gone overboard in more ways than one. And now the man was fixing to chew fire over her dismissal. But if he was still going to be of use, Gus had to step on his lip.

"Sheriff."

Ignoring Matusik, Gus asked his nephew to show him where Bastida had last been sighted.

Castner edged in, moving a cup full of pens, pencils, and Sharpies off to one side. "Here, at Eola Bend," he said, stabbing the river map. "Maybe we should start farther downstream, though. Canvass every—"

"Sheriff, we need to talk. In private?"

Gus didn't move, didn't look at Matusik. "If it's about Cha-vez, we do not."

"Look, she made the right decision. It was my bad that Bastida caught on to us."

Nose snorts erupted from Castner as he sneered at Matusik from over his shoulder. "Was it your bad, too, that she hatched up a piss-poor backup plan?"

"You wanna talk piss-poor? That military cell phone she got saddled with was a piece of crap."

"Yeah, says the guy that—"

"Enough of this horseshit." Gus twisted to his right. "Deputy Castner, shut your cakehole." Then he wheeled back on Matusik. "Now think real hard, son. Before you say anything you'll regret—" Matusik reared back, as if offended by Gus's breath or something. He stepped in even closer. "And then ask yourself, do I want to keep working for this office? For any sheriff's office? Ever?" He knew the guy was still making back payments on that big-ass boat.

Gus matched Matusik's glare, giving him time to think it over, knowing what was going through his head—whether to tough it out or tell his employer to shove it.

Matusik broke off eye contact and turned toward the map. As if nothing had gone on between them, he bent over the table and put his finger on one of several red asterisks Gus and Castner had Sharpied in along the course of the Willamette. "Bastida sightings?"

Gus knew he had Matusik back on track. "Little good they've done," he said with a shrug. "He's all over the map."

"Dates? Directions?"

Gus flicked a hand toward his desk. "Only rough notes."

"Then this search is back to square one."

"Square two," Gus said. "I just put square one behind us."

Gus sent Castner and Matusik off with instructions to nose that riverboat into the armpits of the Willamette—every nook, cranny, and creek mouth—until they found where Bastida parked his butt. He yelled out the last order just as they left his office.

"For God's sake, don't spook him."

* * *

Cleaning out her desk took no time—shove personal items, along with the shame of that morning, into a cardboard box and leave quietly, eyes down. Not much to show for a meager six weeks as acting senior detective.

Then she remembered another box, the one Annie had brought to her and she'd hastily stuffed into Harvey's desk. Why not? It deserved at least as much trunk space as the rest of her junk. One never knew what might get pieced together with enough glasses of red. Yeah, sure.

She found Harvey's desk key and piled the box of shredded paper onto hers.

Darrell was the only one who'd see her leave, but Delia's face was burning as she set down the two boxes, crammed her case files into Castner's mail slot, and leafed mechanically through whatever had accumulated in her own pigeonhole. The one she'd split with Jerzy over the past week.

She started to put back a message marked for him and noticed it was from someone named Chelsea Foushée. She glanced around, unfolded it, and read.

Saving a booth at the Two-Step tonight. It's line dance night.

Delia's arms dropped to her sides as she stared into the blank mail receptacle. Jesus, her day just kept getting better.

Reading again, the note became a white blur in her hand. She told herself to refold Chelsea's invitation. Put it back in the slot and give Jerzy the benefit.

Or not.

But on the verge of balling up the message and hearing it land with a satisfying *ponk* on the trash can's bottom, she hesitated. Instead, Delia doubled over the slightly perfumed paper, slid it back into the shared cubby, picked up her boxes, and banged out the door.

* * *

Driving with a headful of pissed-off hornets, Delia approached a fork in the road. Reminded of what some old baseball sage advised, she took it. Or almost.

Veering right at the last second, she aimed her brother's Camaro west, out of the Willamette Valley and up into the hills. Didn't matter which way, just away.

To hell with Grice. To hell with Castner. To hell with the whole PCSD. *I'll just go off somewhere and work in a grocery store and indulge my fantasy. Write.*

Write about . . . what? Blockbuster cases I've failed to solve? Bizarre killers I wish I'd caught? Yeah. That's me, a budding Josephine Wambaugh, a burgeoning Ramona Chandler.

The tank was nearly full, and Lord knew she had time on her hands. The lower down she felt, the more lead flowed into her foot.

Road therapy. Roll down the windows and numb the brain. Jam that gas pedal and slam those gears. Iron out the curves and roller-coaster the up-and-downs. Leave a crappy day and all those crappy thoughts behind like so much roadkill.

29

Dusk had settled into the skeletal treetops of the Coast Range by the time Delia decided she'd had enough road therapy. Besides, a rip-snorting headache lurked in the wings. Easing off to a sedate seventy-five, she rolled up the windows and swung back toward the Valley, and whatever came next. Now and then, a whiff of good old high-octane exhaust fragrance wafted up through the floorboards. Wetting her fingers, she stuck an imaginary sticky to the dash: *Check header gaskets.*

She'd used up most of a tank of gas that afternoon, boiling down the mush in her brain to a workable threesome: nutjob, botched job, fickle heartthrob.

First, the guy at the bottom of everything. No doubt Bastida was a nutjob. A certifiable Jekyll and Hyde. A boat-wrecking maniac turned last-minute lifesaver. Still, the gut notion stayed with her. Something else lurked beneath all his craziness—a rational individual she'd somehow flipped the switch on during their river face-off. Bastida was a clever, highly troubled fugitive.

Killer or rescuer? How to find out which? And if it wasn't him, who else? Of the one-fifty or so interviewed, she'd pegged a dozen guys running the river that could fill the bill.

She flexed her hands on the wheel. Grice had pulled a fast one, turning her case over to Castner. Lotsa luck catching up with Jekyll, or Hyde.

Switching on the headlights, she turned north onto Kings Valley Highway and goosed the Camaro up to cruising speed. For some reason, the engine sounded louder in the growing darkness.

As for the botched stakeout? Okay, she owned that—the blown river surveillance. But afterward, she'd followed SOP for pursuing a felon in motor vehicular flight. She'd pointed out in her write-up that there was no standard procedure when the motor vehicle was a boat and tearing ass downriver. By playing the insubordination card, Grice had neatly shoved Delia's justification under a rug.

Which led to the bone she'd chewed on for weeks: it had mattered about as much as a perfumed air biscuit whether she screwed up or not.

But it *did* matter. Castner's ineptness and Grice's hamstringing of a murder investigation—for whatever reason—meant a killer would keep on killing. It meant her promise to Zack after Charlie's death was empty as a Sunday beer keg behind the Blue Garden Lounge. And it meant the vow she'd kept inside her heart, to her stolen brother and her long-dead parents, would go unfulfilled. That corny Delia Do-Right one, in Harvey's funky hospital words. It pained her the most. Then, too, she'd have nothing of merit to write about based on a whole month and a half as a hotshot sheriff's detective.

But was she done? No she wasn't. What would Harvey say? KOKO, of course. After all, Delia Do-Right had a reputation to live up to. An obsessed one, but a reputation all the same. She had to keep on keepin' on.

But how?

Off in the distance, a skin of clouds hazed the moon above Dallas, Oregon, casting an unhealthy glow into the evening sky. The sheriff's agenda had moved way past his inbred distaste for "her kind." He'd been desperate to get Delia out of his way. She was onto him—still not onto what. She glanced in the rearview mirror at the box of Grice's cast-off paper shreds. Maybe . . . Nah! But maybe . . .

A sign flashed by. She downshifted, making the left onto the Falls City road again. The Camaro's headlights swept the ditches. Sheets of frost diamonds banded both sides of the route back into the Coast Range foothills. Halfway up that road, a lonely country intersection hosted the Two-Step and a slim hope that bad shit didn't always come in threes.

Heartthrob? Really, Chavez? That achy-breaky crap? A dot of bluish neon showed ahead, and her grip on the wheel tightened.

A hard swallow. Her fault, letting Jerzy Matusik slip past her defenses. It wasn't only his easygoing nature or his good looks. Wasn't because his shoulder had taken the cable aimed at her throat, or because she'd kept the river out of his lungs. Not the sharing of near-death, either. Not even the passion, the hot tub sex. That came later. Simpler things had pulled him inside her heart. He was self-assured, not cocky. Tenacious, like her, yet willing to compromise without patronizing her. More than anything, he listened. His interest in her seemed genuine and exclusive.

Until this morning.

The neon sign at the road crossing hadn't been lit on Delia's earlier prowls past the Two-Step. No Hummer had been parked outside, either.

This time, a pair of electric-blue boots moved back and forth, literally kicking ass on the dark. Beneath those pointed toes and stirrup heels, blinking curlicues spelled out *Suds n' BBQ*. Could the place get any more Texas-tacky?

Jerzy seemed completely out of sync with the joint. He'd never worn so much as boot-cut jeans or Tony Lamas. Or hummed a country tune. He'd quit drinking, so far as she knew. So why the Two-Step? Why this Chelsea woman?

One last roll past that roadhouse; then she'd head for . . . home? To sit at the kitchen table downing shots and piecing together useless shreds of paper? Telling herself Jerzy might show up at any time? Call with some logical explanation?

The Two-Step's gravel parking lot was lit in a jaundiced haze and had filled up. Trucks mostly, and—

"Shit."

The yellow Hummer stuck out like a rubber duck in a rain puddle. Her glance snapped back onto the road ahead, veins pulsing in her temples. She pulled a Hollywood slowdown at the intersection, then rolled through, eyes devouring the center stripes into the distance.

So he'd taken the woman up on an invite. *So what? So your chest feels like you inhaled a bag of traction sand. Get over it and drive.*

Delia drove. West toward Falls City. She'd gas up there and keep going. Up though the ghost town of Valsetz and down the Siletz River road. Graveled and bumpy but passable. Hell, might as well go clear over to the damned coast. She'd stay the night. Down a handful of aspirin, raid the motel mini-fridge, and get drunk listening to the surf.

Fate scratched that notion the second she hit the town center and caught sight of the Falls City Octane Stop. No lights, plywood over plate glass, pumps stripped of hoses and nozzles. She sighed. One more small-town gas franchise undercut by big-box discounters.

Spinning the wheel, she banged a U-ey and headed back, wondering how long the gas needle had been pegged on E. If only she didn't have to set eyes back on that damned roadhouse. If only . . .

Again, the blue kicking boots heaved into view. She came up on the intersection thinking she'd like to kick something. Storm into that place and unload on Jerzy Heartthrob Matusik. Thank him for royally capping off her worst fucking day ever. Then let Chelsea Foo-foo know what an asshole she was hooking up with.

Fuck it. Drive on, Chavez. Drive on. Several heartbeats and she'd pull even with the place. A held breath would get her past it.

She slowed, this time making a full stop at the crossroads. Kitty-corner, off her left fender, only noise spilled from inside the road-house's fake log siding. Then the man she'd saved from drowning, shared her hot tub, her secrets, and her body with, chose that moment to stagger out the front door. His knees were bent under the tepee lean of a short-skirted blonde—busty, of course—her arm draped across his shoulders.

Delia eased out the clutch and rolled across the intersection, dazed by the parking lot spectacle—the cackle of Blondie's laughter, the pair's weaving dance, tottering between parked cars, oblivious to anyone. She shifted into first on autopilot, gawking at the woman who pawed at his shirt collar, like she couldn't wait to get inside his clothes.

As if bogged down in sticky road tar, Delia low-geared it past the place, watching Jerzy drop his latest conquest onto the Hummer's passenger seat. Blinking herself out of a trance, she tore her sight away and punched the accelerator.

Not soon enough. Not before she'd seen Blondie snake out a bare leg, hook it around the back of Jerzy's thighs, and draw him in on top of her.

30

The road down to Kings Valley Highway blurred to a liquid shine, bordered by icy-white shoulders. Delia's temples were pounding. The night closed in as if she were driving through a tunnel. Something had collapsed inside—a lung, her heart, that pocket of hope where Jerzy Matusik wasn't just another horn dog.

Her stranglehold on the wheel wasn't enough. She could feel her frustration grow, turn into something else.

Yelling at the top of her lungs, she gave the Camaro's padded suede dash three quick palm-punches. "You stupid, stupid woman." For good measure, she delivered a couple more jabs. "That's what heartthrobs do."

The ache in her forehead racetracked around her skull, picking up steam. She felt woozy. Needed to pull off. Settle down.

The pavement ran straight and narrow, its sides gashed with deep ditches. No turnouts, only wavering bands of roadside frost outstripping the headlights.

Okay, don't stop. Don't think. Just breathe and go. Outrun the agony.

She cornered south at Kings Valley Highway and tromped the accelerator. Bouncing between hung-over low and boozy high, she seemed detached from herself.

Why not pour it on? Head for the big ninety—the L-shaped widow-maker at Peedee Creek bridge.

Floating across lanes and out into the next straightaway, she mashed on the go pedal. The supercharger yowled, a perfect imitation of Clawed riding the back of a hapless dog out of her yard. She cackled at the image, her laughter sounding hollow.

The speedometer needle bounced past one-forty. The Super Sport streaked down the road, turning highway stripes into flashing yellow dots.

Pumped, yet feeling not one crappy bit better, she twisted at the wheel grip. How could her world go to hell in a single day? Did God have it in for her?

God answered with snow. Big smeary flakes smacked the windshield. Even the weather was beyond real. She flicked on the wipers, lowered her speed to slightly under screaming banshee, and blew into the next curve. Coming out, the Camaro fishtailed but stayed on pavement.

Barrier reflectors gleamed in the distance. The big one was up next. The Super Sport straddled the center line, its tach nudging seven K.

Just imagining, but how shit-faced-easy would it be to fly off into nothing? A slick road in the dark. The snow. Her life in the toilet. Never a better time.

The Camaro lit up a road sign showing an arrow that hooked over a bridge hump. She gauged her chances of power-carving through that ninety. Piece of cake.

A deafening bang snapped Delia's head back against the seat rest. Jolted her into a cold-sober panic as the left front wheel caught the pavement edge and sent the car's rear end into a tire-mauling skitter.

Holy shit. No piece of cake.

The high-compression engine coughed, then sputtered. Kicked on again, then died. The Camaro shuddered, decelerating in jerks and spasms as steam shot out the hood seams.

Still too fast. The car was a silent missile, hurtling at the L-curve with no way to power down or through it. She rode the drift across lanes, then lost control. The convertible traded ends. She hung on, stomping at the hardened brake pedal, gaping at the view going away.

Shoulder gravel spattered the wheel wells with the force of nail guns shot into oil drums. A sickening screech magnified the din. The car shuddered to a backsliding stop, ramming her head against the backrest then nose-first into the horn button. A light show flickered behind her eyes while Enrique's pride and joy brayed.

Lucky was the first thing that popped into her head. Fucking lucky the ragtop hadn't rolled over.

She lifted her head to sudden silence. And a different kind of pain. Tears streamed down her cheeks as she blinked out at the snow glazing the hood. She dabbed beneath her nose with the back of her hand and came away with a dark coating of liquid stickiness.

Mierda, what a night. From whacked-out high to wet-your-pants reality in one easy lesson. Calming herself, Delia snickered out loud. She could write a damn telenovela. Hell, write and star in it. *Spurned rose Delia Adela Chavez returns from the dead to exact double-barreled revenge on* el gigolo, *and* el jefe. The blood kept coming.

The glove box door had popped open, spilling everything onto the front seat. She snatched up a napkin and tore it in half. Twirled two ends into cones, stuffed each up a nostril, and sat there staring out at the irony. A Jersey barrier had stopped her, scalping the side of her brother's classic muscle car.

"Oh, man. Enrique's gonna scalp *me* when he gets out."

A chortle burbled from her mouth. The blood-stoppers hanging from her nose blew upward like curtain gauze. She let out a full-throated laugh, picturing her tamale-shaped brother in an orange jumpsuit, chasing her around his car, scorching her ears with choice lockdown profanities until he bent over, gasping. She laughed, too, for fear of going where the opposite might take her. She laughed until a stitch in her ribs overtook her smarting nose and aching temples and the general sense of life doing her wrong. Nothing like physical pain to clear the cobwebs. She sat up, realizing the torment came from inside. That all the self-pity in the world couldn't get her what she needed: soap-opera justice.

She yanked out the napkins and felt for leakage. The bloodletting seemed over.

Face it, Chavez. Behind Matusik's nice-guy front lurked a player. Whatever she'd thought they had going had been a distraction. But from what? Was he a player in the sheriff's funny business? Was everybody deceiving her? Even Annie, who'd let Grice blindside her?

She felt the bridge of her nose for bone waggle. Nothing moved. Pulling the keys, she got out and popped the hood. A last gasp of steam boiled out as she played a light from her key fob over the havoc. Super-charger belt, MIA. Radiator hose, knocked loose by the exiting belt. Exhaust header pipe, separated from the flange at the weld. Lucky again. No wonder the headache. Her racing machismo. Her imagination gone wild.

Soap-opera revenge required a soap-opera car in working order. She slammed the hood and peered into the night, off toward a yard light at the wide spot in the road that was Peedee.

KOKO, Chavez. KOKO. There was nothing for it but to hike, find a phone, and call her last resort.

* * *

Big Juan wasn't happy about handing Delia the keys to *Jumpin' Jehoshaphat*.

Not after he'd seen the damage she'd inflicted on Enrique's Camaro. But she needed wheels to get back on track. Uncover what drove the sheriff to side-rail a major homicide investigation. Lizard Breath had shoved her outside the box, so she'd work there. KOKO.

Easing out the clutch, she slow-rolled the '51 Mercury coupe away from Big Juan's Low-Down Rides and Tow Service. From the car's rearview mirror, she could see him watching her, combing his fingers through the gray hair he still kept greased back into a D.A.

Big Juan was old-old school, right down to the pegged denims and Camels rolled into a sleeve of his bleached-white T. He wore the same outfit, summer or winter. A Mexican polar bear, she thought as she grannied the car down the street, careful not to hit a pothole or knee any under-dash control switches that might send his prize possession into hydraulic fits of suspension bouncing.

For reasons she knew better than to probe, Big Juan owed her brother big time. Probably from when they'd co-owned the custom car–slash–sometimes chop shop in New Mexico. Enrique made a car super-quick. Big Juan made it super-cool. Her suspicion? Enrique wasn't just doing his own time. Or else Big Juan would not have relocated to Oregon, much less towed the Camaro and agreed to fix it on his own dime.

Turning the corner and coasting out of sight, she grated the unfamiliar column shift into second and picked up speed. Three days, maybe four, she'd have to put up with the loaner Big Juan rolled out only for fiesta parades and dance car competitions.

She could stomach the car's rainbow flame job licking back from the hood. The cholo window fringe, too. But that bobbing hula dancer on the dash had to go. Unfastening its suction cup, she chucked the topless wahine into the glove compartment.

Exhaustion caught up as she rolled toward home.

The wheels of justice could wait.

31

Delia smacked down the snooze button before Selena got off the second *bom* of her Tex-Mex–reggae take on "Bidi Bidi Bom Bom." The digits spelled out 11:00 and the sun was a fuzzy peach in the bedroom window. Ten hours that felt like ten minutes.

She treasured Selena Quintanilla's message and music, especially after her tragic death. But please, not this morning. No lyrics about hearts going crazy. Sitting up, she watched the room spin. Almost wished she *was* dead. New fridge sticky note: *Never chase Sominex with a big red wine.*

Yesterday came flooding back, goose-bumping her bare skin. The idea of eking out justice on her own, together with the cold light of day, sent shivers up her arms. The room kept moving while she thought about the rule of holes and the one she was in. Maybe she should stop shoveling. Drive to Newport and see about getting on at Lincoln County Sheriff's.

Definitely not KOKO, Chavez. Stay and dig. She was beyond hunch Grice was dirty. Not just "the little bite." Dirty in a big way. Rubbing at her arms, Delia wondered whether she'd uncover anything, digging from the outside. At the least, she could find out why the one friend left on the inside had let Grice ambush her.

* * *

Only police vehicles and visitors were allowed in parking behind the Polk County Jail. A colorless overcast and the employee lot suited

Delia just fine. Even better, two prisoner transport vans sat on either side of an open slot directly across from the dispatcher's assigned parking. She backed *Jehoshaphat* into the stall between the camouflaging vans, rolled down the window, and cut the barely muffled flathead V-8 just as Annie's rust-pocked Z-car caromed in.

While Annie parked, Delia slipped on dark aviators, yanked the keys, and took up a third-degree stance at the Merc's front wheel well.

High heels clacked toward her. They scraped to an abrupt stop when Annie saw who was waiting.

"Oh, Delia. Hey." Her glance meandered, then swept past, taking in the flashy car. She edged between the van and the Merc, her attention drawn to the name splashed over its fender. *"Jumpin' Jehoshaphat?"* She must have been off since the night before—sporting a new shoulder bag, manicure, and fresh hair touch-up. She still could have called. Given Delia a heads-up.

Hands on hips, Annie reared back at the waist. "Good God, Chavez. Have you got a Sancho on the side?"

Delia winced behind her glasses. No surprise Annie knew cholo slang for a secret lover—she got around. But this was the wrong damned day for guy-banter.

"They're all yours, Cox. Every last one."

Annie leaned in, a sharper green in her gaze. "What's up?"

Delia shrugged. The air soured in the silence.

Annie nodded at the keys in Delia's hand. "Gonna be back soon?"

"How about never? Is that fucking soon enough for you?"

Annie didn't move, but her eyes went round. "Geez, girl. Who flipped your bitch switch?"

"Why the hell didn't you warn me?"

Annie's mouth went agape, her head tilting to one side. Good acting. "About what?"

"About Grice. That it was an ambush."

"Delia, what happened?"

She felt Annie's hand on her arm and shook it off. "Grice yanked my badge. I'm suspended, that's what happened. Don't act like you didn't see it coming."

"I-I really didn't." Annie lifted three fingers, Girl Scout style. "Truth, girl. Night before last, I left your report on the sheriff's desk. He wanted to pull you in for a dressing down right then and there. I explained the close call you and Jerzy had on the river and got him to back off. He agreed to go easy on you and that's where we left it. Swear to God."

Delia ransacked her friend's face. Read the honesty in her eyes. Felt sick for doubting her. "Okay, Annie. Sorry, but old Lizard Breath's not stopping at suspension. He gets his way, I'm out for good."

Annie broke into a chuckle. "*Lizard Breath*. Nice. I had *Lard Butt*."

They laughed together, but sobered quickly.

"So what about Jerzy?"

"What about him?" Delia snapped.

"Whoa, easy. I just meant, is he in or out?"

Delia rammed her hands into her coat pockets. "Couldn't care less."

Annie peered into her face. "What am I missing? So . . . not a Sancho, but you and him?"

"Me and nobody. Grice put Castner in charge of the case . . . maybe Investigations. Reassigned Matusik to him."

"You're shitting me. Castner? Man's got a mind like a steel trap— welded shut. He botches traffic arrests, for God's sake."

Pulling off her glasses, Delia let out a chuff. "Wanna hear the funny part? Grice called me incompetent."

Annie spun away, stormed out from between the parked vehicles, turned, and stalked back. She took in Delia's jeans and sweat shirt, likely the circles behind her eyes. "When's the last time you ate? I mean, food with protein?"

"I dunno, I—"

"Here's what you do. First, drive over to the Doo-Wop and get yourself a real breakfast. An egg sandwich, at least." Annie stepped past and opened the driver's side door. "Get your mind off things for the day. Go shopping. Shoot targets. Whatever. Then meet me at Harvey's. After my shift's over."

"At Harvey's, huh?" Delia let the question float like a bobber and hook.

Annie masked whatever else was going on with a hook of her own. "Yeah. Time we brought you into our little cabal."

* * *

Relief washed over Delia when she saw no police units in sight at the local cop hangout—no Castner act-alikes in browns, no city roosters in blues to cock-a-doodle-doo over her lowrider, or worse, over the blindside from Grice.

Starving, she wheeled into the Doo-Wop drive-in, parked under its swept-wing roof, and pulled the swing-arm order kiosk in close. She hit the speaker button and broke into the Motown sounds of Little Eva urging everyone to do the locomotion. Listen to that stuff a zillion times and it grew on you.

Nobody there? Duddley must be out back having a smoke. She waited, letting her thoughts wander, wondering whether, more like hoping, the conspiracy Annie and Harvey were hatching pertained to Grice.

A red pickup pulled into the stall opposite her kiosk. Zack slid over and rolled down the window.

"Good news, Detective."

"What kind of news?"

"The sort-of kind. I remember you saying you had no crime scenes to go over—"

"And?" She flipped the speaker out of the way. "Have you got something?"

"No, but the river's gone down. I can get you out where that sumbitch . . . you know."

Where Charlie was killed. The excitement mounted inside her, then sloped off. "I don't have to go by boat, do I?"

A vertical wrinkle showed between Zack's eyebrows and disappeared. He slid back over behind the wheel.

"You okay following in that pearly white lead sled?"

"Let's go."

* * *

Delia had enough trouble navigating the boulder-strewn gravel bar between the Santiam and Willamette Rivers on foot, let alone while shouting questions to Zack.

"Hold up where you think Charlie might've been . . . when he confronted the perpetrator."

Ahead, Zack walked a scum-encrusted waterline, stopping suddenly.

"Here! Where Charlie dropped his shotgun."

She'd parked Big Juan's Mercury coupe on the Marion County side of the Willamette and continued in Zack's pickup along a farm access road, where it ran out just north of the Santiam.

Delia caught up with Zack and swiveled around, scanning, looking for something, any item that didn't fit with the stink and ugliness of every dead thing deposited at the confluence. She could probably stop wishing she still had her evidence bag.

But that dry log above her had been there awhile, before the last high water. She sighted between Zack, now standing with his head bowed where he thought Charlie had gone down, and up to that log. The angle was about right. Worth having a look.

Careful not to slip and bang her knees, Delia negotiated the rocks and got close enough to scrutinize for details. To her shock, one stood out right away, a branch too straight to be a branch.

"Zack, up here." The enthusiasm she voiced drew him to his feet and brought him stumbling up to her.

"Holy crap. Look at that thing. That's what . . . got Charlie?"

"No." It was SOP not to share autopsy photos with relatives. "But this jives with how two other victims were killed."

"Then why's it here?"

"That I don't know." She studied the wicked gleam of its point, embedded in the log. "Wasn't Charlie's hunting coat sliced through at the top of one shoulder?"

"You think this quarrel did that?"

"Could be a miss. You told me you heard Charlie's gun go off. Suggests to me he put up a fight."

He looked at her. "Well, that's something I can hold on to. But it's not near enough."

"I know, Zack. I'll get him. If it's the last thing I do." Who knew how close she might come to speaking truth.

She pointed to the stick that wasn't a stick. "You called this a quarrel?"

"Or a bolt. Used in crossbows. This one's a broad-tip with four hellish-looking razor edges." Until now, Delia had been thinking spear gun. This made more sense. Hunters hunted on top of the water.

"Range?"

"I knew a guy could hit the sweet spot and down a deer at sixty feet with his souped-up pistol-grip crossbow."

"Lay out two of those rags," she said, drawing on rubber gloves from her pocket. She'd seen Zack stuff a packet of new grease rags in his coat.

Chain of evidence was out the door, but this quarrel might still point to the killer.

*　*　*

It was past four when Delia pulled to the curb at Harvey's house, switched off, and gathered up the rag-wrapped crossbow arrow. She wanted to explore options with Harvey before turning anything like that over to Castner—who might toss it in his trunk and forget about it.

She got out, shivered, and zipped her coat. The temperature had plunged ahead of the clouds and a threat of snow. Annie's Z was nowhere in sight, so she retrieved the arrow and hurried up the walkway to Harv's sky-blue, bungalow-style craftsman. Its cheeriness mocked the peevish vein she'd mined into the late-afternoon shadows.

She banged up Harvey's front-porch steps, harboring scant hope an invalid cop, a police dispatcher, and a likely-ex-detective might unfuck a completely fucked-up sheriff's department.

Harvey met her leaning on a single crutch, his arms spread. The strain from hobbling around showed in his face as he looked past her, silently mouthing the name on the fender of her lowrider. Smiling, he said nothing. She stepped into his enfolding uncle hug and felt compensated for keeping on, at least momentarily.

"Crappy couple of days, huh, Dee-Dee?"

"The crappiest. Annie fill you in?"

He nodded, turning and motioning her in. "By phone. Let's go sit so I can get off this leg."

"Oh. Yeah," she said, following him inside. "Your truck accident? No accident. Prints on the e-brake matched a drug peddler's, named Moonshaft Nastry. Heard of him?"

The stress lines in Harvey's forehead definitely flattened, but he kept going. "Uh-uh. Would've remembered that handle."

They sat opposite each other in a living room defined by a fireless fireplace, his Big Man recliner, and a padded chair she'd dragged over from the dining room. A TV tray sat off to Harvey's left. Carving tools and shavings littered the tray. A duck's bill poked out of a wood block. She set down the rag-wrapped arrow.

He wanted her account, so she started in.

She was about to wrap up when there was a single knock and Annie breezed in like she owned the place, kicking the door shut behind her on the way into Harvey's kitchen.

"Hey, Chavez. Hey, Handsome." She put away a bag of groceries in the fridge and cupboards, then cruised over to Handsome's recliner and plunked herself down on one of the arms. "You two get to the heart of the matter?"

Harvey made room, but the outside of his arm stayed in contact with Annie's hip. That modest intimacy spoke more than if they had pawed each other.

Delia gave a mental tongue-click. Harv a confirmed bachelor and Annie a lover of cabana boys. A pair of redheads: one with kinky hair, the other just kinky.

Farfetched, but there it was.

Delia returned to her chair, feeling like a third wheel until Annie got up and scraped another chair close to hers.

Annie's hands took hers and squeezed. "Delia, you have to know this dismissal threat's a setup. Grice wants you out of the way, but we can't figure out why."

"Same here," Delia said. "I'm convinced he's playing a side game that's somehow tied in with Bastida, that military fugitive, and those calls from Virginia you and I got curious about. When I confronted him, Grice fed me a bogus-sounding line that Bastida's not only our killer, but he made off with a secret weapon."

"Wow," said Harvey. "Of course, we are in the era of super-whoppers. And I don't mean burgers. But even if we had any hard evidence—"

"Oh-hoh. But we do." Delia sprang out of her chair, adding, "Well, maybe," over her shoulder as she booked it out the front door. Thirty seconds and she was back with the box of shredded paper she'd been chauffeuring for twenty-four hours. "Anybody up for a game of mix, match, and catch? Tape and glue, find the clue?"

Annie was out of her chair, saying, "Damn, girl. You kept that?" Before Harvey could object, she'd swept everything off his kitchen table: sugar and cream bowls and salt and pepper shakers set aside, napkins gone flying. "Harvey, we need your company table leaves. Quick."

"Hold it, where'd you get that?"

"Street dumpster," answered Annie. "Nineteen eighty-eight court ruling. Fair game." She never ceased to amaze Delia.

"All right, proceed." As if either Annie or Delia needed a go-ahead.

It was anything but quick. Hours later, they had something on Grice. Three photos distinctly labeled by a naval inquiry board. Two depictions caused considerable mirth: images of him on his knees and buck naked in a Barranquilla bordello, a señorita in similar attire riding his back. Delia did some Googling with Harvey's laptop regarding the third photo. It showed Grice in uniform with his arms across the shoulders of two men, one a Colombian general, later indicted for tipping off drug traffickers, the other a cartel kingpin brought down in 2012.

Unsure whether any of it could be used as evidence, Delia started a stack anyway. "I'd say they're blackmail material on a sheriff running for office."

Harvey tapped on the pile. "You can bet I'll follow up on that naval inquiry. What else?"

"We have a winner!" Annie said, taping a last paper strip onto a blank page and handing it to Delia, who described as she perused.

"Two check stubs, dated in early October, from a Navy federal credit union in Little Creek, Virginia. Notice each one is just under ten thousand, the bank-reporting benchmark. I'd like to know for certain whether the signatory is that naval commander who called, and whether the checks are still coming."

"Oh, hey." Annie said, hunching over the table. "You know my brother, Cam." Delia did. Cameron Cox managed the Dallas, Oregon, branch of the Far West Bank. Annie'd once tried to fix her up with him. Nice guy, but apples and kumquats. Not a good fit. "Well, that's where Grice banks."

"Uh, hold that thought," Harvey said. "We're bumping into fruit-of-the-poisonous-tree territory. Bankers can't hand over personal bank records without a warrant."

"Oh, I'm not gathering evidence, just intelligence. I'll casually mention the sheriff's going to the bank a lot and play smiley-frowny face with Cam, like when we were kids. He won't realize he's giving me a thing. Cam should never ever play poker."

Harvey flattened his hands on the table. "Even establishing a pattern, we can't move ahead without a warrant, but we'll have enough to go to Barsch." He lowered his voice. "Grice knows he hasn't a chance of getting reelected, but he's got four lame-duck months to wreck the department before he waddles out of office. However, if Annie's right and we get lucky"—he rapped his knuckles on the wood tabletop—"we might finagle an emergency filing for impeachment on gross malfeasance."

He shifted toward Delia. "Dee-Dee, you've given us a ton to go on. Now you need to back off and give us time to work it."

"I'm not going to sit this out at home, Harv. I've got promises to keep."

"Just don't give Grice a reason to jam you up."

"There's a wrinkle." She stepped into the living room and came back with the roll of grease rags. "We still have a killer loose, and I recovered one of his customized toys. It could have his prints." She unwrapped the bolt and laid it on his lap. "Careful."

The razor-thin spiral blades gleamed jewelry-case bright, earning a low whistle from Harvey. She shook her head. "No way am I turning this over to Castner."

"All right," he said, rewrapping the shaft. "I'll have my OSP contact run it through their lab. But please, stay out of the sheriff's line of sight until we file."

She was glad he didn't bring up chain-of-evidence issues.

32

BOWMAN PARK ON THE WILLAMETTE RIVER
EIGHT WEEKS INTO WATERFOWL SEASON

Big Juan's Mercury was no slouch. Topping one-ten in the straight-aways, Delia covered the forty miles from Monmouth to Albany, Oregon, in thirty minutes. She rocketed off its west-side bridge under a cloud cover. Veering north, she tore up the main drag, blowing through intersections, hoping Zack had waited. Hoping she wouldn't find him laid out on a boat ramp, skewered like duck hunter kebab. He was her last option, and like a good SME, he'd followed her lead.

His five AM call from a truck stop had woken her from a troubled sleep. She'd forgotten she'd given him her home number in case he ran across anything that could put her on the killer's trail. From what he'd said, he just might have.

Delia hooked left at an access road and accelerated toward the Willamette. The Bowman Park entrance sign whizzed past. She caught sight of a boat, a very tiny boat, swinging in the current on a chain tether. Zack stood beside it, flagging her down and definitely nonskewered.

The tension drained from her. She stomped the brakes, and the lowrider shuddered to a stop on the concrete boat ramp. Below, river water boiled around his hip boots, and her gut churned. So much for immersion therapy.

He kept windmilling his arm, motioning her down there. Shit.

Stalling, she canvassed the open parking lot. No sign of the hippie van Zack had described, only Zack's cherry-red pickup hooked to an empty boat trailer. As he clomped up the ramp, she remembered her handgun still held light-grain practice rounds. Hands shaking, she traded out the .44 cowboy loads for Buffalo Bore Magnums and reholstered the never-jam revolver.

A flashlight rapped against the window. She rolled down. Zack leaned in.

"We gotta get moving, Detective. That SOB's goin' after Tweety."

"The former hunting guide?"

"You know about him? I'm worried he always hunts by himself."

She shook off the persistent image of a canary chased by a black-and-white cartoon cat. "Back up, Zack. What about the Volkswagen van?"

"Up behind us. Sumbitch off-loaded his big sea kayak, then parked out of sight. You won't believe what's on the—"

"You've been to the van? Didn't touch anything, right?"

Eye-blinking silence. He pulled back and stared down the ramp toward his pint-size watercraft. "Nah. That was right after Tweety's boat ran past, headin' downriver. The SOB from the van took off in his kayak, paddlin' like a spaniel after a mallard."

"Okay, first things first. Where's the van?"

* * *

In the gloom of a dawn slow to give up the night, Delia recognized the vintage Volkswagen backed into the trees on the park's outer edge. The same van with the faded psychedelic treatment she'd seen puttering past her at the opening day bug-out. Castner had described a kayaker who provoked the shotgun fireworks that broke up the hunting protest. Could it be so simple? An antihunter driven to kill?

She preceded Zack to the back of the van, noted the plate number, then knelt before a partially exposed bumper sticker. Exhaust residue obscured the lettering. She wiped it off with wadded grass. The first line was in tranquil lowercase green, the second in bleeding red capitals. It read:

Don't hunt animals . . .
HUNT HUNTERS!

She stood, trying to wipe the wet off her knees. "Zack. Did you actually see this guy with a crossbow? Any sort of weapon?"

"Hell, I dunno. It was still dark. That SOB packed all sorts of shit into the front hole of his kayak."

On a slow, deep breath, she gazed off across Linn County's Bowman Park, past the cheery lights surrounding a covered picnic shelter, off into the darkness of the river beyond.

"Okay, let's go hunt up this guy named after a canary."

* * *

Delia faced backward in the bow, maintaining a crush grip on the seat braces while the little boat carved a trough through the river. Zack stood at the motor. Suddenly, he kneed the tiller. They banked hard to the left, charging past an upwelling in the river's surface where a reptilelike snout poked up. Images of tree limbs dragging her underwater, squeezing the air out of her chest, flashed through her head. In a blink, the spiky end of the half-buried log disappeared. He leveled the boat and nodded back toward the swirl, grinning.

"Y'know, this river ain't that different from an old crow," he shouted. "Hoards stuff, then just has to show it off."

She couldn't believe he'd just averted near disaster and his hands had never left his pockets.

Not in a million could Delia have imagined wishing to be riding downriver in *Jackie*. Ever. But five minutes huddled in the bow of Zack's wobbling little punt had her yearning for that big jet boat. Forget its driver, whatever and whoever else he was doing. To make things worse, she had only one glove and a wet butt from constant bow splashes, and the flotation vest Zack had loaned her was way too tight. No matter how she sat, the life jacket stretched over the pancake holster and beefy revolver digging into her armpit. She almost wished, too, that she hadn't had to give up her lighter duty weapon.

Doubt burrowed into her brain. Was she on a fool's errand? With no backup in the vicinity? At least she was packing. And legal, with a carry permit. Bow spray chilled the back of her neck, making her turtle into her jacket.

"Here." Zack tossed a brownish-green plaid cap onto her lap. "Put on this Stormy Kromer."

Delia gaped at the ridiculous string bow above the plaid bill, her eyes saying, *Hell no*. But when her bare hand sank inside the pull-down ear band and felt its warm flannel, her fingers said, *What the hell.*

She untied and unfurled the cap, then jammed it low over her ears. A fool might as well look like one.

33

"**C**ut the motor." Still seated in the bow and facing the stern, Delia had to shout over the burr of Zack's outboard.

"Huh?" Still standing with the tiller clamped between his knees, he canted his head.

She repeated, drew a finger across her throat with her ungloved hand, then pointed at the motor.

He bent down and gave the throttle a quick twist. Boat headway dropped so fast she hooked a boot toe under the center seat to keep from toppling over backward.

A chugging grumble replaced the burr.

"What?"

"Gunshots," she said, motioning back over her shoulder. "You didn't hear them? Deep booms. One on top the other." Sounds she'd thought she'd heard before. Twisting sideways, she raised an earflap and listened.

"What kind?"

"Shotgun." Hours at the practice range had given her a keen sense for the reports of different weapons. "Could be just a hunter."

"How far?"

She realized Zack was too near the engine to hear much else. "Not far. A ways downriver."

"Black Dog Slough's closest."

They listened together as the current swept them along. Past a concrete pipe spouting a waterfall. Over a sunken gravel bar marked by bent willow tops.

No shots followed.

She swung around and faced him, peeling off her soaked, useless glove and dropping it on the boat deck. "You see any firearms in that hippie van?"

"Nah." Zack's gaze took on a distant look. "Not that sumbitch. His deal is slinging arrows. Slitting throats." He snuffled against his mitten. "Those shots. Deep booms, huh? You mighta heard Tweety's side-by-side. I seen a ten-gauge double in his boat that time him and me said hello. Old, twin-trigger Ithaca. Barrel holes the size of Ping-Pong balls. Maybe he opened up on those high-flying pintails sailed past us a couple minutes ago. Or—"

He clapped a hand onto the tiller. "We better get down there and make sure." He said the last wrenching the throttle. The boat lurched, causing Delia to grab for seat struts.

In no time, they'd hit maximum plowing speed. She swore *Jackie*'s no-wake troll could beat Zack's metal skiff going full tilt. Time enough to reconsider whether they were heading into something they shouldn't.

None of the shots-fired scenarios she'd trained for—house clearings, tactical drug raids, domestic disputes gone violent—had involved people discharging weapons who could either be legal hunters or active murderers. For sure, none had meant barging into a possible threat scene riding backward in a dinky boat. They still had time to turn around and call in for—

An abrupt drop in engine RPMs signaled they had arrived.

* * *

The mouth of Black Dog Slough crawled past in Delia's side vision, its oily surface the color of rotted leaves. A scant forty yards wide, the sluggish waterway reeked of creepiness.

"Think I caught a glimpse of that booger-green kayak farther downriver. Sumbitch coulda kept goin'." Zack spoke in low tones, as if the knock of his outboard at slow troll hadn't already given them away. "There's Tweety's setup."

From the bow, she scrunched around, craning her head to follow Zack's nod.

At first, she saw only decoys twisting on anchor cords in a large eddy. Twenty yards inside the decoys, a tangle of brush drooped over a low bank. Something partially hidden behind that brownish-green overgrowth caught her eye. Long and low to the water, a uniform weave of darker material rose and fell with the rebounding waves. A mat of evergreens and marsh weeds lay in folds atop a boat. The brush boat she'd seen before. A perfect camouflage when propped up.

Nothing moved inside the hunting blind.

"Don't see him," Zack said, "but the blind's been lowered, like some ducks passed over his dekes and he shot at them." His Jon boat drifted in past the decoys. The deck shuddered with each nervous shift of his feet. Almost like a pee-pee dance. "Yo, Tweety." His sudden shout lifted Delia an inch off her seat. "You out and about?"

He shoved the tiller all the way over, using what was left of their headway to coast in sideways to the larger craft, its far side tethered to a half-submerged tree stump. As they glided past the bow, she habitually noted the decal numbers.

"He must be out after one he only winged. Grab holda that chicken wire toward the back." Zack sounded agitated, like he was in a hurry to be somewhere else. Her sentiments exactly.

Bows nudged and parted before she realized he meant the stuff that held the collapsed mat of dead shrubbery in place. Spotting an opening beneath a frond of Scotch broom, she leaned far out, wove her fingers into the underlying mesh, and pulled Zack's boat in parallel with Tweety's.

The hulls had barely touched when the smaller boat bounced up and down, putting stress on Delia's flimsy grip as well as her knotted stomach. Zack had leapt into Tweety's boat and was yanking up his hip boots.

"Hey, what do you think you're doing?"

"Goin' to find Tweety. The shots you heard prob'ly were at ducks. See that cover crop on the hillside?" He pointed up beyond the tree line surrounding the slough, toward a knoll in a field of knee-high grass. "See that tramped-down furrow goin' over the top?" Zack straddled the shore side of the larger boat and dangled a leg over, as if testing for bottom. "Best I can figure, a wounded bird sailed up that way and Tweety set off to find it. Might've just saved his butt, with that kayaker slinkin' around." He slipped over the far side.

Delia started to get up, then sat back. Her iffy hold on the blind material was all that kept Zack's boat from drifting off.

"Bad idea, Zack. Remember why we're here."

He waved her off. "Just goin' up past the top of that hill, see if I can make him out. Sit tight and keep a lookout for the kayaker. I'll be back in two shakes." With that, he was up the bank and forging through undergrowth.

At last glimpse, the back of Zack's head had disappeared over the edge of the knoll. She'd been right the first time. He needed an excuse to pee in private.

Meanwhile, each minor tug of current on the two boats etched the chicken wire deeper into the tender underside of her bare fingers. She scrunched her body around, scanning the side of Tweety's odd-looking boat for a better grip. She found none. At least none she'd trust.

Even more strange, a bottle floated past. It's neck was rag-stuffed, and on fire.

* * *

Minutes passed—hand-cramping, finger-throbbing minutes. And no sign of Zack. Delia had to do something. Swap hands, maybe. She let go briefly to shake the sting out of her fingers. The boats stayed together, so she leaned forward and searched the underside of her bow seat. Found the single wet glove she'd discarded and wriggled her hand into it.

Feeling motion, she sat up in surprise.

A widening space of water separated the boats. She lunged for a handle of some sort. It turned out to be the butt end of a shotgun poking up from the underside of the duck blind. Her fingers slipped off the stock. The gun disappeared with a clatter into the recesses of Tweety's boat.

"Crap."

Lunging hadn't helped the situation, either. Already Zack's lighter boat was four feet from Tweety's and drifting out toward the decoys.

She searched for a paddle and, finding none, settled her attention on the outboard motor. How hard could it be to start? First, she had to get there without tipping over.

Steeling herself, she took hold of the sides and levered her butt off the bow seat.

The second Delia's knee met deck ribbing, air whooshed past her left side, knocking her cap off center. Splashes followed, sounding like rocks skipping water behind her. Something warm and wet streamed down her cheek, into the corner of her mouth. She tasted it. Metallic, like touching her tongue to a school flagpole. Blood. She slid her hand up past the stickiness, under the Stormy Kromer's dangling flap. A slicing burn made her suck air.

On instinct, Delia hunkered down. She fumbled to get a hand into the life vest while her eyes scanned for the threat—somebody had loosed something at her. Something so sharp it had split her ear nearly in two.

The shooter was somewhere past the end of Zack's boat. Out by that milling log with a darker hump.

Delia's spine straightened in shock. The log moved toward her. And the black hump was a head wearing a face mask. She jabbed frantically for the S&W lodged under her arm. Her fingers tangled in side webbing and she jerked back in panic, trying to free them. Why had she put the stupid glove back on?

She wrested her hand free and tore the glove off with her teeth, her sight glued on the assailant closing in. Green-and-black stripes darkened the skin below and around his mask—special-ops face paint. Bastida? Did it matter? The asshole had shot her in the ear.

She snatched at the life preserver's zipper. She had to shuck the thing to get at her weapon.

Out there, the head disappeared underwater. She fought a brain freeze of fear, got the life jacket unzipped, and yanked. It stayed on.

"Fuck." She'd forgotten the cinch straps. She twisted around, fumbling for the plastic releases, thinking her stupid river phobia might do her in after all.

Four thick fingers curled over the boat rim, making the gorge rise in her throat. A second hand appeared closer to the bow, closer to her. That hand clasped a knife, shiny with newness, its spine notched with serrations. A masked, camo-striped face popped up, flashing a *here's Johnny* grin.

Johnny said nothing. Just hummed a ditty, hanging on to the outside of the boat. Then he lunged, making a vertical blade-swipe that cut into her life preserver. She flopped back and double-kicked. Her right foot missed the swimmer's head. Her left connected with his knife hand. The blade flashed as it spun through the air, clattered off a decoy, and plopped into the water.

Her attacker's grin morphed into a grimace as he scrambled away, hand over hand along the outside of the boat. Out of kicking range, he flapped the injured hand as if shaking out the sting of pain. He slid the face mask onto the top of his head. Bottle-green eyes—rimmed in crusty redness—glared at her. Appraising. Almost familiar. Where?

Still in the water, he yanked down on the boat side, as if testing its stability, then boosted himself partway out. He was getting in. No. Staying out. Rocking.

She clawed frantically for her ensnared weapon. The boat listed toward him. A plastic vest fastener pinged off metal inside the boat. Where was the second clasp? She tore at the knife-slashed vest front.

He sank back into the water and the boat tilted hard in the opposite direction. She lost balance on the roll. A stab of pain shot into her backside. Her tailbone had found the point of Zack's pyramid anchor. She shifted her butt sideways and fought off the nausea. The swimmer rose and sank a second time. Water slopped in and the boat almost went over as she gave a hard, upward yank on the life jacket. The vest flew off her head, her damaged ear smarting as if torn away. Delia's right hand found the holster and closed around the pistol grip.

He let up again and the boat rolled back the other way. Momentum was with him. Another downward shove and she'd be in the water with the bastard. Molding her back into the boat deck, she freed the weapon and thumbed off the safety. Propping her forearms on her knees, she steadied the chunky revolver and snarled an oath.

"No. More. Fucking. River."

He reared up for the final flip. The boat tilted violently. More water gushed in. Her Lew Horton Special jumped twice. The face mask flew off his head. Her brain yelled *no-o*, unable to believe her eyes. She saw no entry wound. She'd missed his head and hit the mask.

The terror inside her yelped *shoot again*, but the boat teetered on the edge of tipping upside down. Her arms flew out on their own, wedging her against the inside of the hull. They were going over, but the bastard would have to pry her off like a barnacle.

In that split second, it struck her that he'd eased up, that only bloodshot whites showed in his upturned eyes. His fingers slipped out of sight and the flat-bottomed hull slapped back the other way.

As her attacker's head lolled back and his face sank from view, she noticed one nostril was narrow, the other rounded. About the size of a .44 Magnum.

34

"I'm not hearing answers I can take to the bank, Lukovsky. Where did you claim you were when Cha-vez was blasting away with her forty-four?"

Half listening to Grice's latest ball-twister, Zack tamped down the slow burn in his gut and lowered his sight to the ruined jacket liner he'd let fall between their feet. Blood oozed from the checkered flannel, veining the cracks in the concrete at Bowman Marine Park. Staining the floor of the picnic shelter they stood under to avoid the freezing rain.

Maybe Detective Chavez had kept her promise. Maybe Charlie's killer was carp food. Zack had already told Grice he'd been off looking for Tweety Bates, heard pistol shots, and found her bleeding worse than a stuck hog.

At Black Dog, she'd used his coat liner to slow the bleeding until they made it back to Bowman Park. Minutes after Zack called 911, the place was a cop convention—Albany Police and county-mounties, all wagon-wheeled around an ambulance.

Then Grice rolled in. Acted like he was running the show. Pressured the Linn County sheriff into sending his patrol boat to search the slough with a couple hours of daylight left. The EMTs were still working on the detective's ear, so Grice had zeroed in on Zack, grilling him, jacking his answers around. Trying to turn blame for whatever happened at Black Dog onto the detective. Or him. Or both.

A dark-red trickle ran under the sheriff's boot toe, reminding Zack of the important thing—the detective had never lied to him. He looked Grice right in his heavy-lidded eyes. "I was close enough to know she didn't shoot a fucking broadhead blade through her own damned ear. Check out that van back in the woods and I bet you find something."

Grice stepped in close. His breath could pickle a live porcupine. "One at a time, smartass. What makes you so sure it was a broadhead blade?"

Zack didn't know what the detective had done with the shaft he'd given her, but he sensed he shouldn't go there. "Because, fat-ass, I found—" In an instant, he was on his toes, yanked up nearly chin to chin with the bigger man. For a chubbo, Grice had lightning-quick hands.

"Guess what, you little pissant. Your sass mouth bought you a night in the bucket."

Zack knew better than to struggle, given the sheriff had a crush grip on the front of his thermals. With his jaw tight against the man's knuckles, he had to spit out words from between his teeth. "Wrong county, Sheriff. Not your jurisdiction."

"We'll see about that." Grice's boozy eyes darted around the parking lot, searching for the other sheriff. Zack figured his mouth had earned him a stay in the old hoosegow when somebody shouted.

"Patrol boat's back. Body recovered."

Grice let go of him and stalked off toward the river, catching up with the other sheriff. Zack knew he should leave. Instead, he followed. The stuff running into his collar was too white to call rain and too wet for snow, but he had to be sure about the body. For Charlie's sake.

Rusted pipe columns punctured the edges of Bowman Park's floating launch dock, allowing it to rise and fall with the river. Only fifteen feet of piling showed. Zack kept the column closest to shore between him and the two sheriffs standing next to their deputies at middock, staring into the county patrol boat that had tied up. Zack planned to slip away after he made sure the recovered body had been the one hunting hunters and not Tweety Bates.

Still, if it was the former under that boat tarp, the killer might've gotten to Tweety before Zack and the detective had made it down to Black Dog.

Or maybe somebody else had been monkeying around in that slough, like Detective Chavez suspected.

Her questions had nagged at him ever since he'd gotten her to quit searching for Tweety and motor back to the park. Questions like: Had Zack seen any scuba gear transferred from the van into the kayak that morning? Had the kayaker been wearing a wet suit? Had he been towing an underwater PWC?

Zack's answers were *no, not sure,* and *what the hell's a PWC?* She should've said *water scooter* first off.

The patrol craft's center aisle stretched a good eighteen feet from an open bow to the OMC Cobra stern drive. Boats like that usually made Zack drool for one of his own. Not this time. Not after they peeled back the yellow tarp over the forward six feet of decking.

The body lay facedown, feet toward the stern. No wet suit. Neoprene short pants, waterproof paddling jacket, and aqua booties, all in puke green. Zack swallowed on seeing exposed body parts. The neck, the lower back where the shell rode up, and the calves were all the color of overripe squid. Something looked wrong with the right hand, too. Like the guy's sleeve had melted onto his wrist.

One of the boat operators rolled the body over. It was the kayaker who'd paddled off from that dock earlier in the morning. He'd been semi-gutted. Torn open with heavy-duty loads at close range.

Zack jerked his head away, taking deep breaths as wet snowflakes skittered across his face. If that was Charlie's killer, Zack felt no satisfaction, only deep sadness. He kept on facing the oncoming dusk, barely hearing Grice yell to somebody at the top of the boat ramp.

"Get Cha-vez down here."

* * *

241

"That's not the one who attacked me. That's not the guy I shot."

The cop crew lining the dockside turned as a unit and gawked at the bandaged side of Delia's head. She rested a foot on the curve of the bow. It was the only spot that afforded her a look inside the patrol boat. Even from a poor angle, one glance was enough.

Grice struggled up off his knees and squinted at her. "Now how in hell could you know that? You can't even see his face from that view."

She sank her hands into her coat pockets and returned the glare. "This one still has the top of his head." Everyone looked inside the boat at once, as if they could've overlooked a guy missing a chunk of skull the size of a pancake. And that burnt hand . . . She flashed on the flaming Heineken bottle that had drifted past her at Black Dog. "Anybody check for ID? Maybe ALF affiliation?"

They glanced her way again. One of the marine deputies tilted the body onto its side. The bulge of grayish-purple intestines from the encircling neoprene caused Delia to step backward, covering her mouth. The deputy groped the body and came up with a billfold. "Shit," he said, displaying the open wallet to the group. "What joker would name his son Moonshaft Nastry?"

"What joker would keep it?" cracked Grice, earning a few sniggers.

"How's your ear, Detective?" At Zack's nearby whisper, she noticed him peering from behind a dock post.

"Fine." Not fine. Not after that sight. Not with everybody staring. Her head felt grossly lopsided, like the EMTs had strapped on a traffic cone instead of a bandage. The whole left side of her face felt saggy, deadened by localized anesthetic until she could get to Albany General for a sew-up. She must look a hell of a lot worse than she felt. "Hurts like crazy, but thanks for asking. Zack, did they say anything about Tweety Bates?"

"Nah. Think the guy who attacked you got to Tweety first?"

"Can't say until they fish out another body, but I have an idea who killed Nastry and came close to checking me out. But Nastry's prints were found in the truck that rolled over our senior detective."

242

"Get out! Harvey Schenkel? Charlie's old boss? Told you that kay-aker was a hyena."

Grice had turned his back to her, was arguing with the Linn County sheriff. She stayed put. Jurisdiction issues, she guessed.

Zack inched out from the post. "I told the sheriff how I'd gone over the hill to look for Tweety. So I can't back you up."

Delia nodded, hoping she could fend for herself on this one. A dicey situation without another body recovery.

She stepped aside as two of the Linn County contingent trooped off the dock behind their sheriff. The confab was over. It seemed they were full up on major crimes at the moment. That left the search-and-rescue pair and Grice at the boat. He crooked his finger toward her, turned, and walked out along the dock.

Delia whispered, "Zack, if the sheriff tries to implicate you in this, I'm your witness."

Tires crunched in the new-fallen snow at the top of the boat ramp. It was Castner's cruiser. Jerzy wasn't with him. Probably off knocking boots with Foushée.

She felt Zack's knuckle-tap on her elbow. "I ain't the one your sheriff's after."

* * *

Grice waited for Delia near the end of the dock, his back to a river boiling with whirlpools. She had to step around the marine patrol deputies bending over the edges of the tarp, grunting to hoist Nastry out of their boat. They lowered his corpse onto the deck and the tarp went slack. Pea-size punctures dotted the kayaker's torso. Much of the shot had clustered, causing innards to spill out where his belly should have been. He'd been shot by a large-bore shotgun. Like the one she'd grabbed on to for a fleeting moment at Black Dog.

With a bare or gloved hand? She couldn't remember.

She stopped a healthy six feet back from the sheriff and a long eight from the end of the dock. Slowly, he faced her, turning her bagged Lew Horton Special over in his hand while shaking his head.

"Cha-vez, Cha-vez. Boy, am I going to enjoy watching you try and worm your way out of this."

She said nothing. No sense giving him more to work with.

"You say you shot somebody? I believe it." Once more, he held up the bagged revolver. "The burnt-carbon stink alone tells me this weapon's been fired." He was having a barrel of fun. "Betcha dollars to doughnuts, the medical examiner digs around in yonder corpse, he's gonna find a .44 Magnum or two amongst the shotgun pellets. But here's what I don't get. With you already on the cusp of dismissal, what in the Sam Hell were you thinking?"

She crossed her arms in front of her. "I used my weapon on an attacker. What shooting I did was in self-defense, and I have a carry permit—"

"That permit is hereby revoked. Did you bring along any other firearms?" He nodded toward the body lying in wait for the ME. "Maybe a shotgun you used afterward? To mask the real cause of death?"

Zack was right. Grice wanted to take away more than her job. She could only stall: a slight diversion before they discovered Tweety's ten-gauge.

"My only weapon was the Smith & Wesson," she continued, hoping to God she'd used her gloved hand on the ten-gauge. "We heard a shotgun before we reached Black Dog. Besides, Nastry's prints were found—"

"Oh, I'm counting on that shotgun," said Grice, leaning to his right and yelling at someone past her shoulder. "Take Lukovsky up and search that boat on his trailer. Move it." She craned her head in the direction he was yelling. Castner stood behind her, out of uniform and gawking at the mangled body.

"Will do, Sheriff."

Grice stepped in close to her. "Now, I'm parked on this crime scene until I sort out the mess you've made. So here's what you're going to do." He motioned toward the parking lot. "Get in your flaming white jalopy up there, drive it home, and confine yourself until further notice."

"What? Like house arrest? You can't do that."

He leaned in, his voice lowering to a breathy growl. "No, I can't. But you've given me a heap of probable cause, and I'd be only too happy to have Castner take you into custody"—a pause like a silent shoe dropping—"if you prefer that to the courtesy I'm extending here."

She was speechless. Shaking.

"I'll set Annie up to be your ankle bracelet."

She unfolded her arms and her rage. "So, it matters not one diddly fuck that somebody nearly split my skull open with an arrow? Tried to drown my ass?"

He glanced at his watch. "You have forty minutes to get home before Annie's check-in call."

"What do I do, skip having my ear sewed back together?"

His gaze brushed over the bandaged side of her head, as if she'd gotten pasted with a snowball instead of shot by a crossbow.

"Oh. Well. Annie's first call will go to the ER at Albany General. Clock starts then."

* * *

With Chavez gone and Nastry's body loaded into the EMT van for transport, Gus wasted no time talking the Linn County Marine Patrol deputies into another sweep of Black Dog Slough. They also agreed to run their searchlights a mile or so downriver along the brush lines where a second body might hang up. Assuming there was one.

Chavez was a giant pain in Gus's ass, but she'd been truthful, and he was desperate to find out whether she'd killed his cash cow. Bannock had been tight-mouthed about why his crew alone had to take Bastida. He'd made it crystal-clear that alive was the only way Gus would see more than the ninety thou he'd collected so far.

His Interceptor had barely started kicking out heat when the radio squawked.

"Sheriff, what's your ten-twenty?" It was Annie. He'd forgotten to call her about Chavez.

"I'm still at Albany. Hey Annie. Are you on the early or late shift?"

"Until twelve, but—"

"Okay, got a situation that might keep you over."

"First, tell me something, Sheriff. Are you expecting company? Like that naval officer from Virginia?"

Gus stared at the mic for a second. "Come again?"

"He stopped by. In a god-awful blood-red Hawaiian shirt and nylon flight jacket. Very military. Rugged-looking, except for the walking canes."

Shit. Shit and holy shit. "What'd he say?"

"Only that you're to call. He's still looking for a place to stay."

Stunned, Gus let the mic slip into his lap. His gaze shifted out of focus. He'd rather swim with cottonmouths than hand Bannock a big goose egg. Or inform him that Bastida might be dead—shot by one of Gus's own people. Maybe he could stall. Say that—

The radio clicked. "Sheriff, you still there?"

Gus lifted his mic hand. "Yeah, Annie. I'll get back to you. Out."

He rolled down and motioned Caster over to him. "Cut Lukovsky loose and park your butt down by that dock. See whether the Linn County patrol boat comes back with another body. If Chavez shot somebody else like she claims, we need to make sure it's not Bastida."

"Oh, ye-e-eah. About that." Castner tapped his forehead. "Uh, with all this shit goin' on, I forgot."

"Forgot what?"

"Happened an hour ago. Right after I got the message to scoot on up here."

"What happened?"

"Me and Matusik figured a way to narrow our search—target vectoring, he calls it. Had his boat pulled out of the water at Independence because—"

Gus slapped the outside of the door with his palm. "Get to the goddamn point."

"We spotted that snake-sided Zodiac. Big as life and haulin' ass downriver."

"Around Independence?"

Castner nodded, enjoying his moment. "Sheriff, I don't know where that Bastida character was coming from or where he was headed. But he sure as hell ain't dead."

Gus gazed out the windshield, blinking. Breathing easier. His cash cow was still milkable.

35

Big Juan had called while Delia was getting her ear sown back in place. She'd met him and swapped cars—him circling the loaner, making sure she hadn't marred his beloved lowrider, her following, thanking him for the free fix-up. If only he had a fix-up for Black Dog.

Twenty minutes later, she slid to a stop in her driveway under falling snow. Why was she still shaking? Not much had happened in the last twenty-four. She'd only taken a life, saved her own skin, and gotten put under house arrest. The kind only judges could impose. This kind, she'd ignore.

She fed the cat, picked up her gym bag and .380 caliber security blanket. Grice might have confiscated the S&W, but her Kel-Tec featherweight still packed a punch.

Five minutes later, she was on the road to Dallas, a bundle of nerves in need of a workout. The little automatic was tucked in the bag. Security checks were nonexistent at Golda's Gym.

Delia stuck to that plan until she reached the storefront gym. And rolled on past. She needed to work something out all right, but not at Golda's. Not if she was going to salvage everything she'd worked for.

Parking a discreet block away from the courthouse, she slipped in through the front doors and made her way downstairs to the sheriff's annex. The two joke-spewing, coffee-drinking deps on duty paid no attention as she light-footed past, reached Harvey's cubicle, and powered up his computer. Waiting, she checked her racing pulse.

With no second body supporting her hunch about the real killer, Grice was sure to try to pin Nastry's shooting on her. Talk about an adrenaline IV. Drip-drip, directly into her jugular.

To stay out of jail, she had to get ahead of the curve. Hell, catch up with it. Too many unknowns—about Tweety, about Bastida, the whole merry-go-round mess Grice had put her on. *So get to it, Chavez.*

She started at the Oregon State Marine Board website using what she had—a memorized boat number—and got an R. T. Bates of Salem, living on River Road South, followed by a series of numbers: 4487-12314. A map showed a rural road running along—she could've guessed—a Willamette River slough. Next, she ran his name through every law enforcement and clearinghouse database at her disposal. Nothing turned up on Tweety, not even a military service record. However, an R. T. Bates Sr. had served during the Vietnam War, distinguishing himself as a SEAL in the Brown Water Navy. She jotted down two questions: *Tweety Jr.?* and *Home sweet evidence dump?*

Time to move on.

As expected, Robert Bastida's name appeared in the FBI's NCIC fugitive warrant file and the U.S. marshal's wanted list. Oddly, he wasn't featured among their fifteen most wanted. She needed to talk to someone. Tapping in the number she found for the marshal at the Oregon district office, she got an actual person.

"Kelly Pearson? Delia Chavez. I'm at the Polk County Sheriff's office." Which she was. "I'm calling about a weeks-old fugitive warrant on a Robert Bastida—"

"Interesting."

"Why's that?"

"A week ago I received a 'be advised' update from my Utah counterpart, that Bastida is an alias, the last name co-opted from a Basque sheepherder who took him in as a youth. One Yuli Bastida who admitted under questioning to harboring this kid from an abusive adult. Said he thought the boy had run away from someplace along a river in the Willamette Valley."

Delia felt a tingle of anticipation at the back of her neck. "Real name?"

"Apparently Yuli had a sudden attack of hermit's amnesia. A few days later, he and his sheep wagon disappeared. High meadows in the Wasatch Range, they figure." There was a pensive silence before he continued. "I've searched Oregon records for a missing youth, but you'd probably have better sources . . ." His words hung in the silence.

"I'll look into it." She gave him an email address. "Send me what you have."

"Great. Check around twelve to fourteen years back." That tingling sensation spread into her scalp. "Oh, and by the way, a naval officer made the same inquiry two days ago. He's stationed in Little Creek, Virginia."

"Let me guess. A Commander John Bannock?" Annie had left a phone message saying Bannock had shown up looking for Grice.

"Close. This John Bannock's a lieutenant, JG. And . . . Detective Chavez, is it?"

"Yes." For now.

"Coordinate with us on this one. Whatever his real name is, Bastida wrecked a special-ops boat unit down in Colombia."

"Anyone killed?"

"No, but rumor has it he made off with millions in drug cartel money."

* * *

Delia keyed in the cold case unit's missing-persons file but got distracted by a hissing sound at the cubicle's opening.

"Chavez, what in God's name are you doing here?" Annie whispered, mixing in furtive glances. "Are you okay?"

"Saving my butt, and my ear hurts like a bitch. You've heard?"

"Hell yes," Annie answered, tapping a dispatch card against her thigh. "Grice wants me doing home checks on you every half hour."

"You know he's way off base." Delia got an immediate nod back. "For what it's worth, I shot someone who almost drowned me, and it wasn't Nastry."

"You must have a guardian angel," Annie said, handing Delia the card. "Call this number with your recorder on. I'll be upstairs with Harvey in the DA's office."

"So Barsch is willing to listen?"

"Maybe. Bring everything you have." Annie was off, heels clicking down the hall. Delia set up her call recorder app and dialed, barely able to sit still.

"Linn County Marine Patrol. Darren here."

"This is Delia Chavez."

"Oh, uh, yeah. I was there. How's your ear?"

"Pierced and painful. Darren, I'm recording our conversation to be able to play it back to our county DA, okay?"

"Fire away."

"First, did a second body turn up at or below Black Dog?" She was on the edge of her seat.

"No, but we dragged the slough and towed that guide's boat up to Bowman Park. Everything we found backs up your version of events." She closed her eyes and swallowed.

"Like?"

"A boat compartment full of scuba gear, a ten-gauge shotgun with the same double-ought loads that hit Nastry. Prints on the handle were too smudged to lift, though." Pent-up tension drained from her like sauce through a sieve. "Oh, and broken bottle glass at the stern that tested positive for a homemade napalm concoction."

She flashed on a Heineken bottle, still aflame and floating by in the slough. "Like maybe a Molotov misfire?"

"Yeah, now that you mention it."

The image of Nastry's body, facedown in the patrol boat, rippled back—the neoprene sleeve melted to his forearm. "The guy must've lit three and tossed one at the boat, had one shatter in his hand, then, so he could put out the fire on his wrist, dropped the one I saw float by later."

"I'd buy that."

"Anything else?"

"One item we grappled up, along with two rubber tires, an ancient fishing rod, and assorted junk, was a pistol-grip crossbow. One-fifty pound test. That what he shot you with?" His tongue clicked. "Man, if that'd hit you center mass . . ."

No reminder needed; she'd been there. Delia thanked him, rung off, and booked it for the DA's office.

*　*　*

Around seven that night, Delia skated and slipped over ice and snow toward Enrique's repaired Camaro, buoyed by renewed hope and purpose. One foot scooted out from under, nearly dumping her on her ass. She slowed, even as her mind raced over what had transpired in Barsh's office.

Harvey and Annie had primed the DA on Grice's "other than honorable" discharge from the Navy and the evidence of his getting blackmailed by a naval officer as well as accepting bribes. But sheriffs were nearly impossible to fire. The topper had been the events Delia outlined on Grice's misdirection of a murder investigation and the new information she'd received from Linn County regarding the shooting incident at Black Dog. Barsch set the wheels in motion for impeachment with the county circuit court judge, leaving his most electrifying move for last.

At Harvey's urging, the DA would explore a temporary appointment for her as district attorney investigator—a first for the county. She'd been left to rectify the troubling fly in the ointment—in Barsch legalese—the missing corpus delicti. Zack had said the river gave up its bodies. Could he help her find what was left of Tweety Bates?

Four inches of snow had turned slick, coating every streetlight, tree limb, and wet surface in sight. Even the shoveled sidewalk ahead shone with a polish of black ice. She baby-stepped down the walkway and around the corner to her recouped ride.

Enrique's Camaro sat in a pool of darkness, its windows crusted over. She unlocked and pulled at the handle, surprised she hadn't needed a hard yank to break an ice seal. Thank God for small things, too. She plopped herself in and cranked the engine, cueing up the Bob Marley disc Juan had left in her deck. With a shudder, she dialed on the heat. Her reward was a blast of icy cold, offset by sun-drenched rhythms. She switched from *floor* to *defrost* and waited for the engine to warm while Bob told her not to worry, not to hurry, and to take it easy.

When the windshield wipers finally opened a patch, Delia put the convertible in gear. The rear superwides spun on ice, then took hold. She maneuvered the overpowered vehicle to the center of the street, then out of town, rehearsing what she'd say on a phone call to Zack.

Not far past Dallas High School, a car approached from the opposite direction. The instant before it passed, she sensed movement behind her and darted a glance into the rearview mirror. Headlight glare lit the inside of her car as the hair on the back of her neck stood out.

In that fleeting glimpse, a pair of eyes stared back.

36

"What the . . . ?" Swallowing a pang of fear, Delia snapped a disbelieving glance over her shoulder, then straightened the car out before it jumped the curb. She'd glimpsed head and shoulders in silhouette. A big man, wearing a flat-brimmed hat. Bastida?

"How'd you get in my—"

"Keep driving." If he was the fugitive, his voice wasn't what she'd expected. Low and resonant. Familiar, yet not.

Don't panic, she coached, chancing a squint at her gym bag. Wishing to God she'd left it unzipped. The bag and the featherweight .380 inside disappeared over the back of the passenger seat. He'd read her mind.

Now panic. No, stall him. Slow down, aim for the ditch, and bail.

"Mister, you picked the wrong car to jack. I'm a law officer, a sheriff's detective." Nothing stirred behind. She eased off a little more on the gas and laid a hand on the door handle. "We're talking major crime here. A throw-the-key-away felony." Now wasn't the time to worry about exaggeration.

Lights flashed by, cars coming from the opposite direction. She heard the creak of coat leather. The door-lock button, clunking down next to her shoulder.

Those mirrored eyes tilted at an angle, then back toward horizontal. A shrug? "One prison or another. Get back up to speed and veer off onto the Dallas-Monmouth road. Like you're heading home."

Her heart boomeranged. He knew where she lived.

She pressed the gas pedal with a shaky foot. Had she been wrong about offing the real killer? Was it him? She swallowed against the dryness creeping down her throat and followed instructions.

"You're Bastida, right?" She decided to stay with the alias.

No answer.

Watching the speedometer needle climb past fifty, Delia slipped a hand between the seat and the driver's side door panel, and found what she needed. Grateful for Enrique's street-racing addiction, she drew the custom seat belt across her waist and timed its fastening with the skank chop of Marley's reggae guitar.

The Chevy glided over the snow-glaze on a sweeping curve and headed southward, into a three-mile straightaway. She was traveling down a dark country road bordered by flat fields with no deep ditches. Locked in with a potential killer who'd taken her weapon. That left one option.

Kill the hijacking son of a bitch.

In tiny increments, she increased pressure on the gas pedal, careful not to telegraph her speed by fishtailing. The Camaro ate up road. Until it was gobbling, she'd need to divert. "So, what's your deal?"

For a while the only male voice in the car was Marley's, wondering if there was a place for the hopeless sinner. Then—

"I almost said something to you on the river." His answer snuffed any remaining doubt over a prior encounter.

"About what?"

The needle crept toward seventy. Killing speed. She felt him shift position and lean forward between the bucket seats.

"Back off on the speed," he growled.

She complied, letting up on the accelerator. A tad seemed to satisfy.

"Now, keeping one hand on the wheel, I want you to reach up and take off the cross and hand it to me."

Delia glanced into the mirror. She had not a clue where this was going—murder, sex, or jewelry heist—but sensed opportunity. She removed the long silver chain, pulling it over the top of her head. Careful not to snag the tight links on her French braid, she flung the crucifix back and downward, extra hard. The car drifted into the left lane and she corrected with no letup on the accelerator. "It's just a family heirloom, not worth anything."

Leather scrunched as he sat back and felt for the crucifix. His hat disappeared below the mirror's line of sight.

Peering ahead, she sighted in on a set of railroad tracks flanked by crossing bars. Each bar was mounted on concrete supports. *Ease up your speed, Delia. Just enough punch.* Marley assured her "ev'ryting's gonna be all right." She cinched the belt tighter.

The railroad crossing on the near-side shoulder loomed in her headlights, its striped guard arm standing at vertical, the metal anchor base sticking up out of the snowy whiteness. She braced her forearms against the steering wheel. The lightweight car gouged into shoulder snow, fishtailing as she goosed the pedal. She adjusted and the big-block Chevy hurtled toward the obstruction.

Bastida flashed into view beside her, diving for the ignition, breaking her grip on the wheel. The engine died like a spent bullet, cutting Bob off at "don't worry." Momentum crushed her against the driver's side door as the rapidly decelerating car shuddered into a sideways skid. The Camaro crossed the road and hit the far signal with a sickening crunch.

Delia's first thought was of how pissed her brother was going to be after Big Juan refused another fix. Her second thought was to get the hell away from Bastida before he could peel his face off the dashboard. She pummeled his back and shoulder with her elbow, at the same time clawing for the belt release.

But he was strong, incredibly strong.

Like a shot he was behind her once more, wrapping an arm around her chest, pulling her into the seat back. Now the safety belt was a liability. She felt compacted, as if struggling inside a body-size Chinese finger cuff. She clawed at anything that resisted but dug into nothing substantial. He held on. She tried a backward head butt and missed, continued struggling until breathless, then gave up in frustration. Still he held on. She gasped for air, glaring at the newly crumpled hood. One headlight beam aimed skyward, the other explored the nearest ditch.

Long after she was quiet, Bastida kept her pinned against the seat back with that titanium arm lock. Seconds more passed. Then his fist appeared, inches in front of her face.

Entwined around his knuckles was a long, thin chain—hers—beside a darker cord. His?

Slowly, Bastida uncurled his fingers. In his palm rested a pair of crucifixes. From the glow of panel lights, each shone with the dull warm luster of Mexican silver. They looked identical. Same size, same unique design.

Delia shook her head. His restraining arm relaxed but stayed put across her breastbone. She snatched at his other arm and caught hold of his wrist. He let her rotate it one way, then the other. Dim light played over the religious pieces cupped in his hand.

Instead of Christ on a cross, Christ was the cross. His body melded into the wood, or in these likenesses, into the silver. The horizontal bars of each crucifix ended in elongated hands. Same for the feet at the bottom of the vertical shafts, the thorn-crowned heads as well.

She knew their contours by heart, having run small fingers over hers as a child, putting herself to sleep dreaming of how her family might have been. Her father's intricate design was not as original as it was striking in the warmth and love it expressed.

She flipped one of the crosses onto its backside. The panel lights revealed crude punch engravings, the imprints of her earliest memories. Okay, that one was hers. She steadied a trembling hand, turned over the other one and inhaled sharply.

"*Puta madre.*"

Both crosses had the same embedded initials. The breath of the man in her back seat whispered past her ear as he spoke.

"It seems we have something in common."

* * *

The red vacancy sign shorted on and off at the Setting Sun Motel, signaling its numbered days. Every few seconds, the ancient motor court was bathed in a cooked-lobster haze—a silent holler at Gus to drive away fast. A black Lincoln Navigator with Virginia plates was backed into a stall at the unit farthest down, the only one that looked occupied.

He stopped by the office and checked the register. That room was rented to a J. Smyth from Richmond, VA. It had to be Bannock. There were no other entries for that day.

No team? he wondered, wheeling his Interceptor toward the end unit.

Gus backed in beside the Navigator and got out. Flicked on his phone light and squinted into the SUV's tinted windows. Nothing but reflected light.

He'd just as soon have been somewhere else. Anywhere else. Like seeing his dentist for a root canal. He reset his belt and knocked.

"It's unlocked."

Gus turned the knob, gave the door a push, and peered in.

"Commander John Bannock?"

"Lieutenant, JG, now."

Gus couldn't help but stare. The man seated in a straight-backed chair beside an unmade vibrator bed seemed—at best—a factory reject of the hard-charging hooyah he'd steeled himself to confront. Bannock sat like he had to prop himself up, one foot planted on the floor, the other crooked around a chair leg. His face looked pinched in, as if he was in constant pain. A pair of hardwood canes hung off the chairback. Had the man been a friend, even an acquaintance, Gus would be asking what in the holy hell happened.

Annie was right about one thing. That Hawaiian shirt was almost beyond description. Birds of paradise detonating over a red tide came close.

"If you're Grice, don't stand there gaping."

Gus stepped inside a cavelike room with fake-paneled walls and a hanging lamp in one corner. A raised toilet seat yawned at him from the open bathroom. He stuck out his hand, aiming to set a friendly tone. "Good to finally meet you—uh—John."

Nothing doing. Bannock stared at the empty glass balanced on his right thigh.

Gus resisted feeling for the doorknob and tried a second time. "Sure was surprised when you—"

"Where's the Bastard?" Bannock's empty hand curled into a fist that he thumped against his thigh.

Gus eyed the toes of his boots. With no phone line buffer, that nickname for the fugitive seemed even more profane. At least he hadn't asked Gus for his money back.

"Trying to drown my people, when he's not killing hunters. The son of a bitch is a phantom. Always moving."

Bannock cocked him a sideways stare.

Sweat trickled down Gus's ribs. He flapped his hands in a lame gesture. "Got a full-time search crew on the Willamette as we speak. We'll find him. I guarantee."

Bannock huffed, held the water glass by its rim, and waggled it toward the far wall. "Pour me one. Neat. Find yourself a glass and park it."

Gus eyed the dresser top, where a decimated case of cheap Scotch vied for room with an ice bucket and an unzipped deployment bag. Still unsettled by the man's appearance, he poured Bannock a jolt and handed it over.

Gus's thirst overcame his confusion. He wiped the back of his hand across his mouth, wishing rum into that bottle. Brandy, even. "Got any coffee?"

No answer. Bannock's head was bowed low. Inspecting for dust bunnies? Silverfish?

Gus counted four empties on his way into the bathroom. A prescription bottle of Percocet sat on a sink fringed with mildew. He dumped a toothbrush out of the one available glass and rinsed it with hot water. Back at the dresser, he loaded in ice and eased Scotch around the cubes. Stalling, he glanced into the bag. The unmistakable retracted stock of a Heckler & Koch machine pistol peeked out from under a layer of clothing.

"Judas Priest, John." Feeling his hand tremble, he set the bottle down and turned around. "John, I don't know . . ."

Bannock's glass was bone-dry, as if he'd licked the bottom. His off-kilter gaze drifted up from the floor and targeted Gus. "You think I'm a sorry sack of shit, don't you?" That last came out sounding closer to *shorry shack a shit*.

Gus took a swig. The whiskey blend went down on an air bubble, hurting his throat. It left a taste in his mouth like a peat bog. He wished he could think of a quick way out and away from this loser—this still-dangerous loser.

Bannock went on. "You're thinking there's no team coming to help us extract the Bastard."

Gus sank onto the end of the bed, away from Bannock. Holding his glass between thumb and forefinger, he appraised the man—the black hair shot with white, the obvious damage to his nervous system, the canes, the Perc. Everything.

"Well, you're right. Grice. It's just me and you."

Gus swirled the amber liquid, waiting to see where Bannock's mind reading was headed.

"You're also thinking there's no way I can go after the Bastard, gimped up like this."

"Hafta admit, John . . ." Gus sat up, perched the glass on his knee, and gave a single headshake. "You, coming here alone? Being at a—a disadvantage?" He clucked his tongue. "Nowhere close to what I expected."

"Well, you're wrong. Grice. Dead wrong. Not when this gimp's got an equalizer."

Gus nodded toward the dresser. "The MP5? You'd need a helluva lot more than that little piss-sprayer. Not the way Bastida leaves bodies in his wake."

"Believe me, he can be stopped."

Gus started to get up. "Now about that, John. I just don't see—"

"*Sit your fat ass down.*" Bannock's free hand was at his side.

Gus noticed a bulge under that butt-ugly Hawaiian shirt and sat. Bannock was still Navy SEAL. Even injured, he'd clear his side arm before Gus could think about unsnapping.

He gave Gus a wave-off. "Relax, Grice. We'll come back to my equalizer. When I'm convinced you're still in." At least he'd gone back to using his inside voice. "One way or another, I'm here to collect. And you're going to help."

Gus drained his Scotch and set his glass on the floor. He might've defied the sit-down order and made for the door, but his paydar had started pinging when Bannock said *collect*.

"You owe me, Grice." The claw-hold Bannock took on the chair arm whitened his knuckles. "But the Bastard owes me more. More than you can imagine."

Gus leaned in. "Tell me, John—how much is more than I can imagine?"

37

Mutilated fenders rasped at the Camaro's radials when she turned too sharply. Delia straightened the wheel and goosed the car off Buena Vista Road, into the farm lane Bastida had pointed out. The snowy field ahead of them lightened the darkness by several shades.

Acres of unharvested corn shocks doubled over, bent from the fall wind and rainstorms. She feathered the clutch, fighting to keep the car crawling ahead as its wheels spun. The car's left beam floodlit a row of treetops, maybe lining a river bluff, while the shaft on the right dove between rows.

Bastida had refused to answer any questions. Just handed back the car keys and said, "Not here. To a place where my brain doesn't numb out."

They were barely a hundred yards up the lane when the Camaro stopped altogether. She pulled the emergency brake. His open palm appeared between the seats.

"Give me the keys and roll down the passenger window." She switched off, peering at the neglected crop as she plopped the keys in his hand.

"This is where you denumb your brain? In a fucking cornfield?"

He made a circling gesture toward the far door. She leaned over the center console and cranked on the handle. Heard the keys drop into her gym bag. Watched the bag fly out the window. He unlatched the door and moved up to the front seat.

She killed the headlights but kept the panels on, then folded her arms across her chest. "Getting cold in here."

He pulled the door shut, rolled up the window, and sat, staring ahead. She studied his profile.

Young, yet somehow older, the man seemed vulnerable, holding his chin so low it nearly rested on his chest. He wore the same boot-length leather coat she'd seen on the river. The hat allowed her to make out only that he was dark-skinned and angular, almost gaunt. His features were decidedly Latino.

"What happened to your ear?" he asked.

Her hand touched gauze. He didn't know. Off the hook? Or could he be one of two—a serial tag team?

"Had a close shave."

He rubbed at his knees in a fury, as if he were trying to spark them into campfires. "I think you know something about me."

"I know the Navy wants Robert Bastida in a brig. I know my boss thinks Robert Bastida is a dangerous fugitive and a serial killer. Which reminds me, uh"– in her what're-you-thinking flash, *dumbest idea ever* lost out to *go for it*—"if you have a knife, I want to see it."

His hat tilted.

"Just show me, then put it back." Her self-hug tightened as her fingers dug in. Protecting what, stabs to her elbows?

For two seconds at most, a fixed-blade knife appeared against the dash lights, then disappeared. Heavy handle. Wicked cutting surfaces—but no serrations. She let up her grip, lowering her hand into her lap. Still . . .

"My hunch? Robert Bastida is someone else. So, who are you?"

He removed the hat and set it on the console between them. Turning, he looked directly at her. "Who do you think I am?"

His gaze stopped her heart. She felt as if she were viewing an old tintype. Distant ancestor? Possibly. From eyes hard as bullets, the features of Emiliano Zapata stared back. All he needed to complete the picture was a mustache and bandoliers across his chest.

J. S. James

One of her relatives had claimed to be a great-grandniece of the famous Mexican patriot. Entranced, her eyes mined for similarities in the face of this disturbed man.

Bastida's hand dove into his coat, and she flinched. Instead of a potential murder weapon, he brought out the two crucifixes, leather cord and silver chain in a tight wad. He untangled and spread them around the brim of his hat. Bastida's gaze met hers in the sparse light. His eyes seemed larger, softer than before. Starved looking.

She buried a fist inside her palm and squeezed. Couldn't be him, could it? Words came on a quiver of fear.

"Your—the other crucifix. Where did you get it?"

His hands tightened over his kneecaps. His silence was agonizing. He looked around the interior, then out at the big moon breaking from a thinning overcast. "Can't say. Had it from way back."

She studied what she could make of his face, then heaved a ragged sigh. He showed no sign of deceit. No *found it on a riverbank* or *bought it at a pawnshop*. Or worse, *took it off a dead boy's body*. But he was holding back.

Once more, his Zapata gaze captured hers. "You have no idea how lucky it is to know who you are."

She swallowed and sat back, her doubts crumbling like the dried mud pies of her dreams. "But you don't? Is that the point of abducting me?"

"The whole point." He leaned over and picked up his cross and held it out in the moon's fullness. "This was how we'd get away from the poacher for a while."

"Who?" she said, baffled.

He jabbed at his temple. "Me, I meant. In here, where my made-up family lives." Then he shook the dangling cross in the space between them. "It was my . . . my house key. Now it rates a boatload of answers."

Her body thrummed with anticipation.

He laid the cross with the cord back on his hat brim. Aligning hers with his, he flipped both onto their backsides and stroked the matching pairs of engraved letters, three sets on each crucifix.

264

"I figure *D.C.* for you."

Trembling, she flexed her hands, curled them up tight, and managed to get off a nod.

He fingered her crucifix, the pad of his thumb pressing on her initials—introduction by way of touch. Then he slid his thumb downward, exposing the next set.

"Who is *E.C.*?"

Delia felt a jagged lump form in her throat but couldn't swallow. Her answer came out a series of croaks. "Enrique. Enrique Chavez. Our—an older brother."

There it was, kinship nearly implied. Tears welled in her eyes. For a while, he just looked at her, his eyes glistening in the naked moonlight. Imploring eyes, the eyes of her family? Her ancestors?

"And *R.C.*?"

The tears ran as her chin quivered with near certainty. "Rob—" Again, the ache in her throat choked off her answer.

He filled in. "Robb? Robbie?"

She swallowed on the hurt and shook her head. "Roberto. Roberto Chavez. The little brother I—I lost on the river." Sobbing shudders racked her body. Her rib cage felt like it had caved in on her spine, breaking up the clots of grief and guilt she had borne inside. In a matter of seconds, the long-gone brother, buried in her heart for all those years, was laid bare.

Tentative fingers touched the backs of her hands, slid over her closed fists, and wrapped them in warmth.

Time passed and the wash of emotion ebbed. Hands withdrew and he retreated to his side of the car. Bending forward, he retrieved a wad of paper napkins from the floor and handed it to her. She took the clump and blew her nose.

"Huh. Roberto." He turned the cross over in the light. "I go by Robb, so it could be—"

"I sure hope so." She said, dabbing her eyes and stuffing the soaked ball of paper in the ashtray. "Papa was a silversmith down in La Paz. He made the three crosses for his children."

"Three?"

She nodded. "Enrique has the other. He's in . . . away for a while. Mama had them consecrated at baptisms." Delia leaned toward him. "Both parents, Carlos and Maria Chavez, are gone. Farm truck accident."

At field's edge, an ice-laden branch broke loose, bouncing off several lower tree limbs on its way to the ground. Snow crystals rained down long after it had landed.

"Do you remember anything? You know, when you were little?"

He shrugged. "Nothing much. Things I'd hear at night. After the bad—"

"Things?"

"Fuzzy. Like I'm hearing it from someone else. From a boat." He reeled off a list as if memorized. "It's smoky all around the boat. Somebody's calling a name. Not mine, but . . ."

Her throat tightened. The name of her dreams—the family endearment she'd screamed across the river toward a boat with a green motor and golden dragons on its sides—was painful to hear in her sleep. Torture to say out loud.

"Tío? Bebé Tío?"

His face took on a tortured look. His head dropped back against the seat rest. He stared out the window, then up at the soft top of the convertible. Anywhere but at her.

When he turned back, his gaze reached past her, eyes vacant. Then he huffed. "Baby uncle?"

Her misgivings in a rout, Delia laughed and laid her hand on his sleeve. "Because Tío was so bright. Could barely talk, but already Papa said he was clever, like a little old man."

The moon shone down from the top of its arc, a disk of burnished nickel.

"I was Dee-Dee. Sound right?"

Hesitating. Giving the barest of nods, he folded her cross and chain into her hand, draped the other over his neck, and drew the hat onto his lap. "How did it happen? To—you know, back when he was . . . little?"

Delia told Robb how Tío/Roberto had been stolen while she looked after him by the river, of the smoking outboard, the man with a brown hat, a yellow-toothed grin, and a clenched pipe—the details kept alive in her nightmares. She told of the failed bridge that took their parents. Nothing about Enrique's absence, but how her older brother had put her though school in the law enforcement program, skipping past the funds coming from stolen-car proceeds. She left out her uncertain status on the outside chance she might persuade Robb to come in. Face whatever he had done.

"How old was . . . Roberto?" he said.

"Two."

"How old were you?"

"Five."

"Then why blame yourself?"

"I don't—" She sat up with a jerk and stared at him. Yeah, as if she hadn't asked herself that a million times, on each one burying the answer deeper. Who else?

At the time, no one had blamed her, but she felt blamed. When Mama and Papa were killed, there had been no one to stop the guilt from coming back as something else. Something not to be trusted.

"It's complicated."

"It's simple. You were a small child. Unpack it from there."

Delia noticed she'd taken one of his hands inside hers. "Maybe you're right, on some of it. Thank you for that." She squeezed, let go, and put her back against the door. "Your turn."

*　*　*

Delia got back only silence from Robb's side of the Camaro.

They traded nervous glances, her patience draining. After what she'd just suffered through, he damn well owed her an explanation.

"Robb, I'll ask you straight out. Have you killed anyone on the river?"

"No. Pretty much rescued the ones who got in my way. You two. A few hunters."

"There's got to be a reason why the sheriff is determined to find you. Your fugitive warrant says—"

"Let me guess. Among other things, that I made off with Colombian drug money."

She looked at him. "How much?"

"Quite a lot. Thirty or so stuffed toy animals' worth. That's how I made the transport."

"How much in, say, a giraffe?"

"Average? Twelve pounds of stuffing, so five hundred and thirty each."

"Thousand? That's . . . ay-ay-ay! Fifteen, sixteen million?"

"A week's haul down there. You want it? Takes up space all tucked away."

Delia had to let that sit. Wrap her head around the implications. She moved on. "Robb, you said something about a poacher."

From him, a snort. She was making progress.

He banged his door open, lurched out, and disappeared.

"Shit. Double shit." Delia shoved at her door and scrambled out in a panic. A bent cornstalk snagged her ankle just as the other foot slipped and dumped her on her tail. Grabbing the Camaro's side mirror, she levered herself up and scanned the field they'd parked in. First back toward the road, then up the slope. The blanket of snow amplified the tired light from a moon in retreat.

She blew out a puff of relief. Robb stood in the farm lane fifty feet ahead of the car with his feet spread and his back to her, the hat beating against his hip. His attention seemed glued on something seventy yards uphill, where the cornfield ended at a tall band of evergreens.

Gaining her snow legs, Delia shuffled uphill and stopped beside him, close enough to realize he wasn't idly staring into the night. If looks could chop down trees, the power of his gaze would turn that stand of Douglas fir into firewood—cut, split, and stacked.

"Do you believe in the devil? In demons?" His tone was hushed, as if ears of unpicked corn might overhear.

She cocked a grin. "Horns on head, pointy tail?"

The thigh-drumming hat paused. He was dead serious.

She shrugged. "I believe in God. Satan, not so much." She stepped out and faced him. "Robb, where's this headed?"

"Better see for yourself." He clapped the hat on and shot his wrist out, checking a black watch with a luminous dial. The kind people dropped several large on. "About time for them to move out."

"Them—who?"

"The poacher. His hog-heavy boy." He sidestepped her and set off up the farm lane in long strides.

She zipped the top of her sweat suit to her chin and followed him up the hill.

*   *   *

Seated less than three feet away at the end of a motel bed smelling of something rancid, Gus felt the contempt in the man's smirk, like actual heat.

"Thought that would get your attention." Bannock slumped back in his chair with a grimace. "Now that I sense your undying loyalty, and before I make an offer you will not refuse, there are things you need to know."

"Okay, shoot." Gus wished he could've taken that back. He eyed his glass on the floor, bent, and picked it up. "How's about I pour a couple stiff ones while you fill me in on your offer?"

Before Bannock could tell him to sit again, Gus had scooted across the room, poured and downed rotgut Scotch like it was premium rum.

"Seven, eight million. Give or take. That's half of what Bastida owes me."

Booze entered the wrong pipe. Gus managed to choke out "Dollars?" as he bent over in a coughing fit.

"Yeah, dollars. The Cartel del Norte was flying out its weekly take to a don't-ask-don't-tell bank."

Gus beckoned to hear more while pounding his chest.

"The Bastard took one of our unit's SOC-Rs and made off for Manaus with a boatload of cartel cash. Fifteen million or more, all in hundreds."

Gus recovered enough to spit out a few words. "Fifteen total? Wait. Back up. Sock what?"

"Special Operations Craft–Riverine. That was after he'd scattered the drug runners, disabled their plane, and ruined the coke shipment. Opened up on those bales with our boat-mounted minigun. When we caught up later, that riverside airstrip looked like it'd snowed in the jungle and stuck."

"Jesus. Where were you when all this went down?"

Bannock's jaw muscles rippled as he spit words through his teeth. "In the Rio Negro, half paralyzed, half drowned."

"Whoa, John. How the devil did he get away with it?"

"Somehow the Bastard caught on to the deal I'd cooked up with Buck Metcalf, our DEA liaison. He had a line on this exchange meet—date, time, and GPS coordinates. My plan with Metcalf was to skip out in the SOC-Rs and bust up their little party." Bannock looked around the dank room, his eyes glazed over. "That cartel money was our platinum retirement card." He tapped on one temple. "In my head I already had a fifty-three-foot Ferretti paid for, delivered, and docked at a villa in Cinque Terre."

Gus leaned his backside against the edge of the dresser, thought about sitting down. Better to keep his distance. "What about your operatives?"

"We'd inserted the unit for a raid on a village of FARC paramilitaries that had river punts. Slow, but the teams could use them to make it back to base camp. Once they figured out Metcalf and me had bailed." Bannock cleared his throat. "Would've worked, too, except the Bastard deserted his group and doubled back to our boats. Swam out and caught us napping, right before we were set to take off. Might've winged him, though."

Gus shook his head. "Damned lucky he didn't kill you."

"Yeah, lucky." Bannock pummeled the thigh muscles in his bad leg, like he was trying to pound sensation back into it. "Only way I'd have been luckier was if he'd rammed the point instead of the hilt of that fixed blade up under my skull."

He was silent for a long while more, rubbing at the leg. "I came to in the water. By then, the Bastard was a half mile downstream. Metcalf was under his overturned boat, screaming about piranhas finding his sorry ass."

"Where's Metcalf now?"

Bannock shifted in his chair and reached up behind his head. "Out of the picture. Demoted to some backwater assignment in Southeast Asia." He brought the canes around and laid them across his knees. "You get Metcalf's cut."

Gus wet his lips. "So mine's seven-five?"

"Close to. Half of what we recover. The Bastard couldn't have spent much of that fifteen mil, and there's no bank traces—in or outside the country. He's got to have it close by.

"But here's something that'll get us closer. The Bastard's name is not Bastida. The Utah relative he'd listed in his induction papers was a Basque rancher who needed the ultimate convincing to give him up. But that's another story." He handed over a piece of paper with squiggly lettering, as if written under duress. "That sheep rancher took him in after he'd run off from a family here in Oregon. Ring any bells?"

"No." Maybe. Something back in his mind's murky recesses clicked about Chavez—a case that had sold Harvey Schenkel on her detecting prowess. Gus sat up. "Not sure. Have to review my files."

The man's eyes blazed, watching Gus like he'd lasered in with a truth scanner. As if a decision were made, Bannock aligned the canes on either side and hoisted himself onto his feet. "C'mon outside. I got a real eye-popper in the back of that Navigator."

Gus set down his glass but stayed put at the dresser. "Whoa up a minute." He waited for Bannock to shuffle around and face him. "I just can't help but feel like we're fixing to rope a longhorn with dental floss. Any other police action, this is where we call in SWAT"—Gus already had his palms up, cutting Bannock off midsnarl—"which, for obvious reasons, we cannot do. But no matter how that kind of money might tickle my testicles, I won't commit suicide."

Bannock explored the ceiling, then dropped his stare back on Gus. "Well, shit. Me neither. Now will you just shut up and let me show you my goddamned equalizer, you dumb son of a bitch?"

38

Delia had nearly caught up when Robb disappeared into the evergreens. She parted the outer boughs and peered in. Faint moonlight shone back from the opposite side, where the evenly spaced tree trunks ended and the hill dropped off into nothing. The narrow grove was less than forty feet across, but Robb was nowhere in sight. Whatever he wanted her to see had to be on the other side. She ducked into the trees.

Coming out at a low bluff, she gazed down on a carpet of whiteness. A stream of fog skimmed the surface of the Willamette, crowding between its banks. Tendrils crept into the upper fields, only to be sucked back into the ferment. She felt but a slight queasiness, mildly clammy skin. The river beneath never let go of anything without a struggle. Not even fog.

She followed a faint trail heading west along the bluff. The trees thinned at the corner of the field where a fence ended and the drop-off was steepest. She found Robb crouched beside an abandoned piece of farm equipment—a honey wagon, judging by the coating of dried cow dung. A rear wheel hung free where the cliffside had fallen away.

He motioned for her to take cover beside him, then pointed toward the middle of the river, where a break in the pall of whiteness bared a dark patch of current. "Now do you believe?"

The fog swirled under the moon's pasty light. The gap below them closed in on itself, void of anything but river and mist-laden air.

"In what?"

He cocked an ear toward the south, listening. "Hear that old Elgin? They're headed upriver, trying to draw me away again."

Except for his whisperings, the night was as still as the Willamette was empty.

He got to his feet. She got up as well, wondering just how head-sick her maybe brother was. She wondered, too, where she'd heard or seen that name. Elgin. Not the wristwatch, something else . . .

His back was to her. She eased past his shoulder and stood facing him. "Robb, help me understand. What in the holy hell are we doing here?"

He plucked at his lip. "Sometimes they come straight at me. Other times, they play head games. Like tonight."

Quietly but firmly, she led into it. "You've been in combat, right?"

"All my life."

"No, I mean in a war. In firefights."

He gazed past her, filling his coat pockets with his hands. "Iraq." After a beat, "Somalia." A long breath. "Couple snatch-and-grabs in Central America. Antidrug actions farther south."

She pointed toward the river and whatever he thought he'd seen. "Flash back on it much? Have anything against hunters?"

"Not like you're thinking. Nothing against hunters, so long as they steer clear of the poacher and his boy."

He stepped over the wagon tongue and gestured for her to follow him to the edge. She did. Had to find out whether he could be salvaged.

Stopping feet short of the drop-off, he leaned his backside against a fence post. She came up beside him. His hat was at his side again, tapping.

"Okay, sure. Been in beaucoups ops where it was balls to the wall and check your skivvies later." He gave a dismissive shrug. "All walks in the park."

"How so?" His attention was locked in on something out beyond them.

"None came close to the hellhole I swam out of right over there."

She traced his gaze across the river, to a stretch of woods where branch tops stuck up from the mist like finger bones. Made out the crumbling roofline of an old house. An uneasy feeling latched on— she was looking down through a time gap. The high-water stone foundation that held up a sagging porch. The paint-bare walls and shot-out windows. The hundred-year willow, its roots littered with broken target bottles. They were standing above the mouth of the Luckiamute, directly across from the Gatlin place.

He toed a rock loose from the field's icy crust and nudged it toward the edge. "That ramshackle excuse for a house makes you think you could waltz right in there. Like Rose could just slip away from the poacher anytime she pleases. Well, you'd be wrong. It's a devil's keep, and—"

Delia stopped his toe with the tip of her Reebok. "Wait. Rose?" He canted his head at her, and she drew her foot back. "So, the man you think lives down in that house, the man you believe uses the river to poach animals—"

"The poacher takes souls."

Moonlight reflected off the snow, magnifying the tension in his jawline. "Willard skins the spirit right out of you. Tacks it to his shed like an animal pelt."

Beneath her workout clothing, a shiver of understanding rippled over her chilled skin. Rose hadn't been the only one who'd suffered from Willard Gatlin's abuse.

"The poacher, him and his boy. When we were too young to fight them off."

"We? You were a Gatlin?"

"Not by choice."

A kick from Robb's boot sent the stone flying off into the darkness. "Soon he'll have all of Rose's soul. I have to get her out of that hellhole."

Delia had the feeling Robb was circling a drain and out of her reach. She hooked a finger inside his coat sleeve and tugged. "No, Robb. You don't."

Latching on to his arm, she spun him toward her, then drew her hand back. There was no easy way except straight out.

"I'm sorry, Rose Gatlin is—is gone." She touched his arm again, more hesitantly. "She's—deceased, I mean. So is Willard. Jess, too."

He was a standing stone.

She swallowed and went on. "Robb, I can show you the grave sites. They're at Buena Vista Cemetery."

Gray light streaked the sky above them. Dawn was a while off. She had no idea whether she was making headway.

Jamming on his hat, Robb reached into his coat, his head shaking like a frond in the wind. Not a good sign.

"No. No, Rose wrote to me." A finger-worn picture postcard appeared. He waved the card in front of her face, then tucked it away. "The poacher made her write, but I know she would never—"

Delia grabbed up his hands, putting urgency into her voice. "Listen to me. You've been chasing ghosts. Willard and Rose shot each other over a note. I was the investigator. I saw the holes she put in Willard Gatlin's belly trying to save herself. Believe me, your poacher is so dead, Jesus would pass him over for Lazarus."

He shook his head again, hands dropping away from hers. "Lazarus rose from the dead. I've seen lights down there, stove fires. Hell, Willard and Jess ambushed me. Knew I was coming from the river and bookended my approach with automatic-weapons fire."

He swept an arm back toward the Willamette. "Since then, I've tried to catch them away from the house. Out on the river where they're vulnerable. But they're chameleons. I close in and they disappear into a slough or up a backchannel. Sometimes into their own smoke."

She cocked her head, arms across her chest, fending off the chill. "How long have you been at this?"

"Dunno, weeks. Boat snares haven't slowed them one bit." He rubbed at his thighs. "I coast along, listening for that Elgin. I close in on their boat till the fog eats them. Grit my teeth when they laugh and start over." He stopped rubbing. "Almost knocked me out of it the night you and your jet boat got on my tail. Now that was kick-ass."

Jesus. She shivered, tightening her grip on her elbows. He sounded like somebody out of that Bill Murray movie. Instead of a time loop, Robb was stuck chasing phantoms, over and over again.

She reached out and drew him close, made him look her in the eyes. "Robb—Tío—I'm your big sister, I think. So I get to say stuff nobody else can, right?" She didn't let him object. "First off, your eyes and your mind play tricks on you. The Willamette is just a river"—God, that came from her?—"The Elgin motor is a rusted-out hulk, and that hovel down there is just a wrecked empty house with a nasty past."

She waited, letting it sink in.

He peered down at the fogbound structure, kneading at the back of his neck for a full minute. He stopped rubbing. "But the lights, the suppression fire. The holes I patched in my boat."

Ha! Took off like a bat anyway, so we didn't— Lonnie. The comeback Bryce had stifled in his twin brother swam up out of Delia's memory. Right place, wrong time.

"Some young guys partied there on weekends. Used that old willow tree for target practice, until I confiscated their toys."

Robb's hand fell away from his neck. "AR-15s?"

She nodded. "You must've been in the vicinity when those idiots cut loose with ARs converted to full auto."

The fog had begun to thin. Early light cut into the gloom and blur of current gliding past the house. She set aside old aversions and imagined herself on that tributary. Looked through Robb's eyes. Down at the water, picturing him on the receiving end.

She voiced her acceptance aloud, as much for herself as for him. "To someone in a boat, moving into the Luckiamute at the wrong moment, it would look, feel, and sound like he'd entered a kill zone. Robb, you're walking wounded. You need to come in and get help. My help, for starters . . ."

Feeling his absence like a stolen breath, Delia spun on her heels. She made out his backside disappearing over the slope of the cornfield and called out. "Robb, Tío. Wait up. Where are you going?

"To shut the lid on hell."

Chingada. "Get your ass back here. You're still under arrest."

Seconds later, she barely heard his shouted reply over the rumbles of twin outboards coming to life.

"Save me a cell."

* * *

"Don't get mad," Gus's mama used to say. "Wait'll the turd sack's takin' a nap and stuff a rattlesnake in his boot."

Still, his gut churned as he drove off from the motel, and not from a bellyful of bad Scotch. He'd looked over Bannock's special ordnance, bitten his tongue, and formed a backup plan.

Dumb son of a bitch, huh? Like the fox that finds a hole in a henhouse and has the patience to wait till dark.

Water Street butted into the Dallas-Coast highway, the pavement shiny in his headlights. Wet snow had frozen, glazed the roadways, and coated the fields in a white crust. He ignored the icy conditions and kicked the Interceptor in the ass. His heart thumped with fear and excitement. What he could do with fifteen million bucks.

Let Bannock take his revenge on Bastida. Gus'd take the rest. Along with a little rattlesnake revenge of his own.

Bannock placed a high value on good intel. If Bastida was who Gus thought he might be and had gone to ground in the old homestead, it would be suicide going in blind. Chavez's closed-case file would give him the name and the property's location, but not its current status. Was it occupied or vacant? Sold or left to go to seed? How about road access? Surprising how much Gus could learn from the county assessor's office. The rest of the time he'd use to make other arrangements.

"You in your car, Sheriff?" That was Castner on Gus's PMR, his private mode radio frequency. Just the boy he needed.

"Craig. You still at Bowman Park?"

"Yeah. Can I leave now? Linn County Marine pulled their boat out hours ago."

"What'd they find?"

"No body recovery. I mean, besides that gut-shot kayaker they brought in earlier. But the boat blind some duck hunter left out there? Everything in it matched up with Chavez's account. No clear prints on the ten-gauge, either." A sour feeling started in the pit of Gus's stomach. "Oh, yeah. And they grappled up a ton of weird shit off the bottom of Black Dog, including a nasty-looking pistol-grip crossbow."

The sourness started to burn. "That screws the pooch."

"What?"

"Never mind." Those findings alone meant Chavez was right about somebody attacking her. Sooner or later, another body would turn up and corroborate her story. He peeled off an antacid tablet and thumbed it into his mouth. The good thing was that Bastida, or whatever he went by, was still alive and kicking. That much he'd known. He crunched the chalky wafer in two and chewed.

So what if that stubborn bitch got reinstated? Ole Gus'd be long gone. Entertaining Playa Venao señoritas at Casa del Grice.

"Sheriff?"

"Uh, yeah. You tell anybody at our shop?"

"About what?"

"Good. Keep it that way."

"Uh, will do, Sheriff. So am I done here? Man, I gotta get some pub grub in me. A beer or three."

"Okay, you do that, Craig. But then we need to meet up. By the way, when's the last time you sighted in that scoped deer rifle?"

"Three weeks back, and it's dead on. Got a four-point in the freezer to prove it. Why?"

"Think you could pull down on a two-legged buck?"

39

Delia had gained early-morning access to the case file storage area, for once thankful the sheriff had neglected his duty, as her office keys remained unconfiscated. Not hearing from the DA about a possible end-run appointment, she'd literally tiptoed past the squad room, down a darkened hallway, and now back to Harvey's cubicle, where she laid out the contents of the Gatlin folder.

She had to do something, anything to get her mind off the craziest twenty-four ever. Too wired to sleep, too conflicted to tell anyone about her encounter with a desperado who might be her long-lost brother, she decided to focus on getting herself up to speed.

After waking Harvey's computer, she made several Google searches based on last June's partial message from Rose Gatlin and background notes printed and filed from Castner's Toughbook. They confirmed that Robb had reason to fear and resent Willard, as had Rose. There was a Robbie, but no other record of his existence. An older boy, Jess Gatlin, had been expelled from school after a bullying incident in junior high. He'd followed in his dad's wild game–poaching footsteps, the citations halting just before a river-drowning report on him. It was left for Robb to clarify—if Delia ever saw him again.

Dead-ended, she sat back, succumbing to the nagging concern that Robb might somehow be linked to the river killings. Was his story plausible? Shaky at best. Did she believe him? She wanted to. Could there have been two . . . ?

She sat up, lifted the file, and snatched from underneath the notes she'd made the night before on Tweety Bates. Ran her finger down the notations and stopped at *Evidence dump?* In particular, the street address notation. Well, a road name followed by some numbers. She fed both into Google, trying several variations. She kept getting map sites and noticed a Halls Ferry Cemetery with no address. At another site, she got a pull-down with the heading "Coordinates." She clicked it and nearly slid off the front of her chair. It gave her 44.8733 N, 123.1439 W, just a smidgeon off the numbers Tweety Bates had listed on his boat registration. That smidgeon seemed to place his location a few points north of the cemetery. Exactly where light reflected off a dull metal-roofed object in the sat-map close-up.

And smack in the middle of an unnamed Willamette River backwater.

*   *   *

Delia's third call got through to Zack as she pulled the Camaro away from the curb and aimed it toward Independence, Oregon. Except his half of the conversation kept getting interrupted by rattles and burps from an unhealthy-sounding outboard motor.

"What?" He must have throttled down, because the background noise dropped to a hiccupping burble. She started in again.

"I said, where are you?"

"Middle of the river, running the carbon out of my Johnson." Delia almost snickered. He meant the boat motor. She kept cop-silent while he clarified. "Had two gummed up sparkplugs from a bad gas-oil mix. You holding up okay?"

"Been better. Doing better." The sickly sound of that idling motor gave her pause as she shouldered the phone to her ear while tugging on the single glove she had left and reminded herself how much was riding on her Google find. "Zack, I need your help to check out something. Can you meet me at Riverview Park?"

"I can make it there in twenty. Seeya."

Nearly an hour later, Delia stood at the top of the Riverview launch area, watching two boats in a line crawl upriver toward the park. The smaller one, getting the tow, was Zack's. The boat doing the towing? *Jackie.* She wanted to climb back into the Camaro with the re-crunched fenders and wonky headlights and rumble out of there. But Harvey was on his way with a search warrant and a new badge.

Barsch had temporarily appointed her the county's first DA detective. It amazed her how an outflow of tension, paired with an influx of relief, had lifted her spirits into the ozone. The last thing she wanted was to have Jerzy Matusik bring her crashing down again.

Twenty feet from shore, Zack loosed the towrope and steered his coasting Jon boat into the bank mud, while *Jackie* glided up against the dock.

Delia turned and hustled away, but Zack caught up and stopped her by the Camaro.

"Sorry, Detective." He motioned down toward his boat. "My Johnson's kaput." She felt not even the slightest urge to smile. "Matusik, down there, came along, and we found out we had a lot in common. I have to trailer my boat, but he's ready to help you out."

"I'll just bet."

Zack looked at her funny, then clomped off toward his parked truck and trailer. She heard footsteps coming from behind. Matusik.

"Delia, are you all right? Annie told me about what happened at Black Dog. I called and stopped by but couldn't reach you. Sounds like you had a super-scary time upriver."

There was nothing to be said. She kept her back to him and focused on Zack, backing his truck and trailer down into the water. Her cell phone rang. It was Annie. Matusik's footsteps faded as he wandered off and started rummaging in his Hummer.

Annie wasted no time. "Got a status update: Grice filled out a personal-leave form and Castner took his annual day. Neither one can be reached."

"So who's in charge?"

"Up in the air for the moment. Waiting on the judge's warrant, Harvey handled the patrol schedules and sent a deputy to Grice's condo. The place was dark."

"All right. Keep us posted." Delia rung off just as Zack's Apache rolled up beside her with his boat loaded on its trailer. He leaned out the open window.

"Sorry I couldn't find the body for you, Detective. Been at it for hours. Even welded up my own grapple. In case I might need to snag that sumbitch's worthless hide and drag it back to shore."

"I'm grateful for all you've done, Zack"—now wasn't the time for a lesson in body-handling procedure or evidence preservation—"but I'm hoping we can clear up what happened at Black Dog when I locate Tweety Bates's houseboat, or wherever he lived."

"I still want to help . . . be in on whatever you come up with."

"Hey, Delia, I found your other glove." Matusik was back. The anger heat rose inside, but she stayed focused.

"We'll see when the time comes, Zack." She slapped the cab frame once, harder than just a send-off tap, and strode off toward—of all directions—the dock, where Beezer sat patiently on guard in the captain's chair of Matusik's tethered boat.

Sounds of some sort of food ordering and money exchange reached her ears. She barely heard Matusik murmur, "Take lotsa time, okay?" Driving off, the Apache's dual glasspacks soaked the air with throaty harmonics.

* * *

A high-pitched whistle brought Beezer leaping out of *Jackie*. Instead of bounding up toward his master, the dog made a beeline for Delia. She crouched down, lavished hugs on the traitor, then continued to the far end of the launch dock. The river was threatening as ever, but she had a statement to make. Even if unspoken, and unlike others, she stuck with her commitments.

Beezer had followed, lugging a stick along that he dropped at her feet. The retriever sat beside her and panted, looking up expectantly.

She ignored his offering. Just stood on that concrete pontoon with her back to dry land, gazing out over the expanse of liquid coldness.

By choice.

Not a small thing—commitments. Big. Like giving yourself to someone who moves on as if it never happened. What she couldn't get past was the betrayal of her intuition—a deep-down feeling Jerzy Matusik was better than that.

She sensed him behind her. To keep from turning and lashing out, she bent and stroked Beezer's ear.

Matusik cleared his throat.

"Your ear doing better?"

No, Chavez. Don't do it.

"I heard yesterday was one hell of a day for you."

She jammed her hands into her coat pockets and said nothing.

"It's great to see you here. Anywhere. Out and about, I mean." She turned slightly and shot him a look superheroes used to melt stone.

He gestured toward her midsection. "I see you're carrying. Does that mean you're reinstated?"

She turned away. "Temporary reprieve." She said that in a voice meant to hang icicles off every syllable.

Beezer whined in the silence, nudging her knee with his big wet nose.

"Hey, Delia. I'm damned sorry for leaving you in the lurch. I should've—"

That's it. She wheeled on him, twisting her lips into a snarl. "Been dancing lately?"

His mouth shut, his Adam's apple rode up and down. "What?"

She pulled her fists out of her pockets, one gloved, one not. "Or did you and Chelsea just skip to knocking boots in your Hummer?"

That jerked his head back. "Foushée? How do you know Chelsea?"

"Mainly by the sight of her pink-thonged butt cheeks poking up between your knees."

Jerzy frowned, his hand running through his hair. "Oh hell. You saw me walk her out of the Two-Step?"

That glimpsed sight again radiated pain behind her eyes, a searing ache in her throat. "We had a . . . a start," she said. "For you, a one-nighter. For me, a really big deal." She glanced away, then back. Glared at him, stabbing two fingers into his breastbone. "I took you to my home"—she jabbed harder—"into my bed. And you blew that start. I—" She made a punching fist, pulled back, then let it drop. "God, what a fucking piece of work you are." She made to step around him, but he caught her elbow.

"Wait a minute. Listen."

She jerked her arm back but stood facing him, the tension mounting inside.

"Look, Delia. What you don't know is that I'm an alcoholic."

She made a Judge Judy eye-roll. "Oh, please. Now you'll tell me booze makes you act so shitty?"

"No, I'm in a recovery program." He dug into his khakis and pressed a metal disk into her hand. "Chelsea is too. On and off."

At first she thought he'd handed her a Canadian loonie or maybe a sex-shop token, then noticed the words *3-year recovery* stamped inside a triangle. "You mean she's a sexaholic? Now that, I would believe."

He waved off her attempt to hand it back. "No, no. Pills and alcohol. Chelsea dropped off the wagon and her sponsor was out of town. I was just filling in."

Delia grabbed up his wrist, slapped the chip into his palm, and pushed his hand away. "I got an eyeful of your filling in."

"Look," he said. "She was bombed and some guys in the Two-Step were plying her with more drinks. I could see what was going to happen. It was on me to get her out of there and drive her home." He tilted his head forward, keeping his eyes steady on hers. "To Chelsea's home, not mine."

She had a hard time dialing down her glower under a glimmer of hope. She chewed at her lower lip. "I'm listening."

Now *he* looked hopeful. She waited for the liar's pause, but he continued right away. "After what you saw, I pushed her off me, boogied on up to Portland, and left her in the care of her roommate. Chelsea's sponsor is back now and she's his headache. End of story."

She paused a moment, then wandered over to a far corner of the dock, her arms hugging herself as she gazed out at the water. He'd shown none of the signs—didn't freeze in place, no head jerks, no repeated words, no neck or crotch covering, no frozen stare. He'd kept his distance and silence, showing the sense to let her make up her mind. No info-dumping, either.

She turned and approached him, much of her anger, the hurt, downgraded to wait-and-see status. She studied him, ignoring how much she'd missed looking into those eyes, their cobalt specks reflecting in the winter sun. "So, I'm supposed to swallow all this because . . . ?"

He looked at her for several beats, rubbing the side of his neck. Then his hand disappeared into a coat pocket and came out with a glove. Her missing glove. "Because we're a good fit." He held the open end to her. "Left and right."

She hesitated, then sank her naked hand into the leather. Instead of letting go, his fingers closed around hers, and he pulled her in close. Their breath mingled in the winter air. "It was a start for me, too."

She searched his eyes, not without doubt, but let his arms enfold her.

"Delia, you might've told yourself you don't need me, but you've got me. You had me way before we climbed into that funky hot tub. Before—"

She arched her head back, feeling the moisture in her eyes, yet giving him a mock frown. "Funky?"

He smiled. "Even before our adrenaline rushes on the river. Can't beat those waterlogged minutes we shared in abject terror. I swear my heart jumped out my throat and flew away."

She chuckled to herself, unzipping the top of his coat and laying her good ear against his chest. "Well, it must've flown back. I can hear it in there."

"No, it has to be hung up in a tree somewhere. Maybe in your backyard shrubs, next to my skivvies."

The chortle she stifled was meant to be tough but came out sounding not so tough. "Sailors still call them that? No, remember? They fell off. Almost drowned my cat."

His arms tightened around her. She didn't resist. At the rumble of trucks—a white F-350 crew cab, trailed by Zack's '55—she pushed away.

"Give me some time. Need to think things through."

"Sure. You must've worked up a pretty big mad over the last couple of days."

"You can't imagine." Already steps ahead, she turned and motioned with a nod toward the parking lot. "C'mon, let's get to work. We'll retrieve your skivvies later."

*　*　*

Feeling the shakes come on, Gus gave up trying to fold the parcel map he'd pilfered from the chart credenza in the county assessor's office. He needed big-picture specifics, more than those puny smartphone maps gave out. But this big picture was too large for his overstuffed briefcase and Miss Busybody would be back in five. It took study time, without a nosy office clerk breathing down his neck. Alerting the wrong people.

His real find happened to be sitting, barefaced, on Harvey Schenkel's desk. That closed-case file for the Willard and Rose Gatlin homicides gave him the confirmation he needed to zero in on Robert Bastida, aka Robert Gatlin. Gus didn't know who'd pulled the file, or why. Didn't care. He had the general location of the Gatlin house— out in the goddamn boonies.

He was glad he'd had the forethought to pocket the jeweler's loupe he'd confiscated from a collar on an old smash-and-grab case. Rolling up the chart, he thanked his stars for its detail. Right down to a break in the woods that might offer a clear field of fire.

With the map tucked under one arm and his leather carryall weighing down the other, Gus hurried across the courthouse lobby. Going straight out the front, he avoided prying eyes. Any deputies who happened to be in the sheriff's office were in the annex behind.

Gus was down the steps when it hit him: he would miss the old pile of sandstone. Well, miss watching Annie sashay her assets out of his office. Miss her tease-talk, lighting a pilot light of hope. Not much else. He picked up his pace and kept his eyes forward. To Annie and the rest, he was on a week's leave. Make that permanent if everything worked out.

He scuttled across the courthouse lawn and got the passenger door of his Interceptor open with no one stopping for chitchat. He tossed the map into the back, wincing at the clinks and clanks when he set the briefcase down too hard. He peeked inside. No broken bottles or rum-soaked firing mechanism. No soggy passport or smeared Costa Rica brochures.

His going-away kit was intact.

The confiscated nine-mil machine pistol was easily concealed, once strapped in under his parka. An Agram 2000 couldn't hold a candle to Bannock's MP5, but it'd make for a nasty surprise.

Just in case his nephew got cold feet.

He stepped around to the driver's side and got in. Noticed his hands were still shaking. Reminded himself Bannock had been consistent on their money deal. Gus wasn't worried about a fair split. He was worried there might not be anything left to split. Bannock was unpredictable. The man had ordnance. Wasn't afraid to blow up his world and everybody in it.

Leaning over, Gus reached inside the briefcase and felt the cocking handle, the cold steel of confidence. He wished now that he'd fired more than a few practice bursts through the jumpy Agram.

Gus started the car's engine and backed out, hoping he'd covered all bases.

It didn't pay to underestimate a man with a cannon and a hard-on for revenge.

40

Well, almost a cannon. Gus figured Bannock's experimental grenade machine gun was just as destructive. Its overkill potential weighed on him as he drove out of Dallas, Oregon.

He curved south onto Kings Valley Highway with big questions riding shotgun. Would Bannock stick to their capture-first, kill-later agreement? Would he load that laser-guided weapon with BZs– the banned knockout gas shells he'd shown Gus—or slip in HEs, high-explosive smart ammo? Bannock was adamant he could send rounds through a window at five hundred meters and airburst the shells directly behind their target's ear. BZs would put Gatlin on his butt but still let him answer questions, especially if they couldn't locate the money. HEs would redecorate the walls in brain.

Bannock was too much about revenge. Somehow, Gus had to get to the carrot before the stick.

Eight miles on, he turned east on the Monmouth Highway then left onto Treehouse Road. A short climb up the narrow back lane, he spotted the ancient tree his nephew had described. The massive white oak crowned a hill, its fan of limbs pockmarked with mistletoe.

But no nephew. Gus parked and waited.

Twenty minutes later, a badly oxidized brown Dodge pickup scrambled up the same road he'd come from and wheeled in beside him.

Craig waved and got out of the pickup. Gus rolled down the window. "Kept me waiting, son."

Decked out in a shag ghillie suit and face paint, his nephew looked like he'd stepped out of an ad for *Turkey Caller's Gazette*. He nodded back toward the truck bed, loaded with six or seven alfalfa bales and a couple of freight pallets. "Had to, uh, pick up the stuff you ordered me to get. Ready to rock and roll, now."

Stepping from his cruiser, Gus overlooked Craig's failure to acknowledge him as sheriff and clapped him on the shoulder. "Good man."

Gus had told Craig little to nothing about Bannock, his potential target, but knew he'd jump at the chance to play sniper. Especially after Gus repeated his promise of a promotion, adding that he'd buy him a brand-new truck. Hell, a camper, too. If Gus had to lay down a smoke screen, he figured he might as well blow it out thick.

"Now, go on around and snag us that county map off the car seat. We've got logistics to work out."

Midday sunlight spackled the satellite image he spread over the hood of Craig's truck.

"Where'd you get this?" Craig asked.

"Never you mind." Gus handed over his jeweler's loupe and motioned to the part of the map where the Willamette River formed the county's southeastern border. "First off, show me exactly how you got to the house where that double homicide occurred. Way back last June."

Craig looked at him, turning the magnifying lens over in his hand. "The Gatlins? I thought we were going after Bastida."

"We are. Turns out he's a Gatlin."

Craig didn't seem all that surprised. "Yeah, makes sense—how he can melt off the river at night." His index finger circled a blue bulge on the map where three rivers joined. "See how the Luckiamute and that bend in the Willamette make a peninsula straight across from the Santiam? Kinda like a hammered thumb? I've bowhunted there."

Gus took the lens from him and leaned in. "What's in that clearing up by the hangnail?"

"That's where the house sits, what's left of it. Look close. There's a double-track lane forks off the highway. That dirt access road runs east through the woods, follows a dike along the river, and swings back into the clearing. The state's been turning it into a natural area, a Portlander's wet dream."

Gus's interest in the river bottom stretched over the next few hours only. After, they could turn it into Six Flags Over Oregon, for all he cared. As for Craig? Well, like any insurance policy, his nephew might not be needed. Anyhow, Gus was the one risking his hide.

"After we switch vehicles, can you wheel in there with my Interceptor without getting stuck? Hide it away and set up ahead of time?"

"You mean find a tree that'll give me a clear shot?"

"Right. From here"—using the rubber edge of the eyepiece, Gus traced a line through a treeless corridor he'd noticed earlier—"to this access road I'll be driving your pickup along. Your target's the hombre riding shotgun with me." He folded and pocketed the lens. "Can I count on you?"

Craig thumbed the corner of the map. His eyes stayed fixed on it as he gave a curt nod. "You park my truck anywhere along the dike, and I'll have my crosshairs on the bridge a that hombre's nose."

"Good enough." Gus snicked the brim of his Stetson. "But remember, only if I lift my hat. Now, let's hear that back."

"If your hat comes off, I shoot."

*   *   *

"Nobody's home, if you can call it that." Delia holstered her weapon after clearing the boathouse and its floating contents of potential threat. "Harvey, you gotta see this. Jerzy, you and Zack help him up out of *Jackie* and I'll get him inside."

She stood on one of two log pontoons the Quonset-type structure rested on. Their boat was tied alongside. Harvey's boot cast hindered his exit, but he made it up to Delia with a man under each wing. Once he was level, she helped him hobble toward one of the Quonset's openings.

Jerzy followed, muttering aloud. "Man-oh-man. Hard to believe you found this place."

291

The coordinates Delia had given Jerzy to feed into his Lowrance Chartplotter had led them on a roundabout but dead-on course, downstream then up a former channel and into a cove notched back inside a river peninsula. On the way, she'd been surprised by how well Harvey and Jerzy had hit it off, aided big-time by the fact that Jerzy's father was Harvey's surgeon. Zack had stayed church-mouse quiet, until Harvey brought up Charlie's funeral and apologized for not being well enough to attend. The full perk-up had come when she mentioned Zack's interest in the Deputy Sheriff's Academy.

"Okay if I work on those swing-out boat doors?" Zack now hovered over *Jackie*'s controls. "Get some light inside this creep crypt?" Delia could tell he was itching to do something useful—anything involving Jerzy's boat.

Halfway through the Quonset's hatchway, she paused and gave Jerzy a look. "That all right with you?"

"Go for it," he yelled over his shoulder.

Delia flicked on her Rayovac, shining it over fifty feet of moored relic. Duck pluckings drifted across its deck like an invasion of spider ghosts. The fuzzy remnants seemed to complement the scum trailing off the old boat's hull.

"Judas Priest," Harvey said, stepping across then leaning against the boat's railing, so his weight was off his injured foot. He gawked around in the semigloom as if he'd boarded a museum piece preserved in mold. "Like stepping into a movie set for an attack scene, downgraded to a horror flick."

"*Apocalypse Now* wasn't a horror story?" Jerzy asked.

"I was thinking much older, like *Heart of Darkness*," Harvey answered.

Delia shrugged, taking photos as she made her way to the open engine bays. "Greed and savagery are sides of a coin. Have a look at Tweety's little workshop of horrors."

Delia watched Jerzy whack his knee on a box-shaped object, knocking one side open. The pungent tang of dried meat wafted over.

Her cell phone flash revealed a half-pint refrigerator that had been gutted and converted into a smoker.

He made it to her side without incident.

Filling the former engine room below deck, a fletcher's workbench displayed Tweety's handiwork. Hybrid projectiles of all sorts featured deer hunter's razor-thin multiblades fused to elongated crossbow bolts and stuffed in quivers.

Delia left Jerzy shining his light toward the target dummy hung on the Quonset's back wall, where she'd already been. Her interest was on the boat deck she'd been examining and snapping shots of ahead of every step. Beyond theirs, only one set of footprints dominated in the accumulated dust and grime. No second set meant no accomplice, no serial-killer tag team. No Robb?

She headed forward, intending to recheck the deckhouse, when a metallic crunch drew her attention to the front of the boat shed. Teeth-grinding screeches followed when *Jackie*'s bow nosed into a crack of light. Zack stood in that bow, prying the boat shed's main doors open, flooding the place with daylight and fresh air. A cottony swirl of down and duck feathers tumbled toward the rear of the Vietnam War–era Swift boat.

* * *

After helping Craig fit the tree stand and the rest of his gear into the Interceptor's trunk, Gus climbed into his nephew's pickup and followed him to Monmouth, where they split up—Craig driving the Interceptor to the woods below Buena Vista, Gus taking Craig's Dodge truck to meet Bannock behind a big-box store that had gone belly-up.

Bannock had nosed the Navigator's grille into an empty loading bay and stood beside the vehicle, swaying on his canes.

Gus backed Craig's pickup to within six feet of the SUV's rear bumper. He gathered up the parcel map and stepped around toward the Navigator's hood. The ever-volatile snake-eater spoke first.

"You have what we need on the Bastard?"

"And more." Gus spread the map and set his jeweler's loupe on one corner. "Here's ground zero." He pointed to the Gatlin house, then trailed the nail of his pinkie finger beside the access road through the woods. "We'll drive up along here, which puts the old Gatlin house to our left—"

"How's he get there?"

"By boat." Gus's stomach was knotting up already.

"How do you know he'll be there?"

"Where else but the place Gatlin grew up? The real question is, how right are you about him packing all that money around, or at least stashing it close by?"

Bannock's attention was on the map. "The Bastard's got it with him, and if it's someplace else, I'm going to enjoy finding out where." He picked up the loupe and bent low over one corner. "Now, load up while I identify a forward position and work out the details."

Gus didn't need reminding he was too damned old to wrestle sixty-pound hay bales around, but he managed to make room for the ordnance transfer. Didn't need the knee-popping told-you-so, either, climbing off the bed of Castner's pickup.

Three crates the color of headstones crowded the Lincoln's cargo area.

From his brief glimpse the night before, Gus knew the larger box housed the core of the weapon system, a belt-fed, squat-barreled grenade launcher on a machine gunner's tripod. A smaller box held its eyes and brain: night camera, laser aiming unit, ballistic computer. The one in the middle was chock-full of metal ammo canisters: four long-lows crammed with blue-tipped, high-explosive fragmentation shells, and a fifth marked *BZ*—silver-nosed grenades containing a nerve-blocking gas. Somehow, Bannock got hold of munitions the military had supposedly destroyed. The two types of shells looked alike. The functional difference was night and day.

Gus set to work, transferring the load. A 48-cartridge belt spilled out when he snagged the lid of a long-low on a crate. The belt lay in segments on the Navigator's floor, so he decided to leave it.

"Unfuckingbelievable," was all he got from Bannock, who bent back over the map.

By the time Gus had manhandled the larger crate and the rest of the long-lows onto the pickup, his parka was clammy. Coolness wormed down his ribs, dampening his shirt and the machine pistol secured inside his parka.

It had been too cold to sweat outside the motel the night before. Yet an icy chill had run down Gus's spine, watching Bannock fondle the grenade launcher's flash suppressor while the man lamented the mess "The Bastard" had made of his life. "The Navy can go to hell," Bannock had said, slurring words. "Only thing I'll miss is blowing shit up and fragging bad guys."

One thing was certain, listening to Bannock had made it feel so right for Gus to have an insurance policy back in the trees.

* * *

Delia joined Harvey and Zack at the Swift boat's railing. Both were looking up with their mouths ready to catch flies. Harvey closed his. "Dee-Dee, you notice what's in the gun tub?"

"Been up there. Disabled both guns first thing."

"How'd you do that?" Zack asked.

"Trick my advanced-firearms instructor taught me. I think we're looking at what might've been Tweety's last stand."

Again the two men gawked at the .50 caliber armament hanging at rest, its twin barrels innocently pointing toward the Quonset hut's metal rafters.

Jerzy strode up and handed Delia one of the crossbow quarrels she'd seen poking out of the practice target. "Boy, was I way off about the guy my dad and I hunted with."

"Lucky, too," she added, shining her light toward the stern. No center-mass shots for Tweety. The straw-filled Gore-Tex camo coat hanging on the Quonset's back wall sported a head with an evil-looking hunter's face drawn on. Between that and the coat, a flesh-toned Styrofoam neck bristled with a quiverful of bolts. Except for the target point, she'd bet this one matched the bolt she and Zack had found at Charlie's death scene.

Zack elbowed in for a closer look. "So this all means the ex-guide Detective Chavez and me boated downriver to warn is the sumbitch that killed my brother. The others, too." He twisted a corner of his mustache. "I figured him for squirrely, but how the fuck did we—"

Delia laid a hand on his shoulder. "I'd suspected as much, Zack, but had nothing to go on without a body." She turned to Harvey. "Any lab results on the bolt I passed on to you, Harv?"

He shrugged. "No blood. Partial prints yielded nothing from the FBI database. For a match check on Tweety Bates, we'll still need a body. But we might have enough here to go on. Ready to call in a state crime lab crew?"

"Not yet." She made to step around, but he stopped her.

"Not yet? This place has to be our tie-in with the hunter killings."

"One more pass-through, Harv," she said, pulling surgical gloves from her coat pocket. It was the link, but she had to be sure Robb wasn't involved with the killings or Tweety, or this sad war relic. Rubber snapped against wrists as she broke off and made for the deck cabin.

Jerzy met her at the rear hatchway. "Can I help?"

She handed him a spare pair of gloves. "I've already photographed down there. You see something, let me know."

Delia assigned Jerzy the forward berth while she searched the pilothouse. Her first gut-clenching discovery came from a box wedged under the chart table. The trophy collection was mounted in a thin, hardwood display case with spaces for sixteen items. The top row of four was filled. Each mounted finger was crooked into firing position. Three were small and wizened, with coppery skin. She'd bet the first belonged to the Yamhill body Harvey had started to investigate. The fourth digit was larger. Fresher. A shudder rippled through her. An odor wafted off the collection. She bent low, sniffed, and popped straight up, nearly gagging. The smell was pungent as beef jerky.

She returned the box. Zack shouldn't be there when she told Harvey Tweety had smoked Charlie's finger, along with the others.

From down below, she heard a muffled thud. Then—

"Ouch. Shit."

"You find something?"

"It found me. Right on the noggin."

Delia joined Jerzy in the Swift boat's deckhouse. Packets of small cigars were scattered across the floor. Jerzy stood before a locker crammed with old military clothing. His index fingers and thumbs delicately pinched opposite corners of a yellow-and-black box with gold lettering—a humidor, she'd learned, on looking up the brand from the cigar butt she'd recovered at the Riverview parking lot.

"The day you hunted with Tweety Bates, he was smoking."

"One of those," Jerzy said, nodding toward the floor.

Another degree of separation. She breathed easier, recalling no hint of tobacco use by Robb during their hours together.

She perched on one of the bunks—her cell phone flashing in camera mode—when the back of her heel made contact with something solid. Kneeling, she slid a small metal chest from beneath the bed and opened it.

On top were piles of photographs. Several appeared to be Vietnam military scenes. Another was clearly more recent. The two figures in that picture wore old-style fatigues.

"The young guy on the left is Tweety," Jerzy said, sitting beside her. "The other must be his dad." They looked alike. Both appeared highly fit.

Delia tapped on Tweety. "He's the one I chased across the River-view parking lot. Got away in his boat. Tried questioning him at the Octane Stop. If I had picked him up either time, the body count might have been halved." From beneath the photos, Delia dug out what she first thought was a photo album.

As if kippered trigger fingers hadn't been enough, that storage chest find was the clincher. On first glance, the bound volume appeared benign. A gussied-up logbook? she wondered. Too ornate. A diary? Nuh-uh.

Though somber, the title on a cover inlayed with mother-of-pearl gave scant forewarning it was anything but a hunting rights sermon:

Why I'm a Hunter, Not a Murderer
A Personal Anthology
by
R. "Tweety" Bates Jr.

Delia opened to page one. They read together in silence.

There are two kinds of hunters, decent and indecent. Decent hunters honor the sacred ethic of the best sport in the world. Indecent hunters violate that ethic every time they go outdoors. They range from out-and-out Concentrics to low-down Hunturds. They have to be culled from the herd because they endanger a natural sport for the rest. That is the mission I chose to accept.

Jerzy tapped on the page. "He called us that. My dad and me."
She glanced at him, then at the book. "Called you what, Hunturds?"
"Decent," he answered. "I thought he meant we were good at hunting, not that he thought us worthy of staying alive."
"Looks like you dodged a bullet. Or a dart from a crossbow." They dipped their heads and read on.

Why, you ask? Guide enough Concentrics and witness the heinous acts of Hunturds over fourteen years and you get a bellyful of reasons. Here's a sample, every one deserving of capital punishment:

– They chase down mallards and blast away, their outboard motors at full tilt while they laugh like maniacs.
– They blast away on the water before birds get airborne then congratulate each other on their kills.

A short way into Tweety Bates's diatribe, she found herself drenched in death thoughts oozing from the pen of a murderer who'd almost killed her. His off-kilter justifications chilled and stunned, each accompanied by a different "stalk and cull" tactic. His nightmare images disturbed and fascinated, drew her deep into the mind that conjured them. Even more disturbing were the flashes of recall they triggered as she scanned down the list.

- *They toss dead birds in the brush so they don't have to pluck, clean or eat them.*
- *One even dispatched wounded ducks by biting down on their heads, showing how macho he was.*

"Sweet Jesus, but the guy lived a skewed life." Jerzy leaned forward, craning to see into her face. "You okay reading this?"

Delia nodded. She had to keep on keeping on, hoping she'd find nothing to implicate Robb.

They had gotten several pages in when Zack dipped his head inside.

"Harvey wants to know if you're done. Says there's weather on the way and thought Detective Chavez would want to call in that crime lab outfit."

She gave Jerzy a gentle push toward the hatchway. "You two help Harvey get settled into *Jackie*. I'll be along."

Jerzy followed Zack. Delia stayed, drawn to the anger.

The final example in Tweety's list was without doubt his last straw.

- *This stinking Hunturd shoots my dog, Trudy, because he forgets to flip on his gun's safety.*

As much as she hated the twisted message, that dark rationale resonated on a personal level, got her heart racing, her head swimming with birds-of-a-feather torments. Had she been culling pedophiles last August? Last year? Where Bates portrayed an unnamed target, she saw the taunting figure of Zedo Camacho in the RV behind that Independence tavern. Had she stalked and culled Camacho? And before him, the skeletal grin of the first one, the chicken hawk she'd winged a year earlier, but wanted to castrate from the neck down? Flexing her stomach muscles to slow the thumping inside her chest, she traced Bates's twisted logic and favored MO for the river killings back to its early roots.

I learned the warrior code from R. T. Senior, my ex–Navy SEAL dad who whipped me into shape with his own brand of BUD/S training. The code: A warrior kills but never murders, so long as he draws a line of conduct he will not cross. I never stalk an unarmed enemy. I make it fair game with only a crossbow or a knife. God made me a righteous hunter. He rewarded me with the thrill of a different kind of hunt.

Delia swallowed, her throat like sandpaper. Those intimate accounts of Bates's kill rushes hit home. Her officer-involved shoots— the two resulting deaths—were justified. But, like Bates, she had enjoyed the after-kill. Shivered through those conscience-numbing adrenaline spikes. The guilt relief they brought.

Ink and yellowed paper blurred together. She now saw her own shootings as revenge for Bebé Tío's childhood abduction.

Doubts aside, the few hours spent with Robb had washed away much of that guilt. But would she apply ballistic therapy on the next pedophile that crossed her path? She'd get no more stay-out-of-jail cards from Harv.

"Ready to shake a leg?" This time it was Jerzy, poking his head in through the hatchway.

She kept her head down. "Almost. I'll see if the OSP crime lab crew can meet us back at the dock."

Her breath took a steep intake as she read Tweety's last line. Words that separated her from Bates by miles and miles.

I knew I was a full-fledged warrior the day I culled Dad.

So, Tweety had lived and "worked" alone, and Robb had nothing to do with the Swift boat. But how was he going to "shut the lid on hell"?

Delia returned the anthology to its storage chest, closing the book on Tweety Bates.

41

Back at Riverview Park, wave tops slopped over the boat dock's wind side, wetting the toes of Delia's chukkas. A dirty mattress of clouds had smothered the afternoon sun. She pinched in her coat collar, peering outside the circle of men she stood among, wondering where Jerzy had gone. He'd disappeared while she, Harvey, and Zack had been busy debriefing three OSP crime lab specialists before their trip to Tweety's Swift boat.

Her overview had included details of their preliminary boat search and Harvey had left it to Delia to sum up her investigation into the river murders, with Zack chiming in as witness-in-chief. The lab crew stayed focused on Tweety Bates and was satisfied she'd kept the chain of evidence intact. When one of the specialists asked why OSP hadn't been brought in earlier, she laid it squarely in Grice's lap. Harvey backed her up, alluding to the ongoing investigation into his conduct.

The group of six wrapped up, agreeing the county should keep the lead on the case while the Staties processed evidence. No one had asked where Tweety Bates's body was, or what a certain military fugitive was up to—neither of which she could answer.

A call from Annie came in on her cell. Asking Annie to hold, Delia turned to Zack. "Are you okay with helping get the crime lab crew set up for a boat trip? Transfer their gear into *Jackie*?"

"Done and done, Detective."

"Go ahead, Annie." Listening, Delia started up the ramp toward Jerzy, who was loading Beezer into his Hummer, apparently following a doggy outing.

"You know the curiosity thing we've been tracking between Grice and that naval officer?"

"The judge got Cam to let us look into Grice's bank accounts?"

"Yeah, and they've been drained. But curiouser than that, I got a call from the CO of NAVSPECWAR in Little Creek, Virginia."

"Bannock's CO?"

"Right. I explained the sheriff was unavailable. The CO wouldn't give me much at first, except Bannock had been reassigned, anchored to a PR desk. Before that, he was Bastida's unit leader in an antidrug operation that went south." Annie chuckled. "That poor, gruff darling commanding officer tried to clam up, but . . . well, you know me." Delia did. Annie could talk the devil out of his pitchfork. "The reason he was so worried was that Bannock took extended leave just when an experimental grenade machine gun went missing from their munitions depot."

"Yipes." Slumping back against the fender of Jerzy's Hummer, Delia pictured multiple explosions going off right over the top of a Zodiac. She rang off and turned to Jerzy, feeling the promise of rain in the quickened breeze. "It might be getting warmer, but my gut says things are about to snowball on us."

He feigned an uphill glance. "Do we try and hold it back or run like hell?"

"I won't be running, if ever," Harvey interjected, stumping up to them. Delia relayed Annie's update to them, adding that she was starting to get the picture, when Jerzy broke in.

"Glad you are. Me? I'm way behind the curve. I know I'm just the boat jockey, but you might clue me in. Like, what's this Bannock character got to do with Tweety Bates?"

Delia flushed. They *had* treated him like a boat jockey. Her especially. "With Bates? Nothing." She glanced at Harvey, then back to

Jerzy. "I should've filled you in sooner. Harvey, Annie, the county DA, and myself have a covert investigation underway. Grice is the focus. Looks like Bannock's been feeding him cashier's checks for several weeks. Payment for slow-walking our investigation." She eyed Harvey. "My take? Bannock bought sole hunting rights on his former team member."

Jerzy's stance shifted. "Let me guess. Bastida, the guy who played water games with us on the river."

Harvey jabbed a finger into his palm. "Right, and now Bannock's here with Grice as his hunting guide." He stared off toward the dock where Zack and the trio from OSP stood waiting. "We're missing major pieces—motive, for one. For another, where they're planning to hunt this fugitive."

Delia tensed, tugging at the sleeves of her coat. This wasn't going to be fun. "Bastida's not the fugitive's real—"

Woo-whoop. They turned toward the sound.

Saved by the whoop. A brown-and-white cut across rows of empty parking stalls and stopped beside them. She recognized Densco, a reserve deputy called up after Grice had "elevated" his nephew.

He gave her a quick nod, Jerzy a passing glance, and focused on Harvey. "You Schenkel?"

"Detective Schenkel. And you are?"

"Just what this department needs. Mike Densco." Nobody responded. He didn't offer his hand. "The dispatcher said I should update you on what I came across at the Buena Vista Cemetery. Somebody dug up two graves, emptied the caskets, and spread both cadavers across the mounded dirt."

Delia edged closer. "Whose bodies?"

Densco checked his Toughbook. "A Willard Gatlin and a Jess Gatlin. His son, according to death records."

"Jesus Martha," Harvey said, kneading the sides of his head as though in pain.

"What about Rose Gatlin?" she asked.

"That grave was left undisturbed. Somebody had laid fresh holly sprigs over the turf." Delia felt her world spin a tick faster.

Densco leaned out. "And hey," he said, glancing left, right, then lowering his voice. "What in the P. Diddy's up with this sheriff?"

"Good question," Harvey answered. "We're working on it."

Delia took Harvey aside. "Densco should stick around. In case we need to follow up on Grice."

Harvey frowned, then nodded. "I'll talk to him."

She pulled out her phone and dialed Annie. "Any word on where Grice or Bannock might be?"

"Funny thing," Annie answered. "Grice has been here and gone. I found the cover sheet on the Gatlin file in our copier and more on his desk. Later, I spotted Bannock in the parking lot beside the jail. You'll never guess who he was huddled with."

Delia had guessed wrong. She rung off with another keep-me-posted and found Harvey. When she told him what she'd learned, his eyes bulged. "Man," he said, giving his head another rub. "And now we've got Castner tied in with Grice and Bannock?"

"That's likely, and they have to be stopped. Can we use your truck?"

"It's almost out of gas. Besides, things are happening way too fast," he said, still massaging his temples. "I missed my venti caffeine dose, and my head's coming apart." He muttered that limping toward his pickup. "Let's get somewhere I can wash down aspirin with coffee and think this through."

"Me for that," Jerzy said as he caught up with them. "Stomach's got my spine pinned to the mat."

"Wait." Delia hooked them both by the arms. "Aren't we forgetting something?"

Harvey and Jerzy gazed back down the boat ramp, then at her.

She was ready with solutions. "I'll put Hotshot Densco on the Quonset with the crime lab crew. He'll love doing crime scene oversight."

"Yeah, okay," Harvey said, kneading at his eye sockets.

She turned to Jerzy. "In case we're gone longer, do you trust Zack to ferry Densco and the OSP lab group to that boathouse—using your boat?"

"Shit." His eyes narrowed. "Longer meaning . . . the Gatlin place?"

Nodding, she reached out and fingered the zipper on his jacket.

He sighed in submission. "I guess. I'll need to call Salem Hospital, though. Get my dad to swing by after rounds and pick up Beezer."

Delia made arrangements and the three of them piled into Harvey's F-350, her at the wheel.

*　*　*

The Octane Stop had only two orange plastic booths. Harvey sat at the inside of a bench seat. Delia dropped in next to him after gassing up his truck. Harvey's boot cast rested on part of the other bench, leaving the rest for Jerzy. She took one of the three coffees he'd bought but nothing from the Hostess fun box.

"Twinkies?" Harvey gibed.

Since Jerzy's mouth was stuffed, she answered back. "The guy goes for them like a Sicilian mobster after cannoli. Now can we get to it?"

"Gimme one of those." Harvey grabbed two Twinkies, but before taking a bite, he glanced over at Delia. "Okay, let's hear it."

"Hear what?" She checked her watch, itching to be where she knew it would all come together. But she had some convincing to do.

"About Bastida?" Harvey *had* been listening.

She took another sip and started in. "Robert Bastida, the military fugitive we've been searching for, was raised a Gatlin. I have reason to suspect Robb might be family."

"Robb?" Jerzy asked.

Harvey swallowed the bulk of his second Twinkie and sat back, looking bemused.

She nutshelled the story of her lost baby brother and the man on the river who'd kidnapped him in front of her—leaving out mention of the lifelong trauma and guilt and fear it had caused. Delia moved rapidly ahead, explaining that when she and Jerzy had gotten wrecked on the Willamette, then rescued by that same fugitive, she hadn't realized it was a turning point . . .

" . . . until one night ago, when he abducted me."

Both men had stunned expressions as she fessed up, admitting she had dropped her guard in the cold and ice.

"He didn't want my car or my life. He wanted to know who he was." She went over the matching crucifixes, his account of being taken as a child, the resemblance. "Everything he showed and told me jibes with what I know and keep in here." She thumped her breastbone above her heart.

Delia took a quick sip of the now tepid brew and leaned in to make her point. "Robb let me go, promising to turn himself in." Did *save me a cell* count as a promise? "He volunteered a motive behind why he's on the run. Why, I think, Grice and Bannock are after him. It's about a ton of money. Revenge, too, if Annie's right about Bannock's injuries."

Harvey shut his mouth. "God, what a story."

"Second that emotion," said Jerzy. "You should write that up. Send it in to a magazine."

Maybe she should. Just go off somewhere and write schlock. Good schlock. But she couldn't. Not yet. "My main worry is that he's very sick. Up here," she said, tapping her forehead. "He did that . . . that graveyard thing, to make sure his childhood tormenters were really dead. Now he wants to shut the lid on hell—in his tortured mind, the Gatlin house. That's where everything's coming to a head. Where we need to be, and pronto."

Harvey's head inclined to the left. "We. Just the three of us." Her hand went for the Crush Ball. And here came that devil's-advocate shit. "We don't know that's all true, for sure. He could be playing you." Jerzy flicked her a nervous glance but stayed silent.

Down inside, her anger burner kicked on, the heat rising. "You haven't been listening, Harv. Sixteen million? Grenade machine gun? Close off hell? My brother?" The flush invaded her cheeks, heading toward eruption. "Robb is going to do *something* to that Gatlin house. That's where Grice was going. We have to stop what's already in motion."

"Delia, listen to yourself. Even when—no, especially when—it's true, we can't go in there on our own. Not up against that kind of firepower." Harvey yanked out his phone and speed-dialed a number. "We go in behind an OSP SWAT team."

Delia crushed the cup in her hand, feeling warm liquid run down her fingers, a white-hot rage ready to touch off. Harvey started talking on the phone. Mr. Careful again.

Jerzy dabbed at the spilled coffee. "He makes sense, Delia."

Her phone dinged again and again and a third time. "What?" she snapped. It was Annie, but they were texts. The first read:

No sign of Grice. Items missing from confisc. drawer, including submachine pistol

The second message read:

Castner spotted S. of Buena Vista in Grice's Interceptor-suited up in bow hunter camo.

The third message was shorter:

Bring Harvey back in 1 piece

She showed him the first two messages.
"Harvey, we can't wait."
"SWAT's on their way. We wait." Mr. Careful again.
She leapt up out of the booth, turned, and leaned over the table, spitting out words. "You two can sit on your asses and wait. Not me." She bent toward Harvey, her glare aimed at the bridge of his nose. "Now, I'm going to use your truck to get to my big brother's hot rod, and I'm going try and save my little brother's ass. If you don't want to be stranded here, you'd better get up out of that booth and ride along."

Harvey opened his mouth. Delia silenced him with a raised pointing finger. "Harv, I love you like another brother, but if you tell me to spritz my Latin fire . . . well, you can just go fuck yourself."

She stormed out of the Octane Stop, raced to Harvey's truck, got in, and slammed the door. Too shaky to fish keys out of her cargos, she gave up and pounded on her thighs. She couldn't believe she'd said that to Harvey.

Yes, she could. And she had. Crap!

Breathe, Chavez. Slow and deep. Get ahold of yourself, then go.

Jerzy rapped on the window. She cranked it down, warning herself not to unload on him, too.

"Hold on, Delia. We're both coming along."

With a curt nod, she retrieved the keys and started the Ford. "I'll take you and Harvey as far as my Camaro, then leave you the truck."

"No. Harvey and I are coming with you—to the Gatlin house." She peered at him, searching his eyes past the nonchalant shrug, the shopworn excuse that came next. "Can't have all the fun."

* * *

Gus pounded heels back to Castner's Dodge truck in a whole lot better a mood than when he'd first trudged down that backwoods lane. Gully-washed in spots and barely passable where the diked farm tracks ran along the river before cutting toward the old Gatlin place, the dirt road had a lot more yonder than he'd expected.

He hadn't liked it one bit when Bannock made him park the pickup and recon on foot. But after what he'd seen getting carted into that wrecked house way down at the end? Shee-it. Might as well paint dollar signs on the walls.

Bannock had his butt parked on a wheel well inside the bed of Castner's pickup. Still tapping on that tactical keyboard and cussing under his breath. Still fiddle-farting with his fancy-dancy grenade chucker.

In Gus's absence, Bannock had centered the wood pallets to serve as a gun mount platform and banked the hay bales against the left wall of the truck bed. The launcher's barrel jutted out from a two-foot-wide firing port. A closed ammunition can—the one with the gas shells, Gus assumed—was parked beside the launcher. But the two canisters containing lethal rounds sat within easy reach of the gunner.

Gus cupped his hands and blew warmth into them, trying to remember which long-lows he had and had not off-loaded from the Navigator. After the hike down that road, Bannock's war prep seemed like total overkill.

"Whoo-ee, John. A cannon-and-mosquito-type deal, if I ever saw one."

Bannock stopped punching keys and jerked around toward Gus, wincing at the effort. His canes lay on the floor of the truck bed. "You saw him? The Bastard's there?"

Gus smiled. "And the Zodiac he rode in on." He sank his hands back into the warmth of his coat. "What's more, I believe we lucked out."

"Why? How was he armed?" All military intensity, Bannock could've shot sparks from his eyes.

Gus sauntered toward the back of the pickup. "Looked mighty light in that department, John." He rested his backside on the tailgate. "Tell me somethin'. What kinda money totes did those cartel mules favor?"

"How the fuck would I know? The Bastard hijacked my whole goddamned plan before I could execute it."

"Think back a sec. Canvas? Maybe molded plastic?"

Bannock shook his head, his mouth a line of irritation. "I dunno." He stared off into the woods, more than Scotch fogging his eyes. "Maybe. My team found nylon hard cases next to that plane, all shot up and emptied."

"Color? Shape? Size?"

Bannock refocused on Gus, blinking. "Fuck that. You're off track."

"Yeah, but John, I just saw our boy humping specialty cases of some kind into that house. Only had glimpses through the cover brush, but they looked full."

Bannock cocked his head, swinging aside the contraption he called a laser guidance system. "Weapons cases?"

"Not that heavy, but something bulky inside. Money bundles are my guess. Gatlin musta had them stashed somewhere else and—"

A cane flashed into Bannock's hand, walloping the lowered tailgate. "Forget the fucking suitcases. Was the Bastard packing weapons?"

"Easy, John. Easy." Gus realized he had inched backward, out of cane range. "It's getting low-light time, but I'm sure he just had a short-barreled shotgun with a pistol grip slung over his shoulder. Nothing spec—"

"How close can you get me?" Bannock had levered himself upright.

Gus started around toward the cab. "I can put us within six hundred yards of the house. Hafta four-wheel around a hellacious dike washout, but the spot I picked will give you clear line-of-sight, and keep us out of sight."

Except maybe from a certain shooter in the woods to the west of that spot. He climbed behind the wheel and whispered a snap prayer that his nephew had set up right and that he'd make the shot.

If Gus was forced to doff his hat.

42

"Dee-Dee, stop," Harvey barked. "Back up."

Delia mashed down the brake. The Ford crew cab skewed to the left. She hit reverse and backed through the woods, fishtailing in and out of the same farm tractor divots they had just bounced over. She estimated it was three miles to the Gatlin place.

Jerzy rode the passenger seat with a two-handed grip on the omigod handle. His face was so taut he might as well have been strapped into the Mad Mouse at the state fair. Harvey braced his recuperating leg across the back seat, less concerned about her driving than them getting sandbagged.

He was right. Grice and Bannock could be anywhere. Ahead, where the lane curved and became a flood dike. At the old river house. Or they could slip up on them from behind.

On the way, she, Harvey, and Jerzy had hatched a makeshift plan—one notch above playing it by ear—and with a limited idea of what waited for them down this river-bottom driveway.

She just wanted to get past the icy lump in her gut and the images frozen in her head. Of a mortally injured, might-be brother down on his face in front of that rotting house, his blood soaking the weed patches. His life leaking away to join the riverside dead of past weeks.

"There," said Harvey. She braked again. "Down that overgrown path forking off to the left. See those flattened vines?"

"Yeah, like they've been driven over."

"I'll give a look-see." Jerzy was outside, across the lane and loping down the pathway before she could say *be careful*.

They waited in silence.

He reappeared with a Z-shaped metal rod in one hand and a small packet in the other, and trotted up to her open window. When he leaned in, the forearm he'd rested on her door came in contact with her shoulder. Warm contact.

"Good eyes, Harvey. Found the sheriff's unmarked car along that beat-down trail." He pulled back, his full attention on her. "Did I hear you say something about Castner driving that car?"

"Yeah, dressed in some kind of hunter's monkey suit."

Laughter rolled out of the back seat.

"Damn close, Dee-Dee." Their glances held in the mirror. "I saw him in a ghillie suit once. He was going bowhunting."

"Well, there is this," Jerzy said, waggling the angular metal rod in front of her.

She felt the threaded point. "And what is this?"

"A tree step. Screw them into the bark and you have a ladder up to a tree stand. I found it in the back seat with the rest of his gear."

"So," Delia said, "either he's coming back, or didn't need it. Why?"

"Maybe the answer's here," Jerzy said, handing her the packet. She unrolled the paper bag and swallowed, sorted through the contents, then passed it back.

"I'm sure you're right."

"Did Castner leave any other bread crumbs?" Harvey asked.

"Whole slices. Sure as hell isn't worried about somebody tracking him."

Harvey cocked a thumb toward the rear of his F-350. "In the mood to do a little ass-covering while we backdoor the party at the house?"

Jerzy broke out in a grin and stepped toward the truck bed.

Via the side mirror, she watched him hoist out a coil of boat rope and walk forward.

"A rope?" she asked, unable to mask the worry in her voice.

Harvey's arm snaked past her shoulder, his hand pointing at the glove compartment. "Hand him my never-fail."

Delia complied, pulling out a beat-up holster with *U.S. Cavalry* imprinted on the flap. A very old Browning automatic was entombed in leather.

"What's this, a World War I relic?"

"A tad older. Rumor has it that hunk of iron went on the 1916 expedition against Pancho Villa."

She checked the magazine and worked the action before hammering down and pressing the .45 into Jerzy's palm. Hands lingered as she fixed him with a stare. "Ever use a handgun?"

"Some."

"There's a hollow-nose in the chute that'll stop a charging NRA lobbyist if you aim between the nipples." Delia loved guns, hated gun mongers, and saw no irony in the sentiment. "Self-defense only. Clear?"

"Clear."

She put the Ford in gear. Wind buffeted the truck while she watched Jerzy slip into the woods and out of sight.

Another rainstorm was closing in.

*   *   *

Tunk-tunk-tunk, tunk-tunk.

Gus barely had the brake set on Castner's truck when Bannock cut loose with his toy. An instant later, the left side of the house at the far end of the clearing blew out, followed by a billowing—of smoke and flames, not the cloud of gas Gus had expected.

"Jumpin' Jesus." Scooting his backside across the cab seat, he poked his head out the open passenger window and yelled, "What in the Sam Hill did you load inta that thing?"

Bannock sat on an ammo canister in the truck bed. His legs were splayed under the grenade launcher, boot soles braced against the hay bales. He was hunched over the tactical computer, his face aglow from the range finder's data screen. Only the corner of his mouth moved, curling up like a scorpion's tail.

313

"Bastard-killers." He reared forward, gave two vicious yanks at the arming bolts, or whatever the hell they were called, and sank his face back into the range finder's rubberized cup. "C'mon, you fucking bastard. Show position and I'll suck the air out of your lungs."

"What about the money?" Gus groped for the right side door handle behind his back, found it quicker than expected, and tumbled out. He hit the ground, falling on the machine pistol strapped inside his parka. A bolt of electricity shot up his rib cage and he gasped for air. Stunned, he blinked the agony away as he watched his Stetson float off on a gust of wind. An odor similar to burnt fireworks stung his nostrils. His future was going up in flames.

Clawing himself up the open door, Gus saw Bannock had swung the launcher's barrel and was targeting something far right of the house.

"No diddle us and dash this time, you maggoty-ass bastard." *Tunk-tunk-tunk-tunk.*

Before Gus could blink, a multi-burst cluster made coleslaw of their quarry's rubber-sided boat.

Bannock had the launcher trained back on the house and was in the process of targeting another volley. Gus couldn't let that happen. He stumbled toward the rear of the truck, anger overriding caution.

"Now just a goddamn minute. You're gonna fricassee the fuckin' money." Too intent on dealing death, Bannock paid no attention to what went on behind him.

Gus didn't think to ask why. He used the truck's back tire as a step-up, hooked a leg over the sidewall, and managed to shinny his belly onto the edge of the bed. He struggled to a sitting position and swung his other leg inside the truck. Repositioning the machine pistol on its strap, he snicked in a round, reminding himself not to stand—his hat was gone and Castner was out there sighting in from a tree.

Gus paused, ginning up the nerve to confront Bannock, when something hard jabbed into his spine.

"Drop the weapon, Gus."

Castner. Coming from behind, his voice sounded strange. Filled with resentment. Gus couldn't believe his bonehead nephew had gotten the drop on him. He slowly raised both hands to show they were empty. The Agram 2000 hung directly below his chest, out of Castner's sight.

"Craig? Son, what are you doing?"

"Cashing in. Real money, not worthless promises."

Tunk-tunk-tunk-tunk. More shells rattled through Bannock's grenade launcher. More distant thumps from detonating grenades.

"You double-cross your uncle? After all I've done for—" Harsh laughter stopped him.

"Sorry, Gus. Not after the years I put up with you scraping me off your boot like dog shit. Now, stand up and turn around. I want to see the look on your face when this Glock tattoos your gut tub."

"How much is Bannock paying you?" Gus leaned forward, lowering his hands as if to push off from the pickup's sidewall. Instead, he swiveled the machine pistol's barrel around under his right arm.

"Ninety now and—"

Gus touched off, shooting through his parka. His own body arched with the return punch of Castner's back-shot. His balance lost, Gus pitched backward out of the truck, knocking Castner off the dike road. Gus would have gone over, too, if he hadn't landed against a tree stump.

By the agony in his shoulder, Gus was sure he'd dislocated it. The real shock was the blood filling his mouth, then spilling out between his teeth. Every drawn breath felt like a stab to his chest. He lay there, afraid to breathe. Afraid not to.

That pain-sick gorge would have been even worse had he not noticed the blood splatters marking his nephew's tumble toward the river. The machine pistol had done *some* good.

Above the V-8 rumble of an approaching truck and the bursts of launching grenades, Gus heard Bannock's send-off.

"You get him, Castner?" *Tunk-tunk-tunk.* "Good riddance. A worthless piece of shit if I ever saw one." *Tunk-tunk-tunk-tunk.*

Gus dearly hoped Bannock wouldn't get his money's worth, but feared he would.

*　*　*

The dike washout's far incline blocked Delia's view of the road ahead as she bounced through the depression, slammed the Ford into four-wheel drive, and punched the gas pedal. At first the F-350 gouged into the slope with its front bumper; then it tilted upward as the off-road tires dug in. The truck lurched up and over the embankment.

Out of the washout and back on top of the dike road, Harvey grunted loudly, mashed against the seat back when Delia hit the Ford's brakes. Both sat there, stunned by what was happening in the Dodge pickup barely a hundred feet ahead.

The truck's open tailgate was aimed toward them, with bales of hay and a figure in its bed seated behind a leftward-facing weapon on a tripod, viciously jerking at the arming bolt.

"Harvey, that's not Grice. I swear I caught a glimpse of him before we dropped into that washout. You?"

"Too busy peeling my face off the upholstery, but that guy looking at us from the truck bed must be Bannock. Hey, what's in his hands?"

Beneath the gathering dusk, she couldn't be sure. Until her sight gelled on the stubby outline of a weapon, a guy in the process of chambering a round.

"*Mierda.* Hit the floorboards."

She flopped hard to the right. The Ford's windshield cobwebbed. Frosty circles the size of pigeon eggs stitched across the safety glass. Each one left a hole like a black yolk.

She stayed down for a second burst, wincing at the *plink-plink-plink* of slugs tearing through grille metal. Engine coolant hissed. Death knells of steam vented out the Ford's hood seams.

She realized her foot had slipped off the brake. Still in drive, their truck crept ahead. Into can't-miss range. *C'mon, Delia. Think fast.*

Harvey voiced the idea forming in her head. "Now, Dee-Dee. Before the motor quits. Run right up his ass."

"I'm on it, Harv." She executed a pop-up, pop-down glance over the dash.

Bannock was turned away, his face buried in a funnel-shaped object on top of a large weapon. A grenade launcher, pointed toward the house. The hellhole Robb had planned to close. The launcher was a sure-kill weapon, and Bannock aimed to kill him.

She sat up and stomped the accelerator. The Ford jumped ahead, just as a belt-load of shells rattled through the launcher.

The F-350 fishtailed toward the Dodge. Over the roar of accelera-tion, she heard the *pomp-pomp-pomp* of forty-millimeter rapid fire. It halted the instant the Ford jolted into the truck ahead.

She stomped down again. The hood of the high-centered Ford rose up and over the stationary truck's tailgate and mounted the Dodge, launching it in motion. The Ford kept going, snorting steam, thrust-ing forward. A hunk of Detroit iron in mating season. The Dodge hit a clump of trees and jolted to a stop. The Ford followed suit when its bumper kissed the cab of the truck beneath.

A concussive whoosh rattled both trucks, and the horizon to her left took on a coppery flush. The house beneath traded its rectangular gray for a globe of flaming orange. A massive fireball rose into the dark, a hot-air balloon painted in hell. Robb. Shit.

"Harv, you okay?"

"Think so. You?"

Shaking off the numbness, she wiped at the blood running from her bandaged ear and unholstered her mouse gun.

Bannock. First, neutralize the threat. Delia got the driver's side door of the Ford open a crack before it stuck. She scrunched her butt around and aimed both chukkas at the door panel. Her kick was interrupted by a low-timbre *whoomph* that shook the truck. Something else had exploded at the house. Stunned, all Delia could do was think cremation and gawk as every space of the structure showing daylight, glowed white hot. The heat came from deeper inside. From the place she was sure Robb had gone.

"Hol-ee buckets." Harvey must have worked himself back up to win-dow level. "That frickin' place had to be packed with fuel and accelerants."

She gave the driver's side door a vicious boot, and it banged open. A snowstorm of loose hay swirled in. She leapt out, twisting to keep her small weapon trained on the major threat as she hit the ground beside the trucks, one stacked atop the other.

That threat was dead. Clearly dead. Bannock's upper torso was crushed between the cab of Castner's Dodge and a heavy-duty electric cable winch mounted on the front bumper of Harvey's Ford. The grenade launcher was also a goner, now a wheel-wrapped linguini of tangled ammunition belt and contorted metal. But had it done its job? Taken away the brother she might've found?

"Bannock has checked out, Harv."

"What about Grice?"

"Good question." The house had flame-lit everything on one side of the trucks, leaving the side to the river in shadows. "Grab those flashlights." She helped ease Harvey down from the two trucks. Taking one of the lights, she made a circuit around the vehicles and returned to Harvey.

"No Grice," she reported, switching off. "And no Castner. I hate loose ends, Harv."

He was about to say something, but turned at the wail of distant sirens. "I'd better hike back and stop them at the other side of the washout." Delia watched his circle of light bounce unevenly along the roadbed as he limped back the way they had driven.

Back! It was the word-trigger she needed to get her thinking straight. After impact, the two trucks had traveled a good forty feet. She traced back along the side to the river, her light playing among weeds, brush, and graying tree stumps. She stopped when the beam lit up a pointed boot toe.

Grice sat with his back against a stump, his chin on his chest. The front of his shirt was bright red, coating over what she took for a machine pistol. He didn't appear to be breathing, but she lifted the strap from behind his neck and removed the weapon. She set down her light and crouched beside him. Feeling for a pulse, she got a weak one. He stirred, lifting a hand toward Harvey, she thought, who stood at the top of the dike washout and flashed his light around. She figured Harvey was having trouble finding a safe way down.

"Cas . . ." Grice burbled, more blood spilling down his chin. His arm dropped, unmoving.

Delia squinted ahead, down toward the water where one of the bushes moved. It crept upward, gaining the top of the dike. She was going for her Kel-Tec when the bush produced a handgun and pointed it toward Harvey. She put two rounds into the bush, which got off one air-shot before she tapped in two more for good measure.

Harvey turned and gawked as Delia retrieved her flashlight. She switched on and lit up Craig Castner's ghillie-suited body.

* * *

Delia Chavez stood as close as she could to the roaring house fire, its heat a fever on her face, the night sky a glower of massing clouds. She peered into the blaze and listened to the clamor of approaching sirens. The wind had died off with nightfall, but cold ground air continued to rush past her legs, feeding the flames.

She'd helped Harvey across the washout, then canvassed the entire outer perimeter of the burning house. A cool-down walk. Twice she'd run her flashlight over every open patch, animal trail, sticker bush, or blade of bent grass that might hint at escape, any shred of possibility Robb had gotten out alive. Something to recoup amidst the evening carnage.

Something to offset the loose ends. Shoot a killer, lose the body. Get abducted, lose a brother. It seemed she'd made a career—a life—out of losing things.

The only tracks she'd found ran between Robb's ruined Zodiac and the front of the place. Or what used to be. The porch faced the dike road and had been fully visible until its sagging roof fell in on the steps. No one could have come out that way.

She watched now as the house collapsed inward, sending beehives of orange-white sparks swirling into the darkness. Bones might survive such intense heat. Teeth. A crucifix. Once the wreckage cooled and the sifting started. Still, she couldn't let herself believe the house, or Bannock, or both, had claimed Robb. Nor set aside her qualms about him. Whether he would have ignored Rose's warning, had he received it. Would have sought Delia out and turned himself in. Acted like a brother. No matter who he was.

She toed an ember, mashing it into dead ash. What had somebody once said about family being more than blood? "It's the people in your life who want you in theirs." But they hadn't said how to keep them in your life.

Delia bit back tears while wiping away the leakage from her bandaged ear. Robb had needed a sister. And she needed—

"Where do I put this?"

She spun around, drying her eyes with the heel of her hands. "Jerzy, Jesus. You okay?" she asked, reminding herself she hadn't lost everything, covering for the pang of guilt she felt for not thinking about him.

"Looks like I missed all the action," he said, showing her a scoped deer rifle. "This was leaning against a monster oak, but I never found our local rent-a-sniper."

"I did."

A procession of colored lights winked along the dike road.

It started to rain.

Epilogue

Sitting in the parked Camaro and reinstated, Detective Delia Chavez glanced at her watch. It had been fifteen minutes since she'd called Zack, two hours since the orchardist's find. Charlie's brother deserved at least some closure. She rolled down the passenger's side window and glassed the site where the three ME crew members in yellow slickers crouched around a darkish lump lodged against the trunk of a cherry tree. Like her, they'd booted up and slogged out there through parts of the orchard still inundated by the Willamette River.

That's the way it had gone. In the month since the Gatlin house had gotten blown up, burned down, then scoured out by impossibly high water, she must have driven every back road along the river, hoping to tie up at least one loose end. What had kept her from making the find on her own? River water, of course. Miles of it. She couldn't count the number of times a roadway had ended abruptly, diving into a temporary lake.

So what had happened? A farmer checking for tree damage had skirted the receding water in his ATV and stumbled across the leavings of the worst flood in years. Yet another fluke in the global-warming hoax.

Hearing the mellow grumble of dual exhausts, she lowered her glasses. Zack's perfectly restored, pearlescent red pickup rolled to a stop across the road, reminding Delia she still had to talk Big Juan into another fix-up on Enrique's Camaro.

She motioned Zack toward the passenger side and he got in, a set of papers in his hand.

"You get me out here for another SME consultation, Detective?"

"In a way. Zack. What's that in your hand?" As if she didn't know. Hadn't put the bug in the new acting sheriff's ear.

"Deputy sheriff application forms. Harvey Schenkel sent them to me. Think I should do this?"

"The sixteen-week academy's pretty rigorous. Think you can tough it?"

"You help?"

"Much as I can."

"Good. We can start with these. One's a recommendation I need from you." He set down the papers, looking around. "Something you wanted me to see?"

She motioned out toward the orchard and offered him the Bushnell's. "Take these and locate the crew in the yellow rain gear." He settled into the eyecups. "Focus on that bump they're crouched around."

"Yeah, got it."

"Now, zoom in."

Zack went still for a while. Then, "That's him? Tweety Bates?"

"Hole in head, bolt quiver, neoprene wet suit and all."

Zack was shaking. "Gotcha, you sumbitch." The glasses came down. He rocked his forehead against the doorsill. She laid her hand briefly on his shoulder, feeling his upper body expand and contract in a motion she took for a letting-go shudder.

There was nothing left to be said.

After a full minute he raised the binoculars, his hands surprisingly steady. Before he lowered them again, she caught his murmured idiom.

"Nyuk, nyuk, nyuk."

"What was that?"

"Charlie's last laugh."

* * *

FRIDAY HARBOR

TWO MONTHS AFTER THE CLOSE OF OREGON'S WATERFOWL SEASON

Delia heard the Chris Craft's salon door slide open.

"Are you decent?" It was Jerzy, back from a foray into town. After renting a boat slip for *Desdemona*, the forty-two-foot classic on loan from Jerzy's dad, they'd spent two sun-filled days exploring San Juan Island on mopeds.

Sun-filled was the operative word after weeks of clouds and rain and rivers swamping the countryside. Ruining crime scenes. She was sick of it all. So ready to give life outside work a fling, she'd jumped at the prospect of two weeks on a yacht in the San Juans, with Jerzy at the helm—and in the galley. She still hated rivers, any large body of water, really, but had come to an uneasy truce—so long as the boat was big and the water stayed beneath her feet.

"Halfway," she answered, stepping out of the forward head. Delia was dressed—sort of. His shorts, her T-shirt, but her hair was still wet.

Sliding in behind the boat salon's nook table, he set down a rubber-banded bundle and a bag of Chinese takeout. "I brought lunch and the mail Annie forwarded. Plus, I found a Laundromat."

"Lucky us." A Laundromat was a must. Jerzy's loaner boxers and sweats were clean and comfy, but they made her look like the *before* shot in an aerobics infomercial.

All in all, she considered herself lucky. For starters, her fair-haired, hash-slinging yacht mate was a great guy. And she had her job back. Also, under Annie's deft campaign management, Harvey had won the

323

emergency runoff for sheriff. Once Delia got back in town, she'd serve as acting sheriff while Annie and Harvey vacationed in Hawaii.

She dragged a wastebasket close by and sat across from Jerzy. News from home was good, too. But for some reason, she wasn't hungry. He pushed the mail across, picked up a set of chopsticks, and dug into the subgum.

Beezer flopped down at her side, tail thumping against her ankle as she disbanded the bundle and started in. Setting aside utility bills and the latest issue of *The Police Marksman*, she tossed the junk mail. A couple of pieces separated when they hit the lip of the basket and fluttered to the floor. She bent over and retrieved them. One piece made her frown.

It was the backside of a postcard. A gaudy banner, scrolled across the top of the message space, read *Hurricane Hole Marina: Paradise Island, Nassau*. Below that, someone had penned six words in block letters.

IN A BETTER PLACE. COME VISIT.

Her fingers started to tremble. She flipped the card over and drank in the image, and waited for her heart to finish a lap around the inside of her chest.

The photo side pictured a fishing charter yacht hauling ass away from the camera and cutting a white wake across a turquoise bay. No question the boat was headed for blue water, big fish, and fun times.

She couldn't make out the identity of the muscular and deeply tanned man at the helm, because he faced forward, but the two women in captain's hats on the aft deck were stunning eye-catchers. Both were uniformed in ripped jean shorts and T-shirts that said *Mate, First*. One waved from the rear of the boat while the other pointed down at the two words emblazoned across the stern.

The boat was named *Bebé Tío*.

Author's Note

I did not pause in taking liberties when faced with divergent information on the places, times, and organizations depicted in this story. Many of the locations along the Willamette River, as well as in and around Dallas, Salem, and Independence, Oregon, are real. Some, I made up. I adjusted physical constructs inside the historic Polk County Courthouse to complement the story. Word has it the Blue Garden Restaurant, which has undergone a few incarnations, has been revived and renovated, yet has preserved its art deco style. It's worth a visit. Drug running is still rampant in Central and South America, as depicted here. I've also taken the reports of Navy SEALs testing of bizarre experimental weaponry one step further. However, portable smart weapons with phenomenal accuracy and firepower are beginning to make their way into conventional use. Most important, the Polk County Sheriff's Office is one of the finer law enforcement organizations in the state of Oregon. I'll have to own any mistakes made in these fabrications.

Acknowledgments

First and foremost, I would like to thank Carole for her never-ending patience and forbearance while I escaped to coffee shops to caffeinate and sweat bullets. Yes, writing is a solitary venture, but putting up with a writer can also be a lonely affair. Loads of thanks to my first readers—Mike Munro, Catherine Hendricks, Keri Clark, Judy Dailey, Myrna Daley, Val Bruech, and Bruce Hansen. Thanks to Pamela Goodfellow, who long ago started the ball rolling and taught me to value critique groups as well as four-sentence writing exercises.

I owe much to the team at Crooked Lane Books and, in particular, Jenny Chen, who saw potential in *River Run* and gave me a shot. Also, thanks to innovative cover designers Lori Palmer and Andy Ruggirello, and thank God for copy editors like Rachel Keith.

Special thanks are due to David Downing for his first-cut edits of a behemoth manuscript, to Lourdes Venard for her read-through and insights on issues of cultural sensitivity, to Clark County Sheriff's Tactical Detective Jared Stevens for his subject matter expertise, to Steven Allen for his military savvy, and to Julie for a couple of no-nonsense but useful edits.

Lastly, thanks to my agent John Talbot of Talbot Fortune Agency, who saw enough light through the forest of this tome to give me a call and speak words of encouragement, advice, and support.